BOUND BY THE BLOOD

Also by Cecilia Tan

Bent For Leather
Black Feathers
The Blossoms of Summer
Bound by the Blood
Daron's Guitar Chronicles, Vol. 1-13
Edge Plays
The Hot Streak
Mind Games
The Mystery of the Bitten Peach
The Prince's Boy
Royal Treatment
Silk Threads: Bonds of Love
Telepaths Don't Need Safewords
The Velderet
Watch Point
White Flames

The Magic University Series
The Siren and the Sword
The Tower and the Tears
The Incubus and the Angel
The Poet and the Prophecy
Spellbinding: Tales from the Magic University
Christmas Magic

The Struck by Lightning Series
Slow Surrender
Slow Seduction
Slow Satisfaction

The Secrets of a Rock Star series
Taking the Lead
Wild Licks
Hard Rhythm

BOUND BY THE BLOOD

BOOK ONE OF
THE VANISHED CHRONICLES

CECILIA TAN

⟡NE

What would you think if you saw a woman walk out onto the George Washington Bridge in the middle of the night with a mysterious black bundle under her arm? Especially if you saw her clutching it in her arms like a baby, bent into the rain and wind. Who goes out for a walk on a night like that, with thunder roaring, cradling a package as if it's precious? What errand was so urgent that it couldn't wait for dry daylight? I can tell you her trench coat is leather but it does nothing to stop the rain from pelting her hair, her face. It's her face that would probably set your opinion, though. Do you see distress there? Angst? Or just a mask of determination. Arriving at this moment has not been easy. Above the bridge's handrail, there is a gap in the decrepit chain link fence—too small for a person, but big enough for this.

Would you think better of her if you could hear the scream she lets out as she heaves the leather-wrapped bundle off the bridge? Does she sound angry or merely afraid? There is lightning in the sky as her burden falls, as it disappears into the river far below.

What do you think of her now?

If you would have looked away and pretended you'd never seen her, then you're not ready for these words. They're for Niko and Saira, Kish and Jair, and whoever comes after them.

After you read this, if you see yourself on that bridge, then these words are for you.

TWO

Let's start with the night I met Clive—boots laced up, my corset cinched, and a bag of whips on my shoulder. I'll start somewhere you might recognize: a nightclub with an upstairs dance floor. The city is full of clubs like it—a thousand different vibes to suit a thousand different crowds. Upscale, downtown, psychedelic, cyberpunk, Bollywood, cowgirl, you name it.

A shirtless man would grab my attention in any of them, but especially in Purgatory.

Before I saw him, I had been asking myself why the hell I was there. The place was goth, but once a month the dance floor turned into a dungeon. People go to these places—all of these places—to hook up. Not just for sex. People go to bars when they're lonely, when they're looking for connection.

I wasn't ready for connection. Not so soon after severing ties with Ethan. But there I was, anyway.

Clive—I didn't know that was his name yet—was standing by the empty deejay booth, looking comfortable in his bare skin. A typical darkwave dance-trance playlist was on, but that night was for a different sort of dance. Two leathermen had been flogging a third on the St. Andrew's cross, but they were mostly done, just running their hands up and down his bare back and buttocks. One of them snapped the elastic waistband of his thong and all three of them laughed. A witchy long-haired androgyne smiled in their direction and then glided down the stairs. A few mixed-gender couples nursed drinks at the tall cocktail tables along the far wall. It was early, not yet crowded, and the spanking bench and other play stations were empty.

I should have been sizing up the possibilities, psyching myself up to meet someone new, but I was trying hard not to think about my ex—which of course meant I was thinking of him—but what would I do if he showed up? I told myself he wouldn't. Ethan had always said club nights were for posers. He preferred to play at private parties, where one could wear less and do more—even sex, if that was your thing.

Parties where you could draw blood.

If you're reading this I probably don't have to tell you why that's sexy. But I will. After all, assumptions are what got us into this mess, and so much has already been lost.

For some of us, sex and attraction and lust are wrapped up in power, and invoking that power through pain or pleasure is what we do. It's how we connect and it's why people arrange club nights like that one, so like-minded souls can meet.

I remember looking at the empty palm of my hand, splashed red by the dance floor lights. Even if Ethan turned his nose up at club play, I might still run into someone who'd been at that party, that disastrous night when he had torpedoed our relationship (and I'd tried to send him down with the ship). What would they say? That I had no right to set foot in a "safe space" like Club Purgatory?

Don't let anyone tell you BDSM is "safe." It's safety-*focused,* but—like parachuting and mountain climbing—danger is part of the attraction. The thrill is the point.

My worries were all in my head: I didn't see anyone I knew. Just that rather enticing-looking guy in black jeans and engineer boots and nothing else. He had a lean-muscled chest and black tousled hair and I closed my hand like I was taking a fistful of that hair and getting ready to drag him to that then-vacated St. Andrew's cross.

He looked up right then. Right at me.

I tightened my fist and read a flicker in his eyes—when you're a thrill-seeker does fear look the same as desire? Was he looking for a goddess in black leather, ready to smite any she chose? And was that what he saw? As I held his gaze, his interest intensified rather than waning. So.

It had been so long that I'd forgotten how to do the next part, the two-steps-forward, one-step-back dance that was flirting.

I've always preferred negotiation over flirtation, anyway. If you could call marching up to him and saying "I have three whips in my bag. Are you interested in seeing them?" a negotiation.

He reflected my courage back to me: "I might be more interested in feeling them than seeing them."

A surge of emotion flooded me at his answer—excitement, lust, curiosity, hunger—I don't know a single word to describe the feeling that comes over me when a potential partner shows their willingness to play—to submit. All I knew was I hadn't felt it in far too long.

I tried to tread lightly—didn't want to scare him away. "Might?"

But there was no scaring Clive. His voice held a touch of bravado. "If you'd like to use them, I'd like to feel them." The lights shifted to white and I saw his eyes were startlingly pale blue.

Me. "I haven't even told you what kind they are."

Him. "And you don't have to."

So. He was either too naïve to know what he was in for, or he was extremely confident about how much punishment he could take. Confidence is sexy. Overconfidence equals disaster.

That was when he told me, with a slight smile, "I like surprises."

Well. He was at least a masochist, a slightly cheeky one at that. But was he *submissive?* I liked self-confidence, but I wasn't into brats

I told myself it didn't matter. It wasn't like I was vetting him for a relationship. I was just going to flog him for a bit of fun. We probably weren't even going to exchange phone numbers, right? He was pretty and he was willing. That should have been enough.

But I never know when to leave well enough alone. "How are you at following directions?"

"Give me some directions and you can judge that for yourself." Rather than being cheeky, these words were delivered with a respectful nod of his head. "Is there a form of address you prefer?"

Good manners. Not a brat, then. "One has to earn the right to call me by a title. Address me by my name, which is Mira."

He drew my name out—"Meerah"—like he was practicing to get it perfect. "Mira, I'm Clive."

I repeated his name back to him, too, liking the way it felt in my mouth, the way my tongue brushed the roof of my mouth before my teeth, a spoonful of something delicious. I held out my hand, fingers angled downward. He took the hint, lifting my hand gently but surely to his lips. That kiss sent a delicious shiver up my arm and I resolved—if he took the beating well—to kiss him on the mouth when his lips would be ripe from surrender.

I asked for his safeword.

He chuckled a little as he said it: "Divinity."

I was sure there was a story behind it, but that wasn't the time to hear it. It was time to set the rules of engagement. "The three whips in my bag are two floggers and one single tail."

He nodded. "Yes, Mira."

"When I meet someone new, I only use the floggers."

"Yes, Mira," he repeated, but did I imagine I heard a hint of disappointment there?

"What are you wearing under your jeans?"

His Mona Lisa smile returned. "I'm legal, if that's what you're asking."

"That is, in fact, what I am asking. Put your boots next to the cross, strip your jeans, take hold of the handles, and then wait."

"Yes, Mira." Again that deferential nod, which almost made my name into a title itself. The thing that really cranked up my anticipation right in that moment, though, was the way he followed my instructions. Sometimes independence and initiative are sexy, but right then total obedience was like a balm on my soul. He did exactly as I asked, no more, no less, and then he got up onto the X-shaped cross and waited.

And waited. I knew from my early experiences in the scene—back when I didn't know the difference between being attracted to a hot dom and being submissive—that a minute of waiting on the cross could feel like twenty. So I didn't intend to have him stand there for too-too long. Just long enough to ratchet up the anticipation.

A little voice of doubt yammered in the back of my head: Get on with it, Mira. Don't wait. He just wants you to flog him. Not everything has to be a test. You're setting yourself up for disappointment when he gets bored and breaks character…

The minute, which I was counting out in my head, had almost passed when a voice behind me said, "Watch out. He's a tough little thing. Your arm may get tired."

I didn't have to glance back to know one of my least favorite people in the scene was standing behind me, a man I knew by the name of Ira Dayton. I didn't know at the time if it was his real name or a scene name. I'd served with Kanna, his wife, on the board of Gotham Kink United, and I liked her just fine, but Ira… Here's what I did know about him: He was a doctor who liked extreme blood play. He would bring his own tarp, scalpels, and matched set of gay submissive puppy players to parties. There was nothing wrong with that. What was wrong was Ira's disregard for the rules.

No, it was worse than that. Ira could couch his penchant for breaking the rules in such a way as to make it seem like he was upholding them. That was my conclusion after one time he had set up one of his extreme scenes right there at Purgatory. Afterward, when the club tried to ban him, he pointed out that in their rules prohibiting fluid exchange they'd failed to mention blood by name. When they pointed out that anyone sensible would know full well you shouldn't be doing anything of the sort, he claimed he only did it to force the club to update their rules "for everyone's safety."

Yeah, right. It had been a dick move and I'd had the sound of puppies whining stuck in my head for weeks afterward.

With a little "excuse me" tossed in Ira's direction, I began to swing the first of the floggers in the air. I figured I'd warm up my arm and maybe drive him away. If he was standing too close and got caught with a backswing it would be his own damn fault. And what did he mean by "little"? That word didn't seem to apply to any part of Clive that I could discern. I'm sure it was just supposed to get under my skin. Being short myself, even in heels, has never bothered me, but Ira didn't know that.

Clive had not moved a muscle. Another jolt of powerlust surged through me. (How's that for a word?) I hadn't bound him to the cross. Above his head, padded handlebar grips were attached to the wood and he was holding them tight as instructed. His shoulders curved enticingly. I don't know who invented the St. Andrew's Cross, but I said a little prayer of thanks to them before I let the suede tails of the flogger come into contact with Clive's skin. Not hitting him hard at all, just swinging the flogger around and around in a circle, thwapping him lightly on each pass, to wake up his skin and get him ready for more.

Every flogging has a rhythm to it, whether you synch up with the beat of the music or let your own body set the tempo. I tend to start with the beats coming quickly but lightly—*tap-tap-tap*—but as I start to hit harder, I slow down and give more time between the blows. It's all about judging when the moment comes to go to another gear. Has my dance partner been lulled into a sense of security that I want to shatter? Or are they literally aching to be pushed harder, to take more?

Clive was one of those who wanted more. He arched into the strikes, muscles bunching and tensing, skin turning a lovely shade of pink. I went from criss-crossing with my wrist to swinging from my elbow, laying longer strokes across his shoulders and his bare buttcheeks. Eventually I used my whole arm, letting all the suede tails thud against his back in unison until his breath was coming in quick gasps.

When his breath lengthened again, as he lost himself in the sensation, it was time to switch floggers. He shivered a little as I trailed the cool tails of the second one down his back, letting him guess what it would be like. The second one had a hide with a stiffer finish; it could sting or leave marks depending how I wielded it. I stepped up to the cross and pulled his hair the way I'd imagined, tipping his head back and taking a quick kiss before he realized I was going to. He brimmed with vigor, his mouth taut with energy.

Number two genuinely caused pain. It did not damage, but it did hurt.

The body always resists pain at first, even with a masochist who craves it. That would be when Ethan would pull at his bonds like he was trying to get free and shout "no!" at me and curse me. But it was an act. He knew that to stop me for real, all he had to do was utter his safeword. Ethan just "needed" to struggle, he told me. At the time I had thought he needed to be relieved of the guilt over wanting to feel something, and lay the responsibility on me for "making" him feel that way.

At the time I failed to understand the true depths of his guilt.

But though I'm comparing the two of them now, at that moment I was not thinking of Ethan or failure. Clive was alive and present in front of me in a way I hadn't connected with another human being in months. (Years, really, if you counted that E. and I had stayed together long past any true connection.) Clive captured my full attention. And as I began laying into him with the leather, harder and harder, he got past the struggle and into that place where all sensation is welcome, where each stroke is another step toward ecstasy. His breath and mine fell into synch, and although he never let go the handholds entirely, his fingers flared against the padding, like tiny fireworks blooming on the horizon.

When I stopped flogging him, it was to lick clean, freshly earned sweat from the back of his neck. Then I kissed him again, and this time the fight was gone. His lips felt supple and yielding in a way they only ever are after surrender. Like he was completely wrapped up in the state of mind known as subspace.

Completely mine.

He opened his eyes slowly—I'd forgotten they were blue.

"Welcome back, angel." That was when I made the decision. "Remember how I said I wouldn't use the single tail on you?"

"Yes...?" Oh, what a hopeful note he struck!

"Be honest. Did you want me to use it?"

"I want you to do whatever pleases you most."

Pure bullshit. I tightened my grip in his hair. "I said 'be honest,' not 'tell me what you think I want to hear.'" (There's a difference.)

"Yes, Mira." He swallowed. "Yes, I would like to feel it."

"I normally won't use it on anyone unless I'm sure they can take it."

"I'm sure I can take it," he said, eyes glittering. Such a courageous heart. "In fact, it would be an honor to."

"An honor, eh?" It was like he knew exactly what I needed to hear to have my choices validated. "All right, angel." That was the moment I decided to take him home.

Just like not using my signal whip on a new person, bringing home someone I'd just met at a club was against my usual rules. You were supposed to have a sober conversation in a coffee shop, and check their social media, and ask around about them before you let a person you just met into your place or went solo to theirs. But he felt too different from all the others—so intriguing, so perfect for me—for the old rules to apply.

Or maybe I was just too desperate. I made him "remind me" of his safeword ("Divinity") and he gave me a nod that seemed to say he knew I wasn't reminding myself of it so much as reminding him that he could use it.

Me. "I'm going to give you three strokes."

Him. "Three?" Plaintively, as if that were far too few.

Me. "I'll give you the chance to opt out after each one and there will be no dishonor in that."

"Ah." He understood. This was going to be a challenge to get through. This was going to *hurt*. And then he asked, "Is this… is this how people earn the privilege to call you by a title?"

So sharp and engaging! He clicked with me on every level. "It's not the only way, but yes, if you take it well, I'll allow it."

"Thank you, Mira."

"Don't thank me yet, angel." I stole another quick kiss, prompting a pang of lust deep in my gut. It had been ages since I wanted anyone that much. I felt almost hollow with hunger for him, and that feeling alone felt like a miracle.

I pulled the braided leather whip from the bottom of the bag, where it lay coiled like a snake. Once upon a time I'd gotten good enough to do demonstrations for BDSM community groups. I could slice paper—or a banana—with it. (It was especially fun if a volunteer held the banana at their belt buckle. I could wrap the end of the whip harmlessly around the fruit from a distance, and then for a truly wicked finale, slice the tip clean off.)

I ran a hand down Clive's bare back one last time, feeling the heat and welts left by the flogging, and letting him know I was there. Then I stepped away, pacing out my distance. I took my stance, left foot forward, whip swaying in my right as I rocked back and forth, preparing myself.

On the cross as he was, back bared to me, Clive couldn't see me, but his head swayed in time with me. I figured it was probably just the rhythm of the music, but I liked the thought that we were in synch. The lights shifted to blue and it was like we were in a bubble under the sea, just the two of us.

The first blow cut diagonally across his right shoulder and I heard the breath go out of him—not a scream or cry, just a breath—followed by a shiver, a tremble. I gave him time to process it and there was no sign he wanted to stop.

I matched the first cut with one on the left, and this time a little cry came forth, and he shook, hands opening as if he could let the pain out faster through his palms.

I drank in that agony, like I could soak it right down to my bones.

When he was still again, and breathing in synch with my swaying once more, I knew he was ready for the third and final blow. The dark red welts from the other two were clearly visible. I knew where the third would go.

My own breath went out of me as I laid a line of fire straight across his shoulders. The welt crossed the previous stripes and made him sing out clearly, an animal cry with a guttural end. A kind of phantom orgasm swept through me at that sound, a shiver of longing so intense it felt like relief when it passed. I pressed myself against Clive, then, tasting the sweat on the back of his neck once more… and sneaking a swipe of my tongue at the blood that beaded on his right shoulder where the two blows had crossed. I hadn't intended to draw blood. No one did that at Purgatory, not since Ira's little stunt.

But no one had to know.

Clive practically vibrated against my tongue, legs shaking, pressing himself back against me. Alive and in the moment with me in a way that was more precious than I can express.

And then he hung his head. It felt almost like a different kind of heat was coming off of him, then. Was he… ashamed?

I ran my fingers into his hair, waiting to see if he'd speak, to see if he'd tell me about the change that came over him.

"Do I… Did I still earn the right to call you by a title? Even though. Um." He trailed off, trying to hide his face. Where had his bravado gone? Had I beaten it out of him?

I turned his head so I could look into his eyes. "You may call me 'my lady.' The fastest way to lose that privilege is to lie to me. What's wrong, angel?"

"Just… my lady, you didn't give me permission to come."

He came from that? No wonder he'd made such a sound. How could he think I wouldn't be thrilled that I could make him come that way? Good god. Another ghostly shiver of near-satisfaction flashed hot and cold through me and I clenched my fists, as if I could grab what I needed from the air.

But what I needed was much more solid than air. "Did I say that was a rule? My rules include no such thing. I have only one absolute rule, and it is that you always tell me the truth, the whole truth, with absolute honesty."

"Yes, my lady," he almost whispered.

I slid a hand between the cross and his abs, until just under the waistband of his thong, my fingers found the truth in his words. A masochist who could literally come from being whipped. What a treasure. I lay a line of kisses along his jaw. "I'm not disappointed at all that you came. The only thing that'll disappoint me is if you don't come home with me tonight."

His breath caught in his throat, his eyes almost starry with hope and anticipation for a moment, before he grimaced, a flare of hot shame enflaming his cheeks.

Here it comes, I thought.

"I'm sorry, my lady." He really looked pained. But I'd just told him I required absolute honesty, and there it was: "I… have another commitment tonight."

The bubble burst. His gaze never left my face but I started to feel the people around us, hear the laughter and voices from the bar. The next couple, impatient to use the cross, lurked beside us. "Oh, really," I heard myself saying, mind whirling. That connection I'd imagined had snapped like a lifeline and sent me tumbling back down the mountain. Reality, like gravity, would not be denied. "Another commitment." That was the sort of thing I would say to slip away from an unwelcome advance.

Had it all been my imagination? My desperation? Maybe he wasn't into me, after all. Maybe he didn't give a damn about me or my rules and was only there to see how many tops he could charm.

Or maybe he was afraid. He'd wanted to earn something from me. Had I coerced him into taking those three stripes and afterward he regretted it? If he wanted to, he could easily accuse me of assault.

I still wonder why Ethan never did.

"I'm truly sorry," Clive went on. "I didn't expect to… to connect to you so well. And even so, I didn't expect an invitation."

He was right. I was far from the only one with a "Starbucks rule." I was the one jumping the gun.

And I could handle disappointment like an adult. I stepped back from him and pointed at the tip of my boot. He hurried to kneel, to place one firm and respectful kiss on the leather, sending shockwaves up my legs. (Good god, I wanted him to place that kiss somewhere else.)

I held out my fingertips, still damp with his issue, and he licked them clean. By rights I should have just said good night, gone straight home, and forgotten all about him.

But before I went home to a vibrator and a pint of fudge ripple, I did one more thing. I gave him my card. He stayed on his knees to receive it.

"That is my number. Let me make one thing clear. I do not chase men. I expect you to call."

"Yes, my lady!" Good god, those eyes. "I'll call!"

Reader, he did not call.

THREE

After that fateful night at Purgatory, we can skip forward to April before there's anything worth noting other than the fact that every day that went by was another drop into the bucket of evidence that Clive wasn't interested in me. And every day I tried not to think about him. Some days I even succeeded.

But once I'd been plied with alcohol, I found myself talking about him. Again.

The cocktail bar we were in was so hip I couldn't even make out the name in the artistic neon lettering over the bar. (I think it started with the letter M?) Wexel—my best friend—had already heard the story of the mystery man who had ghosted me, but he gamely listened to me recount the whole thing. Again.

"I just can't shake the feeling that something really special was about to happen," I told him. "Those times when it's like… magic… are so rare. I even gave him my card. But, not a peep." I kept thinking if he had lost my number, all he'd have to do is ask around in the community and chances were good someone could point him in my direction.

But of course if he asked around about me, someone might have warned him not to end up like my last submissive.

Wex was pragmatic about it: "Anything over a month without contact is definitely him ghosting you." He rolled his eyes and waved his empty martini glass toward someone behind me. "It's been what, six weeks?"

"Three months."

"Not like you're counting or anything, though." He caught the attention of the bartender and rapped a fingernail against the glass to signal for another, then focused on me, brushing recently frosted blond bangs out of his eyes. "Seriously, mija, forget him. He's probably one of those dicks who gets scared off by confident, competent women. Maybe he was just passing through town. Or some Wall Street type slumming for hot chicks in leather or whatever."

I tried to let his supportive words soothe me, but I knew Wex was wrong. Clive—was that even his name? I wondered—wasn't from out of town and he wasn't slumming; Ira had known him. "It's just that he seemed so perfect." Especially *because* he wasn't scared off when I projected confidence.

But maybe he'd seen through me.

"Every toad looks like a prince when you're horny enough. Speaking of which." He made eyes shamelessly at someone further down the crowded bar.

I held up my own glass, which had a mix of aged whiskeys in it and one muddled cherry. "What was this one called again?"

"You've got the Lolita."

I was suddenly less interested in the drink. "Ugh, points off for tasteless naming. Why do hipster bars think that's 'edgy'? It's just rapey."

Wex shushed me nervously. "They might hear you!"

No one could hear us over the din of the crowd or the eclectic worldbeat playlist, but here's why he was concerned. Wex's main gig was as a "secret shopper." A company paid him to visit various establishments—bars, restaurants, hotels, theaters, even a massage parlor once—and write reports on their service. He was supposed to go to great pains to keep his role a secret, of course. One rule of camouflage was he couldn't go alone, so my job was often to pose as his date.

Wex's hobby, though, was definitely hooking up with whatever men he happened across at the sites he reviewed. I didn't know how well the secret shopping gig actually paid, but my guess was the side benefits made it well worth it to him. Being able to take a friend out for free drinks and console her over her love life—or lack thereof—was another perk.

"But he seemed so perfect," I said again, my mind sinking back to the thought I couldn't escape, the name I couldn't forget. "Is that my problem? I'm too much of a perfectionist?"

"No." He accepted a fresh drink—and a wink—from the burly, bearded bartender. "It's that you're not even trying. Have you even been out of your apartment since the night he turned you down? You're not even going to Fitworks anymore, are you?"

I grudgingly admitted that no, I hadn't set foot at my so-called place of employment in months—since even before the night I'd met Clive. I'd been working there as a massage therapist for two years, and after getting certified as a personal trainer I was supposed to switch from the spa to the gym side of the business. But I hadn't scheduled a single training client. I hadn't even been going to Sensei Jack's seminars, and I really liked those. "I just need a break from that place. I'm taking a couple of massage clients a week at my apartment for cash under the table and that's enough for now." Thank god for rent control and a super who wouldn't report me. (I was fixing his frozen shoulder.)

"You know what you'd be really good at? Professional dominatrixhood." He sipped the very pink liquid in his glass, then made a face like it was castor oil. That about matched what I thought of his idea. "Go pro and get out all your frustrations on Wall Street types who'll pay through the nose to be treated like dirt. Or was that what your plan was for being a professional athletic trainer in the first place?"

"Having a whip in your hand doesn't make it any more fun to deal with overprivileged assholes." In fact it would probably take whatever joy I had in domination right out of it. A bad idea in every respect.

Wex tried his drink again. "This is truly awful. Taste it."

I took a sip from Wex's glass and made the same face he had. "Ugh, that's so bitter."

"It's called 'The Ex.'"

"Well, they got one name right, then. There should be one called 'The Sub' and it should seem great at the time but you'll nurse it so long you'll miss the last train home."

He whipped out his phone and made a note for his review. "Not every sub is an overprivileged asshole, you know."

"I'm not talking about you, dear."

"I'm not submissive, I'm a painslut," he sneered, then bit his lip flirtatiously at someone behind me at the bar, maybe the same one as before, maybe someone different. It was too crowded for me to turn around and see.

"Or maybe just a slut." Wexel enjoyed hookups all across the spectrum from kinky to utterly vanilla, so long as the guy turned him on. I patted him affectionately on the arm.

He flinched away. "Mira! Careful. You might scare him off if he thinks I'm bi."

"Oh, honestly. As if he might catch bi cooties from you?"

"Look, I don't make the rules, I just follow them. Some guys can be purists." Yes, they could, and I suspected Wex himself might be one of them. What he said next cemented my suspicion: "It's really too bad women don't turn me on, because the two of us would be so perfect for each other in some ways. Then again, I guess that's why we've never messed up our friendship by sleeping together."

Though I agreed with him about that, I felt it necessary to declare, "Friends with benefits works perfectly well for a lot of people."

He sniffed skeptically. "I prefer strangers with benefits."

Hearing him say it like that gave me the urge to lecture him about safety—not just "safe sex" stuff like condoms but having a safe call check-in—but we'd had that argument before and he'd insisted he had it handled. (Should I have made my point more strenuously?) "As long as you know what you're doing."

"Don't change the subject. We're talking about you, and how you never get out anymore. How are you going to meet the perfect sub—or even one that even meets your minimum standards for getting off—if you never go out?"

"The club scene just isn't for me."

"And you don't go to classes or meetings anymore because you got burned out on leather politics, and you don't go to the parties you used to because you think you'll run into Ethan." He took my hand in his. "I'm going to make a suggestion now. Promise me you won't scream."

"Scream? What are you about to say, Wex?"

"I've been playing with a guy off and on for a couple of months. He's into knives, and I know you've been avoiding that kind of scene—"

"Knives are fine for other people to use." Besides me.

"He's started throwing a very exclusive party at his house in Westchester every month. Ethan is not on his invite list—I checked." Of course he did. Such a dear. "I'm sure I could get you okayed on the invite list for this month. Please say you'll come."

But he seemed overly earnest. I could tell there was something he wasn't telling me. "And you're worried I'm going to freak out if I see you doing a knife scene with this guy? Is that what you're not telling me?"

He broke into a grin. "No, no. He and I don't have plans for this party."

"When is this party?"

"Saturday. I'll text him tonight to get the okay. Okay?" When I didn't answer right away he repeated it more urgently. "*Okay?*"

He must've really meant it to be holding my hand like that. Something still felt off, though. If it had been my birthday I might have suspected it was a setup to surprise me. Wex wouldn't hide something from me without a reason. "Okay."

"I'll send you the address and the rules." He put his credit card down on the bar and it was whisked away far more quickly than our empty glasses. "Now, if you'll excuse me, opportunity beckons." He scribbled his name onto the credit card slip and then snaked off his barstool and into the crowd. He disappeared in the direction of the men's room.

I took that as my cue to leave, as well. I wrapped myself in my long leather coat and headed to the subway. The bar had been shoulder-to-shoulder, but outside? The sidewalk was empty. I made my way down a quiet side street lined with old residential buildings, each one skirted by trash cans chained to low iron fences. I'd been raised with the adage that the city is safest when you're in a crowd and most dangerous when you're alone, but no bogeyman leapt out of the trash.

Underground, the subway station was noisy with multiple buskers—an electric violinist, a saxophonist, and a rapping puppet/puppeteer with a portable beatbox—all their sounds bouncing off the grimy tile and girders running through the platform.

Those girders are the bones of the city, you know. Old and creaking and you have to dig down to expose them.

A half hour later I was on the train home, one arm wrapped around a pole, the other holding my phone, when the train pulled into a station with cell signal and his text came through:

> You're on the list! 7pm Saturday. Take Metro North to Rye and
> they've got a limo to shuttle folks to the house.

He still hadn't told me everything, but that hardly mattered compared to the fact that was the last text I got from him.

By Saturday morning I was calling the police and hospitals.

FOUR

Okay, which should I go into first, Wex or the party?

At first blush it might seem weird that I was going to a play party when my best friend had turned up at a hospital a few hours before, but it made sense, I promise. I wasn't going there to play.

Wex had been found on the Lower East Side, comatose from loss of blood, and he was still unconscious. The police had ruled it a robbery since his wallet was missing, but what kind of mugger leaves cuts all over their victim? He was listed as a John Doe, so when the staff at Beth Israel had put together that I'd been calling around ERs looking for my missing "brother," they'd asked me to come down and ID him.

I hadn't even been expecting it to be him. And I definitely hadn't been expecting to find him marked up like that—thin lines on his arm, shoulder, neck. Like someone had gotten artistic with a razor.

That was when I knew I had to go to the party. There would be blood players there as well as people who knew Wex. They might also know who could've done it to him, and they needed to be warned. It doesn't happen often that we get a wolf in sheep's clothing inside the community, but there are those who prey on kinky folk because they think they can hide among us.

Making sure they *can't* is the best reason to put up with leather community politics.

The trip downtown to the hospital and back had taken all day, so all I had time to do was throw on clothes before I caught the train as directed. I considered myself barely acceptably dressed for a play party: flat-heeled boots, sweater-dress, and jeans, with my everyday leather jacket. I'd grabbed my whip bag out of habit and I clutched it in my lap the whole ride up the Hudson. The tracks went right along the river, out of the city and through the string of towns rich folks traditionally escaped to. A handful of people exited with me at a little commuter station. I was the only one being met by a limousine, though.

Nothing like arriving at a party looking like crap, eh? The limo driver had a sort-of Russian accent and finishing school manners, so he didn't bat an eye at either the fact that I was on the last possible train to make it there before the party doors closed nor that I looked like I hadn't slept in days (because I hadn't).

I was the only party guest picked up on that last run, so I sat alone in the back of the leather-upholstered car with my thoughts. A chilling one hit me: what if the sicko who'd left Wex for dead was at the very party I was headed to? I had wracked my brains for the details of who he'd met at the bar the last time I saw him, but I'd never gotten a look at the guy. Would I recognize him if I saw him? The stats say most victims of assault know their attackers. Had Wex known his? Had he been preyed on, or was it just that the scene went wrong, and the top panicked and dumped him in an alley instead of calling 911? Maybe someone was so afraid of being outed as kinky or queer, they'd risk a life.

The limo driver interrupted my thoughts. "Pardon me, but I received word that we must take a slight detour to pick up a guest."

"Okay." Kink parties like these often have an arrival window, after which additional guests are not allowed in. It fosters a feeling of community and togetherness and ensures the hosts don't have to keep answering the door when they're in the middle of something fun. All I could think was I hoped I'd have time to suss out if a killer was present. "Will we still be there in time?"

"Oh, yes. Don't worry," the driver said. "They won't start until after we arrive."

Before I could think of how to explain what my concern actually was, he was pulling the car over behind an SUV with its blinkers on. Someone on their way to the party had broken down. We were on a twisty two-lane road with woods on one side, and hilly fields divided by rustic stone walls on the other. Not even a half hour outside Manhattan and we were in millionaire country.

The driver got out. I looked at the leather bag in my lap and wondered why I had bothered to bring it, when I had no intention of playing at that party. Autopilot or… fate?

It was full dark by then, and the night was turning chilly. Typical early April in New York: unsure if winter was truly on the way out the door or if it should have one more round. When the driver returned and opened the door for our new passenger, a cold gust of wind came in with him.

"Thank you, Stefan!" said a familiar voice as he slid into the car. Then he turned toward me with a chipper smile on his face. "So sorry about that! Hi, I'm—"

"Clive," I finished for him, as his face froze.

He at least had the good grace to look chagrined. "Mira. I'm so sorry."

I shouldn't have gone right for the jugular, but after no sleep from worry, I was in no mood to be nice. "You said you'd call."

"I know. That's why I'm sorry." The limo pulled off the shoulder and Clive glanced back as we left his vehicle behind. He tried to be delicate: "I got pulled into, ah, something that precluded me getting in touch."

Remember that feeling I had that Wex wasn't telling me everything? I felt it even more strongly at that moment. "You met some self-styled Goddess or dom asshole who forbade you to even text to say 'thanks, but no thanks'?"

He swallowed, but didn't wither under my attack. "Jealousy doesn't suit you, Mira."

"Is that what it is, jealousy? Who told you not to contact me?" Perhaps some friend of Ethan's…?

He set his jaw, the first time I ever saw his stubborn side. "I won't be interrogated about this, Mira."

…Or a dangerous top who was picking up pretty men and cutting them up. My blood ran a little cold as I realized what my eyes were fixating on: a thin line on his neck, a little behind his ear, the same kind of scar that Wex was covered with. Abusers always isolate their victims, forbidding them to contact others, to leave them without support.

I reached for him and he shied back, as if I were going to hit him. That alone was cause for concern. I threaded my fingers into his hair gently and lifted it off his neck, revealing more of the mark, which disappeared under the collar of his bomber jacket. "What's this?"

He sat perfectly still, like he was holding himself back from something. "I just told you I won't be interrogated."

I withdrew my hand slowly. "Fine. Then just listen. I literally just came from a hospital downtown where my best friend has been in a coma for days from blood loss. And he's got marks that look exactly like yours. Someone cut him up and left him to die. So you tell me if I'm overreacting to the fact that now you won't tell me who you've been playing with."

His eyes went wide and his attitude softened suddenly. "Oh, god. I'm sorry about your friend. But, this is not like that. It's not some top keeping me from telling you."

"Your wife, then. Or husband."

"No. I'm not a cheater." He seemed a bit offended that I'd think it. "It's not a relationship thing at all. All right? Please just trust me on this, Mira? I'm sorry. I'm truly truly sorry, both to have disappointed you and for my own sake for missing out on connecting with you. Because I felt like we had… something going on, that night."

That made me feel marginally better about myself. It hadn't been my imagination. And he wasn't avoiding me because he didn't like me. It was something else that he couldn't talk about. The mafia? The CIA?

Before I could let my thoughts go too far down that path, though, he asked, "Your friend. Will he be all right?"

"I don't know. I wasn't even going to come to the party tonight, but I want to make sure people know what happened. He told me he was doing knife play regularly with someone right before he disappeared. Maybe… maybe it's someone people will know. Plus, he was supposed to be here tonight. Have you been to this party before? Maybe you've met him. His name is Wexel."

Clive's mouth hung open slightly. "Wex? Yes, we've met." He touched the spot on his neck where the thin scar snaked. "Listen, Mira, I don't want to be a doubter. But he got marks like this one on the same night I did. In the same scene, in fact." He blushed a little, like he hadn't meant to reveal such an intimate detail. His voice remained calm, though. "So maybe, just maybe, the scars you saw weren't incurred at the same time as the injuries that put him in the hospital."

I looked out the window at the trees going by in the dark. "You're saying I jumped to conclusions."

"Knife play and blood play tend to cause people to. The cops probably would, too."

A bitter laugh caught behind my breastbone and refused to come out. Clive was talking to me like I didn't know anything about knife play. *Ha.* That told me that he didn't know my history after all.

I decided not to enlighten him. "Is that so."

"I'm not saying it's not a factor. I'm just saying… Be careful, I guess. You're right. People tonight will want to know what happened." He looked out his own window, as the limo turned off the road onto a curving driveway. "Wex is a favorite of our host."

I caught sight of the mailbox at the edge of the road, the letter D styled into wrought-iron scrollwork, and felt a sudden chill run down my back. "Who's the host of this party, anyway?" I asked. "Is that who put those marks on you and him?"

"Yes," Clive answered. "Ira Dayton."

FIVE

I suppose it would be accurate to call that house a McMansion. Not quite large enough to be an actual mansion, but it had the trappings of grandeur, including a sweep of wide, shallow front stairs leading up to the front door like the ostentatious train of a Met Gala dress. The front door was flanked by two columns that looked like they belonged on a Roman coliseum, not in the suburbs.

Clive somehow made it out of the car and around to my side faster than the driver—Stefan, Clive had called him—and as Stefan opened my door, Clive held out his hand to help me out. I took it, but I was thinking: Why so service-oriented all of a sudden? Still trying to apologize for ghosting me?

I made a point to thank Stefan for his service as a driver, and to ask, if I needed to leave early, if he'd be available to take me back to the train. He told me he'd be parked on the far side of the tennis court, where the cars of other guests who had driven were parked. "Feel free to come find me if you need." I must have looked very inquisitive because before I could ask the question on my mind, he went on: "I don't go inside. I only drive."

I couldn't even see the tennis court. There must have been more to the property than we could make out from the front.

Clive offered me his arm. "Let me introduce you to some people," he said, as we climbed those ridiculous stairs. "You seem a little nervous."

I was about to snatch my hand back—and lecture him about how I'd no doubt know plenty of people there because I'd been in the New York scene much longer than he had—when I realized he was right. My apprehension level had shot up when he'd said Ira's name. I settled for, "I know the hosts already. Kanna and I used to volunteer together."

"Oh, great." He smiled and seemed relieved. "She's fun, isn't she?" he enthused. "And wicked. She's joining our scene tonight." He suddenly realized that perhaps that wasn't the most tactful thing to tell me and went on a bit more soberly: "Ira and mine, I mean. They, um, haven't told me what they'll be doing to me, exactly."

"Because you like surprises."

Clive looked slightly shocked. Had he forgotten he told me that? Or was he surprised I remembered?

A trans guy I recognized from around town, whose scene name was Cricket, was working the door. He gave Clive a quick hug of greeting and then asked if he could hang my jacket.

I told him no, thanks, since I wasn't planning to stay very long, plus I was still a bit chilly. It was really too light a jacket for how cold the night was getting.

"If you smoke, you'll want it to wear on the pool deck, anyway," he replied. "That's the only place smoking is allowed." Cricket drew a breath like he was about to start a long spiel.

"I'll show her around," Clive said, forestalling whatever recitation of the house rules was about to come forth.

"Great. Nice to see you, Mira."

"You, too. The beard looks really awesome on you." I smiled as he stroked his Van Dyke villainously and then cracked up and waved us into the living room.

The living room had a white shag carpet so thick and luxurious it was like they'd skinned and bleached a hundred Pomeranians. How did they keep it so clean? Especially when they were into blood play? Even the couch was white. White leather.

Clive had the explanation: "The living room, kitchen and dining room are for food and socializing only. The main play area is the great room that opens onto the deck." We passed through the too-white living room into the dining room, where the sideboard was covered with foil chafing dishes. My stomach growled at the scent of Sterno and rich spices. I'd been too upset to eat more than a container of yogurt earlier in the day.

I lifted the cover off one of the dishes. "Is that lamb saag?"

"Probably. There's usually chicken tikka masala, too. Later, there'll be cake." A side table by the sliding glass doors to the great room held pitchers of ice water and bottles of soda. Kink is thirsty work.

My stomach growled again, much more audibly. "Did Kanna make all this?"

As if conjured by the sound of her name, Kanna bounced up behind me: "Mira!"

Kanna is a hugger. She squeezed me hard, squishing her boobs between us. She was wearing a black corset over a frilly white shirt, her eyes dark with kohl, her black hair drawn back into tight bun. She wore a silver nose ring that I didn't remember seeing before, but maybe I'd just forgotten about it. "Haven't seen you in forever! But for the record, no, the food's catered. The only thing I'm raking over coals tonight is this guy right here." She went on tiptoe to give Clive a peck on the cheek. "You ready?"

"Always," Clive said.

"Well, I'm not." She laughed. "I better go finish my prep!"

She hurried away and Clive looked around for the plates and silverware, as if I couldn't find them myself. "If you're hungry, don't wait."

"Indeed," said a voice from the doorway. Backlit by the bright fluorescent lights of the kitchen, Ira stood there in a getup I can only describe as full vampire regalia, from his floor length leather duster and white ruffled shirt right down to the metal claws on the tips of his fingers. Everything short of fake fangs. "As toothsome as delayed gratification may be, we encourage you to satisfy every carnal need without hesitation here. Speaking of which—"

I cut across him. "I have something to talk to you about." Did he really not know Wexel had been missing? And would he be faffing about a play party if he did?

Ira moved faster than I expected from a surgeon, seizing Clive by the hair. "So sorry, Mira. It'll have to wait. This one is late for a scene."

"Late?" Clive yelped in surprise. "But you said—!"

A quick slap across the face silenced him, and before I could interrupt any further, Ira had dragged him away. I'd have to wait until they finished to tell him about Wex. I got a plate and served myself some rice and spoonfuls of various dishes, my mind quietly seething. There wasn't anything wrong with what I'd just seen. Springing something on them suddenly—like making them think they were late, even if they weren't—was a classic technique to get a bottom off balance. Was it all part of Clive's "surprise"? Or had Clive actually lost track of the time between the car breaking down and then showing me around?

Or had Ira decided he just had to literally pull Clive away from me?

I took my plate and sat at the dining room table where I could look through the sliding glass doors into the great room. All the rest of the party guests were in there, chatting and murmuring, while some kind of soothing cello music played. Although I could see a flogging frame against one wall and a spanking bench, no one was playing yet. They all seemed to be waiting for something, which I supposed was Ira and Clive's scene. I made out a few familiar faces. A statuesque blond man with a woman in a ballet tutu. A cheerful-looking triad—two women and a large man with a ponytail—I seemed to recall were from Boston. Or maybe they just looked like people I'd met before.

I could only eat a few bites of the food, even though I was hungry. The thought of having to tell everyone about Wexel made my insides clench uncomfortably. What if Clive was right, and the markings were from a recent scene and had nothing to do with how he ended up in the hospital? Would I get everyone freaked out over nothing? Was I overreacting?

I knew I could easily overreact to anything involving knives. Not that I considered wrapping all my knives in leather and heaving them into the Hudson River an overreaction. No, that had been the most reasonable course of action.

My skin prickled as the music in the next room changed. Intensified. Did the lights dim a bit, as well? The twenty or so guests standing and sitting all around the room fell quiet as if they had, anyway. I got up from the table and slipped inside the glass doors.

From the doorway I could see the whole room. A cathedral ceiling with exposed beams vaulted overhead, a stone fireplace along one wall. The lights did dim, and the glow of the swimming pool lights from outside filled an entire side of the room that was floor-to-ceiling glass. At the center was a multi-level sunken living room but at the bottom, where there should have been a massive 1970s sectional sofa, there stood a steel bondage frame.

The frame was a cube, taller than a person, with rings at each corner for attaching chains or slings or whatever to.

The music intensified again, drums adding to the track, and then some ghostly vocals. There was no fire in the big stone hearth, but a few candles flickered along the mantlepiece. The music swelled dramatically and Kanna and Ira led Clive straight past me then, right to the frame. She had added a long leather coat to match Ira's and had put on taller boots. I caught a whiff of a sweet scent in the air and thought it must be Kanna's perfume. But the scent seemed to build as time went by, so I assumed it was the candles, or maybe incense burning somewhere I couldn't see.

Clive was wearing nothing but a thong, and after they bound his wrists to opposite corners of the cube, Kanna slid a little dagger down one of Clive's hips and cut even that away.

He was beautiful. Every inch of him. Took my breath away.

Ira began to pontificate something about initiating Clive to the mysteries of light and darkness. I dismissed it as some kind of vampire role-playing blather and didn't really listen. All my attention was taken up by Clive. I could hear his breath as Kanna blindfolded him.

They flogged him. Kanna in front, Ira in back, using a matched set of floggers with silver handles. Kanna was the one who made him jump and yelp, as her blows batted his nipples and his inner thighs. From where I stood, I could see Clive in profile and how visibly aroused he was. They worked him over thoroughly, while Ira went on about invoking the elements—air, water, etc.—to "purify" him.

The flogging was just a prelude, though, to the cutting. They circled around him, each holding a ceremonial blade in one hand and a scalpel in the other. I remember in particular Ira saying that before the initiate could undergo the binding, they had to look into his soul, because any flaw could cause him to shatter under the pressure if he wasn't pure.

I thought to myself: That's why I don't go in for role playing: I can't even fake believing in a pure soul. I started trying to guess the direction of the scene. Were they going to pretend to find a black spot on his soul and cut it out? Or what? Don't get me wrong: role playing something like that can be incredibly cathartic. And it's some folks' idea of fun.

But I wanted it to be real. I wasn't a duchess or a goddess and didn't like pretending to be something I wasn't, but if my partner and I agreed on what we were to each other, that became our reality. That's what I'd wanted most with Ethan: a shared reality. But in the end, he couldn't even pretend the rules mattered to him.

One thing about blood: it's very, very real. When you see it, smell it, sense it, every instinct tells you not to ignore it. You can shrug off a bruise, ignore a sore spot, not notice when something goes numb, but not when knife parts skin.

The marking began. Ira and Kanna stood side by side behind Clive, each one drawing a design on a shoulder with the tip of the ceremonial blade. They were leaving scratches rather than really cutting him, and the moans Clive made were deep and sensual. Each of his groans seemed to ratchet something tighter inside me, where lust and anxiety entwined.

Kanna moved in front of him then, adding bursts of pain-pleasure with the tip of her knife swirling across his chest, while Ira prepared his scalpel, showing it to the crowd with a dramatic gesture, like a stage magician.

I felt suddenly hot and had to look away. I looked behind me, at the sliding glass door to the dining room, and in the glass I thought I could see a wild-haired woman, eyes aglow, face striped like a tiger, a goddess predator baring her teeth. Had the incense really gone to my head? Then I realized I was looking through my own reflection at the cans of Sterno under the chafing dishes. Nothing mystical about it, right? But everything still felt trance-y and uncanny.

I dared a glance back. Kanna and Ira were like yin and yang on either side of Clive. Her: dark, in black leather with her glossy black hair unbound. Ira: light, blond and pale and his ruffled shirt so white. They'd shed their leather dusters and their arms seemed to blur as they moved sinuously, cutting designs in the air with a pair of straight razors. Then Kanna put a hand on Clive's chest, the other holding the blade at the point where Clive's neck met his shoulder. Ira had a hand on Clive's back and his blade was poised at the same point on the other side. I could see the sheen of sweat on Clive's skin and almost imagine what it would feel like to have my hand on his beating heart.

"And now, we Open the Gates," Ira said. Those razors were so sharp all they had to do was touch them to the designated spot and let them sink into the skin like butter. Clive went rigid and maybe I was hallucinating but I could've sworn I heard the sound of a gong.

In the next heartbeat, Kanna suddenly slumped to her knees, like she was losing consciousness. And before Ira could get around Clive to catch her, Hell literally broke loose: A gout of flame erupted from the hearth and people screamed. Ira was knocked back on his ass from the explosion and it was like I could see him fall in slow motion. I knew I shouldn't just stand there, but it was like I was under water, and falling deeper into a trance by the moment. The screams got louder as people realized the fire was real and wasn't just a part of the show, but I could barely move. I watched as flames crawled up the stone chimney toward the vaulted roof. The sound of glass shattering reached my ears but as if from very far away. The ballerina had smashed one of huge window panes and I watched as her partner swept her into his arms and out onto the deck, in slow motion, like some avant garde interpretation of Swan Lake.

And then everything snapped back into real time when for me when Clive screamed "Divinity! Divinity!"

His safeword.

I was in motion almost before I knew what I was doing, reaching into the dining room, as the horror of what was going on sank in. Clive had no idea some fire code violation was about to send him to an early grave. He thought it was all a mindfuck, all part of the scene, and had finally had too much. Everyone had fled toward the pool in the panic to get out. Ira was one of the last, dragging Kanna's unconscious body in that direction. The flames were spreading, jumping from the wall to the beams overhead and creeping toward the carpet.

In their flight, no one had stopped to free Clive.

Don't ask me where I got the idea, but I dumped one of the pitchers of water over my own head and then I guess I leaped down to Clive with the other, because it seemed like I was there in an instant. I doused Kanna's discarded leather duster and plastered it to his shoulders. He was panicking and couldn't figure out how to unclip the cuffs himself, pulling at them frantically.

"Clive! It's Mira! Stand still!"

He reacted to my voice and did as he was told, thank goodness. It only took a second to unclip him, and then I was simultaneously pulling his blindfold off and pulling him away from the rising flames, which had spread along the back of the room, cutting off our escape to the pool. I must've been still a bit trippy because the sparks flying looked almost like tiny faces with burning eyes staring at me.

You only get a limited number of seconds to escape a fire like that, before the smoke overcomes you. I didn't dare look up, but I could feel the heat pressing down on us from above. We ran through the dining room. By all that's holy, I swear the sideboard was engulfed in dancing blue flames, as if the Sterno pots had decided to join the party.

The front door was in sight and I thought we were going to make it. But as we were crossing the living room, Clive fell. I don't mean he tripped; he went limp on that plush rug. I dragged him by his feet as far as the front door but once we were on the stone front stoop I couldn't go any farther. I sat there gasping air and trying to think. If I dragged him down those stupid stone steps he'd have brain damage by the time we got to the driveway. The house was going up like it was made of tinder. We couldn't stay where we were, and I couldn't lift him.

But I couldn't leave him.

I couldn't.

I think I cried for a few moments; I'm not sure. I could not make myself leave Clive's side, lying there on the stone porch. I was startled back to awareness when the suburban night was split by cracking sounds: the roof of the great room collapsing. A column of sparks shot into the sky, sending smoke, ash, and embers throughout the rest of the house. Goodbye white carpet and couch. I kicked the front door shut to try to keep the burning ashes from showering us, but it was only a matter of time before the rest of the place came down. We had to get farther away, but even with all the adrenaline in my system I could not carry him.

You know the thing in old movies where they slap someone in the face to wake them up after they've been knocked unconscious? As a kid I thought it was just a hokey Hollywood convention, but Sensei Jack, a self-defense instructor at the gym where I worked and who I liked hanging out with, had claimed there's a grain of truth in it. And I was angry and desperate enough to try anything. I slapped Clive across the face, perhaps a bit harder than I meant to, shouting "Goddamnit, Clive! Wake up!"

His eyes flew open and he blinked, confused, stammering, "M-M-my lady…!"

I didn't have time to question whether it had worked or if it was a coincidence. "Come on!" I grabbed him by the hand and we ran down the steps and then up the sloping, curving driveway toward the road.

He stumbled again as we reached a hedgerow at the edge of the property, falling to his knees in the cold, damp grass. I crouched next to him. Both of us were breathing way too hard, but at least out here the air was clear. Behind us, the house was rapidly being engulfed by flames. Another section of roof fell in, sending sparks into the night sky.

Once we weren't in immediate danger of being killed by fire, my attention turned to the cold. It was below forty and still dropping, and Clive was buck naked. The leather duster had been left behind when I'd dragged him onto the porch. My mind was clicking through the possibilities: had anyone had time to call the fire department? How long would it take them to get here? And would it invite unwanted lines of questioning if the first thing they saw was a naked man? How long would it take for Clive to get hypothermia?

And would there even be anything left of the place by the time the fire engines arrived? I'd never seen a house go up that fast, and I remarked on it to him.

"It's not a normal fire," he told me. Then he suddenly bowed his head. When he raised it again he looked me right in the eyes and asked, "Do you trust me?"

Me. "That's a loaded question."

Him. "It's a loaded situation." His breathing was still rough. "Listen. The thing I couldn't tell you… I think the fire has to do with that. It wasn't an accident."

Nothing like an actual life and death situation to reinforce my suspicion he was mixed up in something like the mafia or CIA. Little did I know. "You think people are after you?"

"Not just me. You told me yourself you think Wex was attacked."

I felt like a ball of ice suddenly formed in my throat and I had to swallow. Wex. "And you think it's related."

"Yes. I know I tried to downplay it before, but we can't take the chance that the same people who tried to kill him and failed didn't also just try to kill the rest of us."

If there was even a slim chance that was true, then we had to get out of there, and I said so, but first I slipped my leather jacket off, my shoulder bag of whips thudding to the ground. I'd forgotten entirely that I was carrying them. My phone was in the side pocket.

"We should hurry," he urged.

"I know. But at least if someone kills you, you'll have some clothes on." I pulled my sweater-dress over my head and handed it to him. While he put it on, I zipped up my leather jacket over my bra.

The sweater was at least long enough to cover his bare ass. He looked down at his uncovered legs. "Well, I'm a little less conspicuous, anyway."

We could both hear the sirens by then—the fire department on the way. No need to call 911, then. I suggested we try walking back to his car.

It was the best plan we had.

We hurried along the side of the road away from the house. The next driveway was at least a quarter mile down. A suburb like that is for rich folks who like their privacy. We'd made it out of sight of the house and around a bend when the sound of the sirens died out. The trucks must have arrived at the fire. I glanced back and saw a new gout of embers and ashes rise into the darkness.

Clive's feet were bare, but he didn't complain as we walked. We turned onto another road he said would bring us eventually to the spot where his SUV broke down. "Maybe it'll even start," he said with a hopeful shrug. "The problem kind of comes and goes."

"But aren't your keys back in the fire with your clothes?"

"There's a spare hidden under the back bumper in one of those little magnetized compartments." He tucked his hands under his arms. "My dad loves to send me useless gadgets he buys on TV."

"Sounds a lot like my dad," I said. "The only thing that keeps him from doing it now is he's overseas."

"Yeah?"

"Yeah. He and my mom relocated to the Philippines. They come back every couple of years, but they run a charity vaccination program. Big crusade to eliminate polio and measles." Chatting made me feel less chilly. Maybe because it was a distraction. He told me his parents were college professors in Colorado and that he'd been raised in Massachusetts. I nattered on to him about finishing massage school and working in an upscale spa and fitness center.

I asked one of the standard questions: "How'd you end up in New York?"

"I'm doing a postdoc at Columbia." He looked away, as if bracing himself for criticism.

"Studying what?"

"Ancient languages." He shrugged. "But I've been thinking about quitting."

"Because of whatever it is you can't tell me?"

"I was getting disillusioned even before that came up," he said. "I'm looking for… something. In life. And I'm not even sure what it is, but I don't think I'm going to find it studying Latin."

"You mean a 'meaning of life' kind of thing?"

"Yeah." He looked up into the murky sky. Between the glow of the big city and the foggy air, not a star could be seen. "Have you ever wanted to be part of something bigger than just yourself?"

"You mean like dedicating your life to a cause?"

"Yeah. To something."

Or someone, I thought.

"Like your parents," he said. "Doing good in the world."

"I suppose. I haven't found something I believe in that much, yet." I kept glancing behind us, but no one was following. "I was raised nominally Catholic, but that just meant when I hit the age where kids quit believing in the Easter Bunny and Santa, I quit believing in Jesus, too."

He chuckled. "Same. Last time I was in a church was for my older brother's wedding. Five years ago, I think? I'd just seen a dominatrix for the first time. She put me through a Catholic school scene, caned me so hard I could barely sit the next day. I thought the pew was going to catch fire from my pure wickedness."

I chuckled, too. "Yeah, I bet your ass felt like fire." It was funny. We'd just been through a near-death experience and were far from safe, yet I felt more relaxed than I had in ages. Maybe part of it was I found Clive's presence genuinely soothing, as if just being with him made me feel something was right with the world. "Relaxed" is not the right word at all, of course, not when I was so alert for danger. The best way to describe it was that I felt more like myself, I suppose. "Five years ago, hm? That was about when I got into the scene. I mean, I was having kinky sex before that, but that was when I got political and joined an organized community."

"I know what you mean."

I found myself saying more than I'd meant to, but somehow talking to him at that moment, I realized something, and said it aloud for the first time. "I thought the BDSM community itself, maybe, was going to be the larger thing I devoted myself to. The thing worth making sacrifices for. To help others. To make a difference. That kind of thing."

"But? I hear a 'but' coming."

"You and your butt," I teased, swatting him on the sweater. "You're right, though. I got burned out, I guess." Ethan had called my activism "crusading" and he didn't mean it nicely. "Even after I stepped down from an official role, my relationship didn't recover."

"When was that?"

"Last year." I shrugged. I didn't want him to think I was on the rebound. No, I'd long since bounced off the rim and rolled to a stop in a dusty corner.

We walked on in silence for a few more steps before he said, "I think I may have found something I can believe in."

"May have? Meaning you aren't sure you really believe it?"

He laughed. "Yes. That." Then he glanced behind us, exactly like I had been. "Ira and Kanna introduced me to some people in the city. Sort of 'spiritual' people. Um, you know how in BDSM there are people who are into the spiritual side of sex?"

"Yes." I had considered myself one of them, once.

"These people are into the sexual side of the spiritual."

"What's the difference?"

"Well, the BDSM crowd has the folks who get spanked and think they see God. These folks… are way beyond that."

"So, like kinky Scientology?"

"No no, nothing like that. They're not kinksters and they're not a cult. I'm not explaining it well. I…" He shook his head. "I shouldn't have even brought it up."

"Then why did you?"

He pulled me suddenly behind a tall, narrow juniper at the edge of a driveway. The bushes were planted along the road and onto the property, lining the drive like a column of soldiers on either side. A moment later a car sped past, the headlights throwing shadows across us. Either we went unseen or that wasn't a carload of murderers looking for us. Clive drew a shaky breath. "Do you believe me when I say someone out there is trying to kill us?"

"Yes."

"The people I'm talking about—"

"The sexual spiritualists?"

"Yes, them. They told me they have enemies."

Even though I was trying hard to believe him, I know I sounded skeptical. "Enemies who are trying to kill them. And you."

"And possibly you, now, which is why I'm telling you this. Even though I was sworn to secrecy." He drew another rough breath and I wondered if he'd inhaled too much smoke. He pulled me deeper between the column junipers. "If you're contacted by a guy named Roland, you can trust him."

"Contacted. What do you mean contacted?"

Clive sank to one knee, his breath laboring. "They told me if… I ever spoke of them to anyone… they'd *know*. And that it didn't matter if I tried to run away or hide. They'd find me."

"So they're the spiritual sex mafia…?" None of this was making sense. "Clive, I should call 911. You look like you're about to pass out."

"Promise me you won't."

"Call 911?"

"Promise. This will prove it's real. The police can't help with this. The only ones who can help us now are—" He made a strangled sound of pain.

"Clive, seriously, you look like you're about to keel over."

"I am," he said. "But if they show up, we'll know it's real."

"If *who* show up?"

"The Circle of Light," he said, and, as predicted, promptly keeled over.

SIX

Smacking Clive across the face again did nothing but put a red handprint onto his cheek and make me feel guilty for doing it. Maybe I had to be angrier, or more desperate for it to work, or maybe he was further gone than before. I cursed him and tried to figure out how much danger we'd be in if I called an ambulance. Would it alert nameless killers to our position, or what? There was too much I still didn't know about who they were and why they might want Clive and Wex—and other people at the party? me included?—dead.

I wondered if Cricket, Stefan, and the others had escaped, but I had to focus on Clive and myself right then and worry about the rest later. I considered leaving him hidden by the bushes and then—what, running to his car? That was never going to work. It would take me too long to get there, and then what if it wouldn't start? I couldn't leave him defenseless.

My heart jumped as I realized the car coming up the road was slowing as it neared. I flattened myself to the ground, the piney scent of juniper and bark mulch filling my senses. I vaguely hoped it was just the residents of the property.

It wasn't. A white van with a logo of a paint can on the door pulled to a stop directly across the road. My choices narrowed to two: If I was interested in saving myself, the thing to do was run (but I knew I wouldn't). If I was interested in saving Clive, the thing to do would be hide and then catch the person by surprise.

Assuming they didn't have guns or firebombs or whatever. I really hated not knowing what I was up against. Made it so hard to plan.

I heard two doors open and shut. Okay, two of them. I positioned myself behind the next juniper over from where Clive lay. In the light from the headlights I could see them: two men. The bearded one was in a hoodie—the hood up. The other had straight shoulder-length hair, a leather jacket, and something about the way he walked made me think he was a soldier. A fighter, at least.

My gaze flashed to something on his leg. Sticking up above his boot was the handle of a knife. Once I saw it I couldn't take my eye off it. Knives. Why did there always have to be knives?

He looked like the tougher one, so I decided he should be taken out first. I'd deal with the guy in the hoodie after.

They bickered a bit as they neared. "Did you bring a flashlight?" "There's one in the glove compartment." "What about your phone?"

My chosen target paused to get the flashlight app open on his phone. I leaped on him and tried to take him down quickly. If the other one drew a gun or discovered Clive, I would have few options.

We hit the ground hard, knocking the wind out of him, and I elbowed him in the head, trying for that speedy knock-out. But he went with the blow, twisting to one side and getting out from under me. An experienced fighter, as I'd suspected. Before he could get all the way to his feet, I lunged at his legs, trying to both knock him down again and grab his knife. He twisted as he fell so he wouldn't go face first into the juniper. Twigs cracked and he cursed, kicking out to keep me from getting control of his legs.

I punched him in the nuts and he balled up like a pillbug. Sensei Jack would've been so proud. That should've bought me a few seconds to deal with the other guy.

But he had found Clive. His back to Clive's prone form, he faced me with his own knife drawn, looking like he wasn't sure what to do next. "Kish!" he shouted.

I heard the van door slam again and my heart sank. Three of them? And even if I could knock them all out, then what? Steal their van? Only if I could drag Clive into it.

Maybe he'd wake up. "Clive!" I called.

The bearded guy glanced back at Clive, who was still out cold, then back at me. "What did you do to him?"

I couldn't answer a question that didn't make sense to me. I hadn't done anything to Clive and if they were going to kill us anyway, why did they care? I kept my mouth shut, my eyes glued on the guy's blade, and shifted my feet. Another car came down the road, this one from the direction of Kanna and Ira's place, and as the shadows of the junipers swung over us, I kicked the knife clean out of his hand and attacked. He cursed as I bore him to the ground.

But the first guy had recovered—how?—and got me in a headlock from behind. Something hard ground against my jaw as I struggled to get free.

"You feel that?" he growled into my ear. "All I have to do to slit your throat is turn my wrist just a little. Don't struggle or you might make me slip."

I was on my knees, one of his legs trapping mine where they were. I was not about to stop struggling since staying still to get my throat slit didn't seem like a good option. "If you're going to kill us, just get on with it."

He made a disgusted-sounding huff. "Roland, what should we do with her?"

That made me stop struggling. "Wait, did you say Roland?" If he was the guy Clive had mentioned, then maybe these weren't the murderers after all. "Clive told me to trust you."

The third member of their party, a Black woman with a leather jacket over her hoodie, helped the bearded guy up. He was rubbing his throat. I guess I had hit him there.

His voice was rough. "We're not going to fall for that. Jair, can you restrain her?"

The guy with the knife—Jair—held me by the hair, the knife still at my neck, while Kish handcuffed me behind my back. She made a short hissing sound as she clicked the handcuffs in place, like she was whispering to someone named Sue, then stepped back. Something glinted on her face: an almost dainty eyebrow piercing.

They began to debate: "Now what do we do with her?" "We should try to pump her for information." "We can't bring her anywhere she could be tracked."

That made it sound like they weren't going to kill me. The bickering and indecision reminded me a lot more of a leather community committee than the Mafia.

That was my first impression of the Circle of Light.

SEVEN

Clive had said I should trust Roland and the Circle, but the problem was that they didn't trust me. I couldn't really blame them, I suppose; I'd attacked them first.

Roland rubbed his beard and sighed unhappily. He and Kish carried Clive to the van. I tried instinctively to follow, but Jair yanked me back. "You won't get another shot at him."

"How about another shot at you." I tried kicking behind me, but he was ready for that.

"Come on, your turn. Into the van." He marched me across the road, one hand still firmly lodged in my hair, the other holding the sleeve of my jacket. He was good at keeping control.

Kish got into the driver's seat, Roland beside her, while Jair held open the back doors of the van so I could climb in. A whiff of paint thinner reached my nose, but inside, where I expect to see shelves of paint cans, two benches faced a center aisle. Clive was lying on the floor of the aisle, his head cushioned on a folded drop cloth. I moved carefully, to avoid stepping on him, but with my hands bound behind my back it was tricky. Jair climbed in and shut the doors behind him. The windows were painted mesh so they looked pretty much opaque from the outside, but from inside I could see through the tiny holes.

Jair checked that his knife was secure in his boot sheath, then said, "You should let me put your seatbelt on. I don't want you landing on Clive—or a live blade—if we come to a sudden stop."

"Safety first, eh?" I no longer harbored any suspicions that these folks were members of a crack arson-murder squad, but I had to convince them that I wasn't one either. I could see a nasty scratch above his eye, a fainter one on his cheek, where one of the junipers got him. "Sorry about that."

"About what?" He reached across me for the seat belt, and I could tell his shampoo smelled like rosemary.

"Your face is scratched."

He dabbed at his cheek with the back of his hand and then examined it. No real blood to speak of. He shrugged. He made the belt a little too tight as he clicked it into place, challenging me just a little. I refrained from commenting that it was the first time I'd let a man put me in bondage since college.

Kish pulled the van onto the road toward the house and I warned her, "You don't want to go that direction."

"No?" Roland turned around to look at me. "Why not?"

I tried to explain. "Clive told me to trust you. So I'll tell you what he told me. We were at a party up the road. The house caught fire and we fled. He said the fire was no accident and I believe him."

Jair let out a "*ha*" but said nothing else.

I kept talking. "I don't know what's going on, but if what Clive said is true, the house isn't a safe place to visit. Whoever set the fire might still be there."

"She's right." Kish hit the blinkers.

Jair eyed me suspiciously. "She could be trying to keep us from rescuing Kanna and Ira."

Kish, though, had made up her mind and swung the van into a U-turn. "I'm turning around just in case. We can figure it out as soon as Clive comes to."

Roland looked me in the eye. He pushed his hood back and I saw his sandy hair was longer than Jair's and tousled. In the glow of the dashboard, he looked like a painting of Jesus, except for the two silver rings piercing one ear. They looked like they matched the one in Kish's eyebrow. "Tell me everything that happened."

I gave him the basic rundown: my first time at one of Kanna and Ira's parties, them opening the party with a big roleplaying scene with Clive, et cetera. Roland wanted details about the scene.

He didn't laugh when I called it a piece of over-the-top vampire role play. I tried to remember what Ira had been blathering about. "Ira announced that before Clive's initiation he had to be purified. Something about needing to see into his soul, to see if his soul was pure."

Jair and he shared a sharp glance. They were not happy. "So, what did they do to him?"

"Flogged him first, then used knives to scratch arcane markings on him, and then scalpels and straight razors. They'd only just made the first real cut, though, when the fire started." And of course they wanted to know how the fire started, but I hadn't the foggiest. "An empty fireplace suddenly went whoosh, and two seconds later the roof was on fire." Then I remembered: "The second before the fire broke out, Kanna collapsed."

"Did you see what happened to her and Ira?"

"Last I saw, he was dragging her out by the swimming pool. Everyone pretty much ran out that way, but then the fire blocked that off. I freed Clive and took him out the front door." I shifted as well as I could in the seatbelt so I could look at both Jair and Roland. "My turn to ask questions."

Jair's jaw dropped. "You're our prisoner! You don't get to ask questions."

"Sure I do. I've already figured out you're not the murderers."

"Oh, yeah? Who are we, then?" Jair sounded almost offended.

"You're the spiritual sex mafia Clive told me about."

Kish tried to hold in a snort, but didn't manage it. "That's one way of putting it."

Roland and Jair were sharing another long look. Jair tried to insist: "We can't trust her. What if she's one of them, went with Clive just to try to infiltrate us, and was about to kill him before we came along?"

"If I was trying to infiltrate you, why would I be trying to kill him?" I shook my head. "Before he passed out, Clive said he would prove to me it was real. That he had sworn not to tell, because if he did, you told him you'd be able to find him wherever he went. So he told me, because he believed if he did, that meant you'd be able to find him."

Kish let out a laugh. "That is... so smart and so stupid at the same time I don't know whether to laugh or cry. Maybe we should've just given Clive our phone numbers."

"He had Ira's," Roland pointed out.

Jair made a disgruntled sound. "It could still be a story. She might have forced Clive to break his oath of secrecy to lure us there."

"If my master plan was to lure you into an ambush, don't you think I would have picked a better place?"

Jair opened his mouth to argue, then closed it again. It *had* been a shitty spot for an ambush.

"Look, I get it. If people are trying to kill you, you're not going to trust people easily. I'm still a little leery of the entire concept myself, but Clive said you'd show up, and you did. So I guess count me among the believers."

"Amen," Kish said.

Roland thought about that for a bit. "What's your name?"

"Mira. Mira Cruise." Once upon a time the family name had been Cruz, but not in a few generations.

"Mira, Mira, on the wall," Jair singsonged, appraising me. "I'd like to believe you, but getting it wrong could be a disaster." He shifted in his seat like maybe his balls were still feeling the effects of our fight. The scratch over his eye looked like it could use a Band-Aid. I guess I couldn't blame him for being careful.

But if we were going to work together, we had to get past the suspicions. "Wake up Clive and he'll tell you."

Jair unsheathed his knife again; it came free silently. The blade was black, only the edge reflecting light. "Oh, don't worry." He tucked a thumb against the guard from the handle that had been digging into me, and cut a swirl in the air. "We'll wake him up."

EIGHT

An office park seemed an unusual place to perform whatever procedure they intended to revive Clive, or so I thought as Kish pulled the van off the main road. A building as nondescript as a beige business suit sat dark except for the lights in a small lobby atrium. "No cars. Not even a security guard's. This is perfect," she declared as she drove around the behind the building and parked where the van couldn't be seen from the road. The back parking lot was surrounded by a steep embankment dotted with professional landscaping but topped by wild woods.

Jair climbed out the back and gestured for me to follow, helping me balance since I couldn't use my hands with them cuffed behind my back like that. The overcast was breaking up and the moon peeked around the ragged edges of a cloud. I shivered a little.

I stood to one side while the three of them lay Clive gently on the pavement. My sweater rode up around his waist and my urge to pull it down so he wouldn't be so exposed made me shift from foot to foot. Roland sat crosslegged at his head. "I can do it myself, but Kish, it'll be easier with your help."

Kish sat at Clive's feet. Jair and I stood off to one side. He asked, "Are you sure you don't want me to take East?"

Roland shot down that idea. "No. Better to keep it balanced." When Roland drew his knife, my hackles went up.

Jair put a hand on my shoulder. "He's not going to hurt him."

I shrugged him off. "Like putting a spell on him that knocked him unconscious didn't hurt him?"

"We don't use the word 'spell.'"

"Whatever. Hypnotic suggestion? Psychic whammy? Is that better?" I was getting angry again, thinking: Who the hell are these people? Just because Clive trusted them didn't necessarily mean they were trustworthy.

Roland cleared his throat and called for quiet.

Far as I could tell, he didn't say anything aloud after that. But he did make a few angular cuts in the air above Clive's head with his knife. Kish reached out once or twice, palms up like she was weighing something.

Then Roland put his palm over Clive's mouth and frowned. "I've undone the binding on his oath of silence, but I can't seem to put it back."

Kish felt the air in front of her: "You taught us oaths have to be affirmed. Maybe we have to wake him up and re-obtain his consent?"

Roland seemed to think it was supposed to work, though. "The original consent should cover re-establishing it, so long as it's the same person. Which I am."

"That feels sketchy," Kish said. "I bet he has to be awake for you to re-apply it."

They debated for a while longer, but eventually Roland gave in and decided waking Clive up was the only logical next step. He put his hands on Clive's face, palms over his eyes, said a word I didn't recognize, and began to slowly lift his hands.

Clive batted his hands away and growled.

Jair cursed sharply and drew his knife. Clive rolled into a crouch and tried to back away from Roland and Kish.

"You're *sure* that spell didn't hurt him?" I asked.

Jair ignored my sarcasm. "Stay behind me in case the containment circle doesn't hold."

Clive stood, my plain knit sweater-dress ridiculously out of place on the otherworldly figure he had become. In the mix of parking lot lights and moonlight it looked like his eyes were glowing and flickering like a fluorescent fixture going bad. He flexed his fingers and balled them into fists as he began to float upward off the ground. All of him glowed, not just his eyes.

"What did you do to him?" I yelled.

"This isn't our doing!" Roland yelled back. "Kish, please tell me you've covered exorcism in your training."

"Nope, not yet."

I was feeling very unimpressed with the Circle of Light at that point.

"We've just got to keep it contained, then," Roland said. "Until it gets bored and moves on." He stretched out his arms and so did she, like they were encompassing Clive in a very wide hug.

Then Clive roared. There's no other word for it. He opened his mouth and a roar came out, and flames sprang up all around him.

How was staying behind Jair going to keep me safe from something like that? "What the hell?"

"There is no Hell," Jair said. He took another step back, forcing me to back up, too. "But that is a demon."

"Explain."

"Hell is a concept cooked up by power-mad religious leaders to control and instill fear in their followers," he said. "But demons. Demons are a real thing. And so is demonic possession."

Which explained Roland's comment about exorcism. "So that's not really Clive?"

"No. So we can't just attack because we'd hurt Clive in the process. Plus I think this demon can probably wreck us all without breaking a sweat."

"Mira," Roland called. "You said something about the scene at the party being a… a ritual of some kind?"

"Yeah, what of it?"

"Did they say they were 'opening the gates'?"

"Come to think of it, yeah, Ira said exactly that."

"And they cut here and here?" He tapped the top of his trapezius, right where people carry their stress.

"Yes."

He cursed. The demon roared again, and the entire sphere he was held by filled with flames—not just the usual red and yellow but blue and purple, too. When they cleared, my sweater was gone and Clive stood there naked, his hair floating upward, as if a powerful updraft were blowing. I'd be lying if I didn't note that it was an awesome sight, though at the time the aesthetics of it weren't foremost in my mind. He roared a third time.

"Is it me, or did it look like the bubble around him expanded just now?" I asked Jair.

"It's not your imagination."

"So what's that mean—the bit about the gates and where they cut?"

"I think it means Clive's soul is out and about, and that left the door open for his body to be possessed. Roland," he called out. "Your containment isn't going to hold. Even Mira can see it buckling."

Roland threw a surprised frown in my direction, then reached inside his hoodie. "Damn. I was really hoping it wasn't going to come to this. Kish, get ready to catch him if he falls."

"All right." She got to her feet.

Clive faced her and roared. So much anger in that sound, so much absolute rage.

"What's Roland doing now?" I asked Jair.

"He's going to try to drive the demon out." Jair backed us up a little further. When Roland pulled out a rosary, though, Jair cursed again and ducked behind the van, urging me to follow. "Come on!"

I found myself too transfixed by what I was seeing to move. Roland thrust the cross toward Clive, chanting something in Latin. The cross looked like an afterimage in my retina, a faint glow blurring in Roland's hand. Each time he thrust it, the flame-filled bubble around Clive wobbled and in my ears it sounded like my head was inside a very big drum.

With one final shout from Roland and a super-emphatic thrust, the containment bubble burst. Heat blasted me like someone had opened an oven door and Clive's roar sounded much louder. His feet hit the ground and he stalked toward Roland, who held the cross between them, but his hand was shaking.

Jair was behind me then, suddenly, doing something to my handcuffs. "What are you doing?"

"Giving you a chance to escape with your life. Run, Mira." He undid the cuffs and then dashed to Kish's side.

I did not run for my life. I didn't know why not other than some part of me thought, dammit, I didn't save Clive from a fire just to abandon him now. There had to be a way to fix this. There had to.

Clive reached Roland and snatched the rosary out of his hand. With a growl, he ripped it in two and flung it away, the cross going one direction, the chain of beads in the other. The beads landed at my feet. I picked up the chain so I wouldn't trip over it.

Clive had knocked Roland to the ground, but then he turned toward me. Jair and Kish both tried to grab him; both were flung away. He was coming for me like a god of destruction and I decided Jair had been right: I should run.

I sprinted for the embankment, thinking if I could reach the tree line, I could hide. I scrambled up the steep slope, my hands and feet slipping a bit in landscaping bark that smelled of wood and rot. I didn't dare look back until I'd reached the top of the escarpment. He was still coming, stalking after me, not running. The other three regained their feet and ran at him. A mere gesture sent them sprawling back again. Not good.

I ran into the trees. There was a suggestion of a path, but I quickly lost it and just went crashing through the underbrush until I was on the far side of a large tree. I pressed myself against the trunk. I had no idea if demons could track people or what. My only chance was that he would miss me, go deeper into the woods, and I could circle back to the others and try to figure something out from there.

But where was he? I thought for sure I would hear him crunching through the brush after me. I dared a glance around one side of the tree, but there was no sign of him even though I was sure he must have come up the embankment long since. So I dared a look around the other side of the tree.

He floated there, about two feet off the ground, light flickering in his eyes like flames, and when he saw me, he lunged. His grip was like iron. No amount of krav maga or self-defense training was going to break that hold around my upper arms. I kicked him in the shins and he didn't even notice it. He bore me to the ground and I could feel his rampant cock pressing against me.

Part of me was wondering if that was just a natural state for a demon or what, but some emotional core of me felt outrage. *How dare he.* I tried to wrestle out of his grip, but only succeeded in twisting myself around in his arms. I went still as I felt his teeth on my neck. But he didn't tear out my jugular. He nibbled beneath my ear, seeking out a hot erogenous zone, his growl turning almost to a purr. Under other circumstances it was a sensation I'd welcome. But these were not those circumstances. My outrage grew. Like hell was I going to let some evil (?) wandering spirit have its way with me. I twisted again and our wrestling match continued.

I once read about a jogger in Colorado who got startled by a mountain lion. What saved her from an attack was that her reflex wasn't to run, but to *scold* it, yelling "Bad cat!" The lion had slunk away and left her unharmed. I suddenly understood that reaction. I got one arm free and smacked him in the face with my open palm. "Clive, *no.*"

That startled him at least enough that I wriggled free and we faced each other, both crouching. I tried to tamp down the irrational anger I was feeling so I could think clearly. Could a demon even understand what I said? Jair thought Clive wasn't home, but what if he was floating around nearby? I wondered if he could get control back or help us if I spoke to him.

Before I could think of what to say, though, Jair tackled the demon and they rolled into the underbrush. I heard someone take a solid hit. It must have been Jair, because only Clive got to his feet. I appreciate that even though he couldn't get up, Jair tried to grab Clive by the ankle, trying anything to slow the demon down as he came after me again.

Clive shook him off and then scooped me upward, hugging me chest to chest as we levitated up the trunk of the big tree. He sat me on the first branch we came to and I stared into those eyes, flickering with the flames of rage and lust—power that was barely trammeled into the shape of a man. I should have been terrified, but I was too busy trying to handle the situation to feel any fear. There had to be some way to put the rampaging genie back in the bottle.

Kish and Roland came together then to hit him with some kind of power. Wind rose up and Clive dropped to the ground, leaving me on the branch. The wind was whirling around us like a dust devil, small rocks and twigs stinging my skin. Jair and he faced each other, Clive crouching again as if he were about to pounce. His back was to me.

I still had the rosary beads in my hand. Could I choke him back into unconsciousness? The demon hadn't been able to do anything while Clive had been out cold, so it stood to reason that getting us back to square one might be the best thing I could do. And I'd had enough.

I dropped out of the tree onto his back, wrapping the beads around his throat. As he bucked, roaring into the swirling wind, I hung on like I was in a demon rodeo. I pulled the chain tight, shouting, "Clive! Stop this at once!"

And, everything stopped. The wind ceased, the pebbles fell to the ground, and Clive dropped to his knees. I put my feet on the ground but kept hold of the chain of beads. Flames flickered under his skin—brightest at the thin lines where Kanna and Ira had marked him—then went dark. His breath was harsh in his throat as he panted, but he didn't claw at the chain or try to free himself.

And to my utter amazement, he spoke these words, in a deeply resonant voice that seemed to come from all directions: "Yes, my lady."

NINE

Clive's answer was the only thing that kept me from tightening my makeshift garrote. If a god-damned demon could hold his rage in check, so could I. "You will cease this nonsense, immediately. You told me to trust these people! You should be protecting them the way they tried to protect you."

Again that voice surrounded me. "Yes, my lady."

"You will not raise a hand to me or to anyone in the... the... Circle of Light without my permission."

"Yes, my lady."

"And you will keep your goddamned cock to yourself." My hands shook. Maybe I wasn't doing such a good job of containing my rage after all. I glanced up to see Kish, Roland, and Jair poised to leap in if necessary. "Can you keep yourself under control?"

The demon spoke again. "Yes, my lady. I remember your rule."

My rule? Did he mean what I'd told Clive about requiring honesty? "Very well. You may kiss my boot."

He turned and prostrated himself, then pressed a kiss to the tip of one boot, sending powerful shockwaves of desire straight up my legs. By all that's holy, apparently nothing turns me on more than controlling a powerful being. Nothing. (And make no mistake: every person has power, just some more than others.)

When he lifted his head, *Clive* was blinking up at me, not the demon. All the glow and flames had faded and he looked... stunned. I held him under the chin. "Are you all right?"

"Um, I think so?" He reached up to touch the rosary and he jerked his hand away like he'd touched a live wire. "What just happened?"

Roland, Kish, and Jair huddled around. "That's what I'd like to know," Roland said. "Because it sure looks to me like a Partisan of Fire just got control of you."

"A what?" I put a hand into Clive's hair and he went stock still. "I just went on autopilot."

"She's not one of them," Clive said. "Mira saved me from a fire at Ira and Kanna's tonight."

"Are you sure?" Roland had his knife in his hand and gestured at me to step away from Clive.

I did no such thing. "Wasn't that why we stopped in the middle of nowhere to wake him up in the first place? So he could verify my story?"

Clive slumped a little and finally leaned into my hand. He had to be cold down there on the ground, and I could hear exhaustion in his voice: "Let me tell you how we met. At Club Purgatory the same night Ira and Kanna recruited me for the Circle. Mira and I played. But I never got back in touch with her because then I was sworn to secrecy."

"So you ghosted her?" Kish clucked her tongue. "Rude. You should've at least made some excuse. Sudden move to Kalamazoo or Kyrgyzstan or something."

"But I couldn't."

Roland faced me. He was close enough to put his hands on Clive's shoulders, but he put them into the pockets of his hoodie instead. "Because she'd already put you under a post-hypnotic suggestion."

"No. Because she told me she requires the whole truth, and I didn't want to disrespect that."

"But if you weren't going to see her, you didn't have to follow her rules, right?" Jair scratched his head. "I mean, why would a sub follow a dom's rules if they weren't going to be their sub anyway?"

"I'm not 'a sub,'" Clive snapped. "No matter how much Ira wants to make me one."

"Okay, whatever." Jair shrugged. "Roland, it's freezing out here. I don't think she's a threat. Can we talk about this in the van, at least?"

"Now you *don't* think she's a threat? But earlier—"

"Earlier she had just punched me in the nuts. Give her some credit for saving our asses."

Roland started to get strident. "Which she may have only done to try to gain our trust!"

Jair sighed. "Kish, you're the tie-breaker."

Kish also sighed. "Clive, describe tonight's party."

Not surprisingly, Clive's account matched mine, and confirmed some details for me. "Ira had planned a scene for me. He didn't tell me what to expect other than they were going to do it at midnight. When I got there, though, at almost eight, Ira hurried me right into bondage in the middle of the main room. They flogged me and said they were going to examine that block you've been sensing, testing me before initiation, and they cut me on the back of my shoulders, and here—" He touched the spot where he had been cut on either side, careful not to touch the beads around his neck. In the dark, I could no longer see the scars, but I knew they must be there. "And that was when an explosion happened? I think? I was blindfolded, but people were screaming and I could feel heat and hear flames. Next thing I knew, Mira was the one rescuing me."

"Which matches her story," Jair pointed out.

Roland stuck to his guns. "Which might only mean that she planted the whole thing in his head, to make herself seem innocent. Clive was blindfolded. She could have set the fire herself when she was afraid Kanna and Ira were going to find out his secret, neutralized them, and then spirited him away."

Jair frowned. "I thought only Barrow had those kinds of mind-control abilities."

"He could have taught someone else."

"Could I at least put some clothes on?" Clive asked, patting his chest as if wondering where the hell my sweater had gone.

"Stand up," I told him. I unzipped my jacket and moved to put it on him, but when Kish saw all I had on under it was a bra, she took hers off instead and wrapped it around Clive's shoulders. She kept her hoodie and buried her hands deep in the center pocket.

Clive put his arms through the sleeves. Kish was busty enough that it wasn't even too small for him. "You know, if Mira *did* have that kind of mind control, she would have long ago gotten the location of The Archive out of me. I vote we get back in the van."

"You don't get a vote until you've been initiated," Kish said. She and Jair shared a long, meaningful look. "But I move we get back in the van."

"Seconded," Jair said.

Roland threw up his hands. "Fine. Let's at least get away from here before the police come looking for the source of all the glowing lights."

TEN

The first place we went was the tree-lined road where Clive had left his SUV, but it was nowhere to be found. We presumed it got towed. We would have to deal with that later. Before long we were headed down the highway, the Hudson on one side and woods on the other. This time Clive and I sat side by side on the bench with Jair across from us. I held Clive close to keep him warm, wrapping one leg over his.

"So the thing you did, where you woke Clive up," I said to Roland. "Is that where the name Circle of Light comes from?"

"I don't think we know where the name Circle of Light comes from, but I don't think it's from that. Although—" Roland furrowed his brow as if no one had ever asked that before. "I really can't answer your questions."

"Because I might be one of the bad guys?"

"Because our whole existence is supposed to be a secret." He rubbed his eyebrows tiredly. "We're the keepers of sacred, secret knowledge."

"Like the Freemasons?"

"No!" he said at the same time Jair said, "Yes!"

Jair laughed. They bickered all the way back to Manhattan. Clive suggested we go to his apartment where at least he could put some clothes on, and which wouldn't give away the secret location of their Batcave. I kept quiet. For people who were supposed to be keeping secrets, they weren't very good at it. I learned, among other things, that the Circle had several other members, and that their enemies, the Partisans of Fire, were trying to wipe them—and their knowledge—out.

It was obvious to me that Roland was the supposed leader—or at least that he'd been around the longest. My guess was he was in his late forties, while Kish and Jair were more like me and Clive, mid-twenties at most. The two of them reminded me of Sensei Jack's buddies, the former Special Forces guys who would let me and the other women at the gym beat them up in the name of teaching us street self-defense—tough as nails, but they stayed relaxed, somehow, despite the danger. Roland, by contrast, was wound tight.

Even through the mesh window covering, I could see the lights of the GWB. There are a lot of bridges in New York City, but I always thought this one was the most elegant. It used to be my favorite.

Clive's place was just west of the Columbia University main campus. We were lucky to find a parking spot for the van only two or three blocks from his building. Out on the street, without really planning it, we walked as a group with Clive in the middle. No one really gave us a second look, though. I suppose in that neighborhood it was not unusual to see a half-naked student being walked home on a Saturday night by a group of friends?

His apartment was on the fourth floor. It had the look of a student place: full of mismatched furniture, hadn't been repainted in decades. The eating counter of the kitchen nook was strewn with books and papers.

Clive's number one priority upon getting into the apartment was to put on a pair of pants. Mine was rehydration. His fridge had little in the way of food in it, but there were plenty of beverages, including beer, water, and sports drinks. I normally hated the taste of Gatorade, but I guess surviving a house fire, walking a mile in the cold, and then fighting a demon can drain a person of electrolytes. Sitting down in the shabby-chic living room, I sucked down an entire bottle in one go. Kish sat next to me on the worn-out couch, sipping hers a bit more slowly. Jair and Roland had gone with Clive into the bedroom.

"You doing all right?" Kish asked.

"Fine, now." I put the empty bottle on a coffee table that was missing one leg. "Why?"

"Oh, you know, you might be a little freaked out after what happened back there."

A little freaked out. "Which part should freak me out more, the fact arsonists are trying to kill us or that I saw someone get possessed by a demon?"

She gave a teensy shrug. "Take your pick."

"I don't have time to be freaked out right now. If someone's really trying to kill us, any freaking out will have to wait until we're somewhere safe."

She raised an eyebrow and I realized this line of questioning could both stem from her concern for my wellbeing and also be an attempt to suss me out. "When they first learn about the Circle and stuff, people are usually at least a little weirded out."

"You know what weirds me out? That Jair and Roland went to help Clive put clothes on."

She snorted. "You haven't taken your eyes off that door since it closed."

"Clive's a grown man. He doesn't need their help." I realized that sounded a bit ridiculous, but my protective instinct was kicking in hard. "I guess rescuing him has made me feel sort of responsible for him."

"They're not going to hurt him." She let out a breath like she was resetting herself. "So, you're a kinkster."

"If you mean I'm into BDSM, yeah." I was still carrying the bag of whips. I moved it from my shoulder to my lap. I could feel my phone in the side pocket. "You, too?"

"Not exactly. I worked as a dominatrix for a little while when I first turned eighteen. I mean, who doesn't like having a man grovel at her feet? But I never got into it recreationally. Maybe I would have if I hadn't fallen in with these guys."

It seemed natural to ask: "So how'd you end up inducted into a secret society of sacred sex-knowledge keepers?"

"Long story," she said. "Ira came out of the BDSM world, too."

"Yeah, I know him and Kanna through the community. And we have another friend in common who Clive thinks was victimized by the Partisans of Fire."

Her posture still looked relaxed, but her attention sharpened. "Oh, that's news. Who?"

"A guy named Wexel." Who happens to be my best friend, I thought, but didn't say aloud.

"Huh. We were supposed to be introduced to him at Ira's party tonight."

That sounded to me like Ira was trying to recruit not only Clive but Wex into the Circle of Light. "He's in a coma in a hospital downtown." How long had Wex known about the Circle? He'd presumably also been sworn to silence or he would have told me, I'm sure of it. It dawned on me suddenly how much Wex had been keeping from me. Remember that feeling I had that there was something he wasn't telling me about the party? I'd thought, when I realized it was Ira's party, that that had been it. But it finally sank in that Wex had known all along I'd run into Clive there. He'd been murmuring supportive noises at me for *weeks* about my missing mystery man, and *he'd known where to find him all along.*

I really needed Wex to survive the coma so I could tell him off about that.

I still hadn't taken my eyes off Clive's bedroom door. "Maybe Wex being attacked is just a coincidence, but I doubt it. I'm starting to be suspicious of everything."

"Good instinct. Keep that up." Kish toasted me with her bottle.

I found myself standing before I even knew what I was reacting to: Clive had yelped. It felt as natural as anything to go busting through the door, Kish right behind me, before I could reconsider.

Clive was wearing a fresh pair of jeans but no shirt, sitting on one corner of an unmade bed, with Roland and Jair both standing back from him, knives out. Jair's was in his left hand and he was shaking his right like he'd been stung.

"I told you," Clive said to them, glaring from one to the other.

"Bet you ten bucks Mira's the only one who can take it off," Jair said to Roland.

Roland was having none of it. "If, as she claims, she's just an innocent bystander in all this, I find it unlikely she could perform such a powerful binding technique." He sheathed his blade inside his sleeve and sat beside Clive on the edge of the bed. "It's more likely the demon's energy is affecting it somehow. Anyway, we shouldn't mess with it. If I'm correct, those beads are what's keeping unwanted demonic possessions out. Clive needs to keep them on."

The dark beads were wrapped around Clive's neck in a double strand. A little silver medallion of some saint had been left behind when the cross was torn off the rosary, which nestled at the hollow of his throat below his Adam's Apple. I kind of wondered at the fact the strands hadn't come loose. It wasn't as if the chain's clasp had been hooked, and I had no clue how it could be staying in place, only that it was.

Clive reached up, but stopped short of actually touching the beads as he asked, "Can you repair what they did?" He meant to his soul.

The idea that a soul could be damaged with a knife was a new one on me.

"If it's actually what we think—that is, if your and Mira's descriptions are accurate—then I think so. If we can get a fourth."

A fourth what? I wondered. "Are you all right?" I asked Clive.

Ask a generic question, get a generic answer. "I'm fine," he said automatically. Before I could ask him something more specific, Roland cut me off.

"Mira," he said. "I want to trust you. But can you see why we can't?"

"Not exactly, no," I said. "I get that you think the people trying to kill you can..." I fished around for the words. "Plant hypnotic suggestions? Which would make eyewitness testimony like mine unreliable?"

He was unmoved. "Plus you might be one of them."

"Which means there's no way you can ever trust me. What are you going to do, kill me?"

Jair sheathed his knife. "We don't kill."

Roland looked at the palms of his hands. "There is a way we could trust you. A way to prove what you say is true."

I felt the fine hairs on the back of my neck start to prickle.

"To do it we'd have to do something like… well… we'd perform a ritual." When he said the word *ritual,* everyone's ears perked up: Jair, standing on the far side of Clive, Kish leaning in the doorway, and Clive himself. "You'd have to agree to be the focus of it."

I tamped down my unease. "Great. What's this ritual entail?"

Roland wouldn't meet my eyes. "It's a form of Gleaning. You've already seen something similar to it."

For a second I thought he was talking about what he did to wake Clive up in the parking lot. Then I realized what he meant. "You mean the whole 'opening the gates' thing Kanna and Ira did to Clive?"

He nodded. "Well, minus the 'cutting the soul free of the body' bit."

"Well, that's good," I told him. "Losing my soul is a hard limit."

ELEVEN

As if I hadn't already had enough excitement for one night, there I was, getting ready to bottom to a bunch of total strangers. A few hours before I hadn't even known this kind of thing was real, and here I was about to let them get ritualistic on me.

"It's probably best if you don't know too much about what's going to happen," Roland said, and I thought of Clive, whose scene had been a surprise, too. "Knives don't even have to be involved."

"I would appreciate that," I said, proud of how evenly it came out.

"Flogging is probably the safest and least invasive method." He rubbed his eyebrows again. "Of course, all our floggers are … elsewhere."

"I have some," both Clive and I said in unison.

"I'm carrying my own in a bag right here." I dropped my shoulder bag onto the bed. It was a nice bag, made of real leather, roomy enough that I could've put a change of clothes and a toiletry kit in with the whips if I'd wanted, though I hadn't. A change of shoes, even. All that was in there was my three go-to's and my phone. "What do I have to do?"

"Let's move somewhere less cramped," Roland said.

"All right if I put on a shirt now?" Clive asked him, sounding a bit miffed. Roland ignored him and left the room with Kish.

"I'd not only put on a shirt, I'd pack a bag if I were you," I said.

"Why?"

Jair stood there listening to us, which was just fine with me. He needed to hear it, too: "What if the Partisans of Fire are the ones who found your abandoned car? What if they connect the dots, lift your address off your car registration, and come looking for you?"

Jair cursed under his breath. "Let's get this over with, so we can get out of here." He gestured for me to precede him into the living room and called to Roland, "We don't need a fourth for this?"

"No, two nodes should be plenty."

"You don't want a stronger containment circle in case Mira goes all demonic on us, too?"

Again Roland ignored the joke—or maybe it wasn't a joke. "We're lowering the barriers into her mind, not her soul." He moved the coffee table carefully aside. "Her most recent memories should be just below the surface and won't be difficult to skim."

As Roland was walking in a circle on the throw rug, drawing in the air with the tip of his knife, Clive joined us. He had an odd expression on his face, like he was trying to smile but was a little too pained about something. Chagrined, maybe.

"Here." Clive handed me a suede flogger similar to one of mine, except the tails were purple. "I thought this would work better as a match for yours."

I pulled the softer one of my two from my bag. He was right: they were about the same length and weight. "Thank you," I said, as Kish and Jair came to inspect them. To them I asked, "But are these too soft?"

Jair gave me a curious look. "Do you like the hard one better?"

"I don't relish being on the receiving end of either of them, honestly," I said.

"Because you're a dom?"

"Because I'm not a masochist," I said. "I'm not one of those doms who thinks feeling their own flogger or touching their knee to the ground somehow erodes their dominant power. I make it a point to know what my tools feel like when I use them. Any sub who'd lose respect for me over something like that isn't worth playing with, in my opinion."

"Uh, sure," Jair said, like he hadn't really followed that.

Kish had removed her hoodie. She was wearing a purple Catwoman T-shirt under it and had draped the purple flogger over her shoulder like a fashion accessory. I slid my jacket off.

"The first part of any circle working is the invocation of will," Kish said. "Do you enter the circle willingly and of your own free choice, and will you allow us to break down the barriers to truth we may encounter?"

"Do I get a safeword?" I meant it as a joke, but it came out sounding serious.

"You can step out of the circle," Kish said. "But if you're trying to prove you've got nothing to hide, I would suggest you don't." She raised an eyebrow. "I know it sounds corny, but say 'I do' if you agree to the terms."

Like the weirdest wedding ceremony ever. "I do."

Jair swung the flogger experimentally. "First time I've done this."

Kish made a figure-8 pattern in the air with her wrist and Jair copied her easily. Then she switched to swinging from her elbow, broadening the stroke and watching to make sure he understood the motion. He apparently did and she nodded. "Okay. You take her back, I'll take the front, and Roland can do the rest, all right?"

"All right."

She helped me slip my bra off and then gestured for me to step to the center of the invisible circle Roland had drawn. "Put your hands in the small of your back."

"Okay." I spread my feet apart and crossed the backs of my hands above my tailbone. No bondage was necessary, plus that position meant I protected my kidneys in case Jair missed his target.

I had only been flogged two or three times since I'd figured out I preferred wielding to receiving. And I had never role-played an interrogation scene, which struck me as ironic just then.

They started to strike me lightly, Jair following Kish's lead in both rhythm and pressure. They synchronized easily, and the similarities between them seemed to become more obvious with each passing moment. Even though she was a curvaceous dark-skinned woman and he was a rangy light-skinned man, they shared a kind of physicality. I'd seen it before in their relaxed-but-alert states earlier, like lions awaiting their prey. Once they had me in their claws, even as their attention heightened, their limbs stayed loose. Soldiers, I thought again. Fighters.

I wondered when they were going to let loose. It seemed odd to me that they would warm me up gradually if they were trying to get information out of me. Maybe it was just to give Jair a chance to get used to using the flogger. When were they going to really lay into me? My back could take a pretty heavy beating, but I never liked pain on my nipples of any kind. So far Kish hadn't hit me that hard, but even a soft stroke would make the flesh sore under repeated blows.

"Think back to the party," she said. "How'd you get there?"

"I took the trai—"

"Hush. You don't have to say anything. Just think it."

Oh. I took a look at Roland, who sat at the edge of the rug in the lotus position with his eyes closed. Was he reading my mind?

He opened his eyes and met my gaze, then closed them again. Hm.

The party. I took the train. The chauffeur picked me up. His name was Stefan, I remembered. I wondered what happened to him? To all the guests? It seemed to me like everyone was able to escape the burning house, but what if the Partisans had been waiting for them out back…?

"Were you surprised to see Clive?"

Very surprised. And a bit pissed off at him, actually. I was still a bit pissed off at him, I realized. Was it really that he didn't want to violate my rule against telling only a partial truth? Or was that just an excuse to avoid having to say *no* to me?

"Did you meet a man named Barrow at the party? British, about the same height as Clive?"

I really didn't have a chance to talk to anyone other than Cricket and Clive.

"You said Clive and Ira and Kanna did a scene?"

To kick off the party, a performance scene, a ritual. The rhythmic blows of the floggers had ceased to feel anything like pain, even on my breasts, and in my mind they matched the rhythm that Ira and Kanna had used in my flashback. It was hypnotic, like drumming, like a deep tissue massage.

"Remember the scene. Remember every detail you can."

I remembered being pissed off all over again at what a pompous ass Ira could be…

"Try not to be angry, if you can," Roland said. "Anger can obscure the signal."

Fine, I thought. It wasn't worth being angry over Ira anyway, not given what happened. I centered my memory on the rapt audience and Clive's gasps and cries, instead. My chest constricted in empathy as the sounds of pleasure and pain he had made echoed in my mind.

The knives, the designs sketched—scratched—onto his back.

The razors. The final cut.

Roland's voice again. "Did you see where the fire came from?"

Maybe? I'd thought at the time that it came from the chimney, from the fireplace. But I couldn't really be sure. A column of flame had definitely climbed the stone. The stone had to be fake. Stones didn't burn. Did they?

Thump, thump, thump. Was that the thudding of the bunched suede against my chest, or the beating of my heart? I was starting to sweat, and the scent of the house fire seemed to rise from my heated skin.

"Why were you the one to free Clive?"

Because Kanna had collapsed. She had slumped to the floor like a marionette whose strings had been cut. And Ira had moved to rescue her first.

"You didn't think to just run, yourself?"

The sound of Clive calling his safeword and no one coming to answer him grated under my skin, even in flashback. I couldn't not answer that call. I ran toward the flames instead of away from them.

My breath deepened like I was starting to run up hill.

I remembered getting Clive away from the heat, escaping through the dining room where the Sterno pots had turned into blue conflagrations.

And Clive falling unconscious. And me reviving him to get away from the house.

I had the strangest feeling, then, like the floggers weren't tearing me down at all, but instead supporting me. I swayed a little under the hypnotic effect but I didn't fall because they held me where I was, patting me on the back, on the chest, clapping on my body like teammates giving me congratulations.

Roland's voice then: "How did you wake Clive up? Where did you learn to do that?"

The gym, I thought. Sensei Jack—the guy who taught krav maga and Hawaiian jiu-jitsu and tricks he learned from Navy SEALs. He had ways to bring back someone who'd been choked out. *Calling their name helps,* he'd told us one time. *When they're knocked out, call them back.*

Wait, is that what "knocked out" means? Was Clive's soul *knocked out* of his body, and did I call it back?

Roland again: "And Clive told you if he broke his confidence to us that we'd be able to find him."

Yes. On the roadside. He was counting on it. I wondered, though, how did they get to Westchester so fast?

Jair spoke, his words flowing with the blows. "We were on our way to the party. Ira had told us the scene would be at midnight. He wasn't supposed to—" He broke off without finishing the sentence but I caught his meaning. Ira had rushed the scene for some reason. And he'd tried to do it before the other members of the Circle arrived. But why?

Jair asked the next question, too. "Why did you attack us when we arrived?"

I had thought they were the Partisans of Fire. Until I heard Roland's name. Before that, I thought they were there to kill us.

Roland's voice: "You fixated on our blades."

Yes, I did. I could still see Jair's sticking out of his boot sheath, Roland's shining in the light of an oncoming car. "Your knives were the most dangerous thing about you."

"Hush," Kish said. "Don't talk. Just picture."

I realized my own eyes had been closed for some time. I pictured the scene, the moments when I thought I had a chance and when I didn't.

The blows were getting harder, faster, and delivered with more force.

I wasn't going to let anyone kill Clive. That was just not happening. Not on my watch. Didn't they understand that?

"She's resisting." "Is she? I don't sense that." "There's a jolt of recognition." "Recognizing danger, not the significance."

The significance of what? The beating was full-on by then, the blows loud, displaced air from each strike on my back making my hair fly. I had passed the point of processing words or sensations individually. I could feel my own wrist in my opposite hand. I was squeezing too hard.

That was the only detail I clung to as my emotions began to shred under the onslaught.

"It's dark, though."

I did not want to cry in front of these people.

"What do you mean, 'dark.'"

"You know what I mean."

"She said she didn't like knives."

"She's had enough."

"Not yet."

I didn't want to cry in front of them because it would make me look weak. But then I realized that thought itself was weak. Why did I care? Why should I have to be anything other than what I was or express anything but what I was feeling?

The mere fact I felt it was necessary to put up some kind of a front, for these people, for Ira and Kanna and the people at the party, for society as a whole… that was the fact I could no longer take.

That was the realization that made the dam burst.

As my tears poured forth, the blows stopped, and I found myself embraced from behind by Jair, his arms solid around my rib cage, his heaving chest pressed against my back. Breaking me had been quite a workout. Kish had a hand on my face, brushing my hair back from my wet cheeks, and saying gentle, nurturing things—at least they sounded like that. I wasn't absorbing words through my own crying. I understood they were trying to get me to move to the couch, but I couldn't. I couldn't even sink to the floor right there. I just had to let it all out while Jair and Kish kept me from collapsing. They held me. They held me up.

I opened my eyes and found myself clinging to Kish. Jair kissed me on the back of the neck and stepped back. I felt something elastic stretch between us, like he was reluctant to let go.

The first voice I understood was Clive's. "Would you like a glass of water?"

I was about to say "yes, please" when the papers on Clive's kitchen counter went up in flames.

TWELVE

The fire began to lick up the wall and spread quickly across the ceiling, just like the flames had at Ira and Kanna's.

"Take the fire escape," Roland urged.

"No! We'll be sitting ducks out there," Clive insisted. Fortunately, he had a better idea. "Follow me!"

I grabbed my jacket and bag and pelted after him, my legs still wobbly from the flogging, but my mind instantly clear. Clive led us down the hall to the rear of the building and then down a different set of stairs from the ones we had come up. He hurriedly explained as we rushed down the back stairs that the basement connected to the building next door. We could exit out the back almost a full block away. If anyone were standing in front, watching his apartment burn, they'd never see us.

In the basement we ran past a series of unlit storage niches and a laundry area that made the whole dingy place smell like fabric softener. We had just reached the far side exit when the fire alarm went off.

Jair stood poised to open the back door. "Guess we don't have to worry about calling 911." I found myself panting, out of breath, and wondering how I was going to manage if we had to run any further. But he pointed and said, "Van's that direction. Walk, do not run. Running'll only attract attention."

I zipped my jacket to the top, my skin still clammy from the sweat of the scene and the sudden run down the stairs. "Anything we should look out for?"

"If Barrow's here himself, you might see a thin British guy, brown hair…" Roland looked at me and Clive. "Whatever you do, don't make eye contact with him."

"With any luck, he's nowhere near us." Jair popped open the door. I put my hands into my pockets as we went out into a service alley and then onto the sidewalk. I'd never felt so exposed on the street before, and crossing a wide avenue felt like crossing a flooded river. But nothing burst into flames around us and knife-wielding ninjas didn't jump out of the shadows, either.

We got back to the van without incident. Kish took the wheel while Jair urged us all to duck down in back. Jair, Clive, and I crammed onto the floor between the bench seats while Roland lay on one of them with a groan.

Clive dug a shirt out of his bag and opened a bottle of water. Both for me.

I took the shirt first. It was heather gray with a university logo on it, too large for me, but that only made it comfortable. The cotton was worn soft and I had to admit it smelled pleasantly of him. I shivered a little even after I put my jacket back on. Clive cracked open the bottled water and I took a sip, but that only made me more chilled.

"Any sign of pursuit?" Jair asked Kish.

"Nope. Nothing," she answered.

Jair turned to me. "You all right?"

"She needs aftercare," Clive answered.

"Don't," I said, more sharply than I meant to. "Don't answer for me."

His reaction was immediate: "No, my lady. I'm sorry." And then he looked away, cheeks reddening, seeming both embarrassed and confused.

"Clive." I tried to be gentle about it. "If you don't mind. Please put your arm around me."

He blinked, mollified but still confused. He put an arm around my shoulders. I hugged my own knees.

"Jair, you too," I said.

He added his embrace around Clive's arm and mine. "Is it always like that?"

I didn't know what he meant. "Is what always like what?"

"I, um, never beat someone until they broke down in tears before."

"You did great, bebe," Kish said to him from the front seat.

"It's funny," he said, still trying to process the scene. "It was like... I could feel it building up, like a sneeze."

"Or an orgasm," said Clive.

"Except it wasn't in me, it was in Mira."

"You were connected with her." Roland threw his arm over his eyes.

"You mean instead of just 'reading' her, I could *feel* it?"

"Is there a difference between those things, though?" Clive asked. "Humans can feel what each other feels just from empathy. How would you tell the difference between 'reading' someone's feelings and 'receiving' them?"

"I've never had an initiate who asked as many difficult questions as you," Roland moaned. "Ask me again when I'm not so drained."

Which of course made me think of more questions I wanted to ask. How many initiates had the Circle had? How long had he known Jair? How long did it take to learn to do what he did? How much of what I saw during the circle working did he "read" or "receive" or whatever?

I asked Jair instead. "So did you see what you needed to? Do you trust me now?"

"We better," Kish said. "Because I'm taking us to The Archive. Anyone opposed, speak now."

Roland had begun to snore.

THIRTEEN

I was relieved to find The Archive was built for stealth. If you weren't in the know, you'd never guess it was the secret hideout of a bunch of arcane sex-magicians, and that was the point. Someone in the 19th century must have planned things this way: The front of the building faced a residential block of the West Village—part of a mishmash of similar townhouses in varying styles, shoulder to shoulder. In back, though, was a tangle of brick-walled gardens, completely unseen from the street. One entered the maze of gardens from the back exit of the small garage where the van parked around the corner.

Jair led the way through a low-ceilinged brick loggia, and we emerged onto a narrow cobblestoned walkway between plots. I was still feeling spacey from the scene and sensory details were jumping out at me. Thick brown vines covered high brick walls, their spring leaves still tentative, unsure that winter was really over. The bricks seemed almost alive with dampness and in the light from the back stoops we passed, Jair's hair was glossier than I remembered. So was Clive's, as he walked beside me, and I took his hand.

As we approached our destination, Kish asked Jair, "So. How friendly did you get back there?"

"Not enough to get her past the aegis, if that's what you're asking," he replied with a snort. "Let's get Roland inside and then figure it out."

Roland weaved a bit tiredly but insisted he was fine.

Everyone was definitely watching me as we drew close to the house. The realization I'd come to while being flogged—that what other people thought of me meant nothing if I didn't let it—was still fresh. Not giving a fuck was even more liberating than I expected it would be. Standing on patio stones that were far older than me, I looked up at the back door. On the top floor, some lights were on but I could make out no details through the gauzy curtains. Was someone looking down at us? I found myself not caring what they saw.

Jair looked up with me at the lit window. "Feel anything?"

"Tired," I answered. That clearly wasn't what he was asking. "Why?"

"Go try the door."

I went up the stone steps. The heavy wooden door had an antique brass handle shaped like a fancy S. What was going to happen? A shock like the one Clive got when he tried to take the beads off?

I grasped the handle. It felt like ordinary brass. The door creaked inward to reveal the back hallway of what had once been some rich family's townhouse. My first look at The Archive. To the right was the kitchen. A few feet down was another door, to the basement I figured, since it was under the stairs. At the other end of the hall I could see the front door as well as wide entryways into the dining room on one side, parlor on the other.

"Told you." Kish eyed me as she came up the steps.

"Don't look at me," Jair replied.

Roland brought up the rear. "It's undoubtedly Clive. Just be happy something went easy tonight. Let's all go into the kitchen. I'm starved and you all probably are, too."

What's undoubtedly Clive? I thought. And what do you mean, all go into the kitchen?

I was not prepared for how huge the kitchen was, at least by New York City standards. No doubt when the place was built they needed room for a bunch of servants to work in there. It was big enough that a beat up table could sit right in the middle of the room. The half dozen mismatched chairs around it were a welcome sight.

"I'll get Niko," Jair said, and I could hear his boots on the carpeted stairs as he took them at a run.

"The Wisdomkeeper," Clive explained. "I've only met him once so far."

"Niko the All-Knowing, All-Seeing," Kish said.

"More like *some*-knowing, *some*-seeing." Roland sat down heavily in a chair, exhaustion setting in. "It's… complicated."

Kish pulled open the fridge and handed him some bottles of water. He put them in the middle of the table and then indicated the seat next to him. "Mira."

I stood with my hands on the back of the chair. I wanted to get off my feet. I did. But I suddenly resisted the idea. "Is anyone going to tell me what that was all about at the door?"

"Yes. Please sit down."

It felt like the vinyl on the back of the chair was going to crack if I gripped it too hard. "How about you tell me first, and then I'll sit."

"Mira, please." He looked too tired to argue.

But I didn't think that was a good reason to give him a break. "I submitted to a flogging to prove that you could trust me. What have you done to prove that I can trust you, though?"

Clive nearly dropped the bottle of water in his hand, as if it were slippery from condensation. He caught it, though, and let out a low whistle, before he came to stand next to me. He looked at Roland like he was very interested in the answer.

Roland unzipped his hoodie and laid it over the back of his chair. Half his sandy hair escaped from a short ponytail. "If you didn't already trust us, you wouldn't have come this far."

"I haven't really had a choice. The main reason I went to tonight's party was to let people know Wex had been marked up and left for dead. I'm not a big fan of Ira's to begin with. The next thing I know I'm saving Clive from an inferno, fighting a demon, and fleeing from psychic arsonists—twice. The main reason I'm here now is you can help Wex and you've got somewhere safe to hide." I looked around the kitchen. "At least I assume it's safe or we wouldn't have come here."

Roland cleared his throat. "I can't go into the exact details right at this moment, but this location, by which I mean this building, was put under aegis over a hundred years ago by the founders of the Circle—"

"He means, 'Yes, it's safe.'" Kish cut him off from where she stood by the phone attached to the wall. "I'm ordering pizza. That all right with everybody?"

Roland put his head in his hands with a sigh. "Sure. Pepperoni, black olives, and mushroom, please."

Kish gave him a look. "I thought you were going vegetarian?"

He looked pained. "Maybe next month."

"All right. Clive? Mira?"

"I'll eat anything," Clive said.

"I know you will," Kish said with a sly smile. "Mira? Any preferences, allergies, whatever?"

"Pepperoni's good. So is plain cheese. I'm not picky."

"Ha. Not about pizza, anyway." She gave me a thumbs up and dialed a number from memory.

I shared a glance with Clive. Was Kish reading our minds or something? Or was I just being paranoid? He didn't seem bothered by her comments.

Jair squeezed past her into the kitchen. "Niko's coming. He was deep in trance. It's taking him a couple of minutes to come back to Earth so he's moving kind of slowly." The Wisdomkeeper. I imagined a little old yogi in saffron robes taking the stairs one at a time. Jair turned the chair across from me around backwards and sat down, drumming lightly on the back. "So. Mira. Clive." He looked back and forth between us. "Is something going on? You guys going to sit?"

"Mira's a bit suspicious of our motives," Roland said.

"Of course she is. A bunch of weirdos spouting gibberish—I recall being pretty suspicious of you myself, Roland." Jair grinned at me. "I'll tell you my motive right now though is to recruit you."

"Well, I don't appreciate being kept in the dark. You were all looking at me like you expected me to fall into a pit of alligators."

Jair nodded. "There's a lot to explain. Like… really a lot. But, sure. Let's start there. The doorway."

Roland gave in. "Normally, only someone who has met certain… requirements… can open it."

That much I'd already figured. "Does that mean I have The Archive's seal of approval now or something like that?"

Jair hid a laugh behind his hand. "Not exactly. It usually means you've exchanged body fluids with someone in the Circle."

"A deep kiss is not enough," Clive said, and blushed for some reason. "Or so I was told." He concentrated on draining the water in the bottle and then lobbing the empty one into the recycling bin.

I wondered what they made him do to enter. "What would have happened if the door didn't open for me?"

"Probably one of us would have pricked a finger for you." Jair held his up like he was making a point. "Assuming you trusted us not to be carrying any blood-borne illnesses."

I flashed on a moment in time, the music of the club throbbing in the background, my hands on Clive's damp skin, as I licked where the welt had broken the skin. "I've tasted Clive's blood. The night we met."

Clive made a small sound in his throat, like maybe he remembered it, too. That sound made me want to pull him close. If he were mine, I would have. I reminded myself he was the one that got away. Unless we negotiated otherwise, I had no right.

But that sound. That memory. I wanted to grip him by the beads around his neck while he sank to his knees beside me, and kiss him until he could barely remember his name.

I was clearly overtired if I was thinking like that.

Roland looked up at us both, brow furrowed, though I couldn't tell if his expression was confusion or criticism. "For the sake of keeping the explanation simple, there's a kind of energy field generated by each living being. When you share blood or other vital fluids, you kind of… how do I put this…"

"You pick up each other's wavelength," Jair said. "The aegis is like a force field on the house that only lets those through who match the right wavelength."

Roland nodded. "The thing is, if you got that taste of Clive's blood months ago, I would have expected the effect to fade by now. Plus that was before Clive had come here. And I would have thought it would only work after we initiated him? But… maybe the aegis is more sophisticated than we know."

Jair grimaced. "There are some gaps in our knowledge."

"That's putting it mildly." Kish pulled the chair up next to Jair and settled back against it. "Fifteen minutes, tops. They'll ring the bell."

Roland gestured at the chair in front of me again. "Now will you please sit?"

I pulled out the chair and sat. Clive did the same after me. I pushed another bottle of water toward him and he cracked it open and drank. I took one for myself, pressing the cool condensation against my forehead. I felt sunburned. Maybe I'd gotten a bit scorched by the heat of the fire. Or the demon. I took my jacket off, and my skin felt extra sensitive against the soft cotton of the shirt Clive had lent me. (No doubt from the flogging.)

"So, after we eat," Kish said, "are we going looking for Ira and Kanna? Or checking out Wex in the hospital, or what?"

"We're recruiting Mira, first," Jair said. "We're going to need her."

"Only if Niko approves," Roland warned. "Let's not get ahead of ourselves."

"Niko's going to love her, I know it."

"Slow down, Jair."

"No, Roland, I will not slow down. We've been moving too slowly as it is." Jair raised his voice. "It's time to speed up, before it's too late."

And just like that, they were in a full blown argument:

"We have to be cautious!"

"We've been cautious about the wrong things!"

"That's your opinion!" The rest of Roland's hair slipped from the ponytail in unruly waves. "It's my job to protect the Circle and all we stand for!"

"No!" Jair pointed a finger at Roland. "That's my job. Mine and Kish's. We're the Guardians, remember? That's what you recruited us to be. You're the Convenor."

"But—!" Roland drove his fingers into his own hair, cutting himself short. "Ugh. You're right. I—You're right."

"Wasn't that the whole point of recruiting?" Jair pressed him. "So you don't have to do it all alone? You can't."

"You're right," Roland repeated. "It's just… I've forgotten what it's like to have a group. And old habits die hard."

"I know. You're suspicious because it's not every day you run into someone who can just jump in like Mira did." Jair looked across the table at me. "But that's exactly why we need her."

"It's just… very unusual to meet someone who can just do what you did out of the blue." Roland looked at me, too. "I know it's not impossible. I know because I was one of them."

Both Kish and Jair's attention shifted from me to Roland, then, their curiosity almost palpable in the air.

"I got recruited to the Circle when I was in my mid-twenties." Roland looked at the back of his hand. It looked normal so far as I could tell. "I had just gotten into divinity school. I thought the answers were going to be found there. One night I… strayed."

(Like a sheep?)

"I met a man. He took me to a… a sex club. It was a test, but I didn't know that. He… tested me."

Jair looked like he wanted to ask how, but he didn't interrupt.

"I lifted him right off the floor. Lifted us both, I mean. Like, twenty feet off the ground. I would've thought he slipped me a drug or something, that it was all a hallucination, but I'd done drugs before and they didn't feel like that. Plus… it wasn't the first time I'd levitated like that."

Jair caught my eye across the table. This story was news to him.

"The first time… I'd been scared to death. I was convinced an angel was dangling me in the air to terrify me into not… not touching myself like I was." Roland's eyes had closed as he dug into his memory. "I was in Catholic school at the time. I was fourteen. What did I know? It was the only explanation that made sense. Angels were literally lifting me off the ground as a warning. I was scared out of my wits and had been caught literally red-handed."

The Church has a lot to answer for making people hate and fear themselves, you know? But that is a subject for another time. I said nothing, but Jair couldn't hold back. "So you swore off masturbating because of that?"

"Yes. But here I was, years later, and it was happening again, but this time I was surrounded by debauchery, and the man I was coupling with was reading my mind. And he told me, *no, Roland, you're the angel.*" He opened his eyes and looked at his palms. "So, I know it's possible to stumble on the powers of the Practice without any training. I know it beyond any doubt. I'm just… naturally suspicious, I guess."

Kish looked at me across the table. "Anything like that ever happen to you before, Mira?"

"You mean, a borderline spiritual-type experience while I was having sex?"

"Yeah."

How to say it? I put it this way: "Um, that's kind of the whole appeal of BDSM for me. It's bonding on a whole other level from just hooking up or dating. Reading each other, feeling like you go to another plane of consciousness, that's kind of what it's all about. For me, at least."

"That's what Ira says, too…" Jair began.

"But he's in it for the power trip," Kish finished.

Clive cleared his throat. "Those two things are not mutually exclusive, you know."

Roland ran his fingers into his hair. "Ira has been pushing us to recruit more in the BDSM scene. It was part of why we agreed to attend his party tonight. If I'd had any idea the Partisans had found us out, we never would have gone." He buried his eyes in his hands. "Has anyone heard from him or Kanna?"

Jair checked his phone. "Nothing. They must have escaped, though. If they were dead, we'd know."

"How would you know?" I asked.

Jair and Roland looked at each other, and I could see them mentally kicking the ball back and forth to figure out which one was going to answer me. Before they could come to a conclusion, I heard the sound of sneakers pounding on wood. Someone running down the stairs. A moment later, a kid with East Asian features in basketball shorts and a warmup jacket appeared in the doorway. He looked me right in the eye. "I'd know," he said. Then in quick succession to Roland, Jair, and Kish: "Her heart is good; Don't you dare; Pizza's almost here."

His last pronouncement was to Clive. "Please reconsider."

"Reconsider what?" Roland asked, as the doorbell rang.

Clive stood. "Leaving," he said. "Mira, allow me to introduce Niko, the Wisdomkeeper."

FOURTEEN

Niko was so different from my expectation that I couldn't stop staring at him. It was remarkable how there was nothing remarkable about him: He looked like a totally normal kid—one who'd been through a growth spurt and hadn't filled out yet.

Kish went to the door to get the pizza delivery. Niko slipped into her chair and leaned against Jair. "It was so weird to have you all gone! That never happens anymore."

Jair put an arm around him in a big-brotherly way. "Are you saying that at age eighteen we still can't leave you alone in the house?"

"Of course not! It was just strange to have the place all to myself." He held out a hand toward me. "Hi. I'm Niko."

I shook it. "Mira." I could feel the weight of something in his sleeve, and see something metallic peeking from under his wrist. My guess was a small folding knife (and I would be right).

"Jair told me you saved everyone tonight from a demon attack?" His eyes were wide. "That is awesome. Clive, you got possessed?"

Clive looked at the bottle in his hand, but I got the feeling that wasn't what he was seeing. "Apparently."

"Is that why you're having second thoughts about joining us?"

Clive sighed. "No. It's just… Mira had it right and I only just realized it. You've made me do a lot to prove myself worthy of being initiated into the Circle. But what have you all done to prove I should?"

Roland prickled. "Sharing the sacred knowledge with you isn't enough?"

"Knowledge I could get killed for having? No one mentioned that getting burned to a crisp was one of the possibilities." Clive crossed his arms. "Or losing my goddamned soul."

"We told you it could be dangerous," Roland insisted. "I know tonight didn't go as planned, and I'm sorry about that, but especially after what happened tonight? This isn't the time to back away. Not when we're the only ones who can help you with your demon problem."

"That sounds like a line," I said, touching Clive's arm lightly. "When someone wants to trap you in an abusive relationship, the one-two punch is 'I'm sorry you got hurt' followed by 'but I'm the only one who can provide for you.'"

Roland opened his mouth to speak, but Jair stopped him with a sharp point of his finger. "No. We got Clive into this mess, we're going to get him out of it, and our doing so can't be contingent on him joining or not joining. How many of us does it take to perform an exorcism?"

Kish put a box of pizza down in front of him. "Bebe, how about you eat before we start talking exorcism?" She plopped another box in front of Clive. "You make a mad dog's decisions on an empty stomach."

Clive looked like he was about to argue, but then she opened the box and he decided to take a scalding slice of extra cheese instead of arguing further, at least right at that moment.

Jair pulled a gooey piece out of the box in front of him and plopped it on a paper plate before it could singe his fingers too badly. "Kish is right, as usual. But I'm serious. Clive, even if you walk away from the Circle, we've got to deal with that before you go."

Roland shook his head. "Walking away from the Circle would be a huge mistake."

Clive studiously ignored that comment, passing me a paper plate and serving me a piece.

Niko, meanwhile, ignored the food entirely. "Could someone tell me what happened, from the beginning? I know I'm good at piecing together information out of order but it'd be great to hear it in sequence."

I ate without speaking and just listened to Roland, Jair, and Kish recount the evening's events, including what I had told them about the fire at the house. They corrected each other a few times, but mostly they got it right and I didn't feel the need to interrupt. Neither did Niko, who nodded intently, barely blinking.

When they were done, the thing he focused on wasn't what I expected at all. "Clive, breaking your pledge was a clever way of summoning us. How did you think of that? Wait, don't answer that now. I need to know what it was like for you three"—he pointed at the others—"when the pledge was broken."

Jair rubbed the knuckles of his right hand. "We were driving along, following the directions to Ira's, when it was like a flare went up. But you don't see it in the air, you see it behind your eyelids."

"For me it was more like a pull." Roland tapped his chest. "Here. Like when you sense something wrong and you have the urge to go fix it? Like remembering you left the burner on the stove and that urgent feeling you have to run back to it."

Niko nodded. "That feeling would be even stronger if Clive were a member of the Circle. You knew it was him, though? You sensed him? Or no?"

Roland shook his head, but Kish and Jair both nodded. "It almost felt like I could feel his name in my mouth," Kish said. "Like I was about to say it."

Niko turned back to Clive again. "What did Ira and Kanna see during the working? Did they get past your mental block?"

Clive shook his head. "I don't think they got there. If they saw anything, I didn't see it myself."

"And we still haven't heard from either of them." Niko pressed his fingers to his mouth and closed his eyes, like he was in deep thought. He didn't open them. "Clive, is that the first time you went Soulwandering?"

"I've had an out of body experience during a scene before, if that's what you mean." He looked at me like there was something he wanted to tell me. "But I never turned into a fiery creature bent on… destruction before."

"And Mira, you're the one who got the demon under control. Why was it you and not one of the others?" He looked right at Roland when he said that.

"I don't know," I said. Sweat prickled across my back as I remembered Clive-as-demon scenting me, hunting me through the trees. "Other than it was me the demon kept coming after."

Jair rubbed his jaw. "I'd say it did plenty of damage all around."

"But once it went after me, it didn't bother with any of you unless you attacked first or got in the way."

Clive's eyes were downcast.

"Interesting," Niko said. "Can you tell me more about how you subdued it?"

"I used Roland's rosary to try to choke him, because I thought if I could choke Clive into unconsciousness, it'd quell the demon. It didn't really work, and I just… snapped, I guess. I was on autopilot."

"She put that demon in its place," Kish said, with an amused smile.

"I guess I did. I was just… so angry." Outraged might've been a better word. "I barely remember what I said."

Jair ticked off the points on his fingers, sounding somewhat amused: "You told the demon not to hurt you or any member of the Circle without your permission, to kiss your boot, and to keep its dick in his pants."

Kish swatted him on the shoulder with a laugh. "Ha. He wasn't even wearing pants."

"Close enough. Mira told that demon what to do and it obeyed. Even the boot-kissing part."

Niko cocked his head like he was listening for something faint. "Very interesting."

Roland stifled a yawn. "I think the demon probably fled as soon as Mira grabbed control, and that was Clive taking over at the end there. Clive, you're holding up remarkably well for having been possessed by a demon that powerful. I was expecting you to at least have bloodshot eyes."

Ira had called Clive a "tough little thing" that time at the club. I rubbed his thigh under the table, my palm sliding along worn denim. "You doing okay?"

"I think so." Clive's gaze dropped to the table. "Assuming this collar doesn't zap my brain. Whenever any of us tries to touch it, I get a shock."

"Even if Mira touches it?"

"I haven't tried." I squeezed Clive's thigh. "Should I?"

Niko nodded. "Would you? If Clive agrees."

"I'm not looking forward to it, but sure, Mira." He stiffened, steeling himself for the pain. "Go ahead."

I reached up and touched the saint medallion that remained where the crucifix had been torn away, then ran my finger along the beads. No shock. No pain for either of us. I could feel the beads were some kind of polished stone, some elongated, others as round as pearls. They were a deep black, and warm from his body heat.

"You owe me ten bucks," Jair said to Roland.

"I didn't take that bet," Roland replied. "I don't think it's just Mira who can touch it. I think anyone can if they're not trying to remove it."

Clive lifted his own hand, brushing mine with his fingertips as he cautiously touched the saint medallion, too. "Huh. You're right."

"Who's that on the medallion?" I asked.

Roland blushed a little as he answered. "Saint Sebastian."

Niko sat up very straight. "I think I know what's going on. Clive, Mira put a bond of obedience on you."

Clive sat stone still.

I let my hand drop to my lap. "What does that mean?"

"It's sort of similar to the binding that connects the members of the Circle," Niko said. "There are a bunch of different kinds of pledge-bonds and the like. I confess I don't know much about this kind, yet."

Clive focused on Niko. "What if, theoretically speaking, I didn't want any binding at all?"

"No one can force you. That's one of the principles of the Practice." Niko changed the interlacing of his fingers to another configuration. "But if you're having issues with Soulwandering, the best way to repair that is with training. As a part of the Circle, you'd learn that, but it takes time. I'd suggest you keep Mira's bond and the collar in place for now as a safety measure."

Roland still didn't want Clive walking away. "What about your spiritual quest to connect with something larger than yourself and do some good in the world?"

Clive stared at the tabletop. "That hasn't changed. And I want to know what's on the other side of my mental block, too. But I was keener on knowing before Ira's stunt tonight." He tapped his temple like he was tamping down his anger—or the powder in a rifle, maybe.

Roland pushed his plate away, the slice of pepperoni half-eaten. "For the record, Ira did that on his own, with no guidance or approval from us."

Clive was looking down, eyes shadowed by doubt. "Still. You don't trust me."

"Because what's behind your mental block could very well be a post-hypnotic suggestion from those who wish us harm." Roland flattened his hands on the tabletop. "It's not you. It's what you could be carrying. Mira, Clive, you understand—don't you?—that our whole reason for existing is that we're secret-keepers? So we can't just tell you everything. Not unless you pledge to being a secret-keeper yourself."

"Fine," I said. "Don't tell us. Keep your secrets."

Roland looked a bit stunned. I guess it had never occurred to him that someone would just say no?

"We can still be your allies." I touched Clive's leg again, lightly that time. "You were right. They are the Secret Sex Mafia."

His eyebrow quirked upward at me, his mood suddenly lighter. "Supposedly, sex isn't all they do. But I've yet to see much evidence of that."

"I didn't hear you complaining about the number of times you came last Saturday," Kish said. She and Jair wore nearly identical smirks.

"Sex is one of the ways to access the… the 'power,'" Niko said. "Maybe the easiest way. Definitely not the only way. But Mira, I sense you have another question on your mind."

I narrowed my eyes. "Are you reading my mind?"

"Not intentionally! Our first principle is the Invocation of Willingness, right? But sometimes people are so loud, I can't shut them out." He rubbed his eyes. "But I can feel you pulling at me very strongly. It's like that when someone really wants to know something."

"Is the 'Invocation of Willingness' the same thing as establishing consent?" I thought about how Kish had asked me to enter the circle to be flogged.

"Seems like it is to me," Clive said. "At least that's how it's been used in what little I've been taught so far."

"Then isn't the elephant in the room that Clive might not want to be bonded to the Circle, but you're all talking about it like his joining is a forgone conclusion?"

They all looked at each other, until Kish blurted out, "Nothing is a forgone conclusion."

I asked the question that had been burning in my mind, then: "And what does it mean, anyway, that I 'bound' him? I didn't do any Invocation of anything."

"But even without a formal invocation, you couldn't have bound him if he didn't consent," Roland said, as if that were some kind of certainty. The rest of them sounded less sure.

"But was that him? Or the demon?" Jair asked.

Niko grimaced. "I think the bond wouldn't take if Clive's will weren't invoked? It is a central tenet of the practice, after all…"

I decided to proceed on their assumptions. "Fine. But consent isn't meaningful unless it can be withdrawn. What does it mean that he can't take his collar off?" I focused on Roland. "If consent is truly central to what you do, then—assuming that I can and a demon won't instantly kill us all—if we were going to join, wouldn't I need to take the collar off him right away?"

Before anyone else could answer, Clive took hold of my wrist under the table, saying, "Don't. Leave it on." He swallowed. "For now."

I confess I felt a measure of relief when he said that. Because the thought of removing his collar—of freeing him—made my heart skip an unhappy beat.

"We should wait," Clive went on, "at least until it's safe to take it off. In the meantime, Mira and I ought to learn more about what a bond of obedience entails."

"And don't tell me we have to join your secret society before you'll tell us that," I said.

"No, of course not," Niko said firmly. He then made a placating gesture toward Roland. "They shouldn't join the Circle until we're sure they can while bonded, anyway."

"We've already initiated a bonded pair, though," Roland said. "Ira and Kanna."

"They're different," Niko said. "I meant our first with a bond of obedience or anything along those lines or power imbalance. Ira and Kanna are a traditional form of partner-bonded."

Jair was trying not to laugh. "You mean 'married.'"

Niko blinked. "Um, yeah. That."

"So what can you tell me?" I asked.

Roland startled. "You mean right now?"

"Yes now, and I'll start," Niko said. "From what we know of pledge bonds, they run a pretty wide gamut. Obedience is the most basic binding between master and slave, which starts a progression from simple obedience at one end and complete physical and spiritual devotion at the other."

I'd heard a similar way of describing BDSM relationships and roles. "In other words there's a difference between service, submission, and surrender?"

"Basically." He shrugged. "I can tell you more after I meditate a bit."

Clive brought the subject back to us. To me. "What about you, Mira? The dom has to consent, too. You didn't ask for this situation."

I looked him over. Clive looked like he'd been through the wringer. There was a dullness to his eyes as he tried to look away from my sudden scrutiny.

I said his name softly as I turned his chin and held his gaze. He relaxed a fraction but I could see how vulnerable and tired and scared he was. It was all so much bigger than either of us expected, and I'll be honest, my protective instinct was kicking in hard. But at the same time, the last thing I wanted to do was make him feel like he had no choice but to stay with me for safety. I chose my words carefully: "I don't want you put at risk. If the bond will keep you safe, I'm content to keep it."

"For now, you mean?"

"For now," I agreed. I could not tell what was going on in his head at all, right then. But I didn't really know what to think about the news that we were "magically" bonded, myself. And still no one had really said what it meant. "I only require one thing if we're going to stay attached at the hip like this."

"What's that?"

"A real apology for ghosting me."

His mouth hung open slightly while he processed what I had said. "Mira." There was an echo in the way he said my name to the way it had sounded that night in the club, like he'd made my name into a title. "I—" He faltered, fishing for the words. "You know I—" He stopped himself before he could go down the wrong path and tried again. "I'm sorry. It was rude of me. I convinced myself you wouldn't care, wouldn't miss me. Instead of facing up to you and taking your feelings into account, I only thought of myself. I'm sorry if my lack of consideration made you feel hurt or… or less worthy in any way."

By the time he finished, his face was as scarlet as if I had slapped him. If we'd been having a normal dom/sub interaction, if we were dating or playing together, I might have. I could practically feel the shame and guilt pouring off him in waves. If we were role-playing, the way to expunge that would be to punish him to clear the slate.

But we weren't playing. The collar around his neck represented something real, something larger than either of us, and held a force in check that was more powerful than us both.

I brushed my thumb across his lips, I suppose because I was thinking about kissing him but didn't feel right doing it right there, right then, in front of everyone.

My voice came out quieter than I expected. "Apology accepted."

FIFTEEN

The group came to a surprisingly quick consensus once we were done eating: our next move had to be sleep. Wex and Ira and Kanna and the Partisans of Fire would just have to wait. Roland could barely get up from the table, and I wasn't feeling too energetic myself. Niko explained that the only way to fill our drained reserves would be a good night's rest. I assumed I couldn't visit Wex again until the morning, anyway.

Upstairs, the house had far more rooms than I expected. There were easily five or six small bedrooms on each floor. As Niko showed us around a little—towels here, shower there—I couldn't help but ask questions. Were the four of them the only ones living here, then? Did there used to be more members of the Circle of Light? Why was their home base called The Archive? Had it always been the Circle's home?

"A full Circle is twelve. Well, thirteen, technically? And there could be even more, so you could rotate in different members for the big circle workings. Members used to live here with their families, even." Niko tossed a few clean towels to Clive from the linen closet. "And it's called The Archive because the original owner was the Wisdomkeeper. The place was built for him and his family in like 1870 or so? But the Circle is even older than that. You can take these two rooms over here, but you might want to consider staying together in one."

Clive hugged the towels to his chest. "Why?"

Niko looked thoughtful for a few moments, eyes focused slightly upward and blinking. "I have a hunch that because of the bond, you'll both feel a sense of wellbeing if you're together. The opposite might also be true: if you're not, you may not." He shrugged. "I could be wrong."

I took one of the towels from Clive. "How can you be wrong if you're the Wisdomkeeper?"

"I'll be able to give you a more definitive answer tomorrow," Niko said. "But I really have to ask you not to ask me any more questions right now."

"Because it's a secret?"

Jair emerged from the shower, then, damp hair plastered to his neck and a thin towel tucked around his waist. "Because he's the Wisdomkeeper. And he'll literally stay up all night giving you answers until you're all sick with exhaustion." He pointed at Niko. "You. Upstairs. Now."

"All right, all right! It's just fun having visitors! I'm going!" He tried to snatch Jair's towel as he dashed away, but Jair dodged him. Niko's laughter could be heard all through the stairwell as he raced up to his own room.

Jair shook his head. "'Fun having visitors.' Someone needs to teach that kid about the secret part in 'secret society.'"

Another flurry of questions rose in my mind. What did Niko mean when he said he'd have more answers tomorrow? He wasn't running upstairs to Google, I was sure. And if he was only eighteen, how did he know all of that, anyway?

Jair stretched and yawned like a lion after his supper. "I'm wiped, or I'd be tempted to pick your brain all night, Mira."

"Oh, about what?"

He shrugged. Jair was—and is—completely comfortable wearing nothing but a damp towel. "Flogging, for one thing. That wasn't quite like any circle working I've been part of before."

Interesting. That made me wonder... what was their "magic" usually like? It seemed clear the ceremonial aspects were more than a mere formality... except when they weren't. More and more questions piling up in my head. At least I wasn't the only one brimming with them? But I yawned, too. "I'll tell you all about flogging tomorrow."

"Okay. We'll go check out your friend first thing in the morning. Promise." He held out his hand and clasped mine like an athlete would a teammate.

"I should probably get some things from my apartment, too, if it's not too much of a risk."

"It's probably fine, but I'll go with you to check it out."

"Okay."

"See you in the morning."

As Jair disappeared into his own room, I heard Clive call my name from somewhere behind me.

I found him fluffing the pillows in a room with two narrow twin beds, one against each wall.

He looked at the pillows instead of at me as he spoke. "Will this do? I don't want to presume."

"Niko said we should stay together," I said lightly. Did he seem a little tense? "With nothing else to go on, I think we should probably take his suggestion, unless you're uncomfortable with it."

"It's fine," he said, voice tight.

I sat down on the edge of the bed next to where he was standing. Niko had been right about us being drained. I couldn't remember the last time I'd felt that tired. But I had learned the hard way not to let little resentments fester between me and a sub. Better if I nipped it in the bud, whatever it was.

"I really need a shower," I declared. I still smelled like smoke and sweat and juniper mulch. "But I can barely sit up."

"Same." He shifted from foot to foot.

"Come on." I stood wearily. "Keep me from drowning."

"Are you sure about that?"

I reached out and hooked my finger under the edge of the saint medallion and pulled him gently to me, until our faces were close. "Are you asking because you're unsure where the boundaries are? Or because you don't like being told what to do?"

He startled, but the collar didn't let him pull back. "That's not... I didn't mean—"

"I've heard you say a couple of times now you're not submissive."

"Submitting is a thing I sometimes do, not something I 'am.'" His nostrils flared.

"A respectable attitude." It was obvious to me Clive was, to put it mildly, conflicted about the whole thing. Well, so was I. "Come on then. At least keep me awake. You don't have to get in. Just talk to me if you want."

He bowed his head in assent and followed me to the bathroom.

The white tiled walls were still steamy from Jair's shower. The stall was large and had shower heads at each end. The fixtures looked antique. "Interesting plumbing. A shower built for two."

"I'd expect no less for a house full of ritual sex practitioners." Clive hung our towels on the rail by the sink.

I turned on the water from both heads. "There. That ought to be enough white noise to block anyone trying to listen in."

That got Clive's attention. So did the question I asked: "So. What are you feeling?"

He looked a bit shocked. "You expect me to just tell you what I'm feeling?"

Was he being cheeky? "You expect to be able to hide it?"

"No! I just… no one's ever been so blatant about it. Or cared that much." He frowned. "And it's not always easy to just put feelings into words."

"Is it difficult right now? Because you seem kind of wound up. I wanted to give you a chance to speak to me without the others listening in. Especially if it's about joining or not joining the Circle."

He shook his head. "I should sleep on that before I come to any decisions. We both should."

"All right. What, then? If it's about our sleeping arrangements we need to figure that out on our own." I saw his gaze flick toward the hall and before he could answer, I asked, "Or is it just that you're jealous…?" He looked away from me. "Of Jair?"

Bingo. "I am not jealous of Jair!" He seemed to realize that his vehemence only confirmed my suspicion. "I mean, *jealous* isn't the right word. Not at all. Jair is Jair. He's just like that." He gestured between us. "And it's not like we're romantically promised to each other or anything."

"But you're feeling some kind of way."

"I suppose I am." He focused on me. "Is it my imagination? You seem very attracted to each other."

"It's not your imagination that he flirts shamelessly." Okay, *flirt* was not really the right word either, but I didn't have a better one for the kind of energy Jair threw in my direction—and maybe in every direction. "And there's no denying he's a gorgeous specimen of manhood, if not really my type."

"No?"

"He's so obviously a baby dom, don't you think?"

That made Clive snort with laughter. "One-hundred percent. You have him pegged there."

"Right? He's so curious about it." I let myself grin at Jair's expense. "Now you see why I didn't want them overhearing what we're talking about."

"And here I thought you wanted to talk about conspiracies."

The room was beginning to steam up and I watched a bead of sweat drip-slide down Clive's temple. "I do think it's important that we figure our stuff out without everyone putting in their two cents all the time. Conspiracies aside, I mean the stuff about just you and me."

He nodded.

"So, back to my question. What are you feeling?"

He let out a long breath, looking me up and down. "I'm not telling you anything new to say

I'm very attracted to you, Mira. And if I'm being honest, that's an understatement."

"An understatement?"

He pressed his lips together like he was holding back the words, but eventually they tumbled out: "I want you in that deep-down way that is beyond reason. I'd…" He faltered, and I waited for him to complete his thought: "I'd forgotten that. Suppressed it, really, when I took the pledge of secrecy. But here we are."

About to spend the night together as a "bonded pair," whatever that meant. "Here we are." I tested the temperature of the water with my hand and turned it down a notch.

"So. You want me to sit out here while you shower?" He had clasped one hand inside the other and I don't think he even realized he was doing it.

"I want you to get in with me. If you're okay with that."

He blushed, gaze fixed on the white bath mat. "I would like to get in with you. I just don't want to overstep my bounds. And—" He broke off, swallowing like he had a sudden lump in his throat.

"Look at me when you speak." I lifted his chin gently. "All right?"

His throat worked, and then words tumbled out. "Yes, my lady. I mean, is that all right? Should I call you that? I—"

"Shh. Hush." I put a hand on his shoulder, trying to calm him. "You earned the right, remember?"

"I would think I lost it again." He nearly looked away, but remembered not to, and held my gaze with his lagoon blue eyes.

"Only I get to determine that." I ran a finger along the beads of the collar and he shivered. "I said I accepted your apology. I meant it."

"I feel like I owe you more than an apology." His eyes fluttered closed as another shiver went through him. He opened them hurriedly. "You saved my life, after all."

"Well, and maybe you saved mine when you told me we should flee the scene of the fire." I ran a hand into his hair and he leaned into my touch immediately. The feeling of power his reaction gave me surged into me. Lust. Desire. Whatever one called it, it felt as red hot and pure as metal straight from the forge. "Clive."

"My lady?"

"You told me you're not a submissive, but that submitting is something you sometimes do. Are you saying that because I saved your life, you feel you should submit to me?"

His answer came out a whisper. "If you'll have me."

He really didn't know that I'd been fantasizing about him for months. "I'm worried that this isn't what you really want and it's just a spell I put on you."

"They don't call it a spell."

"Whatever."

He licked his lip. "Maybe it is the bond making me feel this way. But I accepted it for a reason. I literally owe you my life, Mira. The least I can do is serve you."

In answer, I kissed him the way I had been wanting to all evening, like I was starving for the touch of his mouth, and he for mine. Good god. I was suddenly no longer sleepy.

When I broke free, it was to utter a command—"*Strip*"—and to doff my own clothes as quickly as possible. I stepped into the shower, letting the water sluice away soot and sweat and grime, and then I pulled a properly naked Clive in after me. I couldn't remember being so turned on so quickly ever before. I pushed him to his knees, propped one of my feet on the soap dish, and pulled his mouth into the space I had opened.

For all the talk about spiritual this and that, and the otherworldly powers I had seen on display, this was flesh meeting flesh. This was wetness and heat, pulsing blood and sliding skin, his tongue alternating soft with rough, my breaths alternating between shallow and deep.

The orgasm sent my head spinning—it was that intense—and to help him do the same took only a few slick tugs of my hand. Maybe the bond made it easier?

But even sweeter and more satisfying to me than the orgasm was the washing we gave each other afterward.

SIXTEEN

In the morning, I woke to find myself and Clive tangled together in one of the narrow beds. (We'd left the other bed untouched.)

It felt like it would be the most natural thing in the world to meld our bodies, to find out if he was the kind of guy who liked sex first thing in the morning, before he was really awake. But as I grew more alert I remembered things like the fact we were in a house full of sex magicians, Wex was still in the hospital, and that I had reservations about Clive's boundaries. The night before had he actually said he was so into me it was "beyond reason?"

Yes, he had. Apparently all those months where I had been obsessing about him, he had been doing the same thing. And now, he was at that stage of submission where he had imprinted on me like a baby duck on its mama. The stage where I could swallow him whole and he'd claim to be happy about it. For a while, at least.

And I still needed to know how the demon fit into it all. I had a vivid sense-memory of him carrying me up into the tree, the wind rising around us. Thinking back on it, it really didn't feel like he had been taking me up there to kill me. I would have bet that demon had something else on its mind… except I wasn't even sure at that point if demons had minds.

Speaking of which, Niko had said Clive would need to sleep off being possessed. He barely stirred as I climbed out of bed. I kissed him on the forehead and left him sleeping soundly, then went to find Jair.

He was in the kitchen making breakfast. "You want some eggs?" He had a pan heating on the stove and was whisking something in a bowl. "You can have some of this if you don't mind soy chorizo."

"Sure. I'll take a chance."

He grinned and cracked another egg into the bowl and resumed whisking. "I have nothing against soy except when it's trying to masquerade as something else. But I figured I may as well use these up if Roland isn't going vegetarian after all."

The coffee maker on the counter by the window had a fresh pot under it, and at his urging I poured myself a mug. I didn't feel sleepy right then, but a caffeine jolt would probably help keep me sharp all morning. Out the back window, the gardens looked labyrinthine—a jumble of half-crumbled brick and wisteria gone wild. From the street you'd never even know it was there. Later, my curiosity would drive me to look at online maps of the area, and I would discover that many blocks of Greenwich Village were built with hidden gardens at the center, though I would wager this was the only one with a magically protected townhouse.

Jair scraped the eggs methodically from one side of the pan to another with a wooden spatula and told me a bit about the meal protocol for the group. "Normally we're on our own for breakfast and lunch, but we take turns making dinner." That explained why the fridge had a calendar on it with each of their names written in each day.

Next to it was a list that hadn't been there last night. I moved close enough to read it.

- Wexel hospitalized
- Kanna/Ira missing
- Mira/Clive uninitiated
- Clive easily possessed
- Partisans on the loose
- Lydia on the rampage

He saw me looking. "This bunch loses their focus easily."

"So you wrote a 'to do' list?" I sipped the coffee. It was bitter and bracing. "Who's Lydia?"

"Roland's ex-wife. If the phone on the wall rings, it's either her or a robocall. Hardly anyone has this number." He gestured to a cabinet. "Get plates?"

I pulled two mismatched plates out and set them on the table. "Ex-wife?"

He tipped the eggs onto them. "Yeah, Roland's... complicated."

Instead of pressing him on that, I got out forks and handed him one. "So, I've been thinking."

"I get the feeling you do that a lot." He sprinkled his eggs with hot sauce and sat at the table to eat. "And I mean that in the best way."

I took it as a compliment and sat down across from him. "So. The Partisans of Fire. How did they find Ira and Kanna in the first place?"

"That is a good question. The thing is, Ira gets around, you know? I mean, he's supposed to—he's out there scouting for people who could fill the rest of the slots in the Circle. He was very careful about how he approached both Clive and Wexel. But maybe a Partisan got wind of the party."

"That was a small party with a very exclusive guest list," I told him. "I had to be vetted to get on the list and I didn't even know the name of the host until I got there. It's not like someone who just eavesdropped could have showed up uninvited."

"Yeah, but if we've figured out we can recruit in the BDSM community, the Partisans probably have, too, don't you think?" Jair speared something on his plate with a fork. "Ira might have met one of them while out clubbing and they read his mind."

"I thought you couldn't read someone's mind without consent?"

"We can't. They can."

We can't. They can.

That crystallized everything for me. I couldn't think of a starker division between good and evil. "So... you're the keepers of knowledge. And you only use that knowledge ethically, while they want to destroy the knowledge so much, they'll use it unethically?"

He chewed on that thought for a minute, along with a chunk of soy sausage. "Yeah. It's not just mind-reading. Have I told you the bit about how we also don't kill? Or anything. You haven't seen it in action much, but circle workings kind of boil down to either ritualized sex or blood sacrifice."

"Or both?"

"Or both."

I thought about how someone had left Wex for dead. "Without consent, what you do in one of your ceremonies would be rape, assault, and murder." The Invocation of Willingness made a lot of sense then.

"Seems pretty clear cut, doesn't it?" He put down his fork and picked up his plate. "Obviously I know which side I'd rather be on." He licked every drop of hot sauce off the plate and then sat back.

I refrained from comment, but I think he knew my interest had been piqued. I took his plate and mine to the sink and washed them and the frying pan.

"Niko's right," he said with a grin. "It is fun having visitors."

❧

The hospital was across town, almost directly east of The Archive. The sun was out and our two choices—hoof it or take a crosstown bus—would probably take about the same amount of time. So we walked. The air was still brisk, but I borrowed an assortment of clothes and told myself I'd be warm enough if we kept moving. A cold gust of wind as we crossed Seventh Avenue tested my resolve, though. "Just watch, next week it'll be eighty out and people will complain it's too hot. That's New York for you."

Jair snorted in agreement. "You say that like I'm not from here."

"You're not."

"How can you tell?"

"Well, for one thing, your accent isn't like any New York accent I've ever heard." I'd been trying to figure it out since the night before. Jair had an easy manner of talking that was almost California but without the surfer twang, and some of his vowels were ever-so-slightly shifted. His cadence was different, too, like he'd started with something other than English. "But I also can't place where you're from."

"That's because I'm from everywhere." He stretched out his hands like he was spreading wings. "My folks moved around a lot when I was a kid."

"Military?"

"No. I was born in the States, but my parents moved us to a kibbutz in Israel when I was like three. My earliest memory is of a jet plane in Tel Aviv. I can still see it in my mind's eye, this huge white thing gliding down and down and down, and then a puff of smoke where the wheels touched." He brought one hand in for a landing. "How about you. Are you from here?"

"Yeah, though I went away for college and then came back. Kish is from here, too."

"No. Kish is from Miami."

"Brooklyn," I insisted.

"You just met her! I've known her over a year. I will bet you ten bucks she's from Miami."

"I'll take that bet."

"Ha, shake on it."

We shook hands as we walked. Jair walked fast, yet didn't seem like he was hurrying. He had a bit of a limp, one most people probably wouldn't even notice, except it spurred the massage-therapist part of my brain to think about whether it could be fixed, and how. I soon learned that he'd lived in Oregon, Arizona, Belize, Lisbon, Berlin, both Carolinas, and Vancouver (Canada), all before he was sixteen.

Maybe he was feeling judged. "Does it matter that I'm not from New York?"

Obviously not, but maybe it wasn't obvious to him. "No. You don't have to be born here to be a New Yorker. This is the place people come to become who they're going to be."

"That's deep, Mira."

I shrugged. "Just a fact." Not everyone who comes here finds their destiny, but the one thing you can always become, without fail, is a New Yorker. "So where'd you learn to fight?"

"Who, me?"

"You see anyone else walking with us?" I did a thing Sensei Jack sometimes did—I stuck my foot out like I was trying to trip him.

His reflexes were too good for that. He danced out of the way and lunged to grab me, but I was ready for it. I deflected him and tried to get him in a joint lock. He was smooth, though, twisting the lock back on me until he had my elbow and shoulder in serious jeopardy. I tapped out by reflex, patting him on the shoulder and he let go immediately. We grinned at each other and I raised an eyebrow instead of repeating my question.

He shrugged. "I've dabbled here and there ever since I was a kid. I'm kind of glad I took some filipino knife fighting classes when I was in Florida. Seems like these days it could come in handy."

The main entrance of the hospital was in a cylindrical building on First Avenue. Kind of hard to miss. Once it was in sight, I asked, "So where's your knife now?"

"Same place it was last night. Why?"

I couldn't see the handle, but he was wearing different jeans that covered the tops of his boots. "Just wondering if they'll let you into the hospital if you're carrying it."

"It's not like I'm planning to perform surgery with it."

"I don't think that's why they wouldn't want you to have it. Let me do the talking?"

"I was planning on it." He cringed suddenly. "You don't think they'll be like, giving Wex shots while we're there?"

"I doubt it. Why?"

"I do not like needles." He shivered. "Seriously."

I tried not to laugh. He seemed like rather a tough guy to have a needle phobia.

"I mean it. Do all the ritualistic cuttings on me that you want. Just keep the needles far away."

I suppose everyone has a limit, even Jair.

As it turned out, no one searched us for weapons or anything like that. The on-duty nurse informed me there'd been no change in Wex's condition and gave me some insurance paperwork to fill out, under the impression that I was family, and I did nothing to dissuade that belief. I said I'd have to fill it out at home and bring it back, and she didn't seem to think that was too weird. She led us to Wex's room and said to call her if we needed anything.

He had a roommate, a woman, who appeared to be either asleep or unconscious. I drew the curtain between the beds.

A saline drip in one arm was keeping him hydrated. They'd given him a blood transfusion when he'd first been brought in. Since then his vital signs had been strong, but he'd never woken. To me he looked paper thin.

Jair leaned over the bed. "Is he always this pale?"

"Pretty much." Wexel rarely went out during the daytime. He used to joke that he was more Anglo at night. (The sun-bleached blond look to his hair came from a bottle.) "Can you make anything of the markings?"

Some of the fine lines down his arm were fading, but they were obviously deliberate, with parallel lines and curves.

Jair wanted to look at his back, too, and it seemed best if we weren't caught doing that. Far as we could tell, the hospital room door didn't lock from the inside. I put a chair under the doorknob. It would have to do. We turned Wex on his side, toward the arm with the IV. The heart monitor sped up a little as we did it.

My breath caught in my throat when I saw the markings on his back. It was like someone had played an exotic game of tic tac toe on his skin using unreadable symbols instead of X's and O's. (Circular tic tac toe, I suppose.)

Jair urged me to take a few photos with my phone, and then we eased him back down. Wex did not rouse.

I restored the chair to where it had been at his bedside and sat in it. "Come on, Wex. You're worrying me."

"Do you think talking to him will help?"

"They say sometimes calling the name of an unconscious person helps bring them back to themselves." Or at least Sensei Jack did. I took Wex's hand in mine. "Wexel, come on. You've been gone long enough."

No reaction. Not that I really expected one. "Maybe you should try. You're more his type."

"Oh yeah?" Jair put his hand over both of ours. "Hey, pretty boy. I'm waiting to talk to you." Still nothing.

"Well, it was worth a try. What do you think? Is he Soulwandering? Or just…?" I couldn't say it. Up until that moment I had kept myself from even thinking it. But what if he had brain damage and never woke up again? It was like a fist squeezed my heart and lungs so hard that tears leaked out my eyes.

Jair's grip tightened reassuringly and then he placed his other hand on Wexel's chest. He held it there for a few heartbeats, as if he could use his palm like a psychic stethoscope. "I can't tell what's going on. But don't give up hope, Mira. It doesn't look like he's injured. If it's just that his mind went into retreat, then he'll be back when he knows it's safe."

"Dammit, but how did he get mixed up in this in the first place?" Ira had been recruiting him… but Wex had been attacked *before* the party.

"Let's wait to talk about that." He gave Wex a last pat and then went to push back the curtain. The woman in the other bed had not moved so far as I could tell.

I wiped my eyes and stuffed the paperwork into the inner pocket of my jacket. We exited silently, managing to avoid talking to anyone on the way out.

When we were all the way out on the street I finally asked, "So, do you think it's safe to get some things from my place?"

"I think so." We started walking briskly away from the hospital, Jair glancing behind us. "If we assume the Partisans got Clive's address off his vehicle registration——how would they trace you? It's not like they could find Ira's Christmas card list."

Not in that fire. "And not like I'd be on it, either."

Jair snorted. "I take it your dislike is mutual?"

"I'm pretty sure he thinks I'm a pushy bitch."

"And are you?" he teased gently.

"I get things done. Well, except for lately." When I hadn't been doing squat. "I haven't done much for myself or others the past few months."

"Speaking of others, I'm curious if anyone else who escaped the party has had a suspicious fire like the one at Clive's." He glanced behind us again as I led him to the subway so we could head uptown to my place. "Did you know anyone else there? Can you check if they made it home all right?"

"I know one, at least." Once we were down in the station I checked social media to see if I could find Cricket or any other mention of last night's incidents. I saw nothing in the usual places, but then again the rule about private parties was No Public Posting. I logged into Kinkus—— a site just for folks in the BDSM community——to at least drop Cricket a private DM, and was surprised to see a message *from* him.

> Mira, just checking in to see if you're OK. Crazy what happened last night, right? I've heard from everyone on the guest list now except you and Clive. Well, or Ira or Kanna. I'm freaking out a little. I definitely saw I&K outside, so maybe they're at a hospital, but I never saw you. If you're alive and/or if you've heard from them LMK.

I composed a reply just saying Clive and I made it out safely, before I thought about the risk. Our train came then, and once we were inside I showed it to Jair. He nodded in approval.

Then he took my phone, opened the contact list, and added himself to it.

It was too noisy to talk in the train, but there was plenty of phone signal, especially when we went aboveground. So I texted him: *Looks like the Partisans decided against killing everyone?*

He texted back: *They may be evil, but maybe even they have limits? *Shrug**

A little while later he added: *Nothing in the news about the house fire at all. Which seems a bit odd. There is one little mention of the fire at Clive's, but nothing about arson.*

So the majority of party guests had made it home all right and were fine. Only those connected with the Circle of Light had been targeted. Of course, I wasn't connected to the Circle until *after* the fire… Right?

We emerged onto the elevated train platform to the sound of sirens. It's a common enough sound in New York. You hear them all the time. Ambulances, fire trucks, police cars, rescue squads… they all criss-cross the city regularly. No reason to think the ones we could hear were related to us. But sweat prickled up my back despite the April chill. As we got down to the sidewalk from the platform, a fire truck screamed past. A little old lady shook her handbag at it, cursing a blue streak while holding her ear with her other hand. I led the way toward my building, up the same street the truck had taken.

As we turned the corner onto my block, I could see the other end of the street blocked by emergency vehicles. The sidewalk was full of people gawking, including a few I recognized as my neighbors even if I didn't know their names, like the guy who always wore a track suit to do his laundry or the woman with the two cats, the pair of whom liked to escape into the hall. She had a cat carrier in each hand.

Smoke poured out a third story window on a building. *My* building.

My window.

Jair didn't even wait to ask me. My stricken face probably told him all he needed to know. He hooked his arm in mine and steered me in an about face right back the way we had come, before anyone could even notice us in the crowd. "They might still be here," he murmured into my ear.

"It might be a coincidence," I murmured back, but I sounded skeptical even to myself.

"Hell of a coincidence."

"How did they even know where to find me, or even that they should look for me?" I was starting to tremble a little, as the reality sank in that someone had literally just torched my life. My emotions see-sawed. There wasn't anything in the apartment that wasn't replaceable, not really. Unless you counted the 3-D laser engraving of me and Ethan at Walt Disney World that I'd hidden in the back of the closet. Clothes, books, a bunch of floggers and whips… Some of the whips were valuable, really fine custom pieces, but none of them were my go-tos. That was when it started to feel like Fate that I'd grabbed the bag of my three favorites on the way out the door to the party.

It had already felt a bit Fated that I met the Circle to begin with. But the fire meant I couldn't go back. I couldn't just walk away from them and resume my former life. Not with the Partisans of Fire hunting me.

I hoped no one had been hurt.

"Those bastards." I had started shaking, and I realized it wasn't with fear. It was with rage. "Those utter bastards."

Jair made noises of agreement and steered me past the subway stop we'd come from and kept us walking. For stealth, I guess. I was too angry to think clearly.

"We can't let them get away with this," I said to him at one point.

"No, we can't," Jair agreed. "Or eventually they'll find us and we'll all end up dead."

"Who are they? How many are they?" My brain had clicked right into planning mode. "We have to do something!"

"I one-hundred percent agree. Roland's going to take some convincing, though."

"Three fires in 24 hours isn't enough to convince him?"

"Well, maybe it will. But… We'll talk about it." Jair pulled me into a gap between two buildings and then looked behind us. "I'm sorry, Mira."

"Why are you apologizing? You didn't light the fire."

"I'm not apologizing. I'm sympathizing." He held me by the shoulders. "Listen. If you want to fight the Partisans of Fire, you're going to have to learn to fight on their level."

I knew what he was going to ask next, and I felt like my *yes* was already bubbling up inside my chest. It felt like that time—my first time—when I knew I wasn't going to say *no*. It had been my freshman roommate's older brother. We'd met a few times and we'd been friendly, but not what I thought was flirtatious. I'd been dancing at a frat party with all its attendant groping and ogling and had left because I had hated it. He had pulled up in front of the building in an overpriced sports car just as I stumbled out, flushed and sweaty, and offered me "a ride" even though our dorm was the building right across the street.

I'd known I was going to say yes. And I'd known *that* "yes" meant more than just a ride. I'd known it was going to lead down a path that I couldn't reverse.

What that had taught me was that sometimes all you can do is say *yes* to the opportunity you're presented with. *No* just doesn't even enter the list of possibilities. It's all a matter of when that *yes* will come.

But I wasn't a clueless college freshman anymore. If I was going to believe in free will, then nothing was inevitable. So when Jair, in keeping with his manner, asked me quite directly, "Mira, will you join the Circle of Light?" my answer stuck in my throat.

SEVENTEEN

I put off answering Jair until we'd gotten to our next stopping place, an elevated subway station on the "A" line, over a busy intersection, buses and trucks rumbling by underneath. By then I'd had a few minutes to think about why I wasn't simply jumping at the chance.

"We have to find a way to solve Clive's demon problem, first," I told him. I know, not a typical topic for discussion on the train platform. But no one was remotely within earshot, and I had to remind Jair what was at stake.

"Niko will have some ideas about that by today," Jair said. "I also think Clive will come around. He was just being pissy last night because he doesn't like being pushed around. Which is a little weird for a submissive, isn't it?"

I put my hands together in a prayer for patience. "Jair."

"Uh oh. No one says my name like that unless I'm in trouble."

Ha. That made it more like a conversation I'd had many times before, on subway platforms and elsewhere. "Just what do you think being submissive means, exactly?"

"Did I learn it wrong in school? Submissive means meek, passive. Obedient."

"And does Clive strike you as particularly meek?"

"Well, no, but maybe he's an exception. He's a masochist, too, right? A glutton for punishment?" He tried to give me a winning smile.

That might have worked on his fourth grade teacher, but it didn't work on me. "Okay, first of all being a masochist and being submissive are two different things."

"Yeah, I know—"

"And being the submissive partner in a power exchange doesn't mean you're quote-unquote 'submissive' in personality. You have a top and a bottom, a dominant partner and a submissive partner. The dominant one is in control, the submissive one gives up control. That's it. That's all it means. Anything else about how you act or what you do is up for negotiation."

"Okay…"

"So when you say Clive doesn't like to be pushed around, it means Clive does not like to be pushed around. He doesn't like to be taken for granted, either." I had only known him for what, two days? And that much was obvious to me. "Clive is an adrenaline junkie who likes to have his physical limits challenged, and that's something that's very hard to do for yourself. It's easy to have someone like me do it, though."

"Someone like you. You mean dominant."

"Someone who gets a sexual thrill from taking control, yes." I flexed my fingers. I could almost still feel Clive's hair in my fist. Last night's shower was imprinted on my senses. "I love it when a partner places themselves in my hands. When they give me the gift of themselves to do with as I wish. Their trust in me heightens the emotion and revs my engine. That's a bit different, wouldn't you say, from I just 'like to push people around?'"

Jair chewed on his lower lip, like I was making him hungry for more food for thought. "You make it sound… almost… like a noble pursuit."

"It can be. If you don't abuse your power. The whole point is to not-abuse your power."

He rubbed his chin, where last night's stubble was still growing.

"The whole point," I said again, "is not to abuse the trust you've been given. The thrill is in receiving that trust, not in breaking it. I thought the Circle of Light was really into the whole 'enter of your free will' stuff?"

"We are! But with you and Clive you're talking about something beyond people agreeing to work a circle together. Or even agreeing to mutually have a good time." One hand tapped unconsciously on his leg. "If Ira and Kanna's party hadn't been disrupted, would I have—" He broke off as he looked past me at someone.

I didn't look behind me, just followed his lead as he backed us toward the station wall, away from the edge of the tracks. The train was coming: I could hear it.

A young woman in a leather jacket walked past us, her hands in her pockets. She didn't seem to be paying attention to us, and yet.

The train began to rumble into the station. A belch of exhaust from a truck going by below made me feel like coughing, but I found myself suddenly tense and holding it in.

Jair's voice was light. "You sure this is our train?"

I knew it wasn't a real question. Don't ask me how—I guess it was just obvious to me he was pretending to be clueless. But hopefully not obvious to anyone watching us. I played along. "I'm sure it is. Come on."

The A came to a squeaky halt and the doors slid open. We got on, and one door down from us, so did she.

Then a moment before the doors closed, Jair grabbed me by the arm. "No, we're going the wrong direction." He stepped back onto the platform, pulling me out of the train with him.

The doors closed and the train pulled away. We were alone on the platform. The mystery woman was on her way downtown. Maybe she was no one. Maybe we were being paranoid.

I was fine with being paranoid.

Me: "Why don't we get a cab."

Him: "Good idea."

⁊⁊

Jair told the driver to take us to the White Horse Tavern, and then the second the cab started moving, began texting Roland. I had the urge to do the same to Clive, but not only did I not have his number, Clive didn't even have a phone at that point. It had been left behind in the fire. Not being able to reach him instantly gave me a sinking feeling.

My hands felt idle. I forwarded Jair the photos I'd taken of Wex's marks, but then couldn't figure out what to do with myself. I'd already felt disconnected from my life before the events of the previous 24 hours. I'd been ignoring social media, not going out, not going to work—Wex had been right about all that. Like my life had ground to a halt already. But between the discovery of the Circle and their thing-not-called-magic and the torching of my possessions, I felt like that what shreds of connection to my old life I'd had were gone.

The only moment I'd felt alive in months had been that night Clive and I had played at Club Purgatory. I'd felt that again when I'd leaped into action to rescue him, and from that moment forward I had been low-key aware of my heart beating and the blood pumping through my veins. I guess I'd stopped taking them for granted.

It wasn't just being alive that I liked, but the feeling of having something to live for. And I didn't much appreciate the Partisans trying to take that away. "That woman. Do you think she was one of them?"

He tapped out a few more words before answering. "It's definitely possible. I figured if she wasn't, then no biggie. If she was, well, she's stuck on the train until at least the next station and can't trail us. She looked… sort of familiar to me, though."

He went back to texting with Roland and I looked out the window as we headed down a busy avenue, sidewalks on each side dense with pedestrians. I'd been to LA and Dallas and Miami and Boston and none of them had crowded sidewalks like Manhattan. People, people, and more people. I was accustomed to thinking of a crowd as safety. The thought that any one of them might want us dead rolled uncomfortably through my mind.

The feeling seemed to intensify, becoming a lump in the pit of my stomach. A kind of ache started up in my chest. Strange. Was I feeling grief over my lost apartment…? My lost life? The buildings outside were going by in a blur. *Clive.* I needed to see Clive and make sure he was okay.

Jair cursed at his phone. "We need to hurry."

The feeling of foreboding spiked. "Why? What's going on?"

"Clive's barricaded the door to your room and won't come out, apparently."

"What?" My first urge was to jump out of the cab on the spot and run all the way there. Which didn't make any sense. I doubted I could run that far and the cab would get me there faster in any case. But if I could have flown out the window like a bird, I would have. "Tell them we're coming as fast as we can."

"Already did."

I put my hand on my breastbone. Roland had described a feeling of wrongness when Clive broke his pledge of secrecy, right there, tugging on his heartstrings. That was what I was feeling. "Clive."

"He's calling to you, I think." Jair tapped on his leg with his fingertips. "Was he asleep when we left?"

"Yes. Niko said to let him sleep." Because being possessed is rough on a person. "He didn't say anything about me needing to be there when he woke up, though."

"What do you think's wrong?"

"No idea." Clive and I had talked a little after we got in bed, but not much because we were both too tired. "All he said to me this morning was a sleepy goodbye and then he conked back out."

Jair leaned forward to tell the driver to hurry if possible. "A friend is in trouble."

The guy gave a thumbs up but no promises. My guess was we were still a good ten to fifteen minutes away even if we didn't hit bad traffic. I forced myself to breathe evenly. "How about you tell me everything you know about demons. In case it's that again."

"Okay." He thought for a moment. "I told you before that there's no Hell, right? The idea that demons are some kind of spawn of the devil, you can throw that idea right out the window. Demons are a kind of coalescence." He held up his hands like he was packing an invisible snowball. "Desire is a kind of spiritual energy, right? Think of yourself like a candle. Every time you desire something, or someone, it's like your flame is lit. You light a candle so you can see, but it also sends heat wafting up into the air."

"Sure...?"

"But if you have enough candles combining their heat, you can set the ceiling on fire. The demon is that fire." He looked at me, chewing on his lip. "Maybe that analogy was crap."

"Maybe," I agreed.

"Niko could probably do a better job of explaining."

"How about you just explain how we got from desire to the ceiling on fire?"

He held up his hands again. "When you want something, you send energy out. If there's enough desire, and the conditions are right, that energy can basically coalesce into a force of its own. A demon is a spirit that wants, that hungers. But it can't do anything while its disembodied."

"So that's why they possess a body?"

"Basically. And they're just floating around. You never know when one might be near. It's one of the reasons for the containment circle."

"To keep them in control if you summon one by accident?" Right?

Wrong. "No-no-no, the circle is to keep them out. So they don't possess your body while your spirit is busy doing something else." He shifted uncomfortably in his seat. "The pop culture depiction of the devil-worshipping magician drawing a circle and summoning a demon and telling it what to do is wrong. You can't tell a demon what to do."

"Except that I did."

He chewed his lip. "I don't know, then. Maybe it only looked like you did."

He lapsed into tense silence and I did not ask any more questions. He had at least explained some things. I still didn't really understand what a demon was, but maybe I did get why instead of ripping my head off, it had nibbled my neck?

Talk about a relationship complication.

EIGHTEEN

Jair had the cab driver circle the block before telling him to let us out. He paid cash and we got out a few doors down from where the van was parked. I wanted to run to the house, but Jair held me back with gentle grip on my hand, waiting on the curb until the cab was out of sight. As soon as it disappeared around the corner, though, we rushed through the garage and into the gardens.

Niko was waiting for us at the back door. "I'm not sure what's happening in there. He doesn't answer and he won't open the door for any of us."

"And we didn't want to use force," Roland added, "At least not until we were sure you couldn't talk to him, Mira."

"Was he asking for me?"

"He might have said your name earlier, but mostly he hasn't responded."

I looked up the stairs. "Does that mean the demon's back?"

Niko and Roland shared a glance, and Niko spoke. "It's hard to say. I think it might be some other aftereffect of being possessed. If it's the demon returning…? I just don't know."

"The previous one was… very aggressive," Roland said. "I'd think we wouldn't still be alive if it had come back. But some other spirit might've possessed him?"

"Despite the rosary?" I asked.

"Maybe the binding wasn't that strong and the beads came off?" Roland didn't sound very sure.

"I can feel him here, though." I put a hand on my chest. Was it just my own worry I was feeling? "I sense something's wrong. Niko, you said there could be negative consequences for Clive and me to separate? Could this be that?"

Niko sounded surer. "If you can sense his distress, that sounds like the bond is still in place. Come on. Let's see if you can get through to him." He took the stairs two at a time and I followed him up, Jair and Roland bringing up the rear.

Kish was standing guard, knife at her belt. "I heard a thump a little while ago. He might've moved a piece of furniture in front of the door? I called his name but he didn't answer."

The door had symbols written in chalk on it and around the frame. Some of them looked a lot like the ones I had seen on Wex's back. "What's all this?"

Roland picked up a piece of chalk from the floor. "A weak form of containment, just in case. The aegis on the house is a much stronger one than this."

"Maybe you should all go out into the garden, then." I looked from Niko to Roland. "Just in case."

He tossed the bit of chalk in his cupped palm like he was considering drawing more. "You know you don't have the training to deal with a demon."

"Does anyone? I wasn't exactly impressed by what I saw last night."

Roland blushed to his sandy roots. "I was caught by surprise."

Jair put a hand on his shoulder. "Let Mira try, all right? I've been meaning to ask you what the deal was with that rosary."

"Fine. I'll tell you outside." Roland gave me a nod. "If we don't hear from you in half an hour, we'll come check if you're still in one piece."

"Mira, you need anything from the equipment trunk?" Kish asked. "We've got all kinds of stuff. Rope, chain, candles, ritual flails, a really nice ivory dildo—"

"You don't even have a blade," Jair added.

"I don't need one." I shooed them toward the stairs. "Just go."

They went. My primary worry wasn't that some demon was going to burn everything inside the building including them to a crisp. I mostly wanted privacy. I still didn't know exactly what the limits were on a bond of obedience and if I had to push them, I just didn't want anyone kibbitzing.

I listened for the sound of the back door shutting downstairs and then I knocked softly. "Clive? It's Mira."

I heard something shift against the door, as if what was pressed up against it wasn't a piece of furniture, but Clive himself.

"Clive, if you can hear me, knock twice."

Knock, knock. Obedient as ever. My heart twisted in my chest. What was happening to him in there?

"Clive, open the door and let me in."

The latch clicked and the door opened a crack. I waited a moment, but when it didn't open any wider, I pushed it slowly inward myself. The room was dark, the only light coming from around the edges of the heavy curtains on the window.

It took me a moment to make out that the shape at the foot of the bed was Clive, hunched over in a ball. If he was wearing any clothes, I couldn't see them. I shut the door behind me and latched it before approaching him cautiously.

"What's up, angel?" I asked. His face was hidden. I knelt beside him and ran my hand over his hair. "You doing all right?"

He looked up then, eyes blank, mouth a little slack, his voice so flat it almost didn't sound like him: "He's coming."

"Who's coming?"

He gasped suddenly and buried his face again, forehead against his knees, trembling, voice a terrified rasp: "He's coming!" That sound put a lump in my throat.

"The demon?" I could see the string of beads around his neck. So much for Roland's theory that they'd slipped off. "Is that who you mean?"

He shook his head and shrank away from me, like he could hide by making himself smaller. Like a child.

It reminded me of something. A girlfriend in college who'd got off on the sensation of being spanked. One time she unexpectedly regressed. I just played along like she was role-playing for fun, but afterward she told me it hadn't been conscious on her part.

I didn't know if something like that was what was happening to Clive, but I went with it. "No one's going to hurt you." I petted his hair again and he did not flinch. I swallowed, trying to keep myself calm. "I'm here, angel. I'm here to protect you, remember?"

He lifted his head just enough for me to see his eyes through his tousled hair.

"I rescued you from the fire last night. We're safe here. We're at The Archive with the Circle of Light."

His head lifted a little more and a glimmer of understanding seemed to shine in his eyes.

"You got possessed by a demon yesterday. Do you remember that?"

He looked from side to side, a slight frown between his eyebrows.

"You went Soulwandering. But you came back when I called." I held out a hand to see if he would take it.

He looked at it but didn't reach out.

"Clive? Can you come back to me now?"

He spoke at last, voice rough. "Is it safe with you?"

A pang went through me as I had a flash of Ethan saying *no, absolutely not.* But Ethan could go fuck himself. "As safe as I can make it," I said. I held out both arms. "Come back now, Clive. Come back."

"My lady!" He threw himself into my embrace with a sob.

I held him, rocking him gently like you would a terrified child who just woke up from a nightmare. It was all I could think of to do.

A few minutes went by, I think? I just held him while my mind raced around, thinking, Good god, Clive, what is going on in your head?

His breathing slowed. The next time he raised his head, it was like he was seeing me for the first time that day. "Mira?"

"You okay?"

He blinked. "What just happened?"

"I think you... had a nightmare? Kind of?"

He looked around the room. "Huh. I do sleepwalk sometimes."

"You ever barricade yourself in a room while sleepwalking before?"

"I don't think so." He shook his head. "Was I talking? What did I say?"

"You said 'He's coming.'"

He looked as confused as I felt. "That's all?"

"Pretty much."

"Well, that's vague." He frowned, then focused on me again. "Are you all right?"

"I'm fine. Well, Jair and I tried to go to my place and... it was on fire."

He hugged me tightly. "Dammit. I should've gone with you."

I tried to be nonchalant about it. "You needed to sleep. It's fine. I didn't need any of that stuff anyway." But even as I was saying it, my words felt more and more facile.

"Will you tell me what you're really feeling now?" His cheek was close to mine, his voice close and comforting in my ear.

Part of me wanted to pull away. But I didn't. "I feel like I passed some point of no return."

He held his breath for a moment. "Today?"

I didn't answer his question directly. "Knowing what you do now, about demons and sex magic and whatever? Could you go back to your old life, even if the Partisans of Fire weren't trying to kill us?"

He leaned against me. "I was thinking about that as we were falling asleep last night. Even if we don't become part of the Circle of Light. We can't just run away and forget it all, can we? I don't think I can."

"I don't think I can, either." That sick feeling in my chest of something being terribly wrong had eased, but another ache remained. "I can't go back to my half-asleep life."

"Yeah." He shifted so he could pull back to look at me. "I guess this means we should seriously think about joining the Circle of Light."

"You're the one who had reservations last night. Tell me more?"

He sighed. "Sorry I was so pissy. They'd been leading me on with hints about the Practice and all, but it was almost hard to know if it was real, you know? Like maybe they were just LARPers who took it really, really seriously and never broke character or something. And then, well, you saw how things went at the party."

I got the feeling he didn't just mean the fire. I didn't want to talk shit about someone who might be injured or in serious trouble right then, so I tried to make my words as mild as possible. "You know Ira's not my favorite person."

"I take it you weren't impressed."

"I'm not sure I would use the term 'informed consent' if—just for example—the person I'm performing ritual magic on isn't even sure if magic is real or if I'm just pretending it is." I was starting to feel angry about Ira all over again. Kanna, too, though it really felt like Ira was very much the one in charge. "Am I splitting the hairs too fine, here?"

"You don't have to get all riled up on my behalf, Mira," Clive said. "I know I put myself in harm's way for a thrill. I take responsibility for myself. I know what he'll say, you know, if I confront him with it. If I tell him I couldn't give informed consent because I wasn't suitably informed."

"What, he'll say he swore to keep the secrets of the Circle of Light?"

"No." Clive's eyes were downcast, shadowed. "He's going to say he was doing what I wanted. Because I told him I liked being surprised. I signed up for that."

"You didn't sign up to have your soul cut free of your body." I ran a finger along the chain of beads on his neck. They felt warm from his body heat.

His eyes closed for a moment, and I wondered what he was thinking. Was he thinking about that moment in the woods when the unbridled power of the demon was suddenly quelled, like I was? Or maybe about the fire? Could be either.

Or both. "I'm lucky... you were there." His voice was quiet.

I wanted to kiss him, then, and by "kiss" I mean devour his mouth and his breath until he was gasping for air. The more vulnerable he seemed, the more I wanted to do it—and the less prudent it was. I settled for a peck against his temple. "I'm glad I was there."

"Niko said he'd tell us more today." He shifted, and I felt him disengaging from me, finally, and putting distance between us. I wasn't surprised, but it stung a tiny bit. I reminded myself he hadn't asked to be collared, and that I should give him space, but deep down, my gut urge was to not let him leave the room until I'd put my mark on him and made him mine.

I shook my head. A bond of obedience was a helluva drug, apparently. I let go of him and he got up to dig through his duffel for some clothes. I stayed where I was on the floor, watching him dress. "What do you think Niko's going to tell us?"

Clive moved briskly, donning socks, combing his hair, looking for his shoes. "No idea." He stopped suddenly, and looked down at me, eyes pained.

"What's wrong, angel?"

He shook his head. "What happens if the demon does come back?"

"Clive." I got to my feet, but he moved away from me. "Let's worry about that when the time comes. Right now, let's have some lunch. Then we can find out what Niko has to say about our bond and the markings we found on Wex's back."

"All right." He let me take his hand at the door. As we went out into the hall, he caught sight of the chalk markings around the doorway. "I'm still not totally sure I'm safe to be around."

Well, I'm not safe to be around either, angel. And maybe I never was.

NINETEEN

That afternoon I had my first trip into Niko's domain: a high-ceilinged room on the top floor of The Archive, with an antique skylight and bookshelves that ran from the floor all the way up to the dormer. The late afternoon sun turned the skylight gold. Someone had repainted at some point so instead of the dark polished wood and leather I expected from a 19th century library, everything was plaster white, giving the place an airy, open look. Or maybe that was because shelf after shelf was empty, as bare and open as the ribs on a skeleton.

There were only two little clusters of books. A few tiers near the door held some colorful paperbacks with a lot of teal and purple on their spines. I pulled one out. "Align Your Chakras For Boardroom Success?"

"Oh no, please don't read those." Niko emerged from a door between two shelves, shutting it firmly behind him. "Those books'll just put a lot of confusing junk in your head."

The collection seemed to be "New Age" how-to books of various kinds, mostly from the 1970s and '80s by the look of them. Clive leafed skeptically through *Feng Shui For Cat Lovers*. "Why are they here, then?"

"Sometimes it's useful to see what other people are saying. Or *were* saying," Niko corrected himself with a shake of his head.

The other group of books was an assortment of notebooks, stacked every which way in the corner behind a small computer desk. Some were spiral bound, some were held together with tape. At least two I could see were large three-ring binders, one purple, one red. The computer on the desk looked a little antiquated itself. The monitor stood at eye level, the keyboard sat in a pull-out tray. Next to the monitor was a small electric tea kettle.

In his hand, Niko held a black and white composition book similar to many on the shelf. He invited me and Clive to sit on a thing a few feet from the desk that looked like a giant lima bean but was actually a small, low modernist couch. He himself sat crosslegged on the hardwood floor in front of us, the composition book in his lap. As usual he was dressed more like a track coach than a spiritual one, in dark blue sweat pants and matching jacket. "Okay. I'm going to try to tell you what I can about your bond, but stop me if I get too technical. You guys haven't even learned the basics of the practice yet, so explaining may be kind of a challenge."

"Should we learn the basics first?" Clive asked.

Roland appeared at the door from the hallway, carrying a tray. "Yes, you should, but you have to join the Circle for that. But this is me not pressuring you, all right?" He laid the tray on the floor next to Niko. On it sat a tea service that included a glass pitcher of water, a black iron teapot, and three white ceramic cups. "Need anything else?"

Niko looked up at him hopefully. "You could stay and help with the explanation…?"

"How about I'll pick up when you run out of steam. While Jair and Kish are out, I'm going to try that meditation you suggested last night."

"To reach Kanna and Ira? Yeah, as Convenor you may be able to in a way that even I can't, yeah."

"I'll be in the main room." Roland pulled a rather large piece of sidewalk chalk out of his pocket.

Clive snorted. "And here I thought you were just happy to see me."

Roland just shook his head and left.

"Close the door on your way out," Niko called, but too late: Roland was already on his way down the stairs.

Niko didn't let it bother him. He lifted the lid of the teapot and took out the little mesh basket, inspecting the dry leaves that were already sitting in it. "So. A bond of obedience is not that different from some of the other kinds of bindings between people… except when it is." He set the basket back in the pot. "For example, there's the binding that holds the Circle together. It confers some abilities and makes certain kinds of transfer easier."

"Abilities?" Clive asked, at the same time I said, "Transfer?" The lesson was going to be slow going if we questioned every word he used.

Niko was unperturbed. "Abilities might be a bit strong a term, but for example I can sense that Roland is all the way downstairs." He waited a few beats. "And Jair and Kish have left the building. As they get farther away, my sense of where they are fades. You two might share a sense like that. By *transfer,* I mean… *hmm.*"

He took the pen out of the notebook as if he were going to write something down, but in the end just tucked it behind his ear. "At its most basic level, the practice is about energy. But think about something we think we understand as energy, like electricity. We're science-y. We think we know what it is. Electricity sends signals through your nerves, thoughts through your brain. It's also what creates the thunderclap, when a massive amount of it leaps from a cloud. Is a lightning bolt a thought from a god?" He froze, like a basketball center watching a three-pointer in flight, smiling when it swished through the hoop. "Oh, I like that one." He flipped open the notebook and wrote it down. "Okay, where was I? Oh, the tea."

He poured a little water from the pitcher into the pot and swished it around, then poured it out. "Okay. So what I'm getting at with the bit about electricity is that even with something we think we know, you almost can't consider it the same thing when you talk about what it does in your brain versus what goes on in a thunderstorm. But it is actually the same thing."

"So you're saying there are forces of energy that work one way on the personal, human level, but work differently on a grander scale?" Clive asked. "On a cosmic level?"

"Yeah, exactly." Niko poured water through the leaves again, filling the pot. It seemed weird to me he didn't realize the water was cold. Had he forgotten the water should be hot to make tea? "Okay, listen. Secret or not, I have to give you the basic-basics at least, or this explanation won't make sense."

I glanced at the open door. Everyone was out. "We're all ears."

"What we call 'the practice' is 'the practice of manipulation of energetic extrasensory psychophysiology.'"

"The what, now?"

He chuckled a little. "I know. It's less complicated than it sounds at first, though. Psychophysiology is the effect of your mind and thoughts on your body. Extrasensory refers to things beyond what we can sense with the traditional five senses. And manipulation of energy is what lets me do this."

He held the teapot in his lap, cupped in his hands. He closed his eyes as if meditating, taking long, slow breaths. Beside me I could feel Clive's breathing fall into synch with him.

I've never been good at meditating, and I wasn't sure if that was what we were supposed to be doing just then, anyway. I just kept watch, wondering what I was supposed to see. Or feel. How much time had gone by? I wasn't sure.

The tea began to steam.

Niko opened his eyes and set the pot back onto the tray. "As I think one of you said the other night, it's not all about sex."

Clive pointed at the teapot. "You may as well call that magic."

"And lots of people would," Niko replied. Then, looking down at his hands: "I hear they used to burn witches."

"Yeah, and kill them in lots of other ways," I added. "So you just call it 'the practice,' and it doesn't sound as incriminating?"

"And perhaps more scientific," Niko allowed. "I think our predecessors adopted the terminology in the Age of Reason and we've stuck with it. Anyway. So there is energy being generated within each living thing, and in other things in the natural world, and when you're bonded, you sort of…" He trailed off, his two hands moving from side to side like he was pushing a ball back and forth between them.

"Get on the same wavelength? That's how Jair said the aegis worked."

"Yeah, that's a reasonable way to put it." Niko poured the tea into cups as white, round, and delicate as halved eggshells, and handed them to us by their rims. "But before I can talk about resonance and wavelength, you need to know about a bunch of other stuff."

"Okay." The tea smelled like grass but tasted nutty in my mouth, almost like popcorn.

"I'm trying to figure out where to start." He took the pen in hand, turned to a blank page in his notebook, and drew an outline of a human figure. "The body is like an island. What we see on the map, the way we define it, is by what sticks out of the water. But an island is of course not just the part we can see above the water. It goes all the way to the crust of the Earth. It's part of the Earth, even though we define it as a separate thing because it sticks out of the water. Our bodies are the same: an extension of our whole selves. They're just the part that sticks out into the physical plane."

"And our souls go into the non-physical plane?" Clive waved his hands above his head.

"I'm getting to that," Niko said. "The point is that although we define physical and non-physical parts of our being as if they're two separate things, they're really one thing. Each of us is a whole being." He pointed. "Me. You. Whether we perceive it or not, doesn't make it less than real."

"Okay." That idea wasn't far from some of the teachings I'd had in massage school around some of the eastern healing modalities. "So when you do a ritual-type thing—"

"A circle working," Clive supplied helpfully.

"—a circle working, is that basically a way of getting at the non-physical realm through the physical one? When they were flogging me to get at the truth, was that like… knocking on the door of my mind?"

Clive ran a hand over his own shoulder. "And if they could have just flogged me, did Ira and Kanna not need to cut me also?"

"I can't help but notice," I added, while Niko was mulling over our questions, "that everyone in the Circle carries a knife. Even you. Even when you're safe indoors."

"Oh, this?" He had it clipped to his waistband that day, instead of in his sleeve. He pulled it free and opened it using one hand. It was an almost delicate-looking modern knife, with a shiny spiderweb pattern cut into the blade. "This was a gift from Jair. It's not as flashy as one of the big ceremonial daggers, but it's a lot easier to carry around. And it matches my resonance. But to answer your question, Clive, in your case they had to go deeper than the surface level."

"The flogger only hits the top layer, the knife literally goes deeper?" I asked.

"Yes!" He seemed delighted. "It's not just a metaphor. You've probably gathered already from what's been said that there's a significance to blood in the practice."

"Jair said a droplet of it, transferred from person to person, could allow someone to pass the aegis."

"Exactly. It's not just blood, though. Any 'vital fluid' can carry the signal, if you will." Niko folded his knife up again and picked up his teacup for a gulp before going on. "And a knife isn't the only thing that can penetrate the… well, let's just say the skin isn't the only thing that can be breached." He blushed and sipped his tea.

"Kish did mention a ritual ivory dildo."

Niko nodded. "So here's the theory. All the energy in your being can be accessed through your body. Fluid exchange is a transfer of energy from being to being because it goes through all the layers. The first layer of defense isn't at the skin. It's out here." He held one hand, palm down, about an inch above the back of his other hand, then extended both hands toward us.

I passed my palm over the back of his hand and his forearm, about an inch from his skin, and saw the fine hairs on his arm stand up.

Something like mild static electricity tickled along my hand, barely there. "What am I feeling?"

"There's sort of a cloud layer above the island. It's very subtle, very slight. But when you spank someone or hit them, you break through that layer."

Clive also ran his hand above Niko's. "Is any contact with someone's skin enough to break the cloud layer?"

Niko shook his head. "No. Imagine it's like mist. You could slowly push your finger through it to touch skin, but as you did, your own mist layer would mesh right into it and the cloud cover would remain intact. Whereas if you hit sharply, it's like smacking shallow water. It's driven away by the blow, exposing the bottom of the tub for a second before it pours back in. The cloud layer is thicker at some parts of the body and thinner at others." He drew a cartoon heart in the chest of the figure on the page and then drew an arrow through it. "There are certain points where it can be penetrated more easily than others."

"Like in acupuncture?"

"I confess I don't know much about that! But maybe?" Niko jotted a note excitedly for himself. "After the cloud layer, then there's the skin layer itself, which can be breached different ways. Cutting is different from piercing, for example, and of course intentional, ritual breaches are very different from getting cut in a knife fight."

"Makes sense, I think." I looked at Clive. "But how does that relate to us two being bonded?"

"Um, has anyone explained the different planes of existence?"

"No," Clive and I both said together.

Niko pondered a bit. "Okay. How can I make this make sense." He drew what looked like a large letter M. "You're each one of these islands, and this is the water." He added a wavy line through the middle of it, so that each peak stuck above the water line. "Right? If islands are just the projection of our whole selves into the physical plane—our bodies—then the water is the aethereal plane and the air is the physical world our bodies are thrust into."

He then colored in where the wavy water line met each island. "And this, where the two things overlap, is the liminal plane. This beach, if you will, where the water and the land interact, that's where what we do in the practice takes place."

The explanation seemed reasonable enough, except… "But that still doesn't explain what it means that we're bonded."

He sighed and thought it over, then drew two curlicues rising up from each peak. "Okay. Each one is a volcanic island. As the magma roils around inside the volcano, it makes the water vibrate. That's sending your wavelength out through the ethereal plane."

Clive pointed to the diagram. "And underneath the crust of the earth, we're connected at the same pool of magma?"

"Oh. No. You're skipping ahead. The magma and lava would be like souls in this analogy, which would mean a bond of soulmates, which is something different entirely. The bond of obedience would be like…" He trailed off, staring at the diagram. Then he tore the piece of paper out, crumpled it up, and tossed it over his shoulder. "I don't know. Islands don't really have free will, so… that analogy really didn't work. I get the feeling you two were already resonant with each other before the practice came into play. So now that you're bonded, you're in synch."

Clive and I looked at each other. I asked, "Okay, but where does the obedience part come in, then?"

He considered for a moment. "Your thoughts, Mira—your will—can affect your wavelength. If you ask for something, the person you're bonded with will feel that change in wavelength and do what you ask in order to stay in synch with you. To not do so would cause them distress. Like what you felt when you were apart, and Clive was calling for you."

Clive nearly spilled his tea. "When did I call for you?"

"Earlier today," I said. "When you were sleepwalking or whatever that was." We'd talked that over during lunch but no one had been able to shed much light on it.

"And that's an ability the bond of obedience gives me?" Clive asked.

"Well, I admit I didn't find a mention of that specifically. But it seems likely I just didn't get to it yet." Niko set his empty tea cup down and opened the notebook to a page that was covered in his tiny, cramped handwriting. "Most of what I have here is about collars and necklaces. I should have known this, but necklaces work the same as rings. You might have noticed everyone in the Circle of Light has a matching piercing?"

"Yeah, Kish's eyebrow ring, and Roland's earrings, you mean?" I couldn't remember Jair's, but now that I thought about it I realized Kanna's nose ring and Ira's earring were also that same small silver hoop.

"Exactly. It amplifies and maintains the connection among us so we don't have to apply our will and energy to it all the time. Between the two of you, I believe the collar acts as a focus for the energy and intensifies the effect of the wavelength. The one wearing the collar feels it very intensely if they fall out of synch. And the one who put it on set the wavelength to begin with. It's like you transferred your wavelength to him, Mira. If you take it off again, Clive will return to his own resonance."

"So, you think I can take it off?"

"I think you can. But we have the difficulty that Clive's soul isn't anchored without it."

Clive set his cup on the floor by his foot and sat up very straight. His voice was even, but I could feel the tension at his core ratcheting up. I held my breath, but his next question wasn't aimed at me at all. "So if a bond of obedience is considered one of the lowest levels of pledge, at what level would you put the Oath of Silence?"

Niko searched the ceiling for a few moments before answering. "You know, I hadn't really considered that the Oath was a bond, but… of course it is. It's a little different in that it relies less on matching the wavelength and more on…" He grimaced as he chewed over his word choice. "I'll call it post-hypnotic suggestion, because Roland calls it that, but I'm not convinced that's exactly what it is. For now, though, it conveys the idea."

Clive sat very still. "Did you know what would happen to me if I broke the Oath?"

Niko also barely moved, meeting his gaze. "If you mean that you might be possessed by a demon, no."

"I don't mean that part. I mean, did you expect me to… feel nauseous? Go limp? Or what?"

Niko looked away. "Um. I don't think it's always the same." At that moment he looked a lot more like a teenager who was in over his head than some guru. Like a freshman struggling through his first lab class. "It depends on the person. Will you… will you tell me what you experienced? Please?"

Clive's fingers curled into a fist. "From the moment I began to contemplate telling Mira about the Circle, it felt like something with giant claws was trying to tear my heart out of my chest."

Niko grimaced. "And when you told her?"

"It felt like it succeeded."

"The pain was so intense you passed out." I rested my hand atop his fist. "And you have a very high pain tolerance."

Niko chewed his lip. "You seem… a bit upset about it and I want to understand why. You made a promise and were told the consequences of breaking it could be dire. Are you upset now that the consequences were dire?"

Clive shook his head. "It's not that. What I'm asking is whether you knew how dire they would be. Because it's really hard to have informed consent if you don't even know what you're doing. You-the Circle, I mean, not you-personally, perhaps."

"But I'm the Wisdomkeeper. If anyone should know, it's me." His voice was low and troubled. "You're saying that… basically… the Invocation of Willingness is invalid or meaningless if the consequences aren't known."

Clive and I exchanged a glance. I felt like he was waiting for me to be the one to say it, so I did: "Yes. Consent requires mutual consideration of the risks."

Niko bit his lip and scribbled something furiously into the notebook, then closed his eyes and sat silent for long moments, shaking his head. It seemed like we'd given him a lot of food for thought.

"Niko," I asked. "How did a kid like you become Wisdomkeeper to begin with?"

His eyes flew open like I'd jerked on two window blinds. "That's... I had hoped—" He grimaced like something stung. "I thought we were going to talk about you today, not me. But." He looked at Clive. "Maybe it's important that you hear this."

"Hear what?"

"They story of how I became Wisdomkeeper." Niko let out a long breath. "You're right. You can't give informed consent if you don't know what the heck is going on. And if I'm—if we're—not upholding the principles of the Circle of Light, then there's no point. We may as well let the Partisans win. But, that's the basic problem."

"What's the basic problem?" Clive asked.

"That we don't know what the heck is going on."

I squeezed Clive's hand, but my attention was on Niko. His breathing had sped up and his distress was visibly rising. He gestured to the notebooks behind the computer desk. "Right there, right now, that's the sum total of the knowledge we have to leave for the next generation. As you can see, it's really not much."

"Those aren't just your homeschooling notebooks?" Clive asked.

"No." He refilled our cups, then, forcing himself to concentrate and to breathe, or his shaking hands would have spilled tea everywhere. "Some years ago, there was a... let's just call it a big old spell. Like the aegis, only it covered everything. It was kind of like the Oath of Silence had been applied over the whole city, maybe the whole world. You couldn't betray the oath and speak of the practice to anyone, even if you wanted to, because the words wouldn't even come out of your mouth. This is why the knowledge was called the Unsayable. So until you were initiated into the Circle, you literally couldn't be told about the practice. Anyone who tried... experienced something like what Clive experienced.

"But it went away. We're not even sure exactly when, since no one made it a habit to try to Say the Unsayable, but it's not there now."

I found that thought troubling for a lot of reasons. "So before that, you had to recruit people to the Circle without actually telling them what it was about?"

"Yes." Here he sighed heavily, and swallowed. "There were... raging debates among some of the practitioners about it. But this was way before my time. The Circle was full, though, then, and families were exempt from the rule, I think because of being blood relations. Kids like me grew up knowing about it despite the silencing effect because our parents were in the Circle."

Kids like him. That told me there were others. "So family members could be told."

"Yes, just like they could pass the aegis." He paused, weighing his words. "So it wasn't like they had to go out randomly kidnapping people to join without telling them what was going on. The knowledge was passed down from generation to generation. But there was still this thing, a sort of super-aegis, that kept everyone in the Circle separate from anyone who hadn't been initiated."

Clive nodded, a thoughtful look on his face. "The Circle essentially had an informed population to choose from. So why was this 'super-aegis' necessary?"

Niko grimaced. "The super-aegis, although it demanded silence, had also been keeping us hidden in other ways, we think. Vibrationally, perhaps." He was no longer looking at us, but at his hands as he talked. His voice had a slight quaver in it. "It wasn't long after it went away that Barrow and the Partisans of Fire showed up. Maybe they were responsible for stripping it away so they could find us. Or maybe it faded naturally when we lost the knowledge on how to maintain it. I don't know."

No one had touched their second cup of tea. Niko seemed to have forgotten his. "The Wisdomkeeper when I was a child was a guy named Gabriel. He had practiced the long life techniques so I don't even know how old he was, but... old enough that he had accumulated more knowledge than the average human during his lifetime, plus, due to the way being Wisdomkeeper works, he had all the knowledge of every previous Wisdomkeeper, too."

As Niko's attention focused inward, his eyes closed, but he kept speaking. "There's a circle working to transfer all the knowledge into the new vessel. Gabriel had picked a successor, but then... a great plague came. Many members of the Circle were afflicted with it. His chosen vessel..." He paused, swallowed, sighed. "...died. Gabriel was sickened but lived. But he lost a lot of the members of the Circle. He was forced to recruit new people to help. My parents were among them." Niko drew a ragged breath. "And so was Roland. But he didn't stay."

There were a lot of holes in that story. Maybe I should have just waited for the gaps to be filled in, instead of asking, "What about your parents?"

He swallowed. "They stayed. Until they died."

What do you say to something like that? Clive spoke, but the look on his face said he knew how inadequate his words—"I'm so sorry to hear that"—sounded.

"When Barrow first found us," Niko went on, "my parents and Saira's were the first he killed, and Gabriel was hurt."

I was pretty sure I hadn't heard the name *Saira* before.

"Roland came back to help Gabriel transfer the knowledge to me, to make me the new Wisdomkeeper." He hugged himself then, as if his ribs hurt. Or maybe as if he were holding in the hurt.

"Niko—"

"Don't." He pushed the word through gritted teeth. "Don't ask anything more." He closed his eyes, in obvious pain.

"You don't have to tell us anything you don't want to," I said. Clive held out a hand, like he wanted to help but didn't know how, exactly.

"It's not that. It's just..." Niko held himself until he got his breathing under control again. "You asked how I became Wisdomkeeper. I'm telling you."

"All right."

"The transfer overwhelmed me. I spent... a year or so trying to regain my sense of self. They say... they say I spoke in tongues. Because the working didn't go right. Or—" He noticed the cup of tea sitting on the floor in front of him. He picked it up. "Or maybe that was what was supposed to happen, and I just didn't know."

Clive picked up his own cup, but I could feel him holding back from saying something so he wouldn't interrupt Niko.

"I chose to be Wisdomkeeper," Niko said. He suddenly gulped down the tea as if it were a shot of whiskey and set the cup on the floor with a knock. When he spoke, again, he sounded older. "It was my choice and my desire. But let's say I sympathize with you feeling under-informed."

Clive nodded. "It's like you were expecting an electric shock but you got struck by lightning."

"Exactly." Niko lifted the lid on the pot and examined the tea leaves. He poured fresh water in, and held it in hands like before. "The practice does not always operate on the human scale. And none of us are gods."

The pain on his face seemed to lessen as he centered himself and breathed. When the tea was warm again, he refilled his cup.

I still had not taken more than a sip of mine. "Thank you for telling us that. I didn't mean to make you dredge up painful memories."

He laughed wryly. "Except that's what I'm here for. Literally. Well, okay, they're not all painful. And it is usually pretty cool to have like a thousand years of knowledge in my head."

"'Like?' You don't know how far back the memories go?"

He sipped before answering. "I mostly haven't dared go more than two generations back for answers. The farther back I go, the harder it is to return to myself again. But sometimes the only way to reach an answer is to dig deeper." He pressed his fingers to his forehead. "When I go back to get a memory, I have to write it down before it fades. When I go really deep, I can speak the answer, but I'm kind of in a trance when I do it. I don't retain it for my own conscious knowledge unless I can read it later."

Which explained the notebooks. "This place looks like it was made to hold a lot of books."

"And once upon a time it did. Every member of the Circle kept their diaries here, and they had inherited them from past generations. But the fear of discovery ran very deep. Gabriel decided to rely on the transfer. He read each journal and then burned them, one at a time, over the course of decades. All those pages… are in my head." He winced like he had given himself a headache thinking about it. "So, just think about that. The sum total of hundreds of people's experiences with the practice over the course of hundreds of years is now only to be found in one place: between my ears."

Clive and I shared a glance then, and I felt he must be thinking the same thing I was. All it would take was one Partisan to set the place on fire while Niko slept and all that would be lost.

Maybe Niko was thinking it, too. "The man who killed my parents wants to kill me next. I need help to stay alive. Your help, if you're willing."

I'll admit it: it was really hard to say no to a plea like that.

TWENTY

Getting asked to join a secret society is one thing. Getting asked to help defend a kid (well, okay, he was eighteen, but still a kid to me) from the guy who murdered his parents is quite another.

Clive gave me a look that I interpreted as *you first*. So I started: "Barrow wants to kill us, too."

"Does that mean you'll join the Circle?" Niko held up his hand. "Wait, don't answer that! I'm not supposed to pressure you."

"I said last night, we don't have to join the Circle to join forces." I kept looking at Clive, but his mouth was pressed closed. "Though it seems like there is a lot it would be helpful to learn. And I..." I searched for the right way to put it. "I want to fight the good fight. I feel like life doesn't always give you that chance."

Niko nodded.

"But I don't want to do anything that would endanger Clive. Including severing the bond between us."

Clive finally spoke, his hand clenched into a fist. "Sometimes the world doesn't ask for your consent before fucking you."

"No. But I always will." I put my hand atop his. "We should make this decision together."

Clive turned his hand over, letting his fingers entwine with mine. "And some things are bigger than we are, Mira. It's all a question of whether one believes in those things or not." He looked up at the skylight. "Call me cynical. Call me jaded. I'm skeptical of true love and of promises. But this is... bigger than just 'promises.' Isn't it? This is..." He fell silent without finishing his thought.

Niko picked up the thread as best he could. "No one can be forced to stay in a Circle, if that's what you're asking. And let me be clear, I am here to answer whatever questions I can so you can make a informed choices. But at least now you know the limitations on my answers."

I felt like I must still be missing something. He hadn't really explained what the bond was between me and Clive, had he? I told myself if the bond that held the Circle together was sort of similar, well... maybe I just had to keep asking questions until it started to make sense. Maybe there was just a learning curve. Once upon a time acupuncture had seemed hopelessly obscure, but after a seminar or two I at least felt like I grasped the concept, even though it wasn't my specialty. I figured maybe learning the practice was going to be like that.

Sometimes it helps me to focus on one concrete detail until the bigger picture comes into focus. So I asked about one thing that had been on my mind: "Would joining the Circle mean getting pierced?"

Niko seemed relieved to have a simple question he could answer. "Yes. You may have noticed that things that we think of as symbolic or metaphorical are, well, *actual* when it comes to the liminal and ethereal planes. The ring can be thought of as symbolically linking us—like links in a chain. But it is an actual link in the ethereal plane."

"That's… fascinating. Does it matter where it's placed?"

"The placement can amplify certain effects. Kish's is at her eye because she is watchful. Roland's in his ear was to remind him to listen. The nose might be good for someone who tests or investigates? Someone expressing their loyalty might choose the nipple closest to the heart. There are lots of choices."

I fantasized momentarily about piercing Clive somewhere significantly more intimate than his nose or ear. "The other thing I've been wondering about is what would happen if one of us joined the Circle but the other one—"

Niko suddenly went wide-eyed, the teacup falling from his hand into his lap. He yelped as the hot tea soaked through his track pants and jumped to his feet, eyes still staring into space.

Clive and I were both talking at once: "Niko, what's wrong?" "Are you all right?"

"Jair's hurt."

"What? How?"

"He's… cut. Bleeding." Niko closed his eyes. "That's all I know."

Clive stood. "What do we do?"

I could hear Roland's voice from downstairs. "Niko!"

Niko ran to the railing, calling down the stairwell to him. "Did you feel that?"

I didn't make out Roland's answer, but all three of us ran down to the main room. In what had once been either the parlor or dining room of the house, but was now mostly empty of furniture, Roland had chalked a circle ringed with symbols on the hardwood floor. He stood beside it, shirtless and barefoot, his phone in hand, his eyes glassy.

Niko pulled out his own phone. "I don't see any messages or calls from them."

Roland rubbed one eye with his fist. "Neither do I. And I haven't felt anything since that… that…"

"That cut," Niko said. "We've got to go help them. I'll get my shoes."

"No." Roland's voice was sharpened by fear. "You're their ultimate target. You have to stay here, where it's safe."

Niko's face showed his anguish plainly. "But if something happens to Jair—"

"It'll only be worse if it happens to you, too," I said gently. "Let us handle it, whatever it is."

"Besides," Roland added, "We can't go haring off if we don't even know where they are. We need to stay put until—"

Niko's phone vibrated in his hand and he had the answer. "Text from Kish. They're hiding in the basement of a church building a couple of blocks east of Riverside Drive."

Roland sighed and pulled a beige shirt on over his head. "Are they safe?"

"For the moment. Kish says there are at least two—Barrow and a woman—probably still looking for them. But Jair thinks he saw a third." Niko tapped out a quick reply.

Roland had a hand in his hair and still seemed a bit dazed from his meditation session. He was shaking his head and staring into the middle distance.

"Hey. I can drive the van," I told him. "If we time it right, maybe we can roll right up to the building, they can run out, and we can drive away before the Partisans even see us."

Roland focused on me. "What if it's a trap?"

"Then we should be prepared for a potential ambush."

He shook his head. "You don't have to put yourself in harm's way. I can go alone."

"No," Clive said, voicing what I was thinking: "At least two need to go, one to keep in contact with Kish and Jair, one to drive."

"Plus," I added, "If there are three of them, and Jair's too hurt to fight? We'll be outnumbered unless Clive and I both go with you."

He rubbed his eye again. "Does your brain ever slow down?"

"No. Why?"

"You realize neither of you has even joined the Circle, yet—"

Niko cut across him. "We don't have time to argue about this. Roland, just take them."

Roland stiffened, like maybe he was a little affronted at Niko ordering him around like that, or at least that was how I interpreted it at the time? But then he nodded. "All right. Mira, the keys are hanging under the kitchen phone."

Once we got to the van, Roland got in back and Clive took the passenger seat and my phone. He was already pulling up the address Niko had sent to me. "They're only a couple of blocks from my place."

"I'll take the West Side Highway." I eased the van backward onto the street. Time was of the essence but the last thing we needed was to have a collision. I'd gotten rid of my car when I moved into the city proper (don't ask about my brief exile to New Jersey) so the van took a little getting used to, but once we started moving, I realized it was actually great to be so high up—good visibility. Traffic was a little thick going through the side streets, but once we got onto the West Side Highway I hoped it would be a quick ride.

Something Niko had told us echoed through my ears. Ritual breaches are very different from a knife fight. "So, Roland, how do we fight these Partisans, if it comes to that?"

"We're just going to get our people, not get into a battle," he said, as if he didn't even want to entertain the possibility that things could go wrong.

"But say we have no choice."

"Well." Roland pulled the hood of his sweatshirt up and handed Clive two painter's caps from a crate under the bench. "Let's just hope it doesn't come to that."

The brakes were a little grabby and I may have pumped them a little too hard as we came to a red light. They squealed in complaint. "Agreed. But what if it does?"

Roland buckled a seatbelt in the back and sounded like he was either psyching himself up or hyperventilating.

Clive put one of the caps on and handed me the other. I had no idea if the attempt at disguise would make any difference, but I wasn't going to fight it right then. I pulled the hat on, brim backwards, and tried to sound reasonable. "I'd just like to be as prepared as possible."

"They can't shoot lightning from their fingertips or anything like that," Roland finally said. "But they'll have knives. Try not to get cut if you can help it. Don't let them grab you. And don't let Barrow look you in the eyes."

"Because he has some kind of mind control?"

I was starting to get the feeling that Roland could never let something I said go without correction of some kind: "We think he has the power to plant post-hypnotic suggestions." Which sure sounded like mind control to me. "How he does that just with eye contact, we don't know." Roland scrubbed his face and went silent.

I steered the van onto the highway and we headed north along the river. "Text them and let them know our ETA."

Clive nodded. "Twelve minutes. Take the 125th Street exit. Kish says they're right behind a fire exit door, so if we can pull into the alley, they should be able to pop right out." He glanced back at Roland. In my peripheral vision I could see he had his head bent like maybe he was praying. Clive gave me a small, private smile.

I returned it. His presence was reassuring and so was the scenario. Getting in and out cleanly seemed doable.

Clive fed me directions—where to turn, which street to go down—as we took the exit and neared our destination. That area of the city is sort of strange: a rich neighborhood built basically on top of a poorer one, soaring above on a manmade viaduct. Nineteenth century hubris sure was a thing.

"Go around the block this way." Clive pointed. "And I think that's the alley up there."

Just past a church was an attached building that looked like a small school, or maybe an administrative building. The alley ran between that building and a high cinderblock wall topped by wrapped scaffolding: something under renovation or construction. I scanned the sidewalk and the parked cars lining each side of the wide street, but far as I could tell there were no black-caped villains ready to jump out at us. A woman jogging with her dog, a bearded work-from-home dad pushing a baby stroller while talking on his cell phone, a bicycle food delivery person… but no obvious Partisans. As soon as the bike courier went past, I rolled the van gently across the sidewalk into the alley.

All I could do was pull just past the fire door and hope Jair's injury wasn't so bad that they couldn't get him into the back.

Just as the fire door popped open, someone landed on the van roof. I cursed and pumped the accelerator and then the grabby brakes. A man tumbled off the roof in front of us. I tried not to look at him too closely in case it was the guy with mind control.

Before I could decide whether to try running him over or what, Roland had opened the back doors and Kish was trying to push Jair in.

While she and Roland struggled to get him into the van, the Partisan in front of us had disappeared. One possibility was that he was lying on the concrete right in front of us where I couldn't see him.

Roland heaved Jair onto the floor between the bench seats. The moment Kish leaped in on top of them, before she even closed the doors, I hit the gas and we shot forward, me half-hoping we'd hit whoever it was, and half-hoping we wouldn't. *We don't kill,* I remembered Jair saying. He hadn't said anything about just *maiming* a little, though…

"No, no!" Clive shouted. "It's a dead end."

I slammed the brakes again and the rear doors slammed shut like I'd done it on purpose. "Okay! Everyone all right back there?"

"Just get us out of here!" Kish called from the floor.

I reversed but couldn't go as fast as I wanted to, because hitting someone—or the walls of the alley—could be disastrous. Another thump hit the roof before we made the sidewalk, and hitting the brakes this time didn't dislodge whoever it was.

A tactical knife blade, curved and wickedly notched, punched through the ceiling over Clive's head. Before I could react, he'd opened his window and snaked one arm out. He grunted as he grabbed onto the attacker with one hand.

All I could think was, what if they have another knife? My brain was screaming *no, no, no,* but it took another second or two for air to reach my lungs and words to reach my mouth. "Clive! Get back in here! Get down and don't move!"

He ducked back inside instantly and I gunned the engine in reverse. I prayed there were no dog walkers, baby carriages, or other innocent people on the sidewalk right then, because my ability to be cautious had just gone right out the window. Clive stayed hunched down, at least.

The tires squealed as the van shot out onto the street, but the worst that happened was we got a long honk from a delivery truck of some kind. I whipped the van around to point us back toward Riverside Drive and heard a woman's voice curse as the assailant tumbled off our roof. The knife went with her. As I hit the gas again, in the side mirror I could see her trying to run after us. Roland started to get up onto the bench.

Kish yanked him back down. "Stay down. That bitch has throwing knives, and I wouldn't put it past her to get one right through the damn window."

Jair made a sound from the back that was half agreement and half anguished pain.

"Did you get a good look at her? How many were there?" Roland asked her.

"I only saw two, but Jair thinks there were three."

Our pursuer wasn't superhuman. We left her quickly behind as I sped through an intersection and back to the highway.

Kish cursed softly. "You are bleeding like a mother."

"Don't you talk about my mother," Jair tried to joke, but he gasped at the end. "I think I saw Barrow and two others, that woman and a younger guy."

"What did he look like?" Roland asked.

"Dark hair, a little longer than mine, dunno. I didn't stop to paint his portrait." Jair grunted again with pain.

Kish used her knife to cut a strip from her shirt. "The bleeding won't stop."

I could smell the blood. "Is he going to make it if we go back to The Archive? Or should we look for a hospital?"

"I'm fine," Jair tried to say, but it sounded to me like he was about to pass out as he said it.

"New York Presbyterian isn't far from here," I pointed out.

"Or St. Luke's?" Clive gestured to the east and I realized he'd tucked himself most of the way down onto the floor.

"No." Roland gritted his teeth. "We'll be sitting ducks in some ER somewhere, and doctors may not be able to help, anyway."

The scent of blood was getting stronger. "You'd rather he bled out in the back of the van?"

"No one is bleeding out, goddammit!" Roland shifted his position in back, wedging himself in so Jair's head was in his lap.

I couldn't really watch what was going on and keep my eyes on the traffic, but I could hear them perfectly well. Kish kept insisting that the bleeding should have stopped, that the cut wasn't that deep. Roland asked about the throwing knife and Kish showed it to him.

"Come on, Jair," Roland said. "Breathe. Center yourself."

Jair's answer was another groan of pain.

"He said when we were laying low that his whole body ached like a tooth, and it throbbed when his heart beat," Kish said.

"Come on, Jair. Come on," Roland repeated, but his voice was taking on a desperate note, begging for the bleeding to stop.

That tone mixed with the scent of blood was chillingly familiar to me. I clamped my lips shut: the last time I'd heard it had been from my own mouth.

May as well beg for the Earth not to turn. Someone had actually said that to me; I couldn't be that cruel to Roland, so I said nothing.

Beside me Clive stayed where he was, despite the fact we'd left the Partisans far behind. He was breathing hard and staring at nothing, listening to Roland almost chanting "come on, Jair."

Here's the thing about blood loss. If you bleed so much you pass out, you're already looking at a high chance of organ failure or other severe consequences, even if you survive long enough to get a transfusion. I gripped the steering wheel hard, trying not to think about whether Wex had suffered through something similar.

We hit traffic right around Chelsea Piers and my heart sank. "Roland," Kish finally said, "he's not going to last until we make it to The Archive. Can we center him here?"

"Not while we're moving." Roland scratched his beard, then called forward to me. "Mira, can you find us a place? Parking garage, alley, wherever. Anywhere we can draw a circle big enough to fit him."

"Somewhere we can't be seen, if possible," Kish added. "But I'd take an open parking space in the street if I had to." She began talking softly to Jair then, encouraging murmurs. "Come on, bebe. Stay with me, now. We got you."

I got into the exit lane and started scanning the area. There weren't many spots in Manhattan I could think of where you could really go to be truly alone, but it was a Sunday. Maybe a garage by the Javits Center if there was no convention going on…?

I took us out of the traffic and past the convention center, which was fortunately empty that weekend. There was so much construction going on in that neighborhood. Whole buildings were being razed… which gave me an idea. If construction crews didn't work Sundays maybe we'd find a place.

And we did. Down a side street, I spotted an empty lot where whatever was due to be built hadn't been started yet. On one side sat an empty warehouse, probably slated to be demolished next, on the other, the skeleton of a new building had started to rise. The lot wasn't even fenced in because there was nothing but dirt and gravel on it. I pulled the van onto the narrow strip of hardtop between the construction fence and the dry grit, then turned it ninety degrees to block the view of anyone driving down the street. "How's this?"

"Perfect." Roland sounded calmer than I'd heard him since we'd left The Archive. "Kish, I'll hold the wound. You go draw a circle with cardinal points in the dirt behind the van. We'll move him as soon as you give the ready sign."

"On it." She slid open the door and fresh air wafted in.

"Mira, Clive, I'm going to need both of you to participate."

"Sure. Just tell us what we have to do."

"The four of us are each going to represent one of the four directions. I'll be north and we'll lay him down with his head pointed that direction. You two can be east and west." Roland slapped Jair lightly on the cheek, making sure he was still with us. Jair blinked and squeezed his eyes shut. Was a little blood leaking from his eyes…? "When I say, you call out the direction you represent, and try to stay grounded. Deep, slow breaths, like in yoga. Each time you exhale, like you're sinking into the Earth."

"Okay." I looked up at Kish and saw her waving. I opened my door to get out.

Clive still hadn't moved from where he was hunkered down in his seat. "Mira," he said.

"Are you all right? What's wrong?" I thought that maybe he'd wedged himself in somehow and physically couldn't get free. "Are you stuck?"

His expression was pained, his breath still a little labored. "I don't know what's wrong with me. I just can't make myself move." There was a note of alarm starting to creep into his voice.

"Like you're paralyzed with fear?"

"Kind of? Except I'm not actually afraid of anything at the moment. Well, except that being unable to move is kind of freaking me out?"

Roland and Kish were carrying Jair out the back and hadn't noticed what was going on with us.

I felt a prickle down my arms. We didn't have time for a panic attack or whatever was going on in Clive's head. I went on instinct. "Clive. Get out of the van."

It was like an invisible knot had been untied. He shot out of the footwell, opened the door, and nearly tumbled out. From there he seemed able to hurry over to the newly drawn circle in the dirt without difficulty.

Jair lay at the center. His eyes were closed tightly and he didn't make a sound. I tried not to look at the blood soaking into the dirt through his jeans. Kish knelt at his feet. Roland moved his arms so they were outstretched, one toward me, one toward Clive, and then knelt at Jair's head.

Clive met my eyes as we knelt down. His expression seemed to be asking *what just happened between us?* I tapped my own throat where his collar crossed his neck. It had to be something about the bond, but that was all I could guess at that point.

Roland put a hand on each of Jair's temples.

"No, wait." Jair raised a hand weakly. "Wait."

"What is it?" Roland asked.

"Important." Jair reached into the inner pocket of his leather jacket and pulled out a ten dollar bill. "Mira."

He held it toward me and my breath left my body in sudden terror that I might be about to see him die. "Jair—"

"Take it. You were right. Brooklyn."

I took it just as his hand went limp. "Jair!"

"Places. Grounding. Everyone focus, please," Roland said. "He's still here. He can still hear us. Breathe with me, now." I remembered what he said about yoga breathing. Right. "That's it. Kish. South."

Kish's voice was rough. "South."

Roland took two deliberate breaths. "West."

Clive echoed, "West."

Two more breaths. "East."

"East." As I said the word, a tingle crossed my shoulders as if a chill wind crept up my back. I couldn't look away from the spreading stain on the ground, but the bits of broken glass and gravel seemed to be every color, green, red, brown, blue…The colors seemed to be intensifying.

Sinking into the Earth felt as natural as breathing, even if the two breaths seemed to come in slow motion.

"North." Roland bowed his head.

I looked across at Clive and I could suddenly see every stitch in his sweater, every lock of his hair. His eyes looked very blue in contrast to his dark hair and the color of his lips. I wanted to kiss him suddenly, but he was the span of one Jair away.

"Bring it in, Jair. You know how to do this. Fight it. The knife *lies*." Roland's words didn't make any sense, but then again, did anything?

It certainly didn't make sense to me that the bloodstain on Jair's jeans was getting smaller. But it wasn't my imagination. The cloth went from so soaked through it was shiny, to dully damp, to bone dry and unstained. His chest rose and fell as he sucked in a breath through his teeth and then blew it out gradually, making a sound like "*phewwwww.*"

Phew indeed. His eyes opened and he blew out another breath. His breathing was in synch with mine, I realized. With ours. He stared at the sky.

"Got it now?" Roland asked.

Jair nodded and continued to breathe.

"Can you keep it up until we can actually treat the wound?"

Jair nodded again, showing his teeth with a hint of his usual cheeky grin.

"Okay, then let's go."

Clive and Roland helped him gingerly to the van while Kish erased the circle and rubbed out the bloodstain that had been left in the dirt. It was a lot smaller than I expected. I got back in the driver's seat. The circle working had taken so little time I could still feel warm places on the steering wheel where my hands had been.

Clive climbed back into the passenger seat and buckled himself in, saying nothing. He touched the saint medallion with one finger and did not look up.

I turned the van south on 11th Avenue. Jair leaned against Roland, eyes closed, still breathing in that deliberate and measured way. Kish sat on his other side, one hand on his thigh.

"So what was that business with the money about?" she asked him.

Jair just shook his head.

I held in a laugh. "Tell you later. I promise."

TWENTY-ONE

We made it to The Archive without further incident. Time to find out what they had in the first aid kit there. "You *do* have a first aid kit, don't you?"

"Under the sink." Roland helped Jair lower himself onto the toilet lid in the first floor bathroom. "I don't suppose you know how to suture a wound?" Clive and Kish hovered in the narrow doorway, while I rummaged in the ornate vanity cabinet. A plastic box with a red cross on it was under a value-size package of maxi pads.

Inside the box, a pack of sutures was right on top. I guess if you're going to be making a lot of "ritual breaches" that made sense to have on hand, but… "You're asking me?"

"Yes, you, Mira."

"I've only ever punctured the skin recreationally." The needles in the pack were curved like eyelashes. "Everything I know about sutures I learned from watching reruns of M*A*S*H."

Roland looked downcast. "If only Ira were here."

I was just as glad that he wasn't, though I supposed having a surgeon around could be useful if knife wounds like this were going to be happening frequently. "Let's look at the wound before we make any decisions about what to do."

"Jair, let us get your clothes off." Roland started working the jacket off Jair's shoulders.

We didn't really need his jacket off, since the wound was on his leg, but whatever. Jair's eyes were still shut. "I'm unbuttoning your jeans," I announced, and he gave a curt nod. I dropped to one knee beside the antique-looking toilet and, with his help, eased his jeans down around his knees. Dried blood had glued the denim to his leg hair in a few spots, and I pulled as carefully as I could.

That was when I discovered two things: One, Jair didn't wear underwear. Two, he was living proof that one could wear the Circle of Light initiation ring in a more intimate place than the ear. My attention, though, was on the gash. From the way he'd bled, I'd been expecting a deep puncture wound, but I was confronted with a sort of flap of flesh.

"What's wrong? How is it?" Roland had his hands on Jair's upper arms, steadying him.

"Nothing's wrong." The thrown dagger had almost missed, barely catching his leg on the outside of the thigh. It had sliced a crescent shape about three inches across. It was disconcerting that it wasn't bleeding at all but I supposed I better get used to sights like that since apparently Jair was keeping it from bleeding with the power of his will or something. "We should disinfect this, unless you've got some magic that kills germs?"

"Don't call it magic," Roland snapped.

"Then hand me the Betadine and some alcohol wipes." I disinfected my hands first, and then shook the little brown bottle gently. "Jair, I'm sorry, but this is going to hurt like a motherfucker."

Eyes still closed, he nodded and bowed his head, dark hair falling across his face. Roland stood behind me, then, hands on Jair's shoulders. Jair took hold of Roland's forearms, bracing himself.

As I applied the iodine mixture, an anguished grunt squeezed through his clenched teeth.

"That's good, that's good," I heard myself say, as blood welled up under the flap again. That was my massage-therapist voice, which I hadn't heard for a while. "Let it out. Clean it out." I dabbed the welling blood with a wad of gauze but some dripped onto the white and brown mosaic tile floor.

A second application of the iodine made him curse tightly, chest heaving as he fought to process the pain and regain control.

"That's it," I said. "Breathe. Breathe."

His grip on Roland's forearms loosened as his breaths slowed and the blood once again receded. I wiped the blood away, then swabbed the edges of the wound clean with a few more alcohol wipes. "Hand me the liquid bandage, please?"

Roland sounded surprised. "You don't think he needs stitches?"

"I do think he needs stitches, but obviously none of us are equipped to do that, and I know he hates needles anyway."

Jair made a sound that was half weak laugh, half whimper. I really needed to find out the story of his initiation some time, given where that piercing was.

Roland squinted at the label on the back of the bottle. "This is… essentially Superglue."

"Yes, that's the idea. Should work fine for a wound this shape. I'll glue it shut."

A sharper laugh escaped from Jair. "Like I'm a broken toy." He opened his eyes, but I could see tear tracks in the corners.

I started to apply the glue. "Now maybe you'll even out your limp."

"My whaaat…?" He breathed-spoke.

I hoped there was enough of the stuff. The bottle felt a little light. "You have a hitch in your step, from your right leg. Now maybe you'll have a matching one on the left."

"Huh."

It would have to be enough. I put a bandage over the whole thing to keep it safe and covered, and to keep Jair from scratching it if it itched. He slumped against the towel rail.

Roland sighed in relief and fatigue, too. "Good work, Mira. Everyone. Kish, I wasn't sure we were going to get you two back in one piece."

Kish chuckled. "Two pieces. Jair and I aren't attached at the hip yet." She reached across Roland to pat Jair on the shoulder and then squeezed her way around Clive and out of the bathroom.

I patted Roland on the shoulder. "When you first told us Kish and Jair were in trouble, I wasn't sure you were going to make it."

"Me?" Roland started the water running and handed a damp washcloth to Jair, who pressed it to his face.

"You. I thought you were…" Ready to curl up in a ball and cry. "…going to pass out or something. But while we were in the van you seemed to get a hold of yourself."

"It was hard when I felt helpless. It helped when I felt there was something I could actually do." Roland shrugged and started the water, handing me a bar of soap. We washed our hands, sharing the narrow basin. "Speaking of doing, we had better pack up and move. We've got another safe house we can go to."

That struck me as nuts. "What? Aren't we safe here?" I dried my hands and looked at Roland in the mirror. "I don't think any of us are going anywhere right now, and especially not Jair." Getting him upstairs and into bed was our next challenge, far as I was concerned.

Roland frowned, his brow set. "We don't know if our location might have been compromised."

"How would they find us here? Do you think they tracked the van? Is there a magic spell for that?"

"Stop calling it magic! We don't know! We can't take the risk. I've decided."

"Excuse me, *you* decided?" Maybe I was a little stressed after what we'd just gone through. I was too angry to keep my voice down. "Who died and made you king? Doesn't anyone else have a say? Or does everyone have to bow to you after initiation, dom of all doms?"

"This has nothing to do with dominance," Roland snapped. "You don't know anything about it. And you haven't even been initiated yet!"

"Which is why I don't have to do what you say?"

"No!" He grimaced. "I just mean... I... The Circle works by consensus!"

How interesting. "Then tell me, oh appointed leader by general consensus, why tearing ass out of here is a better idea than staying put?"

One of the perpetual problems of teaching people to be safe in the BDSM community is that it depends on people assessing risks accurately. But people are terrible at assessing risk when they're emotional. And you know what makes a lot of people emotional? Feeling like they're at risk. I'm sure Roland thought he was being logical. He folded his hands in front of him, as if trying to explain something to a child. "If they have a way to track us, then we're not safe here."

He hadn't thought it through at all. "And if they do, and we go to another safe house, all we'll do is compromise that location, too," I told him. "Where is this other safe house? Wait, don't tell me." I put my slightly damp hand on top of his. "Just stop and think. If it was the van they could track, we could leave it behind. But if it's *us* they could track—?"

Roland shook his head like he was trying to clear it. "You're right. I'm just scared."

They really weren't soldiers. Or strategists. Neither was I, but at least I hadn't lost my common sense? "Listen to me. The thing to do now is regroup. Everyone's tired and drained. And I don't know about you, but ever since the working we did in the vacant lot, I feel like I could eat a horse."

Kish stuck her head back into the bathroom. "Rol', she's right. Jair needs some red meat and an iron supplement. You're wiped out, too. And we need to figure out our next move."

"Our next move," Roland said, looking into the middle distance as if he were looking for what that might be.

"We have this, remember?" Kish held out the piece of cloth she had wrapped the throwing knife in, unfolding it to reveal a symmetrical sliver of steel about the length of her hand. "I don't think they can use it to find us. But with this, maybe *we* can find *them*."

I love New York. You can get a meal delivered, cheap, any hour of the day, to just about anywhere in the city—even the secret hideout of your ancient ritual magic cabal. I stuffed myself with as much kung pao chicken as I could stand. Everyone was quiet as we ate. I couldn't tell if everyone was just wiped out or if no one had dared say anything since I took Roland's head off.

Clive in particular seemed quieter than usual, but he stayed close by me, refilling my drink, bringing me a napkin, all without saying a word. Jair nearly fell asleep in a plate of fried rice. Niko helped him upstairs, despite Jair's protests that he didn't need help. (But he did.)

As soon as they were gone, Kish crushed a soda can in one hand and tossed it into the recycling bin. "Okay. What was that bit with the money about?"

"Oh, right." I took the ten dollar bill out of my front pocket, where I'd stuck it. There were bloody finger prints on it. "Jair had bet me you were from Miami. I said Brooklyn."

"Well, I was living in Miami right before I met these guys, but you're right. I grew up in Brooklyn. Still got some family in Queens." She chuckled. "He's a nut. I can't even tell if he was seriously trying to pay his debts in case he died or just making one last joke."

"Joking about it is his way of facing it," Roland said, poking at a container of lo mein but no longer eating it. "Let me see that knife?"

"No," Kish said. "Get some rest. Centering Jair took a lot out of you. We'll look at the knife in the morning. It's not going anywhere."

Roland plunked the container down on the table and stood tiredly. "All right. All right." He left the room nearly as slowly as Jair had.

Kish leaned back in her chair. "You asked before who died and made Roland leader."

"Oh, man." I felt a sudden sinking feeling, as what Niko'd told us about his parents surfaced in my mind. "I didn't mean it seriously. It's just an expression."

"Yeah, I figured, but… Roland's a little sensitive about it. He hasn't come right out and told us, but I'm pretty sure he was planning to become Wisdomkeeper himself when he was in his twenties." She got up and started clearing the plates. Clive hopped up to do the washing.

I stayed where I was, instead of getting in their way. "Niko said Roland came back when the previous Wisdomkeeper asked him to. Jair told me he has an ex-wife, though?"

She stacked the plates in the sink. "I'm not sure Roland and Lydia were married-married, to tell you the truth. Roland makes it sound like they had just split up when the call to return to the Circle came for him, but I kind of wonder about that, you know? She calls here to chew him out sometimes and—call me crazy, but—that doesn't sound like someone who had closure, now, does it?"

I started sealing up the takeout containers scattered across the kitchen table. "I get the feeling Roland has a lot going on underneath the surface."

"Got that right. I think if he wouldn't die from the guilt of leaving his task unfinished, he'd go back to her and his kid in a heartbeat." She shook her head. "Maybe when his job is done, he will."

"Which job?"

"To rebuild the Circle. If you two join that puts him that much closer."

I exchanged a glance with Clive, who'd turned from the sink to look at us.

"Niko mentioned a Circle needs…twelve or thirteen?" I said.

"Hmmm, sixteen, really, though some folks can do double duty. But yeah, twelve Adepts for the Wisdomkeeper, plus two Guardians for the Unbroken."

"The Unbroken? Is that a thing or a person?"

Kish thought for a moment. "I'm probably not supposed to tell you until after you're initiated."

"If we're initiated," Clive said, the first words he'd spoken since Jair's centering. He dried his hands and hung the towel on the handle of the refrigerator. "It doesn't sound to me like you and Roland are going to get along so well, Mira."

"Roland and I get along fine when he doesn't spout nonsense." I did want to know more about how leadership and decision-making were supposed to work in the group, though. "Is the Circle really a consensus organization?"

"It's supposed to be." Kish drew a circle on the table with her finger. "The members are all equal. That's part of what makes it a circle instead of whatever the fuck else. But there is seniority, and also different roles within the Circle are in charge of different things. Roland's been around the longest. He's more likely to know what's what."

"Except when he doesn't," Clive said under his breath.

"I just want to know how it works." Something Kish had said made me think Ira wasn't exactly her favorite person. "How do Ira and Kanna fit in? Assuming they turn up?"

"They're technically still Initiates," Kish told us. "You get initiated first, but you don't move up to Adept until you take on a specific role like Healer or Convenor or whatever. Roland plans to slot Ira in as Healer and he wants Kanna taking over as Bladekeeper."

I wondered if Roland was already thinking about roles for Clive and myself. "Does Ira actually do what Roland tells him?"

Kish snorted. "When Ira gets out of line, Kanna usually puts him in his place. Ira's been a really quick study at the practice, though. He's already way ahead of me and Jair, and we started first." She looked at Clive. "Speaking of quick studies, you ever get that multi-orgasmic thing going?"

He did not blush when he said, "I haven't had much chance to practice it. I suppose if we're initiated I will?" He glanced at me.

Then he blushed.

Kish gave me a knowing smile. "So, most folks who are kinda naturals at the practice have a Blood Talent that makes itself obvious, you know, some thing they can do that's a little different from normal."

"She means a sexual thing," Clive said for my benefit, though he was looking at the table instead of at me.

"It's how they get clued in." She looked over her shoulder toward the door. "Not all of them are as dramatic as Roland levitating while jerking off when he was a kid. Clive, have you showed Mira your party trick, yet?"

He still didn't look up. "Maybe you should show her yours."

Part of my brain was telling me, of course, that what Clive and I should be doing right then was having a clear-eyed and sober conversation about whether we were actually going to go through with initiation. But a different kind of desire stirred in me then.

"What about you, Mira?" Kish asked. "Got a party trick?"

"I can slice a banana with a whip from ten feet away, but I don't think that's what you mean." I wanted to reach out and touch Clive. I wanted to slide my hands over his skin, to feel him shiver under my gently raking nails. I'd wanted to ever since that moment when we'd locked eyes during the centering of Jair, and since there were no distractions left, the desire was growing like hunger in my belly. "Did quelling the demon count?"

Kish's laugh was merry and musical. "Dunno if it's a Blood Talent per se, but yeah, I'd say it definitely counts!"

"After all the Wall Street assholes and self-entitled subs I've had to put in their places over the years?" I interlaced my fingers and cracked my knuckles. "The demon was easy."

Clive flinched. No, he didn't. He didn't move at all, but I felt the flinch. Or did I imagine it? "Clive's not like them," I added, and he relaxed a fraction.

"He's very intriguing, though, isn't he?" Kish grinned at me. "I'm still trying to figure him out. So smart. But so pretty to look at."

Clive's blush deepened. As the blood rushed to his face I wondered if it was my imagination or if the bond really let me sense that blood was rushing to other parts of him, too. Talking about him as if he wasn't sitting right there was a classic dom technique for stirring up submissive feelings. Whether they rebel against the dom's right to do so or accept it doesn't matter: the point is it reinforces who's in control. If you're the type of person who's aroused by giving up control—or by taking it—it's a fine form of verbal foreplay. Kish clearly knew that.

"Very pretty," I agreed. "And for a supposed thrill-seeking masochist, seems like he slides into a service role awful easily."

"Oh, I think he's only that way with you." Kish wagged a finger up and down in his direction. "With Ira he was much more feisty."

"You think that's because of the bond of obedience?"

Kish raised an eyebrow. "I think it's because he's a lot more into you than Ira."

I decided that was the moment to touch Clive. I had a strong urge to do one of my favorite things, which was take a handful of his hair and bend him back for a kiss. But just because I have an urge to do something doesn't mean that's what I do. I put my open hand on the table beside him, palm up.

He swallowed and slid his hand into mine. His grip was strong, like he was holding the safety bar on an amusement ride.

"Is that how the Circle found you?" I asked Kish. "Your party trick?"

"Pretty much. Mine is better demonstrated than explained. If Clive's willing, that is."

He looked up at me. "I'm willing, if Mira is."

"Now you've both got me curious."

Kish stood with a grin. "All right. Come on up to my room, then. And bring a towel."

TWENTY-TWO

Kish's room reminded me of a college dorm—complete with bed, desk, and batik print wall hanging—though I never saw such a pretty purple rabbit pearl vibe sitting out on someone's desk in college. The batteries were lying loose next to it, along with a screwdriver, soldering iron, and some other bits of electronics. "Is this much use in the practice?"

"Nah, I hack vibrators just for fun." Kish sat on the bed, her legs stretched across it and her back against the wall. She propped another pillow next to her and patted it, beckoning me to join her.

I settled next to her while Clive remained standing. He cleared his throat nervously, his hands folded like he was waiting to be told what to do.

In fact, he was waiting to be told what to do. As soon as I suggested, "Clive, why don't you start by taking your clothes off," he seemed to relax. Without being prompted, he folded them neatly and placed them on the corner of the bed next to the hand towel he'd brought in. Some subs would've just dropped their clothes on the floor. Others would have asked incessant questions about what to do or how to do it, which I always found irritating. Some doms wanted to dictate every movement, every detail, which was fine for them. Me, I wanted to have a relationship with a person, not a robot.

He didn't question whether I meant all or only some of his clothes. He knew I meant all. When there wasn't a stitch on him, he straightened up, waiting calmly for me to tell him what was next.

So I did. "Turn around and give us a better look at you."

He raised his arms and turned slowly in a circle, like a statue rotating on a pedestal. I'd say he looked perfect except actually I couldn't help but notice one blemish, a raised mark near the top of adductor magnus—which is to say on his inner thigh—just visible under the crease of his buttock. It looked like the scar left by a puncture wound, like he'd sat on a nail sticking out of a bench or something. Lots of people had marks from childhood mishaps, animal bites, and so on. Sometimes when they were on the massage table I'd mention what I saw and I'd get a whole story about it. Other times they'd say "what mark?" I wondered which reaction Clive would have, but resolved to ask about it later.

If there was one thing about Clive that was perfect, it was what I described to Kish: "He's so comfortable in his skin."

Kish nodded. "Were you always like that?" she asked him.

Clive thought for a moment before he answered. "No. Well, when I was a kid I had no qualms about skinny dipping in the pond or whatever. But I kind of went through an awkward phase—puberty and all that. Took a while to grow out of it again."

Kish settled into a more comfortable position, leaning amiably against me. "Mira, you might find you can control that joystick of his."

"Control?"

"Make it go up and down. He's halfway there already, I see. See if you can get him to rise all the way up."

I wasn't sure what she meant for me to do. "By telling him…?"

"You're the one who's inside the bond. What does it feel like? Do you sense it in a particular way?"

I flexed my hands. My fingers almost tingled, but I'd ascribed that to just how much I wanted to touch him. But I held my palms out and gestured upward, like a conductor urging an orchestra to play louder.

The physical effect on Clive was instantly visible, his spine no longer the only part of him standing ramrod straight.

I examined my palms. "Very nice, but maybe he's just aroused."

"Try reversing it."

I turned my hands over and made calming, tamping-down motions.

Clive let out a whimper as his anatomy followed my unspoken command. "That is… very disconcerting…!"

I looked at my palms although I realized it wasn't my hands that made that work. "All right. I'm convinced." But that made me wonder… "Clive, what's your party trick?"

"I don't know how it works." He wasn't meeting my eyes again.

"You don't have to explain how it works, bebe," Kish said. "Just tell her what happens."

"I can take… extreme sensations and transfer them to someone else."

There was that word again, *transfer*. I felt like I kept hearing it. "By 'extreme sensations' do you mean pain?"

He was already blushing, but I could hear it in his words. "Mostly, my lady."

"How'd you figure that one out?"

"Playing with Ira and Kanna. Kanna tried to shock me with an electrical prod." He looked like he was trying to hide a smile (and it was a wickedly good look on him). "I felt nothing, but Ira got knocked right on his ass."

Kish and I chuckled about that. Part of me want to know how Ira reacted, where that scene went from there… but it was time to concentrate on the people in the room. Kish said to me: "You best pump him back up again, now. If he's not good and hard when I hit him with my thing, it'll hurt like hell."

How intriguing. "Maybe I want him to pump himself back up, though. Clive, what gets you hard? Can you do that for us?"

"Yes, my lady." He licked his thumbs and then ran them across his nipples until the flesh crinkled and stiffened. His head fell back as he then took hold and pinched. The effect was almost instantaneous. I could feel the arousal emanating from him in waves as he returned to readiness.

"Classy." Kish held up her thumb and forefinger in an L-shape. "Most guys would have just yanked right on that thing. All right. You ready?"

Clive's eyes were shut and he gave a nod.

Kish grinned, pointed her finger gun right at his groin, and "fired."

A now-familiar groan escaped Clive's lips as his hips jerked and he shot several stripes of semen onto the floor. A shiver ran through me just witnessing it, a little empathetic ghost-orgasm.

"That is a good party trick," I told Kish. "How'd you figure that one out?"

"Remember I said I worked as a pro domme when I first turned eighteen? One day I ordered a guy to come, and he did, and I was like *oh, that was nice, I didn't even get my hands dirty.*"

That made me chuckle. "Speaking of which, Clive, please clean that up."

He was still panting a little but he nodded. "Yes, my lady." He knelt to his task with the hand towel while Kish continued her story.

"I was too young and naïve to know that didn't happen to every domme. Took a while for me to figure that out, and for the word to get around. I started to get a steady stream of guys with erectile problems. They were telling their friends, you know?" She watched appreciatively as Clive left the room with the dirty towel. As I may have mentioned, he was as nice to admire from the back as the front. "Then my cousin's house in Queens got damaged in a hurricane and I came up here to help her out. We were both broke, she was getting screwed by her insurance, I figured, what the heck. I took out an ad."

"Offering dominatrix services?"

"Nah, just a cure for erectile dysfunction. 'No drugs, no needles, just sweet relief,' it said. Guys were like 'I don't care if it's voodoo or what.' Then one day a plainclothes cop came in. I think he was expecting a 'happy endings massage' kind of situation."

"Yeah, they don't take too kindly to those around here." I could hear the water running in the bathroom down the hall. "How'd you know he was a cop?"

"He told me himself." She smiled like the cat that ate the canary. "He also told me a visit from vice was imminent but that he could 'help me out' if I would return the favor. "

"I can imagine what kind of favor."

"Yeah, no. Not happening to this girl."

"What did you do?"

"I made his nuts erupt." She blew on the end of her finger. "And then I would have hightailed it back to Miami, except not five minutes later, Jair walked in."

Clive returned and resumed standing where he had been.

"Now I'm curious." I sat up a bit. "Clive, would you say it's as satisfying as a regular orgasm?"

Again that thoughtful look before he replied. "It's on par with a quick wank in a public restroom."

"But I thought you said it was painful to do it if they guy wasn't ready for it. Wasn't it excruciating for these guys who couldn't get it up?"

"Oh, but they did get it up." She patted her thigh. "The first part is I'd make 'em pop that boner. I didn't realize at first that that's a different skill from making them squirt. Well, you could do them both with psychosomatic transfer. But making them come without me having an orgasm myself is a different kind of energetic manipulation. Niko will tell you all about that stuff."

"Interesting." I wondered what caused the pain, but I supposed I'd have to ask Niko that, too, and he'd probably have to rummage around in his head for the answer and then scribble it out. "And how does the refractory period play into this?"

Kish chuckled. "You want to see if you can make him go again? I bet you can do both parts with Clive. We know you can get a rise out of him."

I looked into Clive's eyes. "Want to try it?"

He gave me the Mona Lisa smile. "Your wish is my command."

"Say yes, when you mean yes, Clive."

"Yes, my lady." He took a relaxed stance, feet apart.

I raised my hands again, feeling the pull toward him, almost like a magnetic field. My heart raced as heat rose in us both and I realized that what I'd always assumed was just my imagination, just my desire playing tricks on my senses, was actually power.

"There you go." Kish whistled appreciatively. "I think he's even stiffer this time than last."

Clive's eyes had gone glassy, his pupils huge. I could hear my own blood surging.

"And how do you—" I started to ask, but I realized I could feel the answer instinctively before I could even articulate the question. The finger guns weren't necessary, of course, merely stylish. I licked my lips and snapped my fingers instead.

Clive gave a shout and rocked back on his heels as the orgasm hit him. Only a little dribble of liquid came forth, and he panted heavily as the aftershocks went through him. "Guess I… didn't have time… to refill the tank." He groaned. "That one felt… deep."

"Roland insists it's possible for a man to become multi-orgasmic, which means learning to come without ejaculating, but if it was super-easy to do, every guy would." Kish shrugged and gave me a sly smile. "Clive was set to learn it, but maybe with you around he won't have to."

I looked at my hands. "It's certainly an intriguing possibility. There's a lot about the bond we don't know." Clive made a snort of agreement.

"What did Niko tell you?"

"Not a lot. Mostly about the flow of energy between us. But I still don't know how much of that is the bond itself versus, say, the effect of the collar."

"Huh."

Once I began describing it to her, the central question seemed to grow clearer in my mind. "And that energy flow? I still don't get whether it actually gives me some kind of control or if it's just that it makes Clive feel like he wants to follow my lead?"

Clive's eyes flew open. "Do you want me to try to resist?"

"Or would that not work to test the bond, because if Mira wants you to resist, then you'd be doing her bidding by resisting?" Kish raised an eyebrow.

I realized if we were going to test the limits of the bond, we should do it within a scene. "What if I ask you to do something impossible?" I got to my feet, resting a hand on his bare chest. I was wearing only socks which made him a little taller than me. "It's a typical dom thing to do, right? Give the sub a predicament task. If they succeed, you reward them. If they fail, you get to punish them—which is fun, too, if that's what you negotiated."

"I like a good beating." Clive's eyes moved like he was searching my face for something. "But I've never liked needing some trumped up excuse for it. Humiliation has never been my kink."

"Mine either." I wanted to kiss him, then, just because I could. Instead, I said, "There are a lot of paths to the point of surrender."

"There's a difference between reaching the point of surrender," Clive said, "and being broken. And I think some doms don't know that."

"I think some subs don't either." I slid my hand up along his jaw. "If I ever felt the need to break a sub, it'd be a sign that relationship was already broken. And we should both walk away."

Him. "You really believe that?"

Me. "Deeply."

"You'd set a sub free before you'd break them?"

"I'd expect them to walk away of their own accord, if they thought the relationship was broken." Instead of, say, carrying on pretending and then claiming they'd stayed for "my sake."

Clive's gaze flickered. "You expect everyone to be as strong as you are, Mira."

What I was thinking was: You are as strong as me, Clive. But what I said was, "Is that bad?"

"No. But what would happen if your sub couldn't walk away?"

"You can always walk away." Ethan could have; he chose not to. Because lying was easier than facing the truth. I felt angry about him all over again, then resented the fact that he could still make me angry. I petted Clive's hair instead, reminding myself who I had right in front of me. A strong, complicated person. "There's no consent, and no relationship, if you can't walk away."

It didn't strike me as odd that his answer was simply, "Yes, my lady." It felt right.

And then I was kissing him, because not kissing him was an aching need too strong to be borne any longer.

TWENTY-THREE

I woke in the morning pressed against Clive. While asleep, he was as warm and cuddly as a cat. The urgencies of the day rang in my mind like alarms—Wex, Barrow, Ira and Kanna, the dagger Kish had recovered—but I kept my eyes closed and told myself to take five more minutes like that, to savor being so close, so comfortable. I normally only felt that comfortable and relaxed while snuggled up immediately after a scene or sex. But Clive had been too spent—literally— the night before for us to do anything but talk a little before we conked out.

We talked about joining the Circle, of course. After taking part in Jair's centering—not to mention the whole rescue—what the Circle was, and what being a part of it would be like, seemed much more real than it had when we were speaking in abstractions with Niko. If anything, I felt like the Circle needed the two of us as much as we needed it. But we stopped short of saying for sure whether we were going for it. We kept it theoretical.

Clive had asked: *where would you want the piercing?*

I'd told him my ear seemed to make the most sense and asked what he was thinking for himself.

I meant where would you want it on me, he had said. *You have to be the one to decide*—before he slipped into sleep.

The thought of piercing him made me feel warm and fuzzy all over (in a good way), and yet something didn't sit right in my chest at the thought he handed me the decision so blithely. I told myself if Clive was an adult sensible and responsible enough to decide for himself where he wanted a permanent piercing, then he was sensible and responsible enough to abdicate that decision, too. Right? I lay awake for a while, listening to the beat of his heart and thinking it over, my eye tracing the edges of the rectangle of light cast on the ceiling from the streetlamp outside as if that would help straighten out my thoughts.

Maybe there's no straightening out something so kinky.

In the morning, I picked up where I left off, moving the thought around in my mind while I dozed in his arms. Was it that I wasn't comfortable with the responsibility? Or that I didn't believe Clive really *meant* it? Or that I believed deep down it wasn't *healthy* for Clive to mean it?

Or was it that I was used to a sub who would manipulate any situation to make sure he got exactly what he wanted? Had I forgotten what actually being in charge was like?

I opened my eyes, intending to wake Clive and ask about it. The ceiling looked different from what I expected—brighter—not because it was morning, but because it was a different ceiling entirely.

From the look of the posters on the wall, the cars and action figures on the shelf, we were in a young boy's bedroom. It had to be a dream. But Clive was still there in the bed next to me. He opened his eyes.

"I think I'm dreaming," I told him.

He sat up and looked around. "This is my childhood bedroom."

"Huh. I wonder if that means I want to know more about your past?"

He slipped from the bed then, naked except for the collar of beads, to examine the toys on the shelf. He picked up an action figure in each hand: Batman and Catwoman. Catwoman was holding a whip. "Maybe I'm having a subconscious desire for you to meet my family?"

"Except this is my dream."

"Is it?" He turned and looked at me. "I used to fantasize about bringing someone like you home."

"Like me?" I'd always thought of dreams as a way to see your unfiltered subconscious. If so, what was I trying to tell myself? "What do you mean by someone 'like me?'"

"Someone smart enough and strong enough to handle my parents. Someone my older brother would be jealous over."

I wondered if that meant I cared more about what his parents might think of me than I'd admit to when I was awake? Which seemed unlikely. Since he'd mentioned them I hadn't given them a second thought.

Dream-Clive climbed back onto the bed and continued, "Someone who knew the parts of me I wouldn't show to anyone else."

I chided him gently. "Clive, from what I've seen, there's very little of you that you haven't shown to everyone."

"Except there is." A shadow crossed his face as he smoothed the wrinkles in the bedspread with his hand. "There's whatever's behind that block no one can see through."

I ran my fingers into his hair. "Maybe all that's in there is your own self-doubt."

He frowned. "You think?"

"Yeah. Maybe it's literally your worry that no one will love you for who you really are."

"Wait. So you're saying… the thing I won't show anyone is that I'm afraid that if I show them I'm afraid no one will love me…then no one will?" He blinked. "That's… recursive."

"Emotions are fractals." It was definitely one of the weirdest, yet most vivid dreams I'd ever had. "Maybe everyone has something they're afraid that if others knew, they'd reject them."

"Then… what are you afraid of, Mira?" His eyes were that pale blue I kept forgetting.

It was just a dream, right? I could have told him about what I'd done to Ethan, but instead my subconscious went for a different buried truth, one much closer to the present moment: "I'm afraid that if I tell you how much I want you to be mine, you'll resist, and then I'll let you walk away on principle that I don't want to force you."

He drew back as if I'd stung him. "You'd lose me just to prove a point? A philosophical, moral point?"

"Hopefully not?" Truth be told, I felt the prickles of terror at the edges of my mind. Was I going to be forced somehow to choose between my principles and Clive? I tried to reason the fear away. "It's just a philosophical question, though, not a real-life scenario, right? We're on the same page. We already talked about this."

"About what?"

"About how if we don't have the power to walk away, then the relationship isn't consensual."

"Mira," he said, as he touched the collar with the tips of his fingers. "You know you have to be the one, right?"

Before I could ask when he meant by that, someone was knocking on the bedroom door—the door to our room at The Archive. Kish called out, "You guys awake in there?"

I opened my eyes for real. "Yeah," I croaked, voice thick with sleep. Clive raised his head and blinked fuzzily.

"Niko's making waffles. Get up if you want 'em fresh and hot!"

That was sufficient motivation for both of us to hurry to wash and dress. I had my pick of clothes in the closet that had belonged to former members of the Circle, but I preferred to borrow something from Clive. Out of the duffel he'd fled his apartment with came a black T-shirt and a pair of sleek black track pants that were only slightly too long for me. I checked myself out in the mirror. "I'm amazed my ass fits into these."

"The magic of stretch knits," Clive said, pulling on a pair of jeans. "You look positively cat-burglar-esque."

That jogged my memory of the dream, and spurred the nagging feeling we needed to talk for real. At the very least, the dream had to mean there was a disconnect between us.

But, breakfast.

Down in the kitchen, Niko the Waffle Master was wearing headphones and dancing in front of the stove while flipping bacon with a pair of chopsticks. The waffle iron beeped and he turned it over to pry out a perfectly done waffle.

Syrup, butter, and juice were on the table, and the other three were already tucking in. Niko gestured for me to take the fresh waffle on a plate. I brought it to the table. "Clive. Let's split it."

He looked puzzled. "I'm sure we can each eat a whole one."

"So we'll split the next one, too. Then neither of us has to wait." I prepped it with butter, watching it melt into the squares for a few seconds before adding the syrup. I cut a piece and waved it at him on the fork.

He took the chair next to me and accepted the offering right from my fork with careful teeth. "Damn. Real maple syrup."

Feeding him bite by bite more satisfying than eating it myself, I swear. I ended up giving him the entire thing. When the plate was empty, he took it to get a fresh waffle. When he brought it back, he asked, "What happened to 'neither of us has to wait?'"

"Sometimes I like delayed gratification," I told him, while he fussed with the butter and syrup.

He cut me a piece, and held up the fork. "Here. It's only fair."

"All right." It was worth the wait. The bite was crisp on the edges but laden with fat and soft sweetness in the middle. "Mmm. That's good."

Kish and Jair shared a look. "I guess you two are getting along," Jair said.

"I guess we are," I replied, while Clive blushed a little, not meeting Jair's eyes. That rekindled the feeling that we'd been interrupted. What was going on in Clive's head?

Niko brought the last few unclaimed waffles to the table, took his headphones off, and sat down. "Okay! Well. I'm sure you're all wondering why I called you here."

"To worship at the altar of salted butter and tree sap?" Jair guessed, while dragging another waffle onto his plate.

"He's joking, bebe," Kish said.

"So am I," Jair replied, mouth already partially full of another serving.

Niko grinned at him. "I was going to ask how you're feeling but you seem all right."

"I'm great," Jair said, though I thought he looked a little dehydrated, with bluish rings under his eyes. "Thanks to these four. If even one of you had stayed home, I probably wouldn't be here today." He toasted us with a glass of juice. "Mira, Clive, I have to say... if you thought I was big on you joining the Circle before, I'm an absolute fanatic about the idea now."

"Which is the actual thing I wanted to talk about," Niko added.

I shrugged. "I'm glad we were there to help. Though I honestly still don't know exactly what we did."

Roland set his fork down. "Do you want to know badly enough that you'd leave your former life behind just to find out?"

I tried to catch Clive's eye, but he was buttering another waffle, so I answered, "I'd be lying if I said I wasn't very interested in learning how to stop a wound from bleeding with a... a Jedi mind trick."

"Oh, that wasn't a Jedi mind trick," Jair said. "That would be if—" He broke off when Kish did something to him under the table. "I mean, Roland's right. It's all on offer, if you commit to becoming one of us." He licked syrup off his thumb, looking right at me as he did it. "I think you already know what you want, though, Mira. Your heart is already set. It's all a question of whether you've made up your mind. Am I right?"

Kish nudged him. "Don't push, Jair."

"I'm not pushing. I'm just calling it like I see it." Jair's eyes met mine across the table, and I felt like we were time-traveling back to that alley where he'd asked me if I'd join, and I had thought about saying—but had not yet said—yes.

"This isn't just about the pros and cons, though," I said. "My former life was no great shakes. It's logical we should team up to fight Barrow. And we need to know everything about demons, obviously. But that's the thing. It's not just about me, it's both of us we have to talk about, as well as how the bond between me and Clive would be affected."

"Oh! About that," Niko said. "I've—"

"—done a little more research—" Kish and Jair both said, imitating his voice as they chorused along with him.

Roland rolled his eyes and sighed, as if he didn't approve of their antics while we were discussing something so serious, but Niko (and I) took it in stride: "I think as long as we initiate you both at the same time, there won't be any interference between the Circle bond and your pair bond. I don't believe there's any danger one might weaken or break the other if you both do it. Especially with two like you."

Again I felt an echo of the dream. "What do you mean, 'like us'?" Clive put a bite of waffle into my mouth without missing a beat.

"Well, for lack of a better term for it, you guys seem to be..." Niko paused, and then grimaced as he said, "Soulmates."

"I don't believe in soulmates," Clive and I both said simultaneously. We looked at each other in slightly bemused horror while everyone else broke up laughing.

"Why don't you like the term soulmates?" I added.

"Because it's cheesy," Clive said.

"Because it's cheesy, as well as inaccurate," Niko added with a shrug. "Souls don't mate. But I realize 'strongly bonded wavelength-compatible partners' doesn't have the same ring to it."

Jair rubbed his eyes and then licked syrup off the back of his hand. "Now's the time, Mira, to voice your objections so we can work through them. Figure out if there are any dealbreakers."

Clive eyed me curiously.

"Well," I said. "I guess I have two points holding me back. Or, had. One was if joining was going to damage the bond that's keeping Clive safe."

Clive's mouth thinned unhappily, but he said nothing.

So I went on. "The other is that I don't want to dictate everything for both of us just because I'm the dom. Clive's feelings count, too."

Clive sat up very straight suddenly. "I told you that's your choice to make."

I think I blinked at him for a moment. "When? You mean last night? I thought you were asking me to decide where the piercing should go."

"That, too." He looked away from me suddenly, swallowing hard. "I think... you're not listening to me."

That froze me in my tracks. It's so easy, when you're the dom, to just hear what you want to hear, whether because the sub only says things they think you want to hear, or because you tune out or brush off anything that doesn't fit your ideal. "Tell me."

"And you're not seeing what's right in front of you," he added, looking at his hands, which were idle in his lap.

"Do you mean she's not seeing how much you wanted to join the Circle before she came along?" Jair asked. "Or how obvious it is that joining the Circle is the right course of action?"

When Clive didn't say anything to that, I said, "I don't take anything for granted." I held a hand out toward Clive, palm up. He swallowed again and placed his in mine, letting me grip him. "I don't like feeling like any course of action is inevitable and therefore should go unexamined."

He nodded minutely.

"I get the feeling this isn't about the plusses and minuses of us joining the Circle." I squeezed his fingers. "Clive, I need your help. I need you to help me see what I'm missing."

He came at it from an angle, I didn't expect. "If you don't want to do it, fine, but don't use me as an excuse not to."

Whoa. Things clearly looked very different from his perspective. "Is that how you feel?" Well, obviously that was how he felt or he wouldn't have said it. I tried again: "Can you tell me more about how you're feeling?"

He swallowed. "It's just that the longer your reluctance goes on, the more it feels like you're avoiding commitment."

He worded it like he meant commitment to the Circle, but I heard it as my commitment to *him* that he was starting to question. My heart skipped an angry, irrational beat: Where did he get off saying I was the one who didn't want to commit to him? He was the one who'd said he accepted the bond "for now." If I was honest with myself, the thought that he might walk away made me want to chain him down, literally, but I relegated that idea to fantasy not reality. If I wasn't committed to letting him go when he was ready, then I wasn't committed to consent. And if I wasn't committed to consent, I had no business being in a dominant/submissive relationship in the first place.

And that's what I'd been trying to tell him. "Hold that thought, okay? I need you all to realize that my caution isn't reluctance. It's that if I'm going to be making decisions for both of us, I'm going to be doubly careful." That got a small nod from Clive. I felt like we were agreeing to talk about the Circle out loud, but underneath, we both knew we were talking about our pair bond—our relationship—too. I looked at Kish and Jair. "Tell it to us flat out: why shouldn't we join."

Jair's jaw hung open a moment as he realized I was asking him to do the opposite of what he wanted to do. "Other than the whole 'sadistic madman trying to kill us' thing? That's kind of the only downside I can think of."

Roland put in his two cents: "When you pledge yourself to the Circle, to keeping the knowledge and maintaining the integrity of the Unbroken, you get linked with everyone else. That means losing a certain amount of privacy and autonomy."

Jair refilled his coffee. "Yeah, okay, it means giving up your secrets." His eyes met mine over the top of his mug. "If you have any."

Everyone has secrets. Don't forget that. "What happens if, after learning someone's secrets, you decide you don't want them in the Circle anymore?"

Roland cleared his throat. "That was the basic concern behind wanting to know what's hidden by Clive's mental block."

"I thought you were worried the block was concealing a command from Barrow."

"That's just the most dangerous possibility," Niko said. "Though I don't find it likely. If Clive were under Barrow's control, why attack him at the apartment? As for what happens if a member of the Circle has to leave…" He trailed off, fidgeting and eyeing Roland uncomfortably.

Roland finished the sentence. "There's a technique for removing someone from the Circle. It's called Severing."

"Sounds severe," Jair quipped. Everyone ignored him.

"It's not pretty." Roland put his mug down and folded one hand inside the other. "Being Severed creates a kind of psychic wound." His voice grew rough. "Part of the process is… cauterizing that wound. It leaves a scar, behind which the knowledge of all things having to do with the Circle is locked."

A heavy silence blanketed the table, then. I had the feeling Roland was about to get up and leave the room. Niko's fingertips rested on the table like he was about to pounce like a cat.

And then, as if the universe were calling foul, a loud buzzer rang. The doorbell.

"You expecting a delivery?" Jair asked at the same time Niko said, "It's my sister!"

"I'll get it." Jair left the table.

"You haven't met Dag, yet, have you?" Kish asked Clive. He shook his head. Then to me, "You're gonna like her."

A moment later a short woman with wild black hair appeared in the kitchen doorway with Jair, each apparently trying to get the other into some kind of joint lock, laughing all the way down the hall until they got to the door.

She looked in without crossing the threshold. "Oops. Who died?"

"No one, Dag. We're just… talking," Roland said.

She went right to him and caught him in a bear hug from behind. "You're too heavy, sometimes, Uncle Rollie! Give these poor people a break." She reached toward me. "Hi, I'm Dagger. You're the new initiates?"

I shook her hand while thinking *Uncle Rollie??* "I'm Mira, and that's what we're talking about. Whether we are or not."

"Ohhhh, I see." She pulled out Jair's chair and sat.

"And this is Clive."

Clive nodded his head. "I believe we're on the subject of what happens if someone has to leave the Circle."

Dagger didn't bat at eye. "Well, don't let me interrupt. I'm just here for little bro's waffles. For a guy who doesn't eat, he sure can cook." She took a waffle off the stack, prepped it, and then folded it in half in her hand and bit into it like a syrup-butter taco. "If you want my two cents, though, I wouldn't blame you if you decided to run for the hills. Except didn't I hear you have some kind of something going on? A master-slave thing?"

"We don't use the word 'slave,'" Roland said.

She shot him a look, but was undeterred. "So how did it happen? You were like, quelling a demon and you quelled a man, instead?"

"That's the best explanation I've heard yet for what happened." I looked at Roland and Niko, and then back at Clive. "In fact, I'm worried I've quelled him a little too much."

Clive frowned at me. "Because I said you have to be the one to decide for us?"

I didn't have hold of his hand anymore, but I held his gaze this time. "You said it's my decision—and I've decided to take your feelings into account, all right?"

He shook his head. "I appreciate that, Mira, but did you forget I wanted to join so much that I ghosted you?"

No, no I definitely hadn't forgotten that. But. "'Wanted' is past tense. Just the other night, after the party, you said you were having second thoughts." Had I misremembered? "Niko even knew you were, and asked you to reconsider, remember?"

Clive set his jaw. "I'm fine now. I was just having a bad day."

Jair leaned down to say in Dagger's ear: "He gets the crap beat out of him, almost dies in a fire, gets possessed by a demon, and calls that 'just having a bad day.'"

They chuckled and Clive looked a bit sheepish. "It gave me a lot to think about, all right? But seriously, Mira, if you don't want to be part of the Circle, just say so. Right now it's more important for me to be with you than with them."

The beat my heart skipped that time was an excited one, even if he didn't mean that in a romantic way. In fact, I was sure he didn't.

"There are a lot of reasons we shouldn't separate." He worried his lower lip with his teeth. "It's not just a philosophical question. This is a real-life scenario."

The hairs stood up on the backs of my arms as I realized he was referencing something I'd said in the dream. I put a hand over my mouth, but blurted out, "Did I talk in my sleep last night?"

Niko held out his hands like a referee trying to separate two players. "Did you meet in the Dreamscape?"

"Strongly bonded wavelength-compatible partners," Jair murmured to Kish, or maybe she murmured to him.

"I think we did," Clive said. "In my childhood bedroom."

The chill over my skin intensified as I thought about what I'd said. "Did you have a Catwoman action figure?"

He nodded.

That conversation had actually *happened*. Clive described it to the others this way: "Mira's afraid that if I can't consent fully to the bond between us, that we're both going to Hell or something."

"That's not what I said. I said I was afraid I'd… have to give you up."

Dagger had forgotten the half-eaten waffle in her hand. "But, but… Why would you have to give him up?"

"Aren't you the ones who believe that consent is good and non-consent is evil?" I asked. "Isn't that the difference between you and the Partisans?"

"Um, without getting into technicalities… more or less, yes?" Niko said.

"Then it's worth getting this right." I mean, literally, we were talking about the difference between good and evil. That isn't something you want to get wrong, is it? I put both hands out palm up toward Clive and he put his hands into mine without hesitation. "Clive. Here's why I'm going on and on about your feelings and your input." The reasons crystalized while I was speaking. "Basically, what if this isn't what you really want, and that's just the collar talking."

He squeezed my hands as if he were in pain. "You don't believe me?"

"I want to believe you, and I believe in taking my sub's word for things. But I've never dealt with something like a magical demon-repelling rosary before, either. If I'm reading between the lines of what we've been told, it's the force of my will that's holding your collar on."

He blinked, forcing himself to take a long, slow breath. "Okay."

"How do I know my force of will isn't so strong that I'm basically mind-controlling you to say these things?"

He blanched and swallowed. "You don't… you mean you don't even——" He shook his head and started over. "And what if it is? You'd dump me?"

"No. Obviously not, since you're still my responsibility." That came out sounding completely wrong. "Listen. I want us to be a force for good, not evil. Is that wrong?"

"No, that's one of the things that's great about you," Clive said.

"And I want to protect you from harm."

He nodded.

I felt like I was being scalded by the heat of that truth, with all of them watching me say it aloud, but if there were no secrets in the Circle, so be it: "But I worry that if I take your collar off, the fantasy that we're soulmates will be broken. You'll come to your senses and… and… not want to be mine after all."

He winced like thinking about that hurt him as much as it hurt me. And he slipped out of his chair and onto his knees beside me. "Mira. My lady." He swallowed hard, like he couldn't get the words unstuck from his throat.

I held his hands tight in mine. "You promised to tell me the truth, remember? How are you feeling, Clive?"

"Like I've never felt more whole in my life than I do with you." He rested his forehead against our entwined fists.

"Whole?"

He nodded. I think we were both wishing in that moment for it to be true and not a fantasy, not a quirk of the magic. I didn't know what to say that wouldn't seem pessimistic, so I said nothing.

Clive spoke. "And the truth remains: you have to be the one to decide for us both whether we become part of the Circle. I think… I have made my feelings about that clear."

I threaded my fingers into his hair. "All right. Yes. It's the right thing to do and we both want to do it. We should join the Circle. And sooner rather than later."

I took it as a good sign that nothing burst into flames when I said that. My words set everyone talking at once, Niko and Roland debating what the soonest could be, Kish saying she was sure it was okay to skip the fasting beforehand, Jair opining that to speed things up Niko could put us through a guided meditation, and on and on. But my focus was on Clive, and his on me, searching my face for something until I leaned forward to kiss him on the forehead, and his eyes closed.

TWENTY-FOUR

It's rare for life to hand you a moment where you can clearly see two paths, and after you go down one of them you can wonder: if you had gone the other way, what would have been different?

I'm not talking about whether Clive and I should have joined the Circle. I'm talking about which one of us was initiated first. What if things had gone the other direction?

Maybe it's better not to think about that.

Preparing for the double-initiation ceremony was fairly straightforward. They sent us to wash up and put on short white silk robes, and then to meditate (or whatever) in the parlor across from the main room. Once upon a time it must have been the home-schooling room for the kids whose parents were in the Circle. One wall held a chalk board; some old school desks were pushed up against the other. In the center of the floor was a 10x10 workout mat that was good for sitting on while pretending to meditate.

Clive and I sat at opposite corners of the mat. Niko popped by to tell us that normally an initiate would go through a couple of weeks of training and learning before the actual ceremony, but obviously we were skipping that. They'd also usually have undergone STD testing—Clive had—but with me they didn't have any other choice but to trust me. (I'd last been tested before Ethan and I broke up, and there hadn't been a reason to since.)

"Please don't ask me what the ceremony itself entails," Niko had said. "Because first of all it's different for each person, but also… as I understand it, being kept in suspense is part of the experience."

To which I could only say: "Of course it is." At that point it didn't matter to me if the reason was tradition or if it actually had a practical effect on the magic, and I knew if I asked, it would open yet another can of worms.

After he had left us alone, though, I said to Clive, "Suspense, hm? Does the practice hit all your kinks?"

"I don't know about *all*," he said, a touch mulish. "But some of the major ones, yes."

We tried to clear our minds. Maybe he succeeded. I know I didn't. A few minutes later I asked him, "Do you think there will be flogging? Kish mentioned they have ritual flails."

He sounded placid. "I think it's fruitless to speculate, my lady. Unless speculating helps get you in the mood."

I speculated anyway. The skin on the tops of my shoulders was still speckled with fine bruises from the last time they'd flogged me only, what, three days ago? But they wouldn't need to test for sexually transmitted diseases just for a flogging. My bet was that there would be fluid exchange, and not in the form of a drop of wine on a communion wafer or something.

My mind wandered from thinking about myself to others. When Roland left the Circle to get married and have a kid, had he been Severed? And did they have to do something special to reattach him to the Circle when he came back? Could a person be initiated twice… and was that why he had two rings? They said he had the freedom to walk away, but… did it hurt to be Severed, and did it hurt to return?

I supposed freedom of choice didn't mean freedom *from consequences*. Somehow that was the thought that kept returning to me, though I didn't know why. I could see it in my mind's eye, *hear* it being said. I guess in that way it was kind of like a mantra? *Freedom of choice doesn't mean freedom from consequences.*

Freedom is such a fraught word to begin with.

Apparently hours went by without me realizing it, so I guess I was kind-of-maybe meditating a little. I could smell the incense in the air. Jair came to lead us into the main room, where the candles and incense had been lit, and a circle—an oval, actually—had been drawn on the floor.

He reached down to help me to my feet. As I grasped his hand, I had a sudden flash—the taste of his mouth, the feel of his stubble against my chin—and I had to hold still for a moment until my eyesight returned. "What was that?"

"Did you have a vision?"

"More like a whole body sensory flashback, except it was of something that didn't happen in the past." I looked at his mouth, at the lushness of his lower lip. He had held me, but we had not kissed after the flogging at Clive's apartment. I was sure of that. But I was sure I knew what he tasted like.

"Sometimes, when you're about to enter ritual space, perception of time gets a bit weird. You might have had a flash forward." Jair held his other hand out for Clive and helped him up, too. "How about you?"

Clive just shook his head.

"Saira's ready for you now," Jair said. "You haven't met her yet. She's the last secret. She's the spiritual heart of the Circle. She's the pure light at the core."

His words didn't make sense to me. I felt dizzy and they were just words. What could he possibly mean by them?

"Mira, are you all right?" That was Clive. We were both holding Jair by the hand and he was trying to walk us into the other room, but I had to close my eyes to process another rush of sensory overload. Of bodies and breath. Of skin and sweat.

"This is being alive," I said. Like it was something I'd forgotten. Something I needed to be reminded of.

Jair just chuckled and pulled until he'd brought us across the hall and into the main room. The working space was defined by a chalk line on the floor, candles and knives and symbols along its edge, and two figures at either end—Niko closest to the door, and a young woman I hadn't seen before deep in the room. All I could see of her was a pair of large eyes. They were both wearing black robes that covered them completely.

Roland, Dagger, and Kish sat inside the oval, and three small pillows sat empty, facing them. Great, I thought. That means more meditation. I dislike being bad at anything, and meditation is no exception.

Jair was saying some words, maybe something about bringing the initiates, but they slid off my mind. I remembered that before the flogging I'd had to say "I do." Would we need to here, too? I watched Clive for cues. At some point we entered the circle and I don't remember saying it, but I know there must have been an Invocation of Willingness.

What I do remember is a blur of fragmentary sense memories. To call it an orgy wouldn't be accurate, but it felt a bit like one. (A friend once invited me to an orgy because, he said, they needed an odd number. According to him you had to have an odd number and at least half bisexuals in attendance, otherwise you just ended up with a bunch of couples having sex next to each other, which didn't meet his definition of an orgy.) I don't remember when our robes came off. I only know we all started out wearing them, and at the end only Niko and Saira still were.

Words were spoken—by Niko and Saira together, but it sounded like their voices were right inside my head—something about bringing the outside inside, and the inside outside. I remember the sound of the words "ritual breach." Aha. Like Jair offering me a drop of blood from his finger at the crossing of the aegis—which he hadn't done, but he would have—Roland pricked his finger with a needle and placed it reverently into Kish's mouth. I don't remember who offered their blood to me, but I could still taste it when Kish had held me back against her, kissing me, then biting my ear and the side of my neck while Jair breached me between the legs, at first with his finger, but that was not enough, not nearly enough. I drew him to me, suddenly needing to know if the placement of his Circle piercing would generate pleasure for his partner during intercourse. (The answer is yes.) He had a linear cut on his chest that I hadn't seen him get, too perfectly straight to have been a random scratch, and my eye kept coming back to it.

I have a memory of Clive squeezing my hand while Jair took me. But also of seeing Clive's mouth full of Roland. And of both of us kissing Jair. And Kish painting each nipple with a drop of blood and Clive suckling one and me the other. I don't know what order these things took place in. Time flowed in a circle, and so did arousal, spiraling upward through all of us.

The flow came to a stop, though, when Roland held up the piercing needles, one for each of us. Jair closed his eyes and sat in meditation for that part. Kish prepped my left ear with an alcohol swab and it felt ice cold, then took one of the needles. Roland was poised with the other at Clive's ear. I could feel that swirl of erotic energy around us almost like we were in a huge whirlpool, being sucked upwards into a waterspout.

In my mind's eye I imagined I could see the swirling inside the bubble, like when the demon was trying to escape, and I thought: won't the needle pop the bubble like a balloon?

And then I realized that was what was supposed to happen. When the needle went through my ear, it would pop the thin barrier between me and the others and release all that pent up energy. There had been no orgasms in the sharing portion of the working, and that was why. It was all leading to that moment.

But there were two of us. If they'd been coordinated, if they'd both struck with their needles at the same moment, I think it would have been fine.

But they didn't. Roland tried to go first, I think, but he cursed as Clive's head twisted suddenly. Kish's needle went through my ear and I barely felt it, my attention suddenly focused on Roland and Clive, as Roland dropped the needle to the floor. Clive thrashed out of his grip, then, with a "No!" that sounded a bit too much like the demon's roar for comfort. He and Roland fell to wrestling, Clive struggling against him the whole way. I grabbed the needle before anyone could get hurt on it and barked out, "Clive! Hold still!"

He did, arms outstretched, holding Roland at bay.

The next words out of my mouth: "Can I do it?"

And multiple voices answering: "Yes."

"Hold him still, then," I said, though really it was my will that was holding him still.

I pierced him through the left nipple, while Roland and Dagger symbolically held his arms and Kish slid the ring into place. Clive cried out when I did it, sending a shiver that was almost an orgasm through me, but not quite.

I kissed him to silence his cry, like I could eat the sound of his pain, and it was sweet.

I wanted to ride him to completion, then, and if it had only been the two of us, I think I would have. But that swirl of heady arousal was still circling, interweaving the connections between and among us, and it felt to me like it was my role to do something about it.

As I broke the kiss with Clive, I saw his glazed eyes, and he whispered something: "He's coming."

"You all are," I whispered back, as I reared above him, my arms outstretched. It felt like the connections among us all were spiderwebs, and I could sink my fingers into them like I did into Clive's hair, and make a fist and pull them tight... so I did. And as I took Clive's mouth with mine once more, the release that I felt was a full one, rocketing from my body's core up my spine and through not just Clive but everyone in the Circle.

The groans and cries were simultaneous all around me and it felt to me like the floor shook with a small earthquake. Was that real or just a feeling? I collapsed atop Clive, letting aftershocks roll through me while kissing him again.

When I looked up, I looked directly into Saira's eyes. Her hood had fallen back and her hair was askew, and she was staring at me, looking thoroughly shaken.

Dagger was at her side in an eye blink. "Saira. You all right?"

Her voice was light and sweet as spring honey: "I'm fine. Just... caught me by surprise is all. Mira, it is Mira, right?"

"Yes," I said.

"Mira, I think you... just did something unusual." She seemed to gather herself, looking around. The candles had all gone out and the chalk was smudged in places. "Well, maybe it's not unusual. I haven't been part of too many actual workings outside of initiations. Maybe this," she gestured at the others—Jair flat on his back, still groaning a little, Roland seemingly out cold, Kish fanning herself dizzily, "is normal for these guys."

Niko made a high-pitched sound of dismay. "Not exactly? Um. I need to change my clothes." He got up and ran out of the room, and I could see he had been wearing basketball shorts and sneakers under his robe.

Jair sat up. "I don't even believe in Jesus, but Jesus H. Christ, Mira."

Dagger pressed Saira. "You're sure you're all right?"

Saira shrugged her robe off. Under it she was wearing a pink and purple tie-dyed tank top and a short purple skirt. She was younger than I'd realized. "I'm fine. No one even touched me," she huffed.

I turned my attention back to Clive under me. His eyes had closed when the big orgasm had hit, and he hadn't opened them again yet. I stroked his hair. "You doing okay?"

When he opened his eyes, I could see he had a dazed, faraway look. "My lady," he said, but he was not looking at me. He reached up into the air like he was trying to grasp something only he could see.

Roland dragged himself over to us. "What's going on?"

I put my hand on his cheek. "Clive? Are you with us?"

He made what I can only call a grimace of distress. "He's coming."

That was when I remembered he'd said those words before, not only a few minutes earlier, but the other day, when he'd locked himself in his room. "Who's coming?"

"Barrow?" Roland asked, alarmed.

The doorbell rang, its ancient buzzer sound making me jump. Jair looked around for his robe, saying, "Seems unlikely Barrow would ring the bell."

Kish threw her robe on and picked up her knife. "I'll go see."

Clive blinked and focused on me, then. "Is it over?"

"The initiation ceremony? Yes."

He relaxed against my hand. "Good."

Before I could ask him what he remembered or what he'd seen, though, Kish came back in, with a man leaning heavily on her. He was so covered in dirt I barely recognized him, but as he sank to the floor his eyes met mine.

Ira had returned.

TWENTY-FIVE

The last time we'd spoken to each other, Ira had pulled Clive away from me right before their scene. The last time Ira had seen me, I had been pulling Clive away from the fire.

He was even less pleased to see me than I was to see him. "You!" he declared, and lunged from his knees at me. Jair intervened before I could defend myself, grabbing him in some kind of headlock.

"Hello, Ira," I said, wondering what he could have done to get so covered in dirt. He was shirtless but wearing leather pants that looked like he'd rolled down a hill during a mudslide. Even in Jair's grip, he reached a hand toward me.

As his fist closed, a surge of desire flooded me from out of nowhere. What was going on? Ira had to be causing it, but it felt real. Even though I'd just come, there it was—lust—strong and sweet and intoxicating. I swayed, fighting the sudden, undeniable urge to crawl to Ira, to press my body against his, to climb right into his lap and—

Clive curled into the fetal position with a whimper, his hands over his ears. My attention snapped to him, breaking the reverie and dousing the lust that had been burning through me the moment before. "Clive! Are you all right?"

I helped him sit up, our arms around each other.

Ira glared at me. "Fools, all of you. How could you?"

Roland stepped forward. "A lot has happened in the three days since you disappeared."

Ira pointed at Clive: "That one caused the fire. And then this one spirited him away." He swiped at me like a cat with his claws out.

"That's enough of that," Jair said, forcing him all the way to the ground. Ira snarled like a jaguar, his cheek pressed against the hardwood floor. The cut on Jair's pec had started to bleed during the struggle and I wondered if I should get the first aid kit.

"It's the *torst*," Roland said.

Jair looked alarmed. "The which?"

"The thirst. It's normal after going to ground." Roland had pulled his robe back on, but he bared his knife. "Hold him still." He pricked a finger with the tip and then squeezed until a large drop of blood had pooled.

When he thrust it into Ira's mouth, I almost had to look away. Ira's needy groan and the eagerness with which he sucked on Roland's finger were positively obscene.

Clive did look away.

When Roland finally wrenched free, Ira gasped and panted like he'd just guzzled two liters of Mountain Dew. Jair loosened his hold.

But it was too soon. Ira wasn't yet sated, apparently. He turned on Jair and latched onto the bleeding line above his nipple.

"Torst-whatever, *hm?*" Jair made a fist but didn't hit him with it. He lay there, gritting his teeth, his other hand gripping Ira's hair.

After a moment he told Ira, "I'm giving you ten seconds to stop before I punch your lights out."

Nine seconds later, Ira disengaged, and slumped to the floor beside him. "That… that wasn't… very… charitable of you," Ira said, words slurred like a drunk's.

Jair just flexed his fingers and stood up, shaking his head. I imagined I could hear what he was thinking: *So sue me,* perhaps. Or maybe just, *Asshole.*

"Couldn't help myself," Ira added, and then passed out.

Jair brushed dirt off his hands. "I suppose we should get him cleaned up."

Kish nudged Ira with one foot. "Nah, just let him sleep it off and he can clean himself up when he comes to. What do you guys want to eat? Wings? Thai? Mira, Clive, it was your initiation, you pick."

"I could really go for Korean fried chicken, assuming they'll deliver here," Clive said. "Unless Mira wants something else."

"Korean fried chicken sounds great," I said. "Now is someone going to explain what the hell is going on with Ira?"

Roland, it turned out, wasn't red because of how turned on he was by Ira fellating his finger. No, he was livid. About *me.* "How about you explain how you get off drawing both the Wisdomkeeper and the Unbreached into your arousal vortex."

"Word choice," Kish scolded. "He doesn't mean 'get off.' He means… why'd you make us all—including Niko and Saira—come like that."

Clive held out my robe to me.

I slipped it on. "Was I not supposed to? It just felt like the right thing to do."

Roland was so upset he was shaking. "Practitioners of the long life techniques don't sully themselves with sexual… *anything.* They *don't come.* They shouldn't even experience arousal!"

"Or eat," Kish pointed out. "Did you see Dag and Saira leave? I knew Saira wouldn't have any, but I thought Dag'd stick around."

"They bolted the second Roland tried to feed Ira," Jair said. "They don't take chances."

Roland tried to continue his harangue of me. "You've wreaked havoc on months of work for the two of them."

"And how was I supposed to know that?" I wanted to smack him across the face, but I only do that to those who ask nicely. "This is what you get *for not telling me anything in advance.*"

Jair and Kish shared a look and Jair spoke. "She's right, you know."

Roland shook his head and instead of arguing, just retrieved a meditation cushion to put under Ira's head. "I'm not angry," he finally said. "I'm just… scared. We need both of them—all of us, really—at our strongest if we're going to survive Barrow. Having a release like that will leave them both vulnerable for a while."

He didn't say how long, and I took that to mean he didn't know. But maybe he was just being habitually vague.

We decamped to wash up (again) before reconvening in the kitchen. When Clive and I came back down, fully dressed, I poked my head into the main room to see Ira had not moved, but someone had cleaned up the chalk and left him a bottle of golden oolong tea.

Several cartons of savory, crunchy fried chicken had arrived along with a variety of dipping sauces, some sweet, some spicy, some both.

For a while everyone was too busy eating to talk, until Kish said, "The next thing we need to do with you two is get you equipped. But that'll require either a visit to the Sanctuary, or someone making a visit down here."

"You know C.B.'ll complain if we make him haul ass all the way here," Jair said, licking sauce off the back of his hand. "How long 'til Ira wakes up, you think?"

Roland glanced at the clock on the wall and I realized it was much later in the evening than I expected. "We can try waking him up after two hours."

"Be my guest," Jair said, rubbing the spot where he'd been bitten.

I had to ask, "So what's torst, exactly? You said thirst, but I get the feeling Gatorade wouldn't have slaked it."

Niko wasn't there, so Roland answered. "Practitioners of the long life techniques can go into a kind of hibernation. We call it 'going to ground.' But when you come out, torst is pretty common. My guess is that Ira went to ground to hide from the Partisans. Once he went down they wouldn't be able to track his energy."

That explained why Ira was covered in dirt. I dipped some chicken into a spicy red sauce and waited until after I'd eaten it to continue, "Okay, so people doing the long life thing, they don't eat or have sex, but they can… have blood?"

Roland nodded. (His mouth may have been full.)

The one thing that still wasn't adding up to me, though, was that I couldn't imagine Ira giving up sex. But maybe I was making some assumptions about what got Ira off.

Jair pulled down the collar of his shirt to examine the tooth marks there. "And on the third day, he rose. My god, Ira's savior complex is going to be really insufferable after this."

TWENTY-SIX

A voice from the hallway startled us. "Ha ha." Ira stood in the doorway, still dirty and gaunt, but without the rabid look in his eye. "My apologies for my appalling behavior earlier. I was not in my right mind."

"Don't sweat it, I." Jair stretched in his chair. "Have a good nap?"

Ira was deadpan. "If you would call 'being submerged in unconsciousness from psychic exhaustion so profound even your nightmares lack movement' a 'nap,' then, I suppose so."

Roland seemed concerned. "I would've thought you'd still be out cold."

"Roland." Ira shook his head as if he were the one gravely disappointed. "When will you adjust to the fact that I perpetually exceed your expectations?"

Roland moved like a cattle dog trying to herd a bull out of a china shop, his chair scraping noisily as he got up. "Do you need some clothes? There's a ton of stuff in the chest in the third floor hallway." He gestured for Ira to precede him out of the kitchen.

Ira was unmoved. He looked at his dirt-darkened hands, then at Roland. "I have many questions about how Mira Cruise came to be sitting at this table."

Maybe my temper was on a bit of a hair trigger. "And I have many questions about you leaving Clive in bondage in a burning building."

He was instantly on the defensive. "You think I'm strong enough to carry both my wife and him? You flatter me too much."

"I would have thought you'd be sensible enough to simply release him and then he could've carried himself out on his own two feet." I have no memory of getting up from my seat, but I must have because by the time I finished my sentence Ira and I were right in each other's faces.

"The fire was an emergency no one foresaw—"

"You're literally fighting an enemy called the Partisans of—"

"—and I had to make a split second decision between attending to my wife, who had collapsed, and Clive, and be serious, Mira, even Clive understands that 'spouse comes before spice!'"

Clive interjected: "*Spice???*"

"It's just an expression! Goodness." Ira huffed and went on, all affronted puffery: "You're just looking for any excuse to criticize me. As soon as I laid Kanna down outside, I returned straightaway to retrieve him, only to find he was gone—"

"Yes, because I rescued him!"

"—and I truly don't appreciate being criticized by my guests about my conduct in my own home and my concern for my own wife!"

I really wanted to smack some sense into him, but of course, I only hit people who want to be hit. I hit him with words instead: "And the only reason I was even at your party was to warn you—"

"Warn me? About what, pray tell. Did you finally get me banned from Purgatory?"

Smack: "Did you even stop for one second in the lead up to your grand performance to wonder where Wex was?"

Ira's eyes darted to the side, as if he hoped Wexel was standing in the wings. "If I'm not mistaken, it was he who put you on the guest list."

Smack: "Yes. But he didn't show up because someone with a thing for knives left him for dead, bleeding out in some alley downtown."

I shouldn't have been so happy to see Ira taken down a peg, but I was. Under his cover of dirt, Ira blanched and withered. "Wex is dead?"

"No, thankfully. But he's in a hospital and hasn't woken up. At the time I thought I'd show up to the party to tell you something new: that there was someone dangerous out there. But turns out you already knew there was danger."

He put his hands over his face, shaking his head. "They couldn't have... But if they did...?" When he looked up, his usual edge of arrogance had been significantly dulled. "If I had any inkling that Wexel or any other guest was in any danger, we would not have held the party. We thought we were safe." He looked at Roland for backup. "You were all supposed to be there."

Roland could only say, "Everyone was taken by surprise. We've been reacting ever since. Ira, what happened to Kanna after you took her outside?"

"I laid her down in the grass and ran back to try to fetch Clive as well, but by the time I parted the flames, he was gone. And by the time I returned to the spot where she had lain, she had been taken by the Partisans." Ira reached for me suddenly and I shied back. He at least had the grace to look chagrined as he pulled his hand back. "Sorry, I just thought I saw..." He put the hand over his heart. "That's the Circle's ring in your ear, isn't it. What I felt as I was drawing near... that was you being initiated."

"Both of us, actually," I said.

"Ah." His gaze darted to Clive, then back to me. "Ah."

Roland seemed to sense that when Ira was reduced to speaking in single syllables, it was time to make his move. "A lot has happened the past three days." When Roland stepped forward this time, Ira let himself be led away. As they moved down the hall I could hear Roland saying, "Why don't I fill you in while we look for some clothes that'll fit you?"

That left just me and Clive, Jair and Kish in the kitchen. I sat back down while Kish threw one last look toward the empty doorway. "Well," she said, "welcome to the Circle of Light, anyway."

Clive was also staring at the space where Ira had been. "Thanks. I think."

"Anything you want to tell us, now that you can?" I asked.

Jair laughed. "Oh, just, everything. And there's a lot. Kish and I have been here, what, a year? Year and a half? And we've only scratched the surface."

"Yeah. Here's one thing," Kish said. "Not that it probably matters much to you guys, but I figure someone ought to warn you that it goes beyond the whole 'no secrets' thing. Any time you get hot and bothered, the rest of us are going to know." She kicked Jair playfully under the table. "Which means several times a day for certain people."

"So I'm easily attracted to people," Jair said. "So what?"

"Just saying. But seriously, any questions? We got answers."

Clive and I shared a look. "Millions," he said. "I'm trying to think what's most pressing."

I had a few, but the first one was maybe a little obvious. "So what's the deal with Ira, anyway? I'm amazed you guys put up with him."

Jair laughed softly. "He's not so bad once you get past all the posturing. He's a natural at the practice with a ton of power."

"Way more powerful than Roland," Kish agreed, "and picking it up faster than the two of us. Plus he and Kanna are a package deal. And she's just as strong as he is. What she's not is all full of herself." She smirked. "Ira knows his ego's too big and that's why we dunk on him all the time."

"Okay, sure, but did Ira really think Clive caused the fire?" Egotism I could ignore, but being illogical or hypocritical, I couldn't, and I felt like what Ira had just said while arguing with me kind of contradicted his earlier statement. "And what the hell was that spell he hit us with when he came in?"

"It's called the Hand of Lust, but *doooon't* call it a spell," Jair said with a touch of sarcasm.

Kish tapped her chin. "I think Ira jumped to the same conclusion we did: that you've got to be a Partisan, and since you rescued Clive, he must be in on it, too…?"

"There's way too much jumping to conclusions around here." Jair rubbed the spot under his clavicle where Ira had bitten him. "But when you only have scraps of information to go on, you get in the habit of doing it."

Kish shrugged. "Well, they also say 'trust your instincts' a lot."

That was funny for me to hear, since that was basically all I'd done since my first encounter with the practice. I had tried to follow my instincts and draw logical conclusions. So many things about the practice just seemed to fit some intrinsic sense of mine about how the world worked— or ought to. I had to admit, it was a powerful experience to feel so validated.

And I had been right about most things. Though obviously not all: "So tell me why what I did at the end of our initiation was a bad thing. Was it like what Ira just tried to do to us?"

"No, it's different," Jair said. "We all consented to being in the circle with you. It's just that you don't know your own strength."

Kish poked him. "That's not what she means."

"Plus you didn't bite anyone, either."

She poked him harder. "I mean she needs to hear about the long life stuff."

"So tell her! Nothing's stopping you." He dodged as she tried to—I think—tickle him in the ribs, but he managed to bend out of her reach without getting out of his chair.

"Fine." Kish gathered her thoughts. "With the long life techniques you're basically transforming your body into being sustained by aether instead of physical needs like food. The thing is, though, every time you have certain physical experiences it resets you back to 'normal.' Which means you have to start over."

"Yeah," Jair jumped in. "It's kind of like you have a certain amount of mileage on your tires before they wear out. When you perfect the long life techniques, the rubber no longer rubs the road—you glide right over the top."

Kish gave him a skeptical look even though, as I would eventually learn, that wasn't one of Jair's weirder analogies. "You'll still eventually wear down. No one's immortal. But the younger you start and the more you do it… Niko could live two hundred or more years, he thinks."

Imagine being only 18 and wanting to live to 200. When I was 18 my main goal had been to get to 21. "So how was what I did different from what you do, Kish?"

"When I make the champagne cork pop, I don't feel it myself," she said. "Whereas you kind of drew us all into your orgasm and sent us all over the edge."

Jair closed his eyes, and made a sound like he savored the memory. "I've never felt anything like it."

I was surprised. "Really? Even after all you've done in the practice?"

"Mm. I've had a lot of mind-blowing sex in ritual space," he said, "but that was the first time I think I experienced an orgasm with every cell in my entire body? Usually when I come really hard it starts here," he pointed to his groin, "and radiates outward. But this was like what if my whole body was one… giant nerve."

Kish snorted. "I thought you were going to say 'one big dick.'"

Jair snickered. "No, that's Ira."

TWENTY-SEVEN

Jair looked over his shoulder, but it was Niko coming down the hall, not Ira. Our young Wisdomkeeper slumped into a chair. "Hi. Is there any leftover pizza? I figure since I fell off the wagon I may as well." Then he noticed the boxes on the table in front of him. "Oh my god. This is even better."

He proceeded to demolish a good portion of the fried chicken leftovers, the way I'd expect an 18-year-old to. "By the way, Mira," he said, trying to talk even though his mouth was full, "that technique you did at the end, it has a name. That was a Sunburst."

"Yeah, sorry about that," I said. "I didn't know."

"It's all right." He had a piece of chicken in each hand. "I'm only in caesura for 2-3 months at a stretch right now. The main thing is, I guess, with energetic practice, you just have to be cognizant of when you trigger a release. That's what an orgasm actually is."

"Not just a euphemism," Jair said with a chuckle.

"It can create a lot of chaos, so it pays to be careful. Sometimes things will break loose that you may not intend." He wiped sauce from his lip and then picked up another piece of chicken. "I'll tell you one thing, though. I think you didn't just add yourself to the Circle; you actually strengthened the bond of the entire Circle."

"Is that good?"

He nodded, mouth too full to speak for a moment.

That made me feel a bit better, though I could still see the stricken look in Saira's eye whenever I thought back to it. "Will Saira be all right, too?"

"I'm sure she'll be fine. We're both… fine." He blushed and looked up from the food. "Oh, here they come."

Roland and Ira—all cleaned up, with his blond hair damply gleaming and wearing someone's secondhand clothes—came into the kitchen a few moments later. I'd never seen Ira not dressed up in scene clothes of some kind. He looked somewhat out of place in a rather lumberjacky flannel shirt and artfully faded jeans.

The first words out of his mouth were to me: "Which hospital did you say Wex was in?"

I told him and he nodded and left the room immediately.

At the time it seemed a bit brusque. I'd been expecting at least another ego clash or something. But the good news was Ira had some kind of doctor privileges at Wex's hospital. He returned to the kitchen to announce that he and Roland would go and have a look at him, and if it seemed all right, they'd bring him back here.

"How the hell are you going to do that?" I was all for getting Wex out of the hospital if that was what was best for him, but it wasn't like they could just waltz in and carry out an unconscious man.

"I can arrange for him to be transferred to another facility," Ira explained. "And we'll intercept the transfer."

"And what, just sneak him out on a gurney when no one's looking?"

"Some simple hypnosis may be required." Ira spoke with an irritating calmness.

"And that's legal? I mean, allowed by the practice?" I looked back and forth between Jair and Roland.

"The ambulance drivers will come to no harm and suffer no worries," Ira assured me in that forcibly nonchalant voice of his. "Do we have consensus?"

Each of us spoke in turn, and I realized it was a kind of ritual unto itself:

Clive: "I just want him somewhere safe."

Me: "I just want him out of the hospital. He's too vulnerable there."

Jair: "And where the Partisans can't use him as a pawn. Get him on our side of the game board, as it were."

Roland: "And if we can return him to consciousness, which I hope we can, we may be able to learn something important about the Partisans."

Kish: "Something we can use against them. We've been way too defensive. We need to go on the offensive, if we can."

Niko: "I'm eager to have a look at the markings on his back."

"Then it's decided." Ira looked around at us in turn. "I hope you will all lend similar support to the recovery of my wife."

"As if we wouldn't?" Jair asked.

"I merely do not wish for her to be forgotten," Ira said, prickly as a Wartenberg Wheel. "I understand we have a dagger than might point in her direction?"

"No one's been forgotten," Roland said, maybe just a tad irked. "Come on. One rescue at a time."

As they left the house, I could hear Ira speculating to Roland on techniques that might be used to locate Kanna.

An hour went by while they were gone, maybe two? I was in a state of anticipation so keen it hurt. I kept telling myself Wex was going to be fine. He was so close to being safe. The Partisans of Fire probably didn't even know he was alive, much less where he was, and so it wasn't like they were going to jump out and blow up the ambulance. Right? But the images of Clive's kitchen counter going up in flames, the smoke pouring out of my apartment window, the fireball erupting from the stone hearth at the party... I kept seeing them in my mind as I helped Niko prepare a bed for Wex.

"Is he going to need an IV?" I asked. The bed was in a room with a small window facing the back garden. White lace curtains muted the sunlight that filtered through. Niko plopped a heap of bedclothes straight out of the linen closet onto the bare mattress.

"I hope not," he said, as he started picking through the sheets. "I think from what you and Jair described that his condition is more likely ethereal than medical in nature." He handed me two pillow cases and I started wrestling them onto the pillows. "Although maybe it's not accurate to say so. The line between where western medical science leaves off and the practice picks up is a very blurred one."

"I think it's even more blurred in TCM and acupuncture," I said.

"TCM?"

"Traditional Chinese Medicine. That's what the textbooks call it. I only have a passing familiarity with it, really." Right then the acupressure points on my thumb and the palm of my hand felt sore and I wondered if my period was about to hit.

He extracted a fitted sheet from the pile. "Why do they call it 'TCM,' then?"

I took one end of the sheet and he the other and we got it stretched over the mattress without too much trouble. "I'm not sure, but I'm going to guess TCM sounds more modern and science-y than 'traditional Chinese medicine.'"

"Yeah, that sounds a little too much like 'ancient Chinese secret.'" Niko snorted a lot like Jair and I wondered if he'd picked up the mannerism from him. He gestured upward—toward the library—and spoke about his collection of New Age books. "A lot of those how-to and self-help people go on about the Chinese five-element theory and feng shui and stuff and it may as well be about Jedi knights and elven waybread or whatever."

"Because it's a bunch of orientalism that might as well be wholly fiction?"

"Oh, that's just one of the reasons they might as well have just made it all up. In fact, I have to conclude that some of those people missed their calling as fiction writers. I mean, even if there's a tiny grain of truth that served as the inspiration, why would you try to turn your fantasies into advice?"

"Oh, that's easy," I told him. "Lots of those books are part of get-rich-quick scheme. Too much 'faith healing' is about making money, not healing people. Acupuncture's real, though."

"How do you know?" He fluffed out the matching top sheet. "Or is it that people have believed it for thousands of years, and because they've believed it for so long, it becomes real?"

"Well, if the guy who taught our unit on TCM in massage school is to be believed, the roots of acupuncture are scientific, even if a lot of the ancient texts attribute the illnesses to demons." Talking like that was helping distract me from worrying about Wex, for a little while at least. "Chinese doctors thousands of years ago knew that cutting people open had an unacceptably high mortality rate, so they didn't allow surgery. Instead they had to learn to diagnose and treat people through other means. They wrote everything down and tested their hypotheses, and figured out how it worked."

"Huh." He folded the sheet down at the bottom of the bed and I was reminded we were making the bed up for someone unconscious. "And you say it really works."

"Yes, there's no doubt. Even in the English-speaking world, there are thousands of papers proving that acupuncture works and it isn't the placebo effect. What made Western medical doctors so skeptical of it and treat it like mystical woo-woo stuff was, well…"

"Racism?"

He made me laugh a little with that. "Yes, of course." Western cultural imperialism, even. "But I was going to say that it was because they couldn't explain *how* it worked. *That* it worked is not in any dispute, but since they couldn't map it onto western models of physiology, muscles and nerves, etc… they tried to dismiss it as nothing more than hocus pocus."

"Tried to? They aren't still trying to?"

"Well, that's kind of a test of faith for any scientist, right? If you believe in science as a principle, and science can't explain a thing… even though the scientific method seems to proves a thing exists… do you believe in the thing, or not? Most Western medical science came down on the side of 'we don't believe it,' but many medical practitioners were seeing benefits for patients, and so they started to recommend it more and more."

"That's good, right?"

"It's good if people are getting the care they need, yeah. But here's the thing. Some guys had dug in their heels about how it had to be hocus pocus. They said, well, science can't explain it, so I can't believe in it. But the thing is… now science *can* explain it."

"Oh, really?"

"Yeah, and some of these guys who had dug in their heels because they were *soooooo* married to science, turned out to be no better than fundamentalist religious zealots. They still refuse to believe, even though the science has gotten good enough to offer an explanation. They can't revise their worldview even in the face of scientific evidence."

"You mean science can explain acupuncture now?"

"Science is getting close, anyway. Western medicine's explanations started from some bad assumptions, but now that our ability to measure things going on in the body is much much finer than even twenty years ago, some of those assumptions are finally getting overturned." I should have known Niko would soak up stuff like that like a sponge, but I was still getting to know him at that point. I think maybe he was enjoying being the one asking the questions instead of answering them, for a change.

"What kind of assumptions?"

"Oh, like the one that all signals including pain and sensation are exclusively transmitted along the nerve pathways. It seems logical at first that the nerves would be involved, right? But it turns out there is a completely separate pathway for signals to travel throughout the body, which was completely ignored by western medicine until recently. The entire body is interlaced with a network of collagen called the fascia. And where the fascia is thickest is where the acupuncture points are. Turns out that's no coincidence. Western medicine at first rejected the idea that the fascia could carry any kind of signal. But it turns out collagen is piezoelectric."

"Sounds important. What does 'piezoelectric' mean?"

"It means something that generates electricity when you put pressure on it." When I was a kid we'd done an experiment in science class where we'd made tiny light bulbs light up by pressing on a little pad. "Like when you press on an acupuncture point."

"Or put a needle into it?"

"You can even stick a magnet on it."

He turned a bit skeptical at that one: "Is that why sometimes athletes wear necklaces and bracelets with magnets in them?"

"Oh, *those*." I put the pillows at the top of the bed. "It's like you said. There's a tiny grain of truth wrapped up in all the wishful thinking. There's no way a magnet on a string around your neck actually improves your balance or 'energy flow.' But it's probably important for competitive athletes to feel invincible or like they have an edge. If wearing a magnet—or a lucky rabbit foot or whatever—makes them feel stronger, it probably works for them. But I doubt the magnet is ultimately anything more than a good luck talisman."

"That's what I thought." He sat on the bed and looked up at me with a small frown. "The thing is, finding where that line is, between when things work because it's the way things work, and when things work because people *believe* they work and that belief alone gives them power… that's the hard part. And sometimes, like maybe for those athletes, it doesn't even matter. All that matters is that it works."

"I think science will eventually be able to explain everything," I said. "Even the practice, if they ever found out about it. It's just that knowledge isn't there yet. Look at how many scientific theories were considered sound at the time, which now look quaint to us. Like the four humours, or that the sun went around the earth and not the other way around."

"You mean someday maybe that's how humanity will look back on, like, nuclear energy and modern medical practices?"

"Yeah." Which led me to another thought. How did Ira and Kanna, two modern medical professionals, get involved with the Circle of Light? But before I could ask that, we both got texts from Roland saying they were on their way back. With Wex.

TWENTY-EIGHT

So, at last, Wex was at The Archive, all in one piece and looking merely like he was asleep, as if he might wake up at any moment.

Niko, Roland, Ira, and I gathered in the small room by his bedside, Clive in the doorway. Ira kept giving me begrudging looks, as if he still suspected me of nefarious purposes and wasn't sure I had a right to be there.

You bet I had a right to be there. I was Wex's oldest friend, and he mine, and without me they wouldn't have even known where he was.

Ira brushed Wex's bangs away from his eyes tenderly and said something I wholeheartedly agreed with, however: "I want to punish whoever did this to him."

Niko was more concerned with practical matters. "Can we flip him over so we can get a better look at the markings on his back?"

As Roland and Ira reached for him, I said, "You don't have to turn him all the way over. Bend his knee and you can…" I gave up trying to describe the position and just moved him myself. There are ways to work on a client's back without putting them flat on their face. When people lie face down they can't breathe well and their necks get twisted, unless you have a massage table with a head cradle or keyhole for the face. The last thing we needed was Wex smothering in his own pillow.

I put him in position, the sheet draped over his hip and legs. He was heavily limp and unmoving, but we could see the lines engraved into his skin quite clearly.

Ira traced one of the symbols with his fingertips. "The diagnosis seems to have been that loss of blood caused his comatose state. But none of these cuts look like they would've bled that much."

"Tell Jair that," I said, thinking of the way the bleeding wouldn't stop where he'd been cut.

"I don't think this is like that," Roland said quickly, like he wanted to forestall an argument. "Jair got cut in a fight. These marks were made for a different purpose."

Niko pointed to one of the symbols. "That's the sigil that means 'place' or 'site.'" He exchanged a glance with me. He was right. Wex's problem was more spiritual than biological.

"Yes, and this one." Ira framed Wex's shoulder with the L of his hand. "It's seeking or finding, is it not? That answers one question, at least. This is how the Partisans gleaned the location of my home."

Niko opened his notebook to a page with a sketch he had already made based on the photos Jair and I had taken. He jotted down something. "Yes, these two taken together are definitely 'finding a place.' And these two…" He moved Wex's arm slightly and the shape of one of the sigils changed, an oval becoming a circle. "This is the one for self or soul."

"Do you think he's out Soulwandering?" I asked.

"Come feel this," Niko said, moving his hand slowly above Wex's arm. "Clive, you, too. Tell me what you feel."

I ran my hand along the "cloud layer" Niko had described to us before.

"Now lower slowly, until you touch his skin."

I let my fingers sink through and just before my fingertips made contact with his arm, I felt… "Cold?" Just for a moment, like a slight breeze had blown.

"Yes!" Niko beamed proudly at me. "That's what I felt, too." He pointed to another sigil. "This one means basically 'still water.' I think he's in quietude."

"Quietude," Ira announced, as if I couldn't figure it out from the name, "is a dormant state similar to the one I spent the past three days in."

I decided to play along. "Similar to? How is it different?"

"Ultimately, it's not," Niko said, before Ira could answer. "We could put him in a tomb and leave him for a few decades, and he'd ultimately be fine."

"Even though he's breathing…?"

"He doesn't have to," Niko answered, putting a hand on Wex's and squeezing it gently. "Not that I am suggesting we do that, of course."

So much for me worrying we might smother him accidentally. Still, the thought of putting him in a tomb made my own skin feel chilled. Ominous. "And you think the symbols are keeping him… frozen like this?"

"Yes. But…" Roland squinted at the markings, at the lines that went up and down Wex's upper arms, the parallel tracks across the top of his shoulder. "What about these here?"

Niko considered. "I don't think they have a meaning. They must've played a different role in the working?"

"Those marks look pretty standard for a cutting scene," I heard myself saying, even as I was trying to blink away the image forming in my mind of Wex's skin streaked with dripping blood. "Each one is done with a straight razor." My hands were starting to shake. Did he scream while they cut him or was he silent with terror? "Good god."

To my surprise, Ira was the one who took my hands in his. "It's all right, Mira. Wexel enjoyed the bite of a razor. We don't know that he suffered. Maybe… maybe as far as he knew it was a consensual scene and they didn't start using him as a human GPS until after he was unconscious."

"How…" I had to swallow to make my throat work. "How did they even think to do this."

"Usually the circle would be drawn upon the floor." Ira's voice was calm, like he was trying to soothe me, but his words were anything but. "In chalk, or ash, or even blood. I see no reason why it couldn't be drawn upon a person, though. Ingenious, really."

I pulled away. I couldn't shake the fear that Wex had been in terror and grave distress. I remembered what Jair had said about what made us the good guys and the Partisans the bad guys. They abuse consent and we don't. Would they have tortured him just because they could?

I felt Clive's arm around me and I leaned against him.

"I would like to believe that he didn't suffer." Niko's voice was grave and it made him sound far older than his years. "But his mind probably went into retreat because of the trauma. The Partisans would have used the energy of his emotional state to fuel the Finding. And then they sealed him like this." He gestured at the markings. "An untrained person like Wex probably couldn't achieve such a perfect state of quietude by accident. But the markings ensure it. The question is, why? What were they saving him for?"

"To use as a hostage or bargaining chip later?" Clive suggested.

"Perhaps?" Ira joined in. "Or just to keep him out of the way without having to deal with the complication of a dead body and the psychic backlash of a murder."

Niko folded his fingers intricately. "I think we shouldn't try to rouse him until we're ready to deal with healing what trauma he may have."

My fingers closed around Clive's wrist like I was gripping the hilt of a sword. "And tracking down those who did this to him wouldn't help heal that trauma?"

"Well, it might, but he might not be able to tell us much that would help with that. When the mind goes into sudden retreat, you can lose a chunk of memory." Niko shivered a little as he said that.

"We do have one lead, though," Roland said. "We know where he was found."

That shook me from my reverie. (Or at least the blood I was imagining was no longer Wex's.) "We do?"

Ira simply nodded while Roland provided the details: "In the hospital records, Ira was able to find out the address."

"Well, what are we waiting for?" I was already starting my mental checklist of where my phone, jacket, and shoes were, prepping to leave. "Shouldn't that be our next stop?"

"Only if you believe that location to be of greater importance than Kanna's," Ira said, voice as low as a growl.

Roland made shooing motions with his hands. "If we're going to debate our next move, I insist we do it with all present. Hanging over Wexel's bed is not the place for it."

I headed for the kitchen table, since that was where every previous debate had taken place, but Roland gathered everyone in the classroom parlor. We arranged the chair-desks in a circle and sat.

Ira started right in, insisting to Kish, "Let me see this blade you recovered."

Roland thumped his fist against the desk he was sitting in and I swear I heard it echo as if he'd banged a gavel. "I'm the Convenor and I'm in charge of this meeting."

Ira shrank down in his chair a bit, scribbling something in a notebook he'd opened in front of him.

"Oh, that reminds me," Niko said, before Roland could say anything more. He pulled open a cabinet at the back of the room and took out two fresh composition books. He handed one to me and one to Clive. "Now that you're actually members of the Circle."

"Niko, I thought we hadn't decided on that yet," Roland said.

"Decided on what?" I asked, confused if our already-finished initiation was somehow in question, but no, Roland's question was about the notebooks, not us.

Niko folded his arms. "I'm the Wisdomkeeper and this is my decision to make. Every single one of you needs to start keeping a diary ASAP."

"But—" That was all the objection Roland got out. One word.

Niko cut right across him. "No buts. This used to be the common practice, and if Gabriel hadn't been such an egotistical fool, we wouldn't be in this mess right now." He gulped and drew a deep breath. "We're called the Circle of Light for a reason. And I won't leave the next Wisdomkeeper stumbling in the dark."

"Assuming there is a next Wisdomkeeper," Ira muttered.

Niko faced him, something like fury on his normally cheerful face. "If you're not making that assumption, then we've already lost. If you're not living every day like we're going to win this battle, then you may as well go out and slit your own throat in the middle of Fifth Avenue."

Ira nodded. "No disrespect intended, Wisdomkeeper."

"None taken," Niko said, and looked around at each of us. His voice returned to his usual mild tone. "Look. I know keeping a diary is not as exciting as learning to throw knives or trigger multiple orgasms or whatever. But *do it,* okay?"

Multiple answers of "Okay" came from around the room.

"I don't know if we're ever going to replace all that was lost. But we have to try." He took his own seat, between Jair and Kish. It felt to me like he ceded the floor.

Roland called the meeting to order with two simple words: "All right." He laid out two options. "We are here to decide on our next move. We can either check out the location where Wexel was found by the paramedics, or we can prioritize techniques for locating Kanna."

"Kanna is the more urgent issue," Ira said evenly, "because if they break her, then all hope is lost. They'll know everything about us. She is strong, but no one can hold out forever. May I see the knife?"

"In a minute." Kish asked, "What are we thinking of doing with it?"

"It's a question of what the blade knows." Niko had his own notebook out and flipped through the pages. "And how we extract the information."

It was news to me that knives could know things.

"What ways are there to make the blade sing?" Roland asked.

"The Cruelest Cut is the one I've studied most," Niko said. "But I don't know how that would help. It's not like Google Maps. Jair, as the one who got cut, would have to be the one to do that."

"There are other techniques, though," Ira said, "that don't rely on the specific entanglement of wielder and victim. I believe I am sufficiently advanced to not only point in the direction of the person who wielded the knife, but also pick up some of their thoughts or visual memories."

"Just from the knife itself?" Jair asked.

"Yes. Niko, tell him what you know of Ghosting the Blade."

"No." Roland banged his fist again. "I know about Ghosting the Blade and we're not doing it. Too dangerous."

Ira shook his head. "It's no more dangerous than an evening in the dungeon with a toy scalpel. Or shouldn't be. Is the blade particularly jagged or badly compromised?"

"That's not the issue. That technique's effectiveness is dependent upon the victim's fear and resistance and we do not condone that."

"Have we established that?" Ira looked at Niko for an answer, but Niko said nothing. His voice took on a cool, almost medical tone. "This is what I've been trying to say in our previous discussions on the subject: perhaps the effects of a technique can be enhanced by such, but equivalent results should be attainable under entirely consensual, controlled conditions." He looked to me next. "Mira, you know it better than anyone here, I would bet. When you quote-unquote 'terrorize' a submissive in a scene, the *fear* is real. But the *danger* is not."

I, perhaps a tiny bit grudgingly, agreed. "That's true. But what is 'Ghosting the Blade'?"

Roland answered. "It's a technique that allows the person with the blade in hand to pull impressions from it. If I'm not mistaken, Ira is the only one of us who has done it successfully."

He nodded. "Kanna and I tested it in a knifeplay scene mere weeks ago. She held a secret, used the knife in play, then I used it, and I gleaned the secret. A fully consensual scene for all involved, I might add, in case that was unclear."

Clive shifted beside me and I recalled seeing fine scars on him while we'd ridden in the limo to the party. I reached for him like I had that night, gently finger-combing the hair away from behind his ear. Those scars were completely gone and I hadn't even noticed until that moment. (And I felt oddly glad about it.)

Ira was addressing the entire room but I felt somehow that his explanation was aimed at me. "The distress of the person feeding their blood to the blade frees the impressions it carries, and it is not difficult for me to read them as they float loose. I would of course need a completely willing volunteer to ensure consensuality."

Jair got to his feet. "I'll do it."

"No," Roland said. "Not you, because your energy's already tangled in the blade, and may I remind everyone we're still debating whether to do this or not?"

It was clear to me, though, that what we were debating wasn't whether we were going to do it, but when. "How much blood does it take to feed the blade?"

"That might depend on how much information there is to be gleaned," Ira said. "But I am going to guess. For our purposes, I believe it might take a dozen cuts—shallow ones—to get there."

A dozen shallow cuts. "Then, how about me?" I said.

Ira looked me in the eye from across the room. "I appreciate your willingness, Mira, but— not to put it too bluntly—you haven't got a submissive bone in your body. Trying to whip up—no pun intended—the head of necessary emotional foam might be simply impossible for me, with you." He looked at Roland. "And that goes for you, as well, my friend."

Clive caught my eye then. I'd already suspected that he was the bottom in the scene Ira had just described, but the moment our eyes met, I knew it for sure. I also knew he'd offer himself for this circle working… but only if I approved. As we looked at each other, it was almost like we were having a negotiation. Which went against the most important thing I'd been taught about negotiation: the need to state things aloud and not just wish or hope that you both have the same intentions.

But I could read it plain as day. He wouldn't offer himself without my okay. And he also wouldn't do it unless I would be there with him. Was I imagining it, or was I reading it?

And was I imagining the hunger in Ira's eyes as he gazed at Clive, too? Clive hadn't said anything, but he was the only one in the room who hadn't been ruled out. I felt the hairs on the back of my neck prickle.

Niko carried the debate back to its main subject. "Even assuming a best-case scenario on Ghosting the Blade, though, I still think it makes sense for us to check out the apartment first. If we find nothing there, fine. If we find some clues that help us prepare to confront the Partisans, all the better."

"And if we find the Partisans themselves, there?" Ira asked.

"Then we don't need Ghosting the Blade to locate them in the first place." He folded his hands. "Right?"

Quiet nods all around. The Wisdomkeeper had spoken.

Roland raised his hands. "All in favor of apartment recon now, working later, say 'aye.'"

Even Ira said "aye."

TWENTY-NINE

The recon plan, as it was loosely formed, was that we'd go to the building and check it out. One team of two would go up to the apartment to see what there was to be seen while the other two would stay outside the building as backup. I would drive. There were two things we did before we left. One was Jair gave Clive a burner phone to use in case we got separated.

The other thing we did to prepare for the mission was a group meditation. Because of course that's how this crew rolls.

While the others cleared their minds or found inner peace or whatever, I tried to think back over what all had been going on. Over the course of three days I'd gone from binge-watching classic anime online and checking my dwindling bank balance to a life-and-death situation fighting literal forces of evil. There had been a lot to take in and I knew I really wasn't processing it all. I had a nagging sensation in the back of my head telling me I was missing something.

I knew perfectly well that stress could make a person overlook something obvious right under their nose. I also knew that letting go of that stress sometimes could bring it suddenly to mind. Many a time I'd had a massage client on the table suddenly realize something: everything from the fact they forgot to let their dog out that morning to the telltale signs their partner was cheating on them.

So, really, meditating would have been the best thing for me to do.

I would not call obsessively replaying the moments in the parking lot or in the woods while Clive was possessed "meditative," and by the time we got up to go, I hadn't figured anything out. I had thought about how all of it had to be weird for Clive. Didn't it? Or did he feel like his worldview was being validated, too?

Anyway. It was nearly midnight by the time we left The Archive.

The place where Wex had been found was east of us, I think a little bit toward Chinatown. In my mind I had imagined his unconscious body had been dumped in an alley, but apparently not. The building took up half of a residential block and looked slightly modern—maybe 1960? Not really a building you'd take much notice of. I circled the block once while we looked for parking and scoped the place out. The neighborhood was pretty quiet, only one or two passerby on the sidewalk. Another chilly night with not much going on.

The second time around, I took us around a different block and found parking on the street about a block away from our destination. As I angled the van into the space, I asked, "So, you're going to call me if we need to make a quick getaway?"

"Yes, isn't that what we agreed?" Roland asked.

"I've been thinking about it on the drive over and it seems to me it would make more sense if we just stayed on the phone the entire time. I mean unless you guys have some kind of telepathy you haven't told me about."

"Nothing that practical," Jair said. "But I get your point. Maybe we should all be on the phone."

Roland pulled his somewhat older-looking phone out. "I don't think mine lets me do a group larger than three."

Kish looked at hers. "Three's enough. We have three teams, right? So Mira, you connect a call to me and to Jair. Clive, you connect one to Ira and to Roland. And you two are sitting right next to each other."

"That'll work." I had expected them to have some way of communicating already established. But we were all new to being guerrillas, I guess. "Next time, though, we should install one of those team-voice apps like gamers use."

"Why didn't you bring this up before?" Roland asked.

"Because I only just thought of it." I was at least as irked with him for not having thought of it in advance as he was with me. "Go on. Get moving."

Clive and I put our phones on the dashboard and listened while the others went off to their positions.

"The practice of manipulation of energetic extrasensory psychophysiology," Clive said, mostly to himself, spelling out: "T-P-M-E-E-P?"

"Teep Meep?" I said quietly, and we both laughed. "It'll never catch on."

We shushed ourselves and listened again to the sound of footsteps and clothes rustling. It felt to me like it was taking forever for them to walk a block. Sotto voce, I said to Clive, "Remind me why you and I are just sitting here?"

"Because we've got no weapons, no training, and you already proved you can drive the van?"

"Right."

"Niko says we'll be getting our own knives soon." Clive ran a hand over the bit of dark stubble on his chin, as if he could shave it with the mere thought of a sharp edge. "Dagger keeps them."

I felt a lump form in my throat. What if I didn't want a knife?

Jair's voice saved me from having to think about it right then. "Not much of a lobby here. No doorman or anything. Just a door with buzzers and a bunch of mailboxes."

Roland answered him. "Let's walk around back and see if we see anything."

Kish: "I'm almost at the front. I'm going to act like I belong here." I could hear her jingling her keys in her hand and her saying *hi* to whoever was coming out. Another woman's voice answered. I could hear doors creaking and a heavy slam. "Okay, I'm in. Letting Ira in next."

All was quiet while they rode the elevator. Jair and Roland talked in quiet voices as they checked around the dumpsters. I felt my palms sweat a little, like I was expecting them to find a body or something. But no. Nothing like that.

"You know," I said to Clive, "I wonder if we should just get walkie-talkies or something."

"Phones are probably less conspicuous," he said reasonably.

"True." Navy SEALs we are not. "If you see a Duane Reade on the way back, though, we should at least pick up some more liquid bandage. I have a feeling we're going to need it."

Clive zipped up his jacket, his collar disappearing from my sight. "Yeah."

And then we were listening to the voices through speakerphone.

Kish: We're upstairs. At the apartment door. Does that look like chalk to you?
Ira: I think it's just dust. This whole place is filthy.
Kish: Oh shit. Just tried the door. It's not locked.
Ira: The super probably just didn't lock it up again after the police left.
Kish: Or maybe they're coming back.
Ira: Let's be quick.
Kish: Place looks empty inside. No furniture to speak of. Not even a... oh, wait, one mattress. That's it. A hustler squat for sure.
Ira: If they did any kind of circle working here, I don't see any signs. No spilled wax, no chalk or other marks on the floor that we can see. The floor is a very dark color, almost black. You'd think any chalk residue would show up easily.
Clive asked: Are you using a flashlight?
Ira: Yes, I'm using a flashlight.
Roland's voice came through from one phone to the other: There are other things a circle and sigils can be drawn with besides chalk. Get a damp paper towel from the kitchen and wipe—
Kish: There's no paper towel here. This place is empty, I'm telling you. Hm. Let me see.

Silence. And then a hushed curse.

Clive: What's happening? Kish, what happened?
Kish: I licked my fingers and ran them along the floor. Either this paint job's really bad, or there are still traces of blood.
Ira: I'm just going to make sure we didn't miss something in the kitchen or bathroom.
Roland: Still all quiet down here.
Jair: Take one last look around and then let's get out of here, all right, Kish?

All we heard for another minute or two was the sound of Ira's shoes on the floors and some creaking: maybe a medicine cabinet, maybe a pantry door.

Kish: All right, heading down.
And then a door slam, a bolt being thrown. And Kish: Shit, they're here! They're in the hall.

All I could think of was the two windows of my apartment, smoke pouring out of them like dead eyes. "You have to get out of there."

Kish: We'll be targets for knife throwing practice if we go back into the hall.
Jair: We're on our way up. How many are there?

Kish: At least one, but possibly two. It was her, J. Same one.

Ira: Do you smell gas?

"Get the hell out of there," I urged. My phone was in my hand. "Take the fire escape!" All I could hear was rustling and wind, both breathing and air hissing through the microphone.

Clive had his in hand as well, and put it up to his ear. "Jair, are you there?"

I handed him my phone as well, and started the engine. He had one phone on either side of his head and was speaking to all of them at once: "We'll pull the van around toward the dumpsters. We'll hang back as long as we—"

He broke off as we heard something low and loud echo off the high-rises around us. "Was that an explosion?"

My heart felt like it was in my mouth. Through the speaker I heard Kish's voice, though: "Motherfucker!"

At least she was alive. I clenched my jaw as I eased the van around a corner, trying not to attract attention, but I really wanted to gun the engine and speed over. I told myself Kish was cursing at Ira instead of locked in deadly combat with some knife-wielding foe.

Turned out I was right. "Kish says she made it down a few floors," Clive reported, "but Ira's too heavy to drag much farther."

"Tell her to smack him in the face," I said, not even joking. "I see Roland ahead!"

Roland was running toward us. He hopped into the back of the van and pulled the door shut behind him.

"Where's Jair?" I asked.

"Still inside, last I heard from him," he answered. "But the streets are about to flood with people escaping the building." I could already see a woman in a bathrobe, her hair still in its night wrap, pulling a child wearing pajamas and basketball sneakers by the hand.

"He's on his way down," Clive said. "Says he lost them in the crowd. He's almost at ground level."

"Tell him I don't dare get that close to the building or we'll get stuck. I'm cutting up the side street by the basketball courts." We needed to get away from the crowd of people and make sure we didn't get blocked in by any emergency vehicles. As I scanned the sidewalks for Partisans, cops, Jair, anyone who might mean anything, my brain was racing. That was an ambush. We'd walked right into it. We'd tried to be proactive and all we'd done is prove that the Partisans of Fire were one step ahead of us.

Roland patted my shoulder and pointed. "There he is."

I couldn't help but rush up the street to Jair, and then rush away before we could get trapped.

"Keep going," Jair said, as he gripped on to the divider between the driver's seats and the back. "We need to get back to The Archive. Fast."

"Aren't we going back for Kish and Ira?"

Clive put my phone into his pocket. "Fire department's already on the way. She says a paramedic in the building is helping them down."

"Okay, but—"

"Mira," Jair's voice was sharp on my name, and then soft in plea: "I've been trying to contact Niko and I'm not getting any answer."

Everyone cursed one way or another. Roland put his head in his hands.

I made a sudden turn to head away from the building. "This was a setup."

"Yeah, I get that feeling," Jair agreed.

"But even if we walked right into the lion's den," Clive said. "How would that lead them to Niko? It's not like they know where we came *from*."

"Roland," I asked, because he seemed the most likely to know, "is there some way they could have reversed a finding spell on us or something?"

"Don't call it a spell," he muttered. "And we didn't even do a Finding, remember? The address came out of police records."

Right. "Then they must have followed Wex somehow." My skin prickled at the thought.

"From the hospital? Seems a long shot—"

I had to slam the brake a little bit hard as a light changed at the intersection in front of us. "You said the sigils they marked him with were for location and finding, right?"

"Yeah."

"What if the thing they locate is *Wex himself*?"

Roland shook his head, but what he said was, "And the reason they drew the circle on his skin wasn't just to use his blood for the inscription but... Christ, Mira, you may be right."

Jair cursed again. "He was bait and we took it."

I turned the van westward, making as much of a bee line toward The Archive as I could, and wondering if we'd find it in flames. Would Niko flee the building? Would that just drive him right into their hands? What if they'd gotten to him already? And what about Wex, who was lying there, unconscious? Niko wouldn't be able to carry him even if he wanted to.

Jair whooped suddenly. "Text from Niko!"

The text was just one sobering word: *Hurry.*

THIRTY

As I navigated us through the densely packed neighborhood, closer and closer to whatever we would find at The Archive, Roland filled the anxious silence by relaying to us what Kish was telling him.

"Ira's fine. They're a couple blocks away from the fire now. No sign of pursuit. She caught sight of that woman again, for sure, and another man, but not Barrow."

"That's because Barrow is at The Archive," Jair said.

"You're sure?"

"Unfortunately. Niko's hiding in the vault downstairs, but that's making it a bit hard to get texts in and out. He's safe for the moment, at least."

Across the street from the van's usual garage I could see a delivery truck pulling away. That was good luck on our side. I pulled into the spot it had vacated and turned off the engine.

"He says Barrow's inside the building, but it seems like he doesn't know Niko's even there."

Roland looked downcast. "Losing the safety of The Archive is a huge blow."

"Can you worry about that later?" I snapped. "We need to figure out how to get our people out of there. How did Barrow get past the aegis?"

"Probably had a taste of Kanna's blood." Jair unconsciously bit his lip. "I could go in there and keep Barrow busy while Niko escapes?"

"He won't hesitate to kill you," Roland said. "Mira, I'm sorry, but we're going to have to leave Wex behind. If we take him with us, Barrow will be able to track us anywhere."

My skin crawled with cold. "We can't just leave him in Barrow's hands, though."

"We don't have any other choice."

My mind was already racing, trying to cook up another choice. There's always another choice, right? The human brain likes to think things are always either/or, but there are (almost) never only two options. You've never thought of every possibility. "Are those marks permanent? Isn't there some way they can be erased?"

Roland wasn't in the mood to be challenged right then. "As you may have noticed, they were cut into his skin."

"But they were just scratches, really, not deep scars."

"They'd heal in time," Jair said. "But I don't know a way to speed that up."

"Clive had similar markings just a few days ago and now they're completely gone," I pointed out. "Something wiped his slate clean."

Clive ran a hand down his own neck. "She's right. They've been gone since some time the night of the party. But I don't know what caused them to fade."

Damn. I had been hoping there was some kind of simple circle working we could do to heal him. "Could the marks be disrupted somehow, then? Crossed out? Could they be rewritten?"

Roland looked ill. Jair stopped texting with Niko for a moment and touched my arm lightly. "Even if they could, it would mean cutting an unconscious person. That's considered…" He searched for the right word, and came up with: "Wrong."

"I'm sure Wex wouldn't mind us leaving some marks on him if it meant he was no longer a homing beacon for a homicidal pyromaniac," I said.

"How wrong?" Clive asked.

Jair drew his knife from his boot. "Ask yourself if instead of putting this through his skin, we were talking about penetrating him with this." He patted his crotch.

"Are you serious? Penetrative sex and marking the skin are one and the same to the practice of … of… energetic psychopathology?"

"Psychophysiology," Roland corrected me, "and yes, a breach is a breach."

"But if the choice is between being breached and being left to die in a burning building, you don't think Wex would choose not to die?"

"This isn't an ethics philosophy quiz," Roland snapped. "If you breach without willingness, you… you… do damage to your soul. You…you…"

"You go to the dark side of the goddamn Force," Jair finished for him. "You get it now?"

Yes. I got it. That was what the Partisans did. They were willing to rape and kill and perform other feats without consent, and we were not. "What kind of damage to your soul?"

"The kind that leaves you inhuman," Roland said. The dark circles under his eyes were deepening.

"And leaving him here to die is so humane," I snapped, even though I knew it was an impossible choice.

"Maybe if I can get Barrow to chase me out back while we fight, you'll have time to get Wex out the front door?" Jair suggested. He tapped some more on his phone and I wondered if he was relaying everything we were saying to Niko or what.

"That only works if you can beat him," Roland said. "Otherwise he'll just follow wherever we go."

I couldn't even imagine how Jair was supposed to fight someone who would kill him without hesitation, but to whom Jair couldn't do the same. "Does it have to be a fight?" I asked. "What if we could lure him out some other way?"

"Like what?"

"I don't know. Is there some magical way to get his attention?" I knew I'd hit on something when no one scolded me not to call it magic. "You know, like Hand of Lust: That's very attention-getting."

Jair couldn't help but smirk. "That's one word for it…"

"Not very practical, though." Roland looked deep in thought.

"Is there some way for me to flash my metaphorical tits at him?" I asked.

"It shouldn't be you," Clive said. "Why not someone who knows how to fight him?"

"A fight we can't win," Roland said. He looked pointedly at Clive. "I think there is someone else who might seem much more enticing to him, though."

Clive took the not-subtle hint, looking at me for permission. "What do you need me to do?"

And I looked back at Roland. "Why Clive?"

"Because he's the one submissive we've got."

Clive began to object. "You know I think of submission as—"

"Something you do, not something you are, I know," Roland said. "Let me put it this way. When you're in a state to be taken, you'll shine like a beacon to every dominant moth in the area."

"And Barrow doesn't know you." Jair was warming to the plan. "He'll be curious and might approach with some caution…"

"As long as you can lure him out of the house. Then he won't sense us coming in through the front door." Roland craned his neck but The Archive was out of sight, around the corner from where we were sitting.

Jair looked at his phone. "Niko says he can tell Barrow just broke the seal on the chest in the main room. So he's on the first floor right now."

I looked at Clive. "How do we put Clive in a 'state to be taken'?"

Roland swallowed. "That's easy. Just remove his collar."

Clive's face was close to mine, his eyes shining like moonlit water. "I'm willing."

The lump had returned to my throat. Everything I'd said earlier about how much I feared that Clive's submission to me wasn't really want he wanted, and that it would evaporate once his collar was off, welled up and stuck there. My voice came out rough. "I know you are."

He touched his forehead to mine. "It's the best plan."

"Yes, it is." I may have sounded like I was trying to convince myself. Time was wasting. And I could not put my emotional fears ahead of Niko's safety. But I could ask a practical question: "How do we make sure your soul doesn't go wandering off?"

"My lady," he said, and I could feel the warmth of his breath on my own lips. "There are other forms of control."

I kissed him then, long and deep, and a hungry voice at the back of my head asked why I hadn't done it sooner, why I hadn't done it a hundred times before then, plundering his mouth with my tongue like I wanted to meld. When we broke for air, I put my hands on the back of his neck, on the string of beads, and said, "You come back to me."

I felt him swallow. "I will, my lady."

I slipped my finger under the strand, wondering what I had to do to get it off. What was really holding that broken rosary together? Was it really just my will?

I thought about a saying that I used to see a lot on tacky motivational posters—*If you love something, set it free*—and I pulled.

It worked. The strand came loose in my hands and Clive sucked in a little gasp. I held back a sob, clutching the beads to my chest where it felt like there was a sudden, gaping hole.

He shed his jacket and his shirt, then put the jacket back on, leaving a stripe of exposed skin from throat to belt buckle. Then he handed me my phone.

He pulled a pair of wireless headphones from his pocket. "You should stay with the van, my lady. But stay with me this way." He put them in his ears.

I wanted to say "be careful" but it felt ridiculous. The only words that felt right were the ones I had already said: *You come back to me*. I blew him a kiss.

He blew one back and then hurried down the sidewalk toward the garage.

Jair watched him go. "We'll move out as soon as we get the word. I'll tell Niko to flee out the front and Roland and I can grab Wex."

Wex? "I thought we—"

"Niko has a plan for dealing with Wex. If we can get him out of there," Jair said.

That was good enough for me. "All right. Clive, did you hear that?"

"Yes, my lady."

"Stop calling me that right now." I tried to make my tone light, but it was hard to joke about. "You're supposed to be fresh submissive meat for our dom apex predator."

He chuckled, regaining his cheer more quickly than me. Was that because he felt good when freed? "Then I better get off the street, before some wannabe leatherdaddy tries to pick me up." I could hear the sound change as he made his way into the garage and out the back. "It's all quiet back here. Hardly any lights on. I'm almost at the patio."

"Okay. Hush now, angel."

Jair shot me a look. I think it was the first time I'd used my pet name for Clive in front of the group. (Maybe it was the first time I even realized I had a pet name for him.)

Clive, as instructed, was silent.

I put my hands over my own headphones, straining to hear his footfalls against the bricks and stone. I could hear his breath—or maybe that was my own.

Then, a creak and a thump of wood. The back door opening?

Yes. And Barrow's voice. "Well, what have we here?"

I shooed Jair and Roland out, and they hurried around the corner.

I had not been expecting Barrow to sound British, but there it was. "A lost little fledgling come back to the nest?" His voice grew louder as he must have been nearing Clive. "A stray pup?"

"Who are you?" Clive asked.

"You must be one of the new recruits for Roland's army. Someone must have told you not to look me in the eye." He sounded quite close. "Ah, I think I recognize you from Kanna's dreams. You're the one who suffers beautifully."

"I…what? She thinks I'm beautiful?" He sounded genuinely confused. (Yes, Clive, we all think you're beautiful.)

"There is inner beauty and outer beauty, and when you suffer, the inner is exposed. Hasn't Roland taught you that?"

"Not… exactly. Aesthetics hasn't really come up." Clive said.

"What has Roland promised you? Pleasure? Pain so sublime you believe you've ascended? Eternal life?"

I know Clive was trying to keep Barrow talking, to keep him occupied, but I wondered if he meant it when he said, "I'm not interested in any of those things."

"You don't have to fear me," Barrow said. "I know Roland has been filling your head with nonsense about good and evil. If he would listen to the truth, we wouldn't have to be enemies."

Clive didn't answer and I wondered what was happening. Then I felt a downward tug on my heart and somehow knew Clive had fallen to his knees.

"What's your name, puppy?"

Clive did not answer except maybe that was him making a small, high-pitched sound at the back of his throat. I heard a scuffling sound, and then Barrow's voice very, very close in my ear, "Ah-ah-ah, no running away."

And then I heard the unmistakeable click of a switchblade opening, and I was out of the van and running before I could stop myself. When I burst out onto the patio, they were frozen like a modern dance tableau, Clive almost flattened backward on his knees, Barrow arching over him, his knife arm outstretched. In any other circumstance it would have been a beautiful sight, maybe even an arousing one, but all it made me want to do was hurl myself between them.

From his voice, I guess, I'd been expecting Barrow to look like Ira, only older. So I was surprised to find him both much darker and younger-looking than I expected—but maybe he was using the long-life techniques to live much longer than his apparent mileage. His hair and eyes were black and he looked trim and muscular in just a black T-shirt and cargo pants.

"Another lost lamb?" Barrow looked from Clive to me. "Another of Roland's misguided flock?"

Once I was standing there, of course, it occurred to me I'd rushed out there without a plan. I had Clive's collar clutched in one hand, no knife, and no idea what to do. I decided to play dumb. "Um, excuse me? Could you guys keep it down out here?" I remembered we weren't supposed to look him in the eye, so I focused on the edge of a tattoo that showed on his chest above the collar of his T-shirt. "People are trying to sleep."

"Who are you?" Barrow demanded.

"Just a neighbor."

"Liar."

I shrugged. I had to keep him talking until I could figure out how to get Clive away from him. "I take it you are Barrow."

A tiny nod of his head. "You have me at a disadvantage, then."

"Mira," I told him.

"Meera?" He cocked his head, but otherwise neither he nor Clive moved a muscle. "Like… the poet?"

"Like the Spanish word for 'look' or 'watch out.'" I don't know why I told him that. I was just trying to buy time. "I had a nanny when I was a child who said it so often, trying to get me to pay attention, that I thought it was my name."

"Ahhh, a *true* name rather than a mundane name," he said, and I hoped I hadn't just given him some kind of fairy-tale power over me.

"You know, *Look!*" I pointed to the door as I shouted it, and to my surprise, the diversion worked. His head jerked reflexively to look over his shoulder at the house, and Clive scrambled back out of his reach. Barrow slashed at the empty air angrily, sliver blade flashing with reflected light.

Clive got to his feet beside me. It was like two contacts in an electrical circuit meeting. Something flowed through us that I can only call understanding. We knew what we were going to do. It all happened quickly—it had to, with Barrow about to attack—but when there are no words, communication takes no time. We knew. It took one moment for me to put Clive's collar around his neck and in the next moment…

Clive winked as I kicked him in the balls. To my immense satisfaction and relief, Barrow crumpled to the ground. His anguished roar sent a hot feeling like lust, like ecstasy, right through me. I heard his knife clatter against the flagstones, but I didn't stop to try to pick it up. I had already grabbed Clive's hand and was fleeing through the gardens.

Back at the van, Jair was just closing the back doors. Niko was behind him, waving at us to hurry. Roland was in the driver's seat, but he moved over when he saw me coming. They had laid Wex out on a bench in the back. Clive leapt in with Jair, and I pulled us out of the parking space before they even had the doors latched again.

I jammed one of the painter's caps on my head, just in case, while everyone else stayed down. But there was no sign of pursuit. Barrow might not have even stood up yet, and even if he did, it wasn't easy to figure out where in the labyrinth of gardens we had gone. He might think we were hiding, still. At least I hoped that was the case. All I knew was we had to get far enough away to do something with Wex.

When we were a good two blocks away, Roland finally asked, from where he was still crouched, "So what happened? How did you get away from him?"

"We… improvised with our talents," I said, perhaps a bit casually compared to the exultant triumph coursing through me. I wanted to grab Clive and kiss him until our lips were sore. Instead, I checked in. "Clive, are you okay? I kicked you really hard."

He adjusted his pants gingerly. "I can only transfer the sensation, not the physical effects, but I'll be all right. My testicles have certainly suffered worse."

Niko sounded excited. "Oh, you used psychosomatic transfer?"

Jair made a cringe-y noise and Roland looked back and forth between us. "You actually let her kick you in the balls?"

I couldn't help but grin as Clive answered, "Come on, Roland. No judgments. My kink is okay, your kink is okay."

THIRTY-ONE

Niko was pretty crushed by our realization about the markings on Wex's skin. "I really should have figured that out," he said, looking down Wex, who was of course still unconscious, laid out along one of the two benches in the back of the van. "I mean, it's obvious now that we know it, but still." His sigh was heavy.

"Where are we taking him?" I asked. I'd just driven down what seemed like the fastest route away from Barrow and The Archive, but we needed to decide where to go next.

"Uptown," Niko said. "Do you trust me, even though I fucked this up?"

"I trust you." I pointed us toward the West Side Highway again. "What are you thinking?"

"Remember when I said you could bury him for a couple of decades and then dig him up and he'd be fine?"

Roland, as usual, said, "No. You can't be serious. We can't just dig a hole for him somewhere like squirrels putting up nuts for the winter."

"We don't have to dig a hole," Niko said. "We can put him in the Founders' Tomb."

"The what?" Roland sat up and put his seatbelt on.

Jair picked up the explanation. "Remember when Kish and I got attacked up by Clive's apartment? Clive's had been the second stop on our trip. The first was a cemetery."

Roland whipped around to look at Niko. "You sent them somewhere without telling me?"

"I did tell you. I just didn't tell you everything," Niko replied. "They found it, anyway. At Trinity Cemetery. The founders of the Circle are buried there."

"Gabriel was cremated," Roland said stubbornly.

"Gabriel wasn't a founder," Niko said patiently. "He's of the generation after. I'm talking about Samuel and Adelaide Ward."

When Roland said nothing, I assumed it was because that was news to him.

"It's a large tomb," Jair said, "built into the side of a hill. Big enough for several generations."

"I believe the original intent for the tomb was that others of the Circle could also be buried there," Niko said. "But Gabriel, or someone before him, didn't keep up that practice."

Clive tapped on the phone, pulling up directions to navigate for me. "This says the Trinity Church cemetery is downtown, by Wall Street." He tapped a bit more. "And it's where Alexander Hamilton is buried?"

Jair pointed at something on the screen. "There's another one in Washington Heights." They were both silent while they huddled together, reading something on the screen.

"I see. When the cemetery downtown ran out of room, the church built one uptown." Clive told me where to exit and then asked, "You guys never said whether you found anything when you checked out my apartment."

"The only thing I found notable," Jair said, "was that the fire didn't appear to spread much beyond your place."

"I'm not sure what to make of that." Roland looked out the window, peering upward. "Maybe that's normal if the building has good fire suppression?"

"Or maybe they don't want more blood on their hands than necessary," Jair pointed out.

"If you kill enough people, does it damage your soul so much that you can't actually perform the practice?" I asked.

"There are... technicalities," Niko said. "But it could certainly be a motivation."

I decided not to ask about the technicalities right then, because I had a more pressing question. "When we get to the cemetery, will we need to work a circle or something? Because if you're trying not to get accused of witchcraft, I can't imagine that getting caught in the middle of the night breaking into a tomb is going to help that cause."

"No circle necessary," Niko said. "I will need to mark the doors, but I brought chalk for that." He held up a familiar-looking bag: mine. "I grabbed this on my way to the vault and took some stuff from down there that I thought we might need. Mira, I hope your whips are okay smushed in the bottom?"

"I'm sure they're fine." The one thing I wished he'd grabbed was some maxi pads because I was having that feeling I was due to start bleeding at any moment. I hoped it would hold off until we could get to a drugstore. "Once we have Wex settled—" I couldn't quite bring myself to say *buried* or *interred,* "—where to after that?"

"This is the exit," Clive reminded me.

We were pretty close to where Jair and Kish had holed up that time. "You're sure they won't be able to track us to the tomb?"

"I'm sure," Niko said. "Right now the most they'll have is a sense of the direction we went. And the moment we seal Wex inside, the signal will go dark."

The cemetery had large gates, which I assume were locked. How Jair opened them, I don't know, but the winding roadway that climbed the densely-packed hill was wide enough for a hearse—or van. We passed names carved in stone on the doorways and lintels of tombs and on monuments and headstones. Smith. Long. Swords. (Swords? Yes, apparently.) Weaver. Bradhurst.

"Lotta Anglo names," I said.

"Lotta rich people," Jair said. "Oh, look, there's a French one: Jacques."

"Wonder if they pronounced it 'Jakes.'" The van's headlights passed over a perfect circle of twigs on the ground, clearly manmade. "Are we sure we're the only ones doing magic around here?"

"Don't call it—" Roland started, but Jair interrupted him by pointed out another thing: a bundle of sticks tied with red ribbon and left tucked between the stones on one of the big tombs.

"Santeria, I think," he said. "And maybe pagans of some stripe, too."

"Let's be quick about it, then."

"Yeah."

They pointed me at a tomb door and I pulled up so the van's back doors lined up with it. We all got out: I was far too curious to stay in the van. It was too cloudy for there to be any moon, but being right in the middle of a city block, it wasn't what I would call dark right there.

Niko knew how to get the tomb door open. The lintel was low, but once you ducked under it, there were stairs going down a few feet and inside there was room to stand up. He and Roland used the flashlights on their phones to light the way while Jair and Clive carried Wex in by the bedsheet he had been lying on.

They wrapped him in the sheet to keep his limbs from flopping around and then slid him into one of the empty spaces, feet first.

I lit my own phone and looked around a little purely because I was curious. The occupied spaces were sealed with stone, each inscribed with a name. They appeared to have used roughly every other slot, leaving several empty.

Except they weren't empty. I peered into one and could see a few rectangular objects sitting there.

"Niko."

They looked like books.

"Niko, are those what I think they are?"

He came and looked with me, the others quickly following.

"Holy cats," he said, and a moment later he was crawling into the burial slot to retrieve them. "Oh my goodness."

He crawled back out, covered in dust and grime, but his eyes wide with excitement. I held the light steady while he cracked one open.

A diary. A Circle of Light diary.

We quickly scoured the place to see if there were any others. All in all about a dozen diaries were there. We gathered them up and got out. Niko marked the door on the inside with chalk and then added a few marks under the lintel where they wouldn't be seen.

He was ecstatic. "Oh my goodness. There might be all kinds of useful information in these. I can't wait to look into them."

"But please do," Roland urged. "At least until we get to the Sanctuary."

The Sanctuary. That sounds like somewhere safe, doesn't it?

THIRTY-TWO

The Sanctuary was in a part of the city I never knew existed, and maybe that was part of its magic. The Bronx is vast, and besides the urban part that everyone's seen in movies, the borough includes beaches, hills, and even some swaths of undeveloped forestland. Don't believe me? Check the satellite photos on Google Earth. You won't find the house via Google Maps, though. Roland had to direct me into an area called Spuyten Duyvil. That's Dutch for "spitting devil" (or "spouting" if you prefer) and the Dutch apparently weren't too happy about that particular stretch of the Hudson when they named the place.

We left the well-developed stretch behind, heading down a road that looked like it hadn't been re-paved since the 1970s. The stand-alone houses were a mishmash of old and older and they grew less frequent as we went along. Eventually there were no houses, just trees on either side of the road, and we came to the end of the patchy, cracked pavement, staring at a low, stony hill.

"Turn here," Roland said.

"Here?" There was a gap in the trees to the right but it didn't look like a road, exactly. He just nodded tiredly, so I pointed the van that direction and eased us forward.

By the sound of the tires there was gravel underneath, so at least it was some kind of service road. It looped us up a gentle slope in an arc shaped like a mug handle and we crept back down onto pavement. I was beginning to understand why we couldn't use Google Maps to get there. "Is this the same road?"

"The abandoned part," he said. On the left, a rocky cliff rose steeply. Two houses were built against it side by side. Faded, splintered remnants of other buildings dotted the street. "Rock slides happen from time to time so this isn't a great spot to build. Where the road ends back there was where a big slide cut off the road in the 1890s and the city decided to just abandon the rest."

I pulled us past a rusty-looking Cadillac. "You built a place called 'The Sanctuary' where it could be wiped out by a rock slide at any moment?"

"I didn't build it. It was already here when the rock slide happened. And there are safeguards in place," he muttered, but didn't sound very confident about it.

"*Magic*," Jair whispered sarcastically.

The houses were a matched pair of Queen Anne Victorians, probably built a decade or two after The Archive. As I was trying to decide which one to park in front of, Kish burst out the front door and down the steps of the one on the right. Okay, that one. I threw the van into park and jumped out.

"You made it!" we each said at the same time, and hugged, then laughed.

Inside, I found a house that looked like time had stopped around 1950. Antique (or at least old) furniture with handmade doilies on the arm rests circled a living room with a well-worn hardwood floor. An oval braided-wool rug matched the shape of the dining room table.

"I think my great aunt had this exact rug," Clive said.

Through the dining room I could see someone moving in the kitchen.

Dagger came out carrying a platter of cold cuts and other sandwich makings. She was wearing a tank top that showed the tattoos that covered her upper arms and shoulders. Less of a "sleeve" than a shawl, if it had been knitted by your punk ex-roommate instead of your grandma. "Sorry this is all I got." She set the platter on the table next to a stack of plates. "We can't get delivery here like you can downtown. Figured you guys might be hungry."

Until that moment I hadn't realized that I was. The rest of the crew followed in my wake, some sitting down at the table, others taking their sandwiches to the living room. I took a fine china plate to a spot on the couch. Clive followed, but instead of sitting next to me, he positioned himself on the floor at my feet, with his plate on the coffee table. At some point Ira came out of the kitchen bearing a pot of tea, which he shared with Niko. If it was caffeinated, it had no effect on him, as Niko soon fell asleep curled in an armchair like a too-tall cat.

That left the rest of us explaining to one another what all had happened. Eventually everyone had a pretty detailed picture, I think.

"I'm still impressed you thought to do what you did." Impressed or no, Jair was unable to keep from cringing slightly when he thought about it, though.

"I'd contemplated it before, but we hadn't talked about it." Clive said. "But it seemed to make sense since I didn't have any other way to attack."

"Yeah, it just made sense," I said. "Maybe I thought of it because every 'self defense for women' class I've taken has emphasized the kick to the balls? I've literally practiced it a hundred times." As Poor Sensei Jack could attest. Half of what he taught in that class was just to get over the fear of hitting someone hard. Some people have inhibitions about that. "Though that was the first time I kicked a real-live human who wasn't wearing a shit-ton of padding." I petted Clive's hair and then slid my hand down to Clive's neck, massaging the tight muscles there.

He leaned against my knee. I'm not sure who he was reassuring—the group, me, or himself—when he said, "I'm fine."

Ira stood. "Good. I wouldn't want you in too vulnerable a state when we Ghost the Blade together."

My palms prickled. "Did we agree that's our next move?"

Ira pulled himself to his full height. "You have a better one?"

Jair raised a hand. "Whoa, whoa, yes. These two need blades."

"Only I will need a blade for this Gleaning—?" Ira said, sounding confused that Jair brought it up.

"In general. We shouldn't go anywhere until they're equipped."

"We don't have to go anywhere. We can do it right here." Ira spread his hands. "Didn't I hear you say there's a ceremonial space right upstairs, Dag?"

"There is," Dagger said. "But—"

"There's no reason not to get it over with." Ira paced in the opening between the living room and dining room like a summer stock Shakespearean on a tiny stage. "And I would think we would want to strike before the Partisans can regroup."

"What makes you think they haven't regrouped?" Jair gestured at us. "We've regrouped."

"I just mean while they are back on their heels."

"They're not back on their heels." Jair shook his head. "They just sprang two traps on us at once, successfully. They lured us out of safety, attacked us, and discovered our safe house. They have all the momentum right now."

"Is there any way they can find this place based on what they can find at The Archive?" I asked. "Deeds or records or whatever?"

"No, they shouldn't," Roland said. "If it weren't for Kanna still being in their clutches, I'd say we should hole up here to train our new initiates and disappear entirely for a while."

Ira cleared his throat. "I fear for her safety. What if they decide they no longer need her to reveal our location, and dispose of her?"

Jair shook his head. "No. They'll keep her alive because she's a bargaining chip. They know we want her back. There's also probably plenty of information they still want to squeeze out of her."

Clive spoke up from where he sat at my feet. "Barrow said he'd seen me in her dreams."

Everyone was silent for a moment, contemplating that kind of invasion.

Dagger broke the silence. "Look, Ira, no one is taking the situation lightly. But you all look like you're about to fall over from exhaustion. It's three in the morning. Wouldn't it be a better idea to get a good night's sleep before doing anything?"

Jair yawned, but said, "I've never been one for a blood ritual first thing in the morning, though."

"Except when I'm on the rag," Kish joked, nudging him.

I put my hand on my uterus with sudden alarm. "Oh. That reminds me—"

Dagger and Kish both burst out laughing. "Forgot to tell you," Kish said. "Everyone synchs up to me."

"Everyone *what?*" Jair asked.

"I don't know whether to count that as a Blood Talent or not."

Niko looked up sleepily. "Count what?" He dozed back off before he could hear the explanation, though.

"That happened in my college dorm," I said. "Menstrual cycles getting in synch, I mean. I took months to happen, though."

"That's a thing?" Jair looked bemused.

"It's a thing, bebe." Kish assured him. "With the practice, it can happen really fast."

"That explains a lot." Jair whistled appreciatively.

"It does?"

"Sure. Think about it. If the women around you are all going through PMS at the same time? Just think of the geopolitical implications."

"Pig." Kish whapped him on the shoulder with the flat of her hand. "Mira, the closet by the second floor bathroom's got a stash, if I remember right."

"Yeah. Might as well put you and Clive in the room next to it." Dagger got up, as if to set up a guest room or whatever, Ira sat down and poured himself another cup of tea, and that seemed to be the end of the meeting.

I took the opportunity to bring Clive with me upstairs. While no one was actively trying to kill us, we needed to talk.

⁂

The bedroom was very blue, with ivory lace curtains trimmed with blue ribbon and a blue bedspread and pillows. The headboard was to the right of the door in the opposite corner from the windows and something about it felt familiar. Then I remembered that was the arrangement of Clive's childhood bedroom in the dream we had shared. Dagger told us to help ourselves to any clothes we could find that might fit us. Like at The Archive, there was at least a generations-worth of clothing left behind.

As soon as we were alone in the room I pulled Clive into a hug. Or maybe he pulled me into a hug. That's probably more likely because I felt like I never knew when to stop moving. I was probably already getting ready to dig through the closet or something, and that was right about the time when he was learning that he was the one thing that could stop me in my tracks.

"Are you sure you're all right?" I murmured against his neck, where I had tucked my face.

"I was not kidding when I said my testicles have taken rougher treatment." I felt his face muscles tense as he smiled. "I did a week-long camp with some pony players in Connecticut. One of the mistresses was very into CBT."

The thing is… cock-and-ball torture involves a lot more finesse than just rearing back and kicking as hard as possible. But point taken. "I know I was supposed to stay in the van, but when I heard him draw a knife on you… I just couldn't stay put."

"I'm glad you were there."

"It was almost like I was compelled."

He was silent, but I could almost feel him thinking. "Mira," he eventually said, "what would you think if it turned out you were?"

"If I were what?"

"Compelled."

I can be so thick sometimes. "You mean like what if Barrow had mind-controlled me to show myself? It didn't feel like that."

"A compulsion probably doesn't." The vibrations of his voice were soothing, even if his words weren't. "You probably feel like it's your own idea, but once you start, then you can't stop yourself."

I started to get the inkling he was trying to tell me something. "Clive, have you been compelled like that? Magically or spiritually or whatever you want to call it?"

"Yes."

The word hung between us like he'd rung a gong and I couldn't speak until the echoes were done bouncing around inside my skull. Yes, he'd been compelled… "Recently?" I asked.

"Yes," he said again, and again I heard the weight behind the word. The weight of confession.

And I was still being thick, thinking he meant he was worried that Barrow had hypnotized him or something like that. "When?"

His sigh was nearly as heavy as the word. "Mira—"

A tap came on the door then, and Dagger's muffled voice. "Mira, have you got everything you need?"

"Um, are there towels in the bathroom?" I called out.

"Yep, in the cabinet."

"Then we're fine. I'm going to take a shower and then go to bed." I loosened my hold on Clive and looked into his face.

He was searching mine, but I don't think he found whatever he was seeking. "Shall I scrub your back, my lady?"

"You can scrub more than just my back." Shall we say, the itch I felt then was not dry skin.

The bathroom was as pink as the bedroom was blue, including the towels and washcloths, the curtain around the white claw-footed tub, and a doll of a dancer with a roll of toilet paper hidden under her pink, crocheted skirt. "Not a lot of room in this tub, but we'll make do."

"Yes, my lady." Clive started the water while I looked around for a comb to run through my hair and his.

Hot water felt good and I held him again, just letting it run over us, washing away the stress of the attack and our flight from The Archive. "This must be where Saira and Dagger stay," I said, "but I didn't see Saira."

"I think she's in the house next door." Clive leaned his head back into the spray and I ran my fingers into his waves, massaging his scalp. He groaned in pleasure. "Wow, that feels good."

"Years of practice," I said. Before long I had him groaning again, this time with my hands a good deal lower on his body. As his arousal grew, it felt to me like the whole rest of the world—the Circle, Barrow, everything—disappeared, leaving us in a bubble where there was nothing but him and me.

And when there were no distractions and no one else to think about, I could see him so much more clearly. I brought him to the brink of release, then backed off, stroking him slowly under the spray, and saying, "You were telling me about feeling compelled."

His throat was tight with desire. "Yes, my lady."

How had I not seen it before? It was obvious once I gave it the slightest thought, and I felt a flush of shame that I had missed the signs—or that I had ignored them. That was the thing. I had "seen" it, but I hadn't really understood it. Sometimes it takes time for a fact to become knowledge. "You mean, by me."

"Yes, my lady."

"You've been trying to tell me for a while, haven't you?"

He was already so flushed with arousal I couldn't tell if it deepened as he bit his lip and said, "Yes, my lady."

"Clive. Angel." I leaned down and nipped him on one nipple with my teeth. "If I'm being thick-headed, please tell me. Please don't think it's your job to put up with me when I'm being an idiot, just because I'm the dom."

His voice came out a whisper. "Yes, my lady. But… it can be hard."

"Did you feel compelled not to speak up?"

"No, my lady. But… you do have the power to silence me." He blinked water from his eyes, meeting my gaze. "You realize that now, don't you?"

"I do realize it. Now." I know I was supposed to feel conflicted about it. I was supposed to go into a spiral of self-doubt, as my carefully constructed morality around consent was shattered by that revelation. I could literally tell him to do anything and he would have no power to refuse. But all I felt in that moment was a kind of searing joy, an ecstasy so superheated it almost hurt to experience.

He was mine.

I took his hand and guided him to where that heat seemed to gather, where my legs met. "Do you mind?" I whispered.

"I love making you come," he answered.

"No, no, I mean, do you mind that I have the power to compel you?"

He thought for a moment, letting his fingers work while he did. "No. Because I trust you. And I know I can trust you, now that you know."

I nodded. "You were in the most danger when I didn't know. I might've inadvertently ordered you to do something I didn't intend." It was all so clear. "That's what was happening in the van, that time off Riverside Drive, wasn't it?"

"Yes. You told me to *get down and stay down*. I think I literally could not get up until you told me otherwise."

"Why didn't you say something at the time?"

"I don't know." He threw his head back suddenly as I brought him to the brink again with my hand. I backed off once more to let him answer. "I think at first I wasn't even sure that's what was happening? My mind kept trying to convince me it was my own idea. But then I when I tried to bring it up, and you didn't pick up on it right away… I thought… maybe you… didn't really want to be bonded together."

I slid my hand lower and gripped him by his sopping testicles. "Clive. Let's get past this right now. I want you to be mine more than I want anything else in the world."

"My lady!"

"And I didn't say that sooner because I thought *you* might not really want to be bonded to *me*." Especially seeing as how he really seemed to have no choice in the matter.

"You might have noticed—" He paused to gasp with arousal, then continued. "That my feelings didn't change when you took my collar off."

Yes, I had noticed. It was one reason I'd felt so exultant after thwarting Barrow.

"I knew my feelings weren't going to change because I felt that way before you put the collar on in the first place." He bit his lip so hard I thought he might draw blood. "Mira. My lady." He hung his head. "I've wanted to be yours since the night we met."

I remembered him saying that once he met the Circle of Light he didn't dare contact me because he knew he'd fall so hard for me he'd break his vow of silence. It just hadn't really sunk in for me at the time what that meant. "How long has it been? Since… you felt like you were mine?"

He shuddered as I gave my hand a twist. "Since you rescued me."

Since I had literally saved his life.

"I feared you'd reject being… forced into such a relationship," he said. "And I worried you'd—or that we'd both—reject it as coercive."

I thought over some of the actions I had taken since then. "I think the bond compels me to act, also." That impulse I had to throw myself between Barrow's blade and Clive's skin… I had come so close to doing it, too. "But I don't think the bond creates feelings I didn't already have. Maybe it just makes them stronger."

"Remember what Niko said about the difference between a spark and a lightning strike? I feel like we're playing with electricity. I like it. I like it a lot. But I worry it could be too much for one or both of us."

"Same, angel. Same." I kissed him hard and tasted a tinge of blood. "We'll figure it out, okay?"

"Okay."

"Now let's see if psychosomatic transfer works for pleasure as well as pain, hm? I'm going to make you come, angel. Let's see what happens if you send that sensation my way."

Honestly it wasn't a good test because I was so close to coming anyway. When the orgasm hit, I saw spots in front of my eyes and Clive had to keep me from falling into the pink-tinged water.

THIRTY-THREE

In the morning I learned I wasn't the only one who'd had a womb-squeezing orgasm the night before—some solo, some with help, I think. Kish had told us everyone in the Circle would sense when any one of us was aroused, but I hadn't really thought through the implications of that. We are empathetic creatures. What one of us feels, we all feel—even without the aethereal bond. By morning, Kish, Dagger, and I were all having a full-on visits from Aunt Flo in all her gory glory.

Dagger and Saira were the first ones up. Clive and I went down to the kitchen and I was a little surprised to find Saira there. She had dark circles under her eyes and a hot water bottle on her back. "You, too, hm?"

She nodded. "All of us. Like clockwork."

I asked what I thought would be a straightforward question. "Given the importance of blood in the practice, does menstruation affect it at all?"

"You'd have to ask Niko that," she said, then got up from the table. She squeezed Dagger's hand and gave her a kiss on the cheek. "I'm going to go check on C.B. See if he'll join everyone for breakfast."

Dagger was whipping eggs in a bowl. "You know he'll say no."

"But I can at least ask." Saira wafted out the back door like a scarf on the breeze.

"C.B.'s the only person we haven't met yet." I took the bowl to finish beating the eggs while Dagger got bacon out of the fridge.

"Yeah, and you probably won't. He mostly keeps to himself."

"Why?"

She lit the stove with a match and dug the pans out of the drawer at the bottom. "He's of Roland's generation, a survivor." When she swept her thick black hair into a knot and fanned the back of her neck, I got a better look at her colorful tattoos: a fish, a bird. "His word, not mine. He's HIV positive is what I'm trying to say. He's afraid he leaves negative vibes in his wake or something so he mostly keeps to himself. I think it's overkill. It's not like we'd accidentally prick his finger on a spindle or something, you know? But he's only around when we really need him."

"He's Roland's age? Did they know each other?"

"Yeah, back in the day." She shrugged.

My curiosity about C.B. only increased, then. I was sure he'd have some interesting stories to tell. "So it's just the two of you here, usually? Are you separated from everyone else for a reason?"

"Saira's supposed to have two guardians, like Niko, but until we can recruit and train someone new, there's only me." She swirled a little oil in the bottom of a pan. "The isolation is mostly a precaution to keep Saira from getting overexposed to the practice."

"Is that a nice way of saying it's less likely she'll have accidental sex if she's not around a bunch of horny people like us?"

"Heh, yes." Dagger chuckled as she lay bacon into the pan. "I like you. You're like Kish. You say what you mean." (I got the feeling Dagger herself was also like that.) "The thing about the accidental sex… well, that's apparently how they got Saira in the first place. Her mother was the previous Unbroken, but… it didn't last. I don't know the exact details. I was a baby myself at the time. You could probably ask Niko if you're really curious."

"Ask me what?" He bounced into the room and did a lateral fake pass and pirouette with the empty kettle before sticking it under the faucet.

I was not caffeinated yet, but I still remembered my previous question. "How does a woman's monthly cycle affect how we practice the, uh, practice?"

He set the kettle on the stove and lit the burner with the same match his sister had used, transferring the flame out from under the pan she was frying in. "We're not totally sure."

"Really? I would think that it would come up a lot."

He thought about that for a long moment, eyes searching the ceiling, before he spoke. "I think in most ways, it doesn't matter. Like, it shouldn't stop you from working a circle or really affect how you transfer energy. Remember, the real action of the practice happens in the liminal plane."

"But no one wants to have to clean a pint of blood off the floor after a working, so we mostly try to schedule around it," Kish finished for him as she came in and opened the fridge. "Personally I think I'm a little more sensitive and vulnerable for the first day or two. And I don't mean emotionally."

"I think all people probably have some kind of cycles, both monthly and yearly." Niko got a large iron teapot off a shelf. "No matter what biological sex your body presents. But the practice itself doesn't really go into detail about it."

"Are there trans practitioners?" Clive asked.

"Yes," Dagger and Niko said simultaneously.

"Wait a second." I remembered something Niko'd told us before and I tried to put the thoughts together. "So if the body is only the projection of the aethereal self into the physical plane, then biological sex characteristics are… what? Do they mean anything?"

"Ohhhh, hm." Niko's gaze returned to the ceiling and as his eyes moved back and forth I wondered if that was him accessing his ancient memory banks. Was he literally reading the memory of some long-lost practitioner's journal? "That might depend on what you mean by 'mean.'"

"I guess I'm just asking if it's random? Whether someone comes out male or female, or intersex?"

"Oh, well, that's a function of cell biology, where the parents—"

"She knows about the sperm and the egg, bebe," Kish told him gently. "I think she means… do souls have gender, too?"

Niko put his hands on his head. "Now we're getting all the way down to concepts of selfhood. This is way too deep a lesson to go into before caffeinating."

"I think the short answer is no, though," Dagger put in, as she flipped the bacon with chopsticks. "The spiritual sea that fills us isn't gendered, only the container you pour it into is. In the liminal plane you retain your gender identity only in that you retain your sense of self and identity in the first place. If you believe in reincarnation, then you can come back as a being that isn't even human much less the same sex you were the previous time, right?"

"Do you believe in reincarnation?" I asked.

"Oh, hell no," Dagger said with a laugh. "I'm just saying, you know, in theory. Hey, Little Brother, go round up the rest of the troops and find out how many want eggs."

Niko dashed off to do that, and I was drafted into making a pile of toast.

When Kish was done setting out plates and forks, she came to stand beside me at the counter. "I think now's a good time to pick your blade."

I had been avoiding that moment as long as possible, for reasons I wasn't even allowing myself to think about. "Now, you mean right now?"

"I mean today, at least, while you're on the first day of your cycle. I think you'll make very strong connections today."

"Okay," I said blankly. "Are we doing this other thing first, though? The thing Ira was going on and on about yesterday?"

Kish looked back at Clive, who had been tabbed to keep turning the bacon while Dagger started the first round of eggs scrambling in another pan. "Only if the two of you are okay with it. I feel like the discussion was kinda rushed."

Roland dragged in then, hands buried deep in his central hoodie pocket. "What discussion?"

"About Ghosting the Blade."

Ira was right on his heels. In an Oxford shirt and slacks, he looked more like himself and less like he was cosplaying a lumberjack than he had the day before. "I thought we already determined that is our next move?"

Roland looked back and forth between Kish and him. "Kish seems to feel the discussion was rushed. And I don't think we should undertake such a significant working without a formal vote."

Ira gave him a nod. "Well, you are Convenor. It's within your power to compel it."

There was that word again. Compel. That sounded more like it was being used in the legal sense than the psychic one, but with the Circle I couldn't make that assumption.

Clive was picking the bacon out of the pan with chopsticks and laying it on paper towels. "I'd like to get more details."

"Fine." Roland nodded. "No more discussion until after we've eaten, though. Dag, please tell me you've got coffee here somewhere?"

"Oh, you know what...?" She looked around. "I think CB's got the machine over in the other kitchen."

Roland offered to go retrieve it and left. I supposed that gave him a chance to visit his old friend, too.

Jair and Dagger put hot sauce from a jar on their eggs and Dagger ate hers on rice. "You guys are making me miss my mom," I told her. "She eats her eggs like that. But with Spam or corned beef instead of bacon, and ketchup as well as hot sauce."

"I like to just fry the egg until the yolk is still runny and put that on rice, too," she said. "Both my parents liked it like that, with some kimchi fried in the pan next to the egg. My dad would make it as a midnight snack."

"Middle of the night is the best time to eat breakfast," Jair said, licking hot sauce from the corner of his mouth. He quickly amended: "Although it's great now, of course. Thanks for cooking."

"If you really appreciate it, you can wash the dishes," Dagger said with a toothy grin. "Speaking of food and division of labor, we better figure out a grocery strategy if you're all going to be here for a while."

"Well, we won't be going back to The Archive anytime soon," Niko said with a heavy sigh.

The discussion of logistics of course quickly had to turn to what we were going to do next. I didn't want to say that if what we learned from the blade Kish and Jair had recovered led us into a deadly confrontation, that would leave a lot fewer mouths to feed. No one likes to sound so pessimistic. But I was thinking it.

After breakfast, Roland formally convened the meeting in the living room. I was expecting it to be a fairly short discussion, a formality really, given that we'd already talked about the topic. I think Ira thought it would be quick, as well.

We were both wrong. Kish brought the knife down and laid it on the coffee table, atop the square of purple silk she'd kept it wrapped in. No one touched it directly. Niko sat crossed-legged on the floor, poking it with a chopstick from time to time as he examined it. "It looks fairly new. Not a lot of scratches or wear."

Jair rubbed the spot on his thigh where it had sliced him. "The nicks we see are probably from it hitting the brick wall after it went through me."

"Well, but that's good," Ira said. "The impressions on it should be fairly fresh and un-muddied."

Roland asked him, "You're sure you can do this?"

"Yes. It's a subtle technique, but my visualization should be quite clear."

"Never would've pegged you for a Seer." Kish gave a little shake of her head.

Ira was sitting in an armchair against the wall, still nursing a cup of tea. He set the cup down on a coaster. "You doubt the veracity of my claim?"

Kish shook her head again. "I didn't say that. I'm just remarking."

"All of us should develop some ability to See," Niko said. "It's not a unique talent, and it should be developed in every one of us. Ira, I would suggest you do a full Clearing before you begin, to be sure you aren't just Seeing what you want to See."

"Of course." Ira dipped his head.

"That's assuming we go ahead with it. I notice that we still haven't said who'll be on the receiving end of the blade," Clive said. He was sitting on the floor next to Niko, legs under the coffee table, while I sat on the couch behind him. The living room wasn't that big; it made sense that to fit everyone in, two had to be on the floor (or bring chairs in from the dining room).

But it felt right having him at my feet. I'd missed that feeling. Not just of having someone at my feet, but of having someone constant in my life, someone at my beck and call. Someone under my protection.

I kept quiet, though, and let him speak for himself. "Seems likely I'll be the one donating my blood to the cause."

"With Mira's permission, of course," Ira said quickly. "Or your bond might create a barrier."

I said nothing and let Clive continue. "Tell me again what this ritual entails?"

Ira folded his hands on his knee. I imagined it was the pose he struck when explaining necessary surgery to a patient. "Once the containment is drawn and willingness invoked, the blade will be made to sing by the drawing of blood."

"You're sure you shouldn't use my blood?" Jair asked.

"Quite sure." Ira waited until Niko had also nodded. "Your impressions are already going to be quite strong and could overpower the ones we're trying to extract from your attacker. Fresh blood is necessary." Maybe I'm biased, but it seemed to me that as he said it, Ira was looking at Clive with an expression of pure desire.

Clive's eyes were on the knife. "And where will the blood be drawn from?"

"Your back would be best," Ira said. "It's the widest canvas."

Clive sat silent, then, chewing over that thought. I could feel the tension in him, twisting tighter all the time like a spring inside a watch.

"If you don't want to go through with it, you don't have to," I said to him.

He finally looked up at Ira. "I won't do it without Mira."

My heart had skipped a beat. That was what I had thought (or hoped?) he was thinking, the previous time the subject had been discussed.

"She'll be right there," Ira said, voice even. "The whole Circle will be there."

"What do you mean by 'with you,' Clive?" I asked.

"I'll do it if you can be inside the containment circle with me." His head bowed and his voice dropped to almost a whisper. "Holding me."

"Of course." I ran a hand into his hair by reflex, trying to soothe him, but I felt him bristle. "Assuming that's allowed?"

"It shouldn't interfere," Ira said lightly. "In fact, given the energetic bond between the two of you, it might even be necessary. Niko, don't you agree?"

"Yes, that seems likely." Niko moved the blade with the chopstick. It was perfectly balanced on a point between the handle and blade, leaving it spinning slowly, like the pointer in some macabre board game.

"Clive, are you sure?" I asked him.

"Is there no way to have Mira do it?" Kish asked. "Could she learn the technique?"

"We don't have the time," Ira said. "And even if we spent the days or weeks to teach it to her, there's no guarantee she'd grasp it."

"We'll only get one chance with this blade," Roland added. "But I would like to make sure if there are any objections that they are fully aired. Mira?"

"If Clive wants me in the Circle, and he's fine with continuing, then I am fine with it," I said. "But the decision is his to make."

"Clive?" Roland asked.

Clive sat silent again, tension radiating through his shoulder blades. When he spoke it was to the group, but his eyes were on Ira. "You all know what happened the last time I did a scene with a knife. Right?"

When no one said anything, Ira took it upon himself to answer, using his most calming—or perhaps I should say condescending—bedside manner. "The Partisans attacked us. That won't happen here, Clive."

Clive's voice was icy, slicing with cold: "I was referring to the fact you severed the connection between my body and soul."

"Ah." Ira swallowed and gathered himself. "Yes, well. I know better than that now."

I felt a strange lightness in my head, as if I were beginning to float on a strange, strange sea. As if Clive's ire had filled the room with hydrogen and the entire place was rising like the Hindenburg.

"You don't know everything, Ira," Clive said. "Don't let what little knowledge you have go to your head."

"We practiced this one, though, remember, Clive?" Ira was still using the condescending voice. "We know it works. We can do it. I believe in you. But I need you to believe in me for this to work."

"Bullshit," Clive said. "The only person you believe in, Ira, is yourself."

Ira's pale face showed when he flushed. His voice tightened as he spoke through a stiff jaw. "You don't know what it's like to be a surgeon. How necessary it is that I have complete faith in my own abilities. Literally every time I open someone up, their lives are in my hands. If I doubt myself, if I go in ruled by fear, it becomes a self-fulfilling prophecy."

Have you ever lost a patient? I wanted to ask, but I didn't want to interrupt Clive. He and Ira stared at each other.

"I can do this, Clive." Ira said. "We can do this."

"Christ." Clive swore. And Clive never swore. But he lifted his metaphorical boot from Ira's metaphorical neck. "I'm sure it'll be fine. Let's do it. But it's you, me, and Mira in the circle."

"And the four of us," Kish said, indicating herself, Roland, Jair, and Dagger, "on the cardinal points. We've got your back, Clive."

"And you," Dagger said to Niko in what was clearly her big-sister voice, "ought to go hang out with Saira while it's taking place." A few glances came my way. No one wanted a repeat of last time.

"I miss her," he said. "That'll be good." Then he looked up from the knife, which was continuing to spin slowly on its perfect balance point. "Ira, did I already tell you you'll need to do a full Clearing?"

"You did," Ira said with a nod.

"Do you need me to lead you? Or are you all right on your own?"

"I can handle my own meditation, thank you. Just give me an hour."

"Great," said Dagger. She pointed at me and Clive. "That should be enough time for at least one of you to get a blade."

"Let's not rush into things." Roland held up his hand with a sigh. "Why am I always the one advocating caution?"

"Because it's your Myers-Briggs type?" Kish muttered under her breath and I had to hold in a laugh.

"The last thing we need is the two of you charging into battle with weapons you can't even use." Roland looked at Jair. "You said yourself a woman with a weapon isn't better protected.

She's in more danger because the weapon is more likely to be used on her."

"When did I say that?" Jair looked around. "And even if true, I don't think that applies here."

"It took you weeks of training to be able to connect to your blade," Roland pointed out.

"Mira and Clive are light years ahead of me and they haven't even sat down for a formal lesson. They're already using transitive sadism, for Pete's sake." Jair appealed to Niko. "What do you think?"

Niko folded his hands. "I think it's nuts to wait any longer and they both need knives right away."

Roland wore that kicked-puppy look. "Fine. Which one of you wants to go first?"

"Clive first," I said automatically, without giving a reason. Thankfully no one asked for one. The blade spinning on the table finally came to a stop, pointing right at Clive, as if it agreed with me.

THIRTY-FOUR

That night was when I learned that Dagger was a nickname; it was customary for the Bladekeeper to take a name that fit the job. She had all the knives we could choose from in a drawer upstairs. The attic that contained the house's ceremonial space had sloping ceilings and creaking pine floors. We climbed a steep stair-ladder through a trap door into the space. The air was warm and smelled of old wood.

A trunk sat in the far corner—the twin to the one at The Archive that we'd had to leave behind—an antique-looking chest of drawers in the corner beside it. Roland, Kish, and Jair came upstairs with us.

The top drawer of the chest held supplies: candles, incense, matches, a bucket of children's sidewalk chalk in every color. Dagger took a candle out and set it in a metal candleholder atop the chest. She lit it and held her hands together like she was saying a little prayer. She turned to Clive. "Now you."

He imitated her without question. What prayer did he say, I wondered?

Dagger pulled open the next drawer down. In it were a few dozen bundles, each one wrapped in cloth or suede or leather and tied with string.

Each one was a knife.

"Reach in and see if you feel a pull from one direction or the other," Dagger said.

Clive pulled out a bundle wrapped in what looked like a fine dinner napkin. He set it on the top of the dresser to undo the string, revealing a shiny, silvery-looking blade, four or five inches long. The handle looked like twine or rope had been wound around a core and then cast in metal. He wrapped his fingers around the grip and a small, satisfied smile settle on his face, as if the knife evoked some gratifying memory.

"Does it feel so right it's like holding your own dick in your hand?" Dagger asked with an eyebrow raised.

"That's one way to put it," Clive said.

"Then we have a winner! That was quick." Dagger looked at me. "Usually folks have to try a few."

"Should I pull another to compare?" Clive said, but he was already kind of holding it to his chest like he didn't want to give it up.

"No no, that definitely looks like a great match," Dagger said. "Okay, Mira. You want to have a go, then?"

I sucked in a breath. I had been avoiding the moment so long, I did it by reflex. "Right now?"

"No time like the present."

I realized that if I fought it any longer, though, they'd know something was wrong. They'd know everything I was trying not to think about. In hindsight, of course, I knew on some level that I couldn't keep my secrets forever. The Circle, and Clive, were going to know everything, and they were going to probably know sooner than later. But when you've spent so long with your mind shying away from a topic, when you've carefully constructed your own blinders because without it you'd run yourself into the ground, that narrow view and those honed instincts have become part of who you are. And changing that doesn't come quickly or easily.

"Okay, what do I do? Pray?"

"Just give yourself a moment at the candle," Dagger said. "Let the light fill your eyes, then close your eyes and let it fill your mind. When your mind is quiet and full of light, reach into the drawer."

Fine, I thought. I stood in front of the candle, pressed my palms together, and stared long enough that when I closed my eyes I saw the blue-purple imprint of the flame inside my eyelids. *Let's do this.*

I reached into the drawer and let my hands skim over the bundles, like feeling for the cloud layer. "What should it feel like?"

"It's different for each person. But does one feel warm? Or like it's giving a magnetic pull to your fingers? Is one lighting up?"

If I felt anything there was a slight buzz like static, but it wasn't coming from any particular bundle. I pulled one out at random. It felt heavy and it made a thump on the wood when I put it down to unwrap it. It was pretty: the haft had an art deco look to it. But it felt even heavier when I picked it up in my bare hand, my wrist sagging.

"Definitely not," Dagger said. She took it from me and re-wrapped it. "Try again."

I watched my fingertips as they moved past the bundles, like I was trying to decode a message. There was one wrapped in a maroon bandanna. The bandanna reminded me of Girl Scouts, of wilderness camping and self-sufficiency, and I concentrated on that and not on the last time I'd cut a person. I plucked it out, but nearly lost my grip on it the bundle felt so feather-light. "Whoa."

Dagger chuckled and took it before I could even unwrap it. "Not that one either. Come on, Goldilocks, let's find something that's just right?"

I took a deep breath and tried again. There was one bundle against the side of the drawer, almost completely concealed under another, but what I could see looked to be wrapped in gray suede with a bit of black piping? Like someone had cut a piece out of a suede miniskirt to wrap that one up.

I pulled it free to find it wasn't tied, merely rolled several times over with the ends tucked in. I set it on the dresser and unrolled it. The knife I revealed had a blade as black and wavy as Clive's hair—or mine after a home perm.

"Gorgeous," Clive said.

I picked it up. The hilt was silver and patterned in snake (or dragon?) scales. At the very tip and along the edge of the black blade it shone silver where it had been sharpened. The tip was as sharp as a needle and I had the sudden urge to see what kind of line it would leave on Clive's skin. I clamped down hard on that feeling and tried to put the knife down.

But I couldn't let go. I thought for a moment maybe that meant it was the right one? But tremors ran up my arm as I tried to will my fingers to to open. With my fist even tighter than before, I stabbed the blade down, jamming the point into the wooden top of the dresser. The impact jarred my hand loose and I stepped back quickly, before I could feel that compulsion again.

"Okaaaay, definitely not that one, then," Dagger said, working it free of the wood and wrapping it up again. "You know what? I think maybe we should all do a little Clearing meditation before the working."

"That seems like a good idea," Kish said.

"Yeah," Roland agreed.

"I'll sweep the floor," Jair offered. "Mira, why don't you get the cushions out of the bottom drawer."

Jair was savvy. He gave me something to do so I wouldn't just stand there, flexing my fingers and stewing in swirl of negative emotions I couldn't name.

THIRTY-FIVE

Niko returned to consult with Roland on the drawing of the circle and turned it into a lesson for me and Clive. He pulled a bright pink piece of chalk out of the bucket and, without using any tools or measuring, drew what looked to me to be a pretty much perfectly round circle on the floor.

"We call it a circle," he said, "but of course you should think of it as a sphere, and the line demarcates where the sphere intersects the floor."

"I've seen that," I told him. "The night the demon broke through, it looked like a soap bubble."

"It usually takes people a few weeks or months to be able to see things like that." He regarded me for a moment. "I wonder why you're naturally good at it?"

"I bet it's her training in the healing arts," Jair said from where he was shaking out a robe before putting it on.

Kish poked him in the ribs. "Or maybe she was drawn to the healing arts because she's already got the sense." He tried to grab her finger and the two of them tussled a moment, each trying to joint-lock the other and failing.

Niko ignored them. "The thing about seeing the bubble… It's difficult to figure out if you're actually seeing something that your *eyes* actually sense, or if your *brain* is sensing something and the best translation it can give to your consciousness is a visual one. Another person might also sense the barrier but instead of visually it might be through some other part of the brain. We say we have five senses but really there's only one reality, one sense, and it's just our biology that splits it into separate experiences. When you're fully attuned, you probably will sense it with every sense, not just your eyes."

That made sense to me philosophically, but it only created more questions in my mind. "So what is the barrier made of, then? What is it?"

"It's not exactly 'made of' anything, I don't think?" Niko held out a hand in the air like he was feeling for air currents, and oriented himself toward the front of the house. "The bubble where the working takes place is basically just a blob of the liminal plane that's been pulled up onto the beach of our physical reality."

"The same way our bodies are a projection of our whole selves into this space?" Clive asked.

"That's a good way to think of it," Niko said, then laughed at himself and pointed at something on a bare wall stud. A tin letter N nailed to the wood. "Here I've been trying to sense North and I forgot someone marked it generations ago." He bent down to mark it on the circle and went on to describe how most circles should be marked with the cardinal directions. "Since this is the spot where we're overlapping the planes of existence, and, as you've seen, stuff can happen like out of body experiences, some of this is to make sure everyone can find their way back."

"Does the color of the chalk make a difference?" I asked.

He looked at the piece in his hand. "No. I just like the bright ones." Then he paused. "Actually, wait. Do I *know* that color doesn't matter? Or am I just assuming that...?"

"How about saying 'so far as we've noticed, color doesn't seem to change the outcome,'" Roland said. "Would that be accurate?"

"It might be, but it dodges the question." Niko rubbed his forehead. "I'll have to think about it later. Now let's add glyphs."

That was the part he and Roland had to discuss. Some were standard, like the one that meant "holding" or "containing." Some would help those at the nodes channel their energy into maintaining the bubble. Clive and I would be putting our energy into the blade via Clive's blood, and Ira would be pulling the energy out and reading it. One symbol I recognized from before meant Clarity. They also added one that would keep wandering spirits out.

Clive was fascinated. "So does each symbol represent a word?"

"Well, each one has a meaning, but not necessarily a single word, at least not in English." Niko draw another that looked like two parallel squiggles with a triangle.

"But the symbols have names."

Niko paused, chalk in the air. "They do, but I don't want to overload you with a lot of stuff to memorize right before a working that's probably going to wipe it all out anyway. I guess the thing is, the name of the symbol isn't the same thing as the word for the meaning it represents? At least... I don't think it is?" He sat down on the floor and leaned his head on his hand. "You're giving me a lot to think about."

"What I'm getting at is that if it's the meaning of the symbol that matters, how does the symbol itself affect the way things work?" Clive stared at the squiggle-triangle. "Would it work just as well to write, in English, 'Clarity'? Or is part of it dependent on the training of the practitioners, and their mental associations of certain symbols with certain meanings?"

"Or is it the alphabet demons know?" Jair put in, joking.

"It is not the alphabet demons know," Niko said, as if the question had been serious. "But I think we're back to that question we ask a lot, which is how much of what our predecessors did was because it was necessary for the practice to work, how much of it was to maintain secrecy, and how much of it just seemed kinda cool?"

I didn't want to sidetrack us too much, but maybe I was a little bit happy to be delaying the scene to come. "May I ask one more question before we get going?"

Niko sighed. "Yes, but my queue is getting long."

"Okay, but I hope this is one you can answer. Why does the victim have to be submissive?"

"We don't use the word 'victim,'" Roland said, sounding horrified.

"No, we say 'sacrifice,' because that sounds soooo much better," Jair said. He was bouncing on his toes like he was warming up for a race.

"Let me rephrase. Why does the person whose blood-energy is going into the blade have to be submissive?"

Niko got up and dusted off his hands. "I think you just answered your own question. The direction of the energy flow for this one has to be very purely one-directional. Some techniques require resistance and release, or a back-and-forth flow, but not Ghosting the Blade."

That idea intrigued me extremely. In BDSM what happened in a scene was called power exchange, but we meant it more like who had the power of will, who was in charge, but here it was literally power in the form of energy flowing from one participant to another. And the idea that one could manipulate that power in different ways, resisting or not, to create different effects, just made a whole lot of sense to me. "What happens if someone resists too much when they're not supposed to?"

A voice came from the stair ladder. Ira's head and shoulders were poking up through the hatch. "Well, that's the point of meditating beforehand. To be open to what's going to happen without fighting it."

"Which doesn't answer my question."

"Let's just say," Niko said, "that in some workings, if the sacrifice can't let their energy flow when it should, then the whole thing can kind of blow up. But I want to be clear about one thing."

"We really should get going," Roland told him.

Niko went on as if he hadn't heard him. "Technically speaking, any person should be able to play the so-called submissive role, or the dominant role, if properly prepared. It's just less difficult and less prone to backfire with people who are predisposed to one or the other. I discovered something in my meditation last night."

Everyone hung on Niko's words then, no one moving, barely breathing.

"I wasn't going to tell you until later, but now that it's come up..." He looked at Ira and then at me. "The Circle did try to recruit BDSM tops and bottoms at one point. But too many initiates were rigid about their roles and it blocked their advancement. To become adept, they had to be able to switch sometimes."

He moved over to the hatch. "And then the virus came, and they weren't ready."

"Virus. You mean the 1918 influenza?" Ira asked as he climbed the rest of the way into the attic.

"No no, not that long ago. I mean HIV." Niko looked at Ira. "Try to remember that, will you? That circumstances could call any of us to wield the blade, or to yield to it."

Ira bowed without speaking and Niko descended.

Dagger came up right after he departed. "Last chance to change your tampons or take a leak, folks. No one? All right, then." She closed the hatch door with a thud. "Everyone ready?"

No, I thought, but it was definitely time to get it over with.

THIRTY-SIX

Before we began, while everyone was doing their deep breathing and positive visualization and whatever, I took Clive aside for a few moments. We held each other's hands and breathed. I hadn't even intended to say anything, but he did: "What's wrong?"

I shivered. "It goes against every grain in me to put you in harm's way like this."

He nodded. "You know I like a challenge, but…I don't think I could go through with it at all if I didn't know you were with me. Maybe it's the bond?"

"Niko did say there could be a kind of backlash if we're separated. Being on opposite sides of the spell bubble would count."

"Don't call it a spell," Clive whispered with a conspiratorial smile, and I wanted to squeeze him and not let go.

Thinking back on it, it's obvious we were just saying things to soothe each other. If we'd really been trying to be logical we'd have probably said different things.

"I'm going to be fine," he murmured into my ear. "And if I'm not, well, at least you'll be there to put me back together?"

Like I had Jair. "Definitely." I gave in to the urge to pull him close. He felt so new to me, so fresh and unexplored, and some part of me resented that I couldn't simply forget everything, pull him into the bed downstairs, and not emerge for days except for the occasional bathroom break. I wanted to memorize the scent of him and learn every inch of his skin. Letting someone else mark him was the last thing I wanted to allow.

But we'd agreed. And like Niko said. Any of us might need to be the one under the knife. I'd already tried to volunteer. We'd been through all the options. This was the course of action we'd all agreed to.

It was time to go through with it.

I looked up to find everyone already in their places, candles lit, robes on over their clothes. Ira was standing at the center of the circle, hands folded around a knife, wearing only a robe and looking as placid as a statue. I nodded to Clive and he stripped down to nothing, not even his socks—his nakedness symbolic of his willingness to be vulnerable, to be the sacrifice. I put a ceremonial robe on over my clothes.

Roland told me to take Clive's hand, and then invited us to express our willingness to participate by stepping over the line of chalk.

It seemed brighter inside the line, ringed by tea lights in their tiny cups. My adrenaline spiked upon realizing what was next to Ira on the floor: a kneeling pad for Clive and a stool for me to sit on. It felt a lot like the last, disastrous time I'd tried to submit to a sexy, sadistic dom. That time

I had looked at the array of devices the guy had laid out and realized I was in over my head.

I reminded myself that no permanent harm had come from that scene (except maybe to the dom's ego). Clive wasn't having an organ transplant here. A dozen cuts at most, that's what Ira had described. I swallowed. Being hyped up for the scene was part of the drama, part of what gave a ritual its power. It didn't mean there was actually anything to fear.

Clive took his position and I mine. I sat on the stool and he knelt in front of me, his hands on my knees, mine on his shoulders. Ira said something—I don't even remember what—but Clive wrapped his arms around me then, clasping his hands inside my robe, behind my back. One of my hands cradled the base of his head, immobilizing him against me. The other I settled in the small of his back. I could feel each of his breaths.

Clive was the canvas, I was the easel, and Ira was goddamn VanGogh.

Ira raised the slim, symmetrical knife in his hand and got ready to work. I couldn't help but focus on the tip of the blade, as sharp as any needle. The people around the circle seemed to fade into the distance, as if we were at the top of the globe and they were below the horizon. I think they had been chanting—maybe they still were but the sound no longer reached us, or maybe they had stopped because it was time.

The first thing Ira did with the knife, though, was cut the tie of my robe at the neckline, letting it fall back over the stool and getting it out of the way.

He leaned close. "I'm going to scratch a design lightly at first." Clive did not move but I nodded. Clive was breathing like he was putting himself into a trance, making himself ready to receive whatever was to come.

Can you imagine making yourself that receptive? That open? I couldn't. Not then.

Ira touched the point of the blade to a spot on Clive's shoulder and just held it there, anticipating the first cut. I felt my mouth water. That was the way I would have done it, too—to build anticipation and to savor that first moment when the knife would bite into flesh, the pain about to ripple like a pebble dropped into a pond.

Did the knife in Ira's hand feel like his own cock? I had to wonder. His eyes were dark with concentration, his pupils huge, as the first drop of blood was drawn, and Clive skipped a breath.

He shivered as the blade moved along his skin and I felt my own palms itch. I knew what it felt like to be the one holding the knife. I knew what it was like to love that feeling, to love feeling like my lover's life was in my hands, even if all I was doing was leaving a mere scratch at the time.

Ira was drawing a circle. As he came around to close the design near Clive's spine, Clive drew a shuddering breath, clutching me tight, and all my apprehension morphed into arousal. He was never more gorgeous than when he was surrendering to sensation, riding it like a hit of a drug, become more and more vulnerable with each passing moment.

"I'm drawing the face of a clock," Ira said, ostensibly to both of us but I'm not sure Clive was hearing him. "I'm going to make cuts going counterclockwise, representing movement backward in time." He looked me right in the eye, then. "Stay focused and you may catch some of it, too."

I could only nod in assent. My voice felt buried deep in my throat.

As with a straight razor, the blade was sharp enough to cut without a slicing motion. All it took was gentle pressure for the honed edge to part the dermis and draw fresh blood to the surface. The first cut Ira made was on Clive's left shoulder, where I could just see the darkening around the blade.

Ira froze, blade in the air, his eyes wide and unfocused as what he was seeing then was no longer anything in the room. He sucked in a breath, and whispered, "She's Barrow's," as if that were too scandalous to say louder.

Of course she's Barrow's, is what I was thinking. We knew that. Or did he mean the way Clive was mine…?

The next cut was down further, beyond the curve of Clive's shoulder, so I did not see it, but I saw Ira's eyes light as the cut was made and I felt Clive's arm tighten around me, a moan escaping him that sounded far more like pleasure than pain. The division between those two things is false, you know? There is only sensation and the judgments we put on it. If a sensation creates happiness, shouldn't it be considered pleasure? Clive's moan reminded me of the night we met, of him climaxing from the touch of my whip.

That must have been the first time we were connected on the liminal plane. Hadn't I told Wexel I thought something special was going on? (Had I used the word *magical*?) I felt the near-vertigo again that came with being proven right. The connection between Clive and me really *did* start before that inadvertent collaring in the woods of Westchester.

Ira, meanwhile, processed what he saw into words: "The woman. She's a *slave*." He dragged his voice over that last word like an obscenity. "The other man we've seen isn't. Only she is slavebound so deeply that she has almost no thoughts of her own. So deeply that he could kill her with a thought. Monstrous."

Surely I misheard him, I thought to myself. Surely he said Barrow could kill her *without* a thought, i.e. without regard for her. He couldn't have meant that a thought could kill?

The cut at nine o'clock on the circle on Clive's back brought forth hisses from both of them. I felt Clive's jaw clench.

Ira stared at the blade instead of into space. "Her name. Her name is Anlyse."

I heard sounds of amazement from beyond the circle. I guess I should have been impressed with Ira, but I didn't know that level of detail was unusual.

"They traveled from the Lower East Side the day they attacked Jair and Kish."

Probably from that building we had visited, I thought. Meanwhile, Clive was still clenched tight. I kissed his temple, reminding him I was there, slowing my own breathing to encourage him to relax again.

Every muscle in him tensed up again as the next cut came over his ribs. He was probably extra-sensitive there, a fact I tucked into my mind for later. I massaged his neck with my fingers where I was holding him and drew breath to murmur something encouraging…

But before I could, I was caught up in a vision of my own. I was seeing Club Purgatory. Not the night that Clive and I met, but the first time he had met Ira. Ira drawing him in with a haughty yet smoldering look, a smart word, a clever turn of phrase, a domineering mien.

I was no longer hearing whatever Ira was narrating about the woman and the Partisans. My attention was wholly on Clive's memories unspooling, also moving backwards in time. Ira had said the working would reveal the past of she who'd held the knife, but had he known it would reveal Clive's past, too? At the time I could only guess, and my guess was that only I could see the visions seeping out of Clive's consciousness.

The pony mistress that he'd mentioned to me once, she was there. And as Ira continued to work backwards, there was Clive—twenty-first birthday, maybe?—bound for the first time in a professional's dungeon, his balls aching while the dominatrix strapped a gag into his mouth and flogged him. No sex—a "performance only" pro domme—followed by bone-shaking relief and shame when he came in the back of a taxi, unable to wait even for the privacy of home. Shaken to tears by his own reaction.

Oh, angel…

His answer was a heaving chest, a shuddering breath.

Ira made the cut at six, right along the spine, and I felt the blood trickle over my own fingers. The vision was shockingly intense: Clive, bent over a desk, gripping the far edge while the fraternity hazing paddle was swung again and again, full force, at his ass, the sound of laughter and screams of other pledges mixing in his ears like a raucous carnival.

In my own ears I heard a weak laugh. Of course I wasn't the only one seeing the visions: Clive was seeing them himself. I hushed him and reminded him to hold still. "Halfway there, angel."

Stay with me. I swear I heard the words as if he'd said them aloud, yet I was sure his mouth hadn't moved.

"I'm right here," I told him.

The next vision put me right into the bedroom I'd seen in our shared dream. Clive knelt naked on the rug, wrapping his balls with a shoelace, while on a screen a science fiction movie showed an interrogation and torture scene: a confession wrung from the hero by an alien queen while Clive wrung his cock dry with desperate tugs.

How far back were these visions going to go into his past? He was shaking in my arms, and I tried to get him to breathe with me, to once more be calm and still for the next bite from the knife. I looked up at Ira, willing him to do the same, until all three of us were taking long, slow breaths, Clive finally falling into synch with us, his shoulders settling and his head tucked into my neck.

He may have been ready for the next cut, but I was not at all prepared for the scream that came out of him along with it, nor for the sheer terror in how he clung to me. The vision was of pure darkness, the blackness the color of fear.

I held him as tightly as he held me, calling his name, but he was deep in whatever vision it was that I could not see. His mind had snapped shut like a trap. Ira had dropped the knife and had bent over, both hands over his eyes. Whatever he was seeing must have also been terrible, but he was on his own.

"Clive," I called. "I'm here."

He called my name and writhed as if he were in physical pain, as if the cut were continuing to burn. "I can't."

"Can't what, angel?" I stroked his hair, trying to restore calm.

"Can't get through it."

Ira looked up then, and placed both his hands on Clive's shoulders. So close to me, it looked like his skin and hair were suffused with a golden glow, but maybe my eyes were simply dilated. The knife was somewhere on the floor.

Ira gritted his teeth. "We're nearly there."

"I can't," Clive repeated.

"Maybe you can't," Ira said. "But! I! Can!" He punctuated each word with an open-handed smack right onto Clive's cut flesh, each blow harder than the last. Clive's anguished cry was loud in my ears and I felt the blood spatter—I don't know which thing triggered my reflexes, but I kicked Ira right in the stomach, sending him flying one direction and me and Clive the other, as the stool toppled backwards. I held him as we went down, landing on my back, keeping his wounds from touching the floor.

"I've got you, you're with me," I was saying to Clive, while he rode out the waves of pain Ira's impact had unleashed. I could not see any visions and I didn't know if Clive could, or if his reaction was purely physical. "I'm here."

He was sobbing, shaking, on the verge of screaming. And I could hear the comments of the others then, as if from far away: about how Ira had been kicked clear out of the circle, about how much blood there was, about how that wasn't supposed to happen. Was it the knife, the one that had made Jair bleed so much?

I remembered something Roland had said to Jair: *The knife lies.*

Voices were calling my name, but I couldn't answer. I was too busy calling Clive's. "Clive, angel? Are you all right?"

He was bleeding too much, exactly like when Jair's blood wouldn't stop flowing. I could feel it, slick and hot, and the overdose of adrenaline turned my heart to acid.

I could hear Jair's voice from very far away saying, "Breathe."

Breathe. Yes, just as he'd been told to do. I did that. Drew air into my lungs and let it out slowly, and tried to get Clive to do the same. "Clive, breathe with me." He did, as if some part of him still followed my commands, even while the rest of him was still riding out some kind of agony, body twitching. I pulled his head back and his eyelids were fluttering.

My heart was screaming: It's too soon to lose him! Not now! Not when we're just—!

"Clive! Don't go where I can't follow!" It felt like he was slipping deeper into darkness and I had to bite down hard on my own tears. I rolled him off me and onto my discarded robe. I didn't want to slap him like I had that time he'd been unconscious at Ira's. That didn't feel right. But what should I do? What could I do?

And from what I could hear, it seemed the others were trapped outside the circle. Why? It couldn't be another demon—Niko said the circle wouldn't allow outside spirits in. It was just us in there.

Just us. I began to suspect that I was the one keeping the others out. I didn't know how I was doing that, but I was. Which meant I didn't know how to undo it. I was on my own.

Clive gasped like he was drowning and I pressed my lips to his like I could give him oxygen. He seized me, pulling me down to him like I was everything he needed. Could you even call the state we were in then "arousal"? That barely describes the desperate hunger clawing at me, despite the danger. I had to do something besides just kiss him while he struggled with whatever internal fight had trapped him.

The bond between us could be a leash, I thought, or a lifeline. He needed to be freed from the trap in his own mind so he could center himself and draw himself in the way Jair had done the other day.

He needed to be released.

My bloody hand slipped down his chest to find him so stiff and hard it felt like it should've been painful in itself. Blood is not good lube. But it was enough to slip my hand up and down him. I could feel his spirit rousing, rallying, fighting against the undertow pulling him down.

"Come on, Clive," I was saying. "Come back to me. You're mine, remember? You belong to me. Your heart, your soul, every bit of you. This bit of you." I stroked faster and felt his own natural lube start to flow. "Your pleasure, your pain, all mine. Your voice, your will, all mine. Did you forget that?"

A whine sounded from the back of his throat, but his eyes remained clenched shut, his body shaking. He was trying so hard. But he couldn't break free.

"Are you ready, Clive? Are you ready to give yourself to me?" Such an archaic turn of phrase, but it seemed apt.

He gasped out a word, "Can't."

He couldn't push himself over that finish line. But I knew a way to trigger release. I got my jeans off and wrapped one of my legs over his, rutting against him. So close myself. Close enough that riding his leg would be more than enough.

I found the rhythm that matched his shudders and quite suddenly I was at the brink. "Come now, angel, come for me."

Clive cried out, his voice mixing with mine as my orgasm exploded, ripping through us, rippling through the liminal plane and swirling inside the containment bubble, prolonging the sensation like water taking a long time to circle a drain.

Wherever he had gone inside himself, he was present with me once again. I found myself kissing him, and his mouth was joyfully supple, all tension gone.

"Breathe," I said, when I could pull myself away. "Breathe."

"Yes, my lady," he said, eyes sparkling with candlelit tears.

THIRTY-SEVEN

A moment after the barrier came down, Jair was there, kneeling beside us, a hand on each of us. He sounded out of breath. "Are you okay?"

"I'm fine," Clive said automatically.

"How's the bleeding?" I asked him.

That gave him pause. "Um, I think it's all right. Now, anyway."

"Let me see." I slid off him and let him roll over onto his front so I could survey how badly he was cut. To really do that I needed to wipe away some of the blood. Good thing Jair had brought a pack of disinfecting wipes with him. "This is going to sting like a motherfucker."

"I can take it," Clive said with a little chuckle, as if he hadn't just been in intense psychological—or at least psychic—distress moments before. Ira had been right when he called him "tough."

"Here." Jair handed me a washcloth and a bottle of water, and I used that instead, sluicing it along Clive's skin, using my hand like a squeegee, and then following with the cloth.

What was revealed was nowhere near as bad as I expected. In fact, Clive's cuts were already healing. The first two incisions, at eleven and ten o'clock, were barely visible.

"How does it look?" he asked.

"Surprisingly fine." I took a disinfecting wipe after all and used it, but he barely hissed. "The marks are already disappearing. You're not even going to need a Band-Aid." I kissed him on the back of the neck and then tapped him twice on the back, my usual signal to clients it was time to turn over. Clive didn't know that, but he did it and sat up.

There was still blood everywhere. I wondered where everyone else was.

"Roland and Dag took Ira downstairs after you knocked him on his ass," Jair told me. He'd apparently needed some help getting up, but wasn't injured enough to stop him from immediately trying to write down everything he could remember.

Kish held open a trash bag while Jair, Clive, and I cleaned up as best we could—at least enough that we could get to the shower without leaving bloody handprints everywhere.

I took stock of myself as I wiped up. I was unharmed and mostly worried about Clive, despite his seemingly quick recovery. "Are you feeling anything? Pain? Vertigo?"

"I told you I'm fine," he said, getting to his feet. "I'm mostly curious about what the hell happened there, though."

"That's true for all of us, I think," Jair said. "Go get cleaned up for real. We'll take care of cleansing the space up here, and then we can do a post-mortem while we eat."

Clive helped me to stand. My legs were wobbly but held me well enough to climb back down the ladder-stairs and into the shower.

Clive wrapped his arms around me and we just stood there in the hot water for a while. "Why does it seem like the only time we get alone is in the shower?"

"Because that's the only time we're not busy saving the goddamn world," I answered. "So what happened there? Ira was doing his thing, and then you seemed to hit a wall."

"More like a stepped off a cliff into the abyss." Clive leaned back to let the water run over his face, then looked at me again.

"I got the feeling it was a lot older than that. I was seeing your memories," I told him. "Going backward in time."

"So much for the theory that the block everyone's been sensing in me has anything to do with you or the Partisans." He ran his fingers into his hair, soaking his head. "I'm sorry I ruined the working."

"Ha. I doubt you ruined it, angel. More likely that was me, trying to kick Ira in the balls." I'd hit him squarely in the stomach and shot him across the room like my leg was a loaded spring. "I wonder if he saw what was behind your mental block this time? I know I didn't."

He sighed. "I didn't, either. I'm still sorry for failing."

"Hush." I kissed him under the water and ran my fingers over his hair myself. "You're mine right now, remember? Only I get to judge whether you succeed or fail at anything."

His breath caught and then he smiled. "All right."

"Besides, I think we'll see what's in there when the time is right. There's a right time for everything." I kept telling myself that, as well. The empty ache where my legs met intensified suddenly. One of those times I was going to take him inside me. It was becoming more and more clear to me that only that would do. But not right that second, obviously. He was so utterly spent from what we'd just done, and I doubted that my ability to manipulate his state could counteract that. Plus the others were awaiting us.

"How did you know that would bring me back, though?" he asked, picking up the soap as we separated to do our actual washing up.

"You seemed trapped. I remembered what Niko had said about orgasm being a release and about how the power it unleashes can kind of knock things around. It seemed worth a try."

"Well worth it," Clive said with a smile.

⁂

By the time we got downstairs to the dining room, pizza had arrived. I expressed surprise that delivery could even get to the house and was told that C.B. had to go and pick it up. I had missed meeting the mysterious C.B. once again. Everyone was tucking in except Ira and Niko, who were sharing a pot of tea at a side table.

My next question: I wanted to know if a working could leave a person with heightened senses. "Because this pizza seems to be even more of a sensory feast than usual. I mean, look." I tore off a bite from a slice. "The crust is perfectly rippable, satisfyingly chewy. The cheese and sauce have melded together into a new substance that incorporates all four food groups."

Jair nodded in agreement but asked, "What are those again? Dairy, meat...?"

"Salt, fat, acid, heat," Kish said, and I pointed to indicate she knew exactly what I was talking about. My mouth was too full to answer any other way by then.

Niko looked like a sad puppy dog. With a sigh, he got up and tore himself off a slice.

"It's all right, little bro," Dag said. "No one expects you to become the freakin' Buddha overnight."

"I figure I'm off the wagon anyway…" He might have said more but I couldn't make out any other words among the chewing. He basically inhaled a slice with pepperoni and sausage and then sat back with a look of bliss on his face. "Ahhh." His stomach gurgled, though, and his expression grew concerned. "I keep forgetting that when I eat cheese it doesn't go down well."

"We got pills for that, bebe!" Kish put a bottle on the table. "I'm lactose intolerant, too."

He snagged it. "If I'm eating it regularly I do okay, but when it's been a while… Yeah."

Roland stood. "If everyone's fed, let's clean up and move to the living room?"

The group moved as one, everyone's chairs scraping as we went into action. While I wiped down the table, I asked Jair, "Is that *because* he's the Convenor? Or is Roland just the type who wants to organize everybody? Or is that *why* he's the Convenor?"

"Roland is actually *not* the type who wants to organize everybody, which is why I end up being the one making out the to do lists and cooking schedule." Jair sounded ever so slightly resentful about that, but I couldn't see his face. He was playing fridge Tetris, slotting the boxes of leftovers in wherever they would fit. "He's the Convenor because Gabriel, the previous Convenor, bestowed the role on him. I'll tell you something, though, Mira, I feel like since you showed up, Roland's been taking a more active lead."

"Because of me?"

He closed the fridge and looked at me. "Maybe. Or maybe just now that there are more of us, the cat herder really has to take action." He grinned. "That's what I hear in my head, you know, whenever someone says Convenor. Cat Herder."

I grinned back. "Are there other roles like that?"

"No, that's the only one I have a nickname for."

I couldn't tell if he was being too literal to goof with me or if he was sincere. I decided to take it as sincere. "I mean, what are the other named roles?"

"Oh. You already know some of them. Wisdomkeeper, Bladekeeper." He put a hand on his chest. "Guardian."

"Is there a list of all the roles somewhere? Besides in Niko's head, I mean."

"We'll get to that." Jair washed his hands at the kitchen sink. "I assume we'll resume formal training when we're not in the middle of a rescue operation."

Kish had mentioned before that some people got roles when they moved from initiate to adept, but… "Does everyone get a role?"

"Sometimes more than one. No one person should have too many roles though, or it consolidates power too much." He shooed me toward the living room. "Gabriel was Wisdomkeeper, Convenor, and Healer, and even he knew it was too much but he did it anyway."

In the living room I took the same spot on the couch that I had before and Clive settled without question or hesitation at my feet, leaning against my leg. The borrowed sweatpants I was wearing felt fluffy against my skin, and I had a sudden yearning for that group of people to be sitting down together for a less dire reason. To watch a movie or play a game or discuss group vacation plans or celebrate a birthday. To have my lover sit playfully at my feet where I could tousle his hair because we'd negotiated our role-playing for our mutual satisfaction and not because he owed me a life-debt.

But I wasn't sorry at all to have him there.

He was also wearing sweatpants, and had put on a long-sleeved shirt but had left the front unbuttoned. (Just the way I liked it.)

Roland sat down beside me with a notebook and a ballpoint pen, which he clicked nervously. I must have been looking at him incredulously because he mumbled, "Thought we might need to, you know, make a list or something."

Jair caught my eye and gave me a told-you-so nod.

"Why don't we start with Ira," Roland suggested. "And what you Gleaned."

Ira cleared his throat. He was seated at the edge of the room, in an armchair beside a small table, still nursing a pot of tea. "I am pleased to report that the operation was successful. I learned far more than I expected." He paused, before beginning a recitation of all he'd seen, though, to nod toward Clive and me. "Thank you, Clive, for allowing me in so deep. And you, Mira."

The thanks felt sincere, and the acknowledgment felt appropriate, if unusual to me. "You surprised me at the end, there," I said.

"For which I apologize. I got carried away by the moment and the prize. The surge of the flow brought me a wealth of knowledge, however. Such as…" He poured himself another cup of tea, and cradled it as if he needed the warmth. "Her name is Anlyse. And she is Barrow's slave."

"And this is a bad thing?" Clive asked.

"Yes. This is not a mutual pair bond such as you share with Mira. Perhaps 'thrall' would be a better word. It is a one-sided connection that allows him to control her, even to drain her."

"Without her consent?" I assumed.

That turned out to be a thorny assumption. Ira and Roland looked at each other like they were playing a mental game of rock-paper-scissors to determine who had to explain.

Ira lost. He hunched his shoulders and went on. "Consent is a complex concept within the practice. She no doubt believes she is acting of her own free will. But so do suicide bombers."

Clive sat up straight suddenly. "Wait, are you saying that someone who chooses to sacrifice themselves for a cause can't do it of their own free will?"

"No, of course not." Ira looked at Roland helplessly. "I am the wrong person to explain this."

Niko spoke from where he sat on the rug, cross-legged at the coffee table across from Clive. "Stop thinking about 'consent' and concentrate on what's going on energetically. There's a balance between Mira and Clive that is missing between Barrow and Anlyse. Our view of the practice puts a value judgment on that."

"In other words, it's evil," Jair said. That fit with what he'd told me before, about the lengths the Partisans would go to for their ends. "Ira, you said at one point in the working that he could kill her with a thought."

Ira simply nodded. I felt a chill and put a hand on Clive's shoulder.

Ira poured again, from the iron pot into a matching cup, the liquid making an almost musical sound as it poured. "A third man is less clear in the visions, because Anlyse is not bound to him, only to Barrow. It was her knife and her connection to the other is more tenuous.

"I received clear visual impressions of two places, though. I've sketched them." He handed a piece of paper to Jair, who was the nearest to him.

"I believe one is the location where they have Kanna. The place Anlyse went most often is south of here, and I have a strong impression of going under water, and of a tunnel. I have a clear vision of a tunnel approach but I confess I have no idea which one it is." He gestured for Roland to hand him the notebook and quickly sketched another drawing onto one page.

Jair passed the drawings around. Ira wasn't a half-bad artist. The sketches were full of recognizable detail and depth. I suppose surgeons have to have excellent hand-eye coordination. (But then how do you explain why so many doctors have terrible handwriting? Just one of the mysteries of life, I guess.) The building where he thought Kanna was being held was boxy and rectangular, like an old factory or warehouse.

"Did you see Kanna?" Kish asked him.

"No. The only impressions I have are of Anlyse, Barrow, and the one other male we've seen with them."

Roland chewed his lip. "I wish I could believe that's all of them."

"Either Barrow limits her contact with others, or that is the entirety of this cell," Ira said. "It would be very good news for us if there are only three of them."

"Do you think the guy is also a thrall?" I asked.

"I don't know. Perhaps." Ira held up the sketch of the tunnel approach. "I think she fears the tunnel, going under the river. That's why this is so clear."

"But not clear enough for you to read the street signs?" Kish asked.

"I think if we go down around the tunnels we might be able to figure out which one is a match, though?" Niko said. "And by 'we' I mean someone other than me, obviously."

"I might be able to sense it," Ira said. "Many of the impressions I am left with are non-visual."

"This time can we install some walkie-talkie apps before we go rushing off, though?" I asked. "We need to be able to stay in contact if possible."

"There are techniques for maintaining group contact in the liminal space," Ira said, "but I hesitate to suggest we try them."

"Why?" I asked.

"Because then you cannot accuse me of working a circle just to get between your legs." The asshole eyed me over the rim of the cup as he sipped, but at least he was being an honest asshole. "Also our ability levels are too disparate, it would take too long to master, and there is the question of what happened to Clive just now."

Yes, that. "You mean what you did to cause Clive to bleed uncontrollably?"

Ira's mouth tightened. "I do not believe the overbleeding was my doing. I was referring to the way Clive retreated into himself."

As if the cause of Clive retreating into himself was not what Ira had done. My outrage begin to simmer.

"Had it not been stemmed, Clive's retreat could well have resulted in him being in a state like Wexel's," he continued, which did nothing to cool my feelings on the matter. "Clive, I assume that the reason I met such resistance was the fact that I encountered the block we previously discussed?"

Clive's voice sounded as acid as I felt: "Maybe you just hit my limit."

"Perhaps your bond with Mira made it more difficult for me to sense when I was nearing those limits," Ira said. I would have ripped into him for shifting blame if he hadn't quickly followed it with: "I thank you again for allowing me to delve so deeply, and apologize for any trespass."

"Clive," Niko said, "if it isn't too much for you, could you describe what you were going through? It felt to me like you were… shrinking."

"That's how it felt to me, too," I added. "Like you were getting smaller and smaller."

"Like receding into the distance?" Niko asked.

"Or into himself." I couldn't help but touch his hair, then. "Like you were curling into yourself tighter and tighter."

Clive nodded as he leaned a little into my hand. "It felt a lot like the ego death you get sometimes on a psychedelic drug trip."

Blank and concerned stares all around. Clive chuckled. "I take it psychedelics aren't part of the practice, then."

"We have enough other ways to alter perception," Roland said carefully, but somehow what he said came out sounding very judge-y. "Drugs are, shall we say, largely eschewed."

I found that amusing, honestly. The Circle was fine with group orgies but found drug use morally questionable? Roland probed, "Have you had many psychedelic experiences?"

"Yes, several, in college and grad school." Clive chuckled again. "Linguists hang around a lot with the neuroscience and cognitive psych people, and they always have the best drugs."

I didn't like drugs in general because I didn't like being out of control, but I didn't mind if other people did them. "So what's 'ego death?'" I asked. "Because it sounds terrifying."

"It can be," he said, "because you lose your sense of self, but if you don't let that frighten you, it can be very euphoric and freeing."

I kept my hand on his shoulder. "It didn't feel like what you experienced was euphoric and freeing."

"No." His head bowed slightly, but he said nothing more.

"Is this different from an out of body experience?" I asked.

"Yes," Niko said. "But with the self in retreat, it's also a time when it's possible for possession to occur."

"Which you seem to be prone to," Ira said to Clive.

"*Prone to?*" Clive snapped. "I wasn't 'prone to' anything until you untethered my consciousness."

"I have already apologized for that unfortunate consequence," Ira replied, "but if you hadn't been putting up so much resistance to us seeing what was beyond your block, such a push would not have been necessary. There was definite backlash coming from your direction. It is why I initially believed you caused the fire."

Clive was having none of that: "You were the one responsible for whatever happened while I was in your power."

Ira's face darkened. "You can't blame us for thinking you were hiding something."

"And if I was?" Clive rose to his feet, taking a step out of my reach. "I never gave you permission to break down my fucking mind, Ira. Or to cut my soul free. I let you do a lot of things to me with your leading me on with hints about the Circle, but we never negotiated anything close to that."

"Well, with the Circle, you see how much is at stake here." Ira spread his hands as if showing vast wealth. "If we had any hope of getting beyond your block, it had to be a surprise."

"No, it didn't." Clive's hands shook. I think he was trying hard not to ball them into fists.

"It's very hard to sit here and listen to you get on your high horse about Barrow and Anlyse when you had no actual qualms about fucking up the inside of my head for the supposed sake of the Circle. Anlyse is sacrificing her body, her mind, for Barrow's cause? Maybe that's her choice. I didn't get a choice. You didn't give me one."

Ira's blush suffused his entire skull. I half-expected him to explode with rage. But his voice was quiet. "I thought we were quite clear with the possibilities of where we might go with that scene. But perhaps we were not, and for that, I apologize. But listen to how vehemently you're opposing me, Clive. Don't you think that's a symptom of how deeply averse you are to breaking down the block? You have never challenged a dominant in this fashion before. Whatever's in there is causing you to overreact."

I couldn't stay quiet on that one. "He's not overreacting. You're trying to make him think he is, to protect yourself."

Ira's "harrumph" came up almost like a belch. "Protect myself from what?"

"From admitting that you made a mistake. Your fragile ego can't take that you were in the wrong."

"And I suppose you've never made a mistake with a submissive, Mira? Never pushed one too far, never left their psyche in tatters? That is a mighty high horse you're—"

Clive cut him off, trying to defend me. "Of course she hasn't."

My heart was suddenly lodged in my throat, trapping the words I'd been about to speak: *Of course I have.* My fingertips barely touched the tail of his untucked shirt, as I reached out, trying to silence him before he could say more. Everything suddenly seemed so fragile, his skin, his mind, the new tendrils of emotion that were growing between us. *Of course I have.*

Clive sensed me reaching for him, I think. Or at least he stopped speaking. I cleared my own throat so that I could say what I needed to: "It isn't my 'perfection' as a dom that gives me the authority to criticize you, Ira. It's my experience."

I felt as if I were on a tightrope, like the wrong word would send me tumbling down, so I tiptoed through them carefully. "Yes. I have left a sub in tatters." I sucked in a breath, or maybe that was Clive. "Yes, I have pushed them too far." I had the urge to clutch at the fabric at the back of his shirt, in case he tried to run away from me. *Yes, I have been the one with blood on my hands.* "I know how important it is to admit the mistake. That's how I know."

I wanted Clive to turn and look at me, to see complete empathy and understanding in his eyes, a look I had already grown so attached to. But he stood stiffly—facing Ira, controlling his breathing—and that stiffness felt all too much like a refusal, like he was trying not to hear me.

I never asked to be idolized, I thought, though I wondered if it was true. *It's easy to be devoted to a goddess. Is it hard to serve a fallible human? Too hard?*

Ira's eyes glittered as his gaze darted from Clive to me. "If my error is that I aggrandize myself too much, yours is that you sell yourself short," he said. "If you wade into a working without complete confidence, you will drown when the first rip current hits you. And when you go down, you will both be lost. How can we trust you under pressure?"

Kish made a noise. "Mira's the only one of us who's any good under pressure! Have you seen what a mess we are? If it weren't for Mira, none of us would be here right now! Clive would be dead, Niko would be in Barrow's hands, and the rest of us might not have made it this far either."

Arguments erupted all around, Kish and Jair and Roland and Ira raising their voices, but I couldn't make out the words. All I could hear was Clive's breath, the rush of blood through his ears, and feel the tension and fear crackling along his skin.

And I could feel power gathering in the hand that was reaching for him. It felt like if I made a fist, I could crush his resistance like a soda can. I could make a hammer and shatter him. I could split an atom that was never meant to be split and take all that energy for myself, making Clive a part of me, an extension of me and nothing more.

I blinked back sudden tears of terror. Jair and Niko had called it evil. Did they truly not know that evil was right there in my grasp? My bond with Clive wasn't inherently virtuous. I could almost taste the fear in the sweat on the back of Clive's neck, under the beads of his collar. If he didn't like what Ira had tried to do to get past his resistance before, how would he feel about the fact I could obliterate it entirely? Could obliterate *him* entirely?

Terrifying. I couldn't move. Could barely breathe. It was like being on the edge of a cliff or a very high roof and fearing I might fling myself off in a moment of insanity.

Then something touched my fingertips. Clive, shifting backward just enough that I felt the small of his back again. I did not move as he lowered himself until he was again at my feet. My hand, frozen in place, came to rest once on the edge of his collar. As if it had always been there, always belonged there.

The moment he bent his head, I could breathe again, and sound rushed in, the last few words of the argument echoing even as everyone's heads turned to look at us. The moment he had settled into place had drawn their attention like the sound of a shotgun being primed.

"Don't ever try to tell me I don't understand what's at stake or question the lengths I'm willing to go to," Clive said. "I'm ready to do whatever Mira needs me to do. I don't expect any of you to understand that."

He looked back at me, then, and his eyes were clear and compassionate, as if he were saying, *Except you. You understand it perfectly well, don't you?*

I wouldn't say I understood it, no. But I accepted it. I gave him the smallest of nods and saw the hint of a smile ghost his lips. That emptiness at my core that only he could fill ached again.

Ira spoke, his voice low, perhaps even humble. "It was never my intention to put Clive at risk to get Kanna back. I cannot be the one to gauge whether the risk of his overbleeding, retreat, block, or possession is worthwhile. But she is my other half. Our pair bond is one of balance. Without her... I am half-empty."

I knew what he was feeling. I remembered screaming, just a short time ago, to Clive, telling him not to go where I could not follow, because being without him would be impossible to bear. I gathered we'd reached the point of the discussion where the only thing holding us up from running off to try to find Kanna right that second was that Clive might be in danger. So I threw Ira a bone. "I think if you leave Clive to me, he is not at greater risk than the rest of us."

Ira bowed his head in acknowledgment.

THIRTY-EIGHT

Before we went searching for Kanna, though, I needed a knife of my own. And before I could choose a knife, I needed to clear my mind.

And before I could do *that,* I needed to say something to Clive. Every instinct I had, actually, was telling me to pull him into the bedroom, lock the door, and have passionate, intense, utterly vanilla sex with him. No magic, no power games, no pain, no bondage, just two bodies moving together in space and time until the need to move was sated. But if Ira was going to respect Clive's and my bond, I felt it important to honor his and Kanna's, and get her back as fast as possible. Time was not a luxury we had.

So I pulled Clive into the bathroom with me while I dug around for a fresh maxi pad and tried to gauge whether a tampon was or was not a good idea from a psychoenergetic standpoint.

I kissed him and then bit him on the neck until his knees went weak, them caught him by the collar as he sank to the floor.

Clive looked up at me. "You didn't tell them what you saw during the working."

"No, I didn't, and given the smackdown you delivered to Ira about exceeding your limits, I decided I wasn't going to, either." I stroked his hair back from his forehead "But the block is still there, isn't it?"

"Yes. I've been thinking. Could it be a repressed memory from when I was a kid?" Clive swallowed and said softly, "Memory loss is often associated with a blow to the head."

True, but… "Somehow, I don't think you're blocking out how you fell off a bicycle, though."

Clive agreed. "Probably not."

"All the memories leading back to that one were of kink, of sex."

"I know." He let out a long breath.

"How old would you have been? If each memory was a leap backward from the previous?"

"Fourteen? Thirteen, maybe?"

Someone in Clive's past had hurt him and I wanted to hurt that person. My hands itched with the desire.

"Stand down, my lady. You can't protect me from my own past."

"I know." I made a fist. "But if I own you, Clive, I own all of you, including your darkness, your pain, your secrets. And some day I'm going to need to see into that darkness."

He nodded soberly. "When the time is right, you said."

"Yes. And I know your reflex is going to be to do anything you can to keep me out, but—"

"I'll try not to resist."

"Hush, that's not what I'm asking you." That was the crux of it. The thing I knew I needed to say, sooner and not later. "What I'm saying is, I won't take your resistance as a sign of disobedience or failure. If you fight me, so be it." I bent close enough that my lips brushed his as I spoke. "But if we fight, you know I'll win."

"Yes, m—" His words were swallowed in my kiss.

A knock told me that was all the time we had. It was time for me to get a blade.

❦

Upstairs, Dagger pulled the entire drawer out of the chest and laid it down in the middle of the floor. I sat across from her, crosslegged, Niko right beside me on one side, Clive on the other. Roland sat off to one side, too. Everyone else was downstairs but it was like I could feel their presence; I suppose that I could, through the bond of the Circle. The floor was completely clean, but was it slightly damp? Or was I imagining that?

I rubbed my fingers together. I was about to hold a knife in my hands for the first time since I'd sworn off using them. Well, not counting the one I'd picked up earlier today that had gone all stabby. Was that going to happen again? I tried not to think about it. Niko encouraged me to empty my mind of negative thoughts. I wondered if Ethan was doing all right…

So much for emptying my mind of negative thoughts.

I moved my hand slowly over the wrapped bundles, wondering what I was supposed to feel. Hot? Cold? I tried one at random and nicked myself trying to unwrap it. Dagger plucked it away from me as I stuck my finger in my mouth. Definitely not that one.

I tried again. "I'm not feeling anything, really."

Niko frowned. "You don't feel any slight pull or attraction?"

"No. If anything I feel the pile pushing me away."

"We did have an adept in the early nineties who used acupuncture needles instead of a blade," Roland said. "But there were techniques she couldn't adapt."

"Well, I don't know any techniques in the first place," I pointed out.

"But you will." Niko pressed his hands together and then held them palm up toward me. "Put your hands on mine?"

I touched my palms to his, which were warm and dry. He searched my eyes.

"Try again, now."

I hadn't felt anything while we were touching, but as I pulled my hands back, my palms were tingling. That tingle increased as I got near one area of the drawer, so I picked through the bundles there. One felt like it was buzzing like a cell phone—a scrap of denim tied with a shoelace. I undid the bow and stared at the blade in my open palm. It was silver with a black matte hilt. I pulled the denim out from under it and grasped it with my bare hand.

My fist tightened so much my arm trembled. I tried to let go and couldn't. "It won't let me drop it!"

"Deep breath, relax!" Roland barked.

"Yeah, right!" My arm shook so much that the point of the dagger came dangerously close to Clive's face.

Clive grabbed my wrist and I felt the blade trying to stab him. He flattened me, trapping my arm against the floor, while everyone else scrambled around us.

"Suggestions?" Clive asked through gritted teeth, while he held me and the knife still.

Niko squeezed his eyes shut. "I got nothing."

Clive met my eyes and gave me a speculating look.

I knew what he was thinking. "No."

"Just a scratch," he said. "Could it be worse than last time?"

"What if it is?"

"Let me try."

"All right. Of your own free will." I fixated on the pointed end of the knife.

Clive managed to get one hand free. He made a fist and then ran the back of his hand along the tip, leaving a red scratch in its wake.

My arm went limp. Thank goodness. Clive took the knife carefully from my still-bent fingers and handed it to Dagger, who cleaned and sheathed it.

"How did you think of that?" Niko asked.

"Read a lot of old fantasy books as a kid," Clive said with a shrug.

"Ah!" Niko brightened. "It's like in the fairy tales—once the cursed knife was drawn it had to draw blood, is that what you were thinking?"

"Yes, but are these knives cursed?" Clive asked as he helped me sit up.

"No," Dagger said. "But maybe there's something about the way Mira's energy combines with the vibrations these that makes them…thirsty."

"Bloodthirsty." I stood up to leave. "Maybe it's just not a good idea for me to have one."

"There's one you might want to try that isn't in the main bunch," Dagger said. "Hang on." She hopped up and opened another drawer in the chest, returning with a small wooden box. It was a puzzle box, I realized, intricately carved, and if there was a knife in there it had to be quite small.

She sat down and I was forced to get back down on the floor to see. She pushed at the design on the box until it opened, revealing what at first glance looked like a toy sword in a tiny sheath, as if made for a doll. When Dagger plucked it out of the box, I could see it was a necklace. The knife, including the blade and handle, was only about two inches long.

"Mom used to say if you were only using it for ritual purposes, only a size queen needed a knife bigger than this." She laid it in my palm.

So small, and yet even a knife the size of a toothpick could be deadly. "So what happens if I draw this one and can't let go of it?"

Clive knelt beside me, holding up his other, unmarked fist. "Make it match?"

I took a deep breath and pulled the tiny blade from its sheath. Since I was prepared for it, I wasn't overwhelmed by the surge of desire that seemed to race from my center to the fingers holding the blade. It throbbed with my heartbeat, echoing in the empty space I longed for Clive to fill. My entire body was growing warm, arousal blossoming through me as if I were being coaxed to readiness by whispered words and feather-light touches. I found if I didn't fight that desire, but embraced it, I could hold the blade in check…

For a while. But like the last one, I needed to feed it before it would go quiet again. I took another breath and pressed Clive's hand against his chest, his palm flat over his heart, getting ready to scratch a matching mark to the other.

It struck me then that this was what the little knife was for. It was never meant to be used for self-defense. It was the right size to use as a drawing tool, for writing glyphs on skin.

It seemed to take forever to touch the sharp tip to Clive's hand, as if time had slowed to a crawl. It took even longer to leave a design. I drew a stroke—curved at the top and then straight downward—and it felt as if I had just stroked all of the nerve endings between my legs. I drew another and gasped as the arousal redoubled. One more and the design would be done. One more.

Clive cried out as I finished the third and final stroke, not in pain but with the bellow I recognized as his orgasm cry. A pleasure peak swept through me, too—not a full release but a peak nonetheless. I sheathed the blade smoothly and time returned to normal. I was panting. So was Clive, his hand still over his heart as if he were pledging allegiance, and there on the back were three curved lines, nearly identical, each touching the other at the tip of the curve, making it look as if a cat with three claws had accidentally made a fancy letter M.

It wasn't an accident, of course. At some level I had known I was putting my mark on him. I licked away the beads of blood that had gathered at the bottom of each stroke like calligraphy ink. Clive gasped again and I felt another surge of lust, of the hunger to sate my needs, to use this gift from the universe as he was meant to be used—to satisfy every desire I could imagine.

Whew. "You okay?"

Clive licked his lips. "P-perfectly fine, my lady." He looked at his hand and his eyes shone with pride and need.

"Did you come?" Niko asked, eyes wide with curiosity and amazement, hovering to one side.

Clive looked down and shifted the visible prominence in his sweatpants. "I did, and yet I didn't."

"Same here," I told him. "What on earth was that?"

"You…you both…" Niko's hands fluttered as he tried to come up with the words to explain it. "You get that sex is a primal access to the liminal plane, right? And all these things we do, with knives and ceremonial objects, they're just a more sophisticated access to it. With the pair bond you have, you two are basically, um, having sex in the liminal plane whenever you do something like this."

"So we both came on the liminal plane—" I began.

"—but not on the physical one," Clive finished.

Roland stood. "Well, that's fine then. Aroused is the right state to be in to do battle with the Partisans. Drained is not."

Clive made a desperate noise but nodded in agreement.

"Mira, just be careful about drawing your blade," Roland said. "I think the reason you feel the way you do—compelled to draw blood—is that you've got a circuit open that's trying to close."

My womb felt heavy, ripe. I'm not sure I'd ever really felt my womb before. "Are you sure I'm safe to be around?"

"Do you think the blade would have been satisfied with anyone's blood, or only Clive's?" Niko asked.

Clive and I looked at each other. "I think it felt like it wanted Clive, but maybe it's just that I want Clive."

Niko blushed a little. "I suppose that could be it, too."

Roland looked a bit worried. "Did you have a bad experience with knives before?"

I sighed as I held out a hand to help Clive up. "You could say that."

It was the closest I'd come to talking about Ethan since the day I'd thrown my knives into the Hudson.

Clive kept hold of my hand after he stood. "You can tell us about it later. I don't need to know right now. Ira was right. We're going to need all our confidence to succeed." He squeezed my hand and I knew he was telling me he was ready for whatever I might dish out.

He was more ready than I was.

THIRTY-NINE

While I'd been getting equipped upstairs, Ira, Jair, and Kish had been planning our next move. A little Internet searching revealed that the tunnel approach Ira had drawn led to the Holland Tunnel. The lair of the evildoers was apparently in New Jersey.

The moment Niko joined them, though, Jair fell to his knees, digging his fingers into his hair, his breathing suddenly labored. "I can't."

I hurried over. "Are you having a panic attack?"

"No." Niko was right behind me and he put a hand on Jair's forearm. "He's feeling the backlash of leaving me unguarded the last time."

"Whew," Kish said. "That explains why I feel like puking my guts out. We've never had a problem with you releasing us before, though?"

"I think me actually getting into jeopardy has a backlash effect," Niko said, putting his other hand on Kish's shoulder. "Even though I'm fine now."

Niko had told us there were different kinds of bonds, including between Guardians and those being guarded, but I hadn't expected anything like what I saw happening to Jair.

"Don't make me leave you," Jair rasped, voice rough, as if he were in intense pain and trying not to cry.

"I won't," Niko said. "Kish?"

"I'm all right," she said. "Jair's bearing the brunt of it. He can stay put while I do whatever you need me to do."

"Then… Go out and confront my enemies," Niko said, and his voice had a formal ring to it. I could feel the weight of the order reverberate like a bell had rung. I wanted to ask about it, but not right that second.

The rescue party—Kish, Roland, Ira, Clive and me—climbed into the rusty Cadillac parked outside. (It was C.B.'s) Kish was the shortest so she sat in the middle of the back seat and didn't seem to mind at all that I ran my arm along the top of the seat so I could touch Clive. Roland drove and Ira navigated.

It was a long, tense ride down to the opposite end of Manhattan. I found myself getting drowsy, but whenever I would drift off to sleep I could feel a phantom knife in my hand and that would wake me up again.

We came out of the tunnel on the far side of the river and Ira directed Roland to pull off the highway immediately, into the neighborhood surrounding the tunnel approach. Some parts of New Jersey that closely faced Manhattan had gotten very tony and expensive in the last couple of decades. The area we went wasn't one of them. A few intrepid condo towers had sprung up but the area was still dominated by old warehouses and industrial spaces. Who wanted to live right next to the perpetual traffic jam of the tunnel approach? Rich folks had better options in Hoboken and other places where gentrification had already swept through.

Ira employed various techniques of the practice to seek for Kanna, drawing on his pair bond with her. He could sense her proximity if he was sufficiently aroused. At one point I whispered into Kish's ear, "Is he using his actual dick as a divining rod?"

She nodded and said, "Cop coming." Ira covered his lap with his jacket. It wouldn't do to get pulled over for indecent exposure. The cruiser passed without incident.

"Make a right," Ira said, and we turned onto a side street. "Now left…"

At that time of night, the area was basically deserted. We wove through, block by block, but it didn't seem to me like Ira's dick was very accurate. I said nothing, though. He was searching for his own wife. He was plenty motivated and probably anxious enough without me criticizing his masturbation techniques.

But we were definitely circling the same block we'd been on before. Could the signal between partners bounce around like a GPS getting confused by concrete and steel buildings?

Just when I thought I should say something, Roland beat me to it. "We've been down this street twice before. If we circle again, it's going to start to look suspicious."

"As if anyone is around to notice," Ira snarled. "That cop didn't give us a second glance."

"I meant our enemies might notice," Roland said patiently.

"We have to assume the Partisans will think we're going to try this," I added, "if they know you're husband and wife. Is there something they could do to block or misdirect your connection?"

"Unfortunately, yes," Roland said, putting an empathetic hand onto Ira's shoulder.

"No, I'm sure we're close," Ira insisted. "I can feel she's near—"

The windows on the top floor of a warehouse building up the street suddenly lit up as if a bolt of lightning were trapped indoors. There was no missing that. I blinked after it faded and could still see the outline behind my eyelids. "Did you all see that?"

"Weird night for a rave," Clive joked.

Roland pulled the car to the curb and threw the gearshift into park. "I'd say we found them."

We walked the half-block to the building. The front door was chained shut, a *For Sale or Lease* sign plastered across the windows. One of the first floor windows was shattered, held in place by cardboard taped from the inside.

In the back, we found a fire escape that could be reached if we climbed atop a dumpster.

Another flash of light came from above.

I had to ask. "Isn't that going to attract a lot of attention?"

"I bet only we can see it," Roland answered. "It's kind of like the flashes of light you see when you come. If they're in the middle of a working, this is an ideal time for an ambush. Rescuing Kanna should be our priority, but if we have a chance to do more…"

"What do you mean, *do more?*"

"Obviously, don't kill anyone," Roland said. "But anything we can do to harm their pursuit of us, or mess up their ability to perform the practice, is fair game."

The look on Ira's face made me think he was fantasizing about castrating Barrow.

The top floor was six flights up and the fire escape brought us to large windows that let us look directly into the wide open space that had once been a factory floor, only a few brick columns here and there. Far across that open floor I could see three people—two standing, one bound face up on a steeply tilted St. Andrew's cross. The bound figure was naked, the other two were draped in black.

"That's Kanna on the cross," Ira whispered, crouching below the level of the windows. "With Barrow and Anlyse. I don't see anyone else."

"Or sense them," Roland said, opening his eyes. "Whoever the third partisan is, he's not here. How should we proceed?"

"Presumably the trick we used to fool Barrow before won't work again," Clive said.

"I can probably pop his cork," Kish suggested. "I get the feeling he's good and aroused right now. That should knock him out of action for at least a minute."

Roland nodded. "Okay. Kish and I will take on Anlyse while you three work to free Kanna. Ira, if Barrow gets up, you'll have to deal with him since Mira and Clive have no real fighting techniques to draw on."

Nods all around.

It was as good a plan as any, really. There was no real way to sneak up on the Partisans. We slipped through the window. Kish rubbed her palms together, held one hand to her mouth, and blew a kiss in Barrow's direction.

I was already sprinting toward him as he bucked backwards and crumpled. He didn't stay down long, though. We'd reached Kanna but Barrow was already starting to get up. Ira didn't do anything fancy, opting instead to kick the leader of the Partisans in the face and then leap on top of him.

I hoped that would keep Barrow busy long enough for Clive and I to figure out how to free Kanna. She was bound to the cross with ropes that wound around her limbs in intricate ways. I don't know if there was some significance to the pattern or not. Clive began to work on her wrists and arms while I turned to her ankles and legs, but I froze when I realized what I was seeing and said "Kanna, don't move."

Between her legs was a post; in dungeon play, a dildo might be mounted there. But what I could see bound to the post looked chillingly like one of the knives I'd tested earlier at the Sanctuary. Only the hilt was visible because the rest was hidden by Kanna's body.

Inside her, I mean. The world seemed to narrow to the place where the weapon and Kanna's body met. The textured hilt was bound to the wood with thin crisscrossed cords. Her eyes were closed.

"Kanna, can you hear me? We're here to rescue you. Nod if you can."

Her head bobbed once.

"Hold very still, okay? Don't move." There was no way to undo the knots or even figure out where they were exactly. I just drew my tiny sword and sliced through the bindings. Bits of cord fell away and I steadied the hilt of the intruding weapon with one hand while sawing through the rest of the strands until the last of the wrapping was gone.

I couldn't see any blood and I took that as a good sign. I closed my hand around the hilt—the intense urge to get rid of it as quickly as possible battling with the absolute necessity to be careful. I eased it from the notch in the post, then slowly, slowly, pulled it free of Kanna.

The blade was clean, no evidence of blood at all. As it came free, the sounds of the fight behind me seemed to rush in, Roland and Kish shouting, a grunt from Barrow. I tried to fling the dagger away.

And I couldn't. Dammit. Dammit dammit dammit.

Clive had drawn his own blade and had sliced Kanna's arms free. Ira had torn through the ropes holding her legs. He heaved her into a fireman's carry.

"Go, go!" I shouted.

He did. Maybe he was running toward an exit? I hoped so. I could sense Anlyse, Kish, and Roland moving in the same direction, though who was pursuing whom, I didn't know. My hands were full of an entirely different problem.

"Mira," Clive said.

"Stand back." I pressed the two blades together to stop the shaking briefly, sucking in air, trying to get the energy flow through me. The little knife I could handle. I wanted nothing more than to inscribe my name across Clive's back—fantasizing about it and realizing, *no, even better, on his chest.*

The dagger that had been holding Kanna in place was a different story. Like a man who'd been pulled off a woman before he could finish, it wanted to plunge deep into flesh, to stab and stab and let forth a torrent. I turned in the direction the others had fled and there was Barrow, lying unconscious on the floor.

"Don't," Clive said. "Don't kill him. Mira, you can't."

Oh, but I could, I thought. Hadn't Niko called him evil? Did he deserve to live? He had killed Niko and Saira's parents and he would kill the people I loved, too, if given the chance. I could be the one to end that... The knife was telling me all kinds of things like that.

But I knew Barrow's life wasn't mine to take. I kept up my deep breathing, letting lust rage through me. I had to do something while I could still control myself. "On the cross. Quick."

Clive stepped into place and I was on him in a moment, tearing away his shirt with the big knife, exposing the skin of his chest. I dipped my head to suckle a nipple and tasted the sweat of exertion, salty and intoxicating, while repeating over and over in my head: *The small knife. The small knife.*

I didn't think I could keep the big knife in check long enough to write my entire name, so I settled for another "M", carved with the blade that was my own, in the same manner as before: one, two, three—

—orgasm. Clive cried out, his head flying back, exposing his throat—

—and I leaped onto Barrow and plunged the larger blade into his thigh.

It was a good plan, given the information I had. A very good plan, actually. I was able to let go immediately after stabbing him, as expected. And then we would have run away.

The information I didn't have was that Barrow wouldn't be incapacitated by the wound. If anything, he seemed energized by it. The instant after the knife plunged into him, he grabbed me by the throat. I flailed, my hand seeking the knife handle again, but I could not find it. I felt the back of my head hit the floor, and Barrow's fingers on my throat, and the black edge of the world grew bigger and bigger until all that was left was blackness.

FORTY

I awoke in Clive's arms. My eyes were closed, but I was very aware of his presence, both physical and otherwise. And I found his voice inside my head: *Are you awake?*

Are we alive? I thought in answer.

We are.

Details. I could feel my cheek pressed to his chest. I was lying between his legs. He must have been sitting up against a wall. In the background I could hear a kind of rhythmic scratching sound. I could feel the air on my skin.

Where did our clothes go?

No idea, Clive thought. *Neither of us is wearing a thing. Well, except my collar. Barrow tried to break it and failed.*

I would've thought that would be a good thing, but then he told me Barrow had used the collar to shackle him to the wall.

And how are we doing this? I asked. I'd never heard Clive's voice so clearly in my head before. We'd had moments where we seemed like we knew what each other were thinking, but this was a whole different level.

Melded on the liminal plane, I guess? If I'm quiet and still, I can even see your dreams. He told me I'd been dreaming about having to go back to school years later to take a final exam that I had missed. He also told me Barrow was just a few yards away from us, sharpening a blade.

That was the sound I was hearing. Then came Barrow's voice. "I can feel you quickening, slaveboy," he said from nearby. "Are you thinking about fucking her while she's senseless? Naughty naughty."

I've been trying not to answer him, Clive thought. *But he seems to know I'm not asleep.*

Or he says things to you to make you believe that he can sense you're awake. Barrow was right about Clive quickening though. I could feel him under me.

"I can feel her responding to you, too, slaveboy," Barrow said. "Do the two of you fit together like a hand in a glove? Does your key unlock her secrets?" His voice was suddenly nearer. "Are you like an incubus that can seduce her as she sleeps?" I hadn't heard him move, his footfalls were silent.

I couldn't help it. I raised my head and looked right at him. "I'm not asleep."

"Mira," he said. Of course he remembered that I'd told him my name.

"Barrow," I answered. "Sorry about your leg."

That startled a laugh out of him. "Did you not intend for me to come to harm?" In his hand he held the knife he had been sharpening. I recognized it as the one I'd stabbed him with. He was wearing black cargo pants and a black T-shirt, a Velcro brace of some kind around one forearm; his feet were bare. "Or are you merely sorry you failed to strike something more vital."

What a pompous ass. "I would've fled without hurting you if I could have. But I had a bit of a problem and had to put it somewhere You were convenient. What are you going to do with us?"

"That, my dear, really depends on you." His eyes were so dark it was hard to see his pupils. "Obviously I need to know everything you can tell me about that Circle of yours."

"Which isn't much." I sat up as he took another step closer to us.

"Every little bit helps." He drew waves in the air with the blade. The brace on his arm made me wonder: did knife-sharpening cause a repetitive motion injury? I was looking for any weakness he might have. His voice was calm. "I suppose you've been warned against trying to kill me?"

"Why, will you split in two or something?"

He laughed again. "Oh, I like you. If only, my dear. That would be quite a feat."

I was mostly trying to keep him talking until I could figure out what to do next. The room was windowless—like a closet, but bigger—with brick walls and a concrete floor. To me it looked like the same building we'd rescued Kanna from, but I wondered why Barrow would stay where the Circle could find him....

Unless he was keeping us as bait?

Clive and I kicked that thought around. *Why not just kill us?*

Perhaps he's as wary of killing us as we are of killing him?

But we could have been killed in how many fires they set...?

It didn't add up. I also wondered how likely it was that the Circle would come back to try to rescue us. If protecting Niko and Saira was really the number one priority, they should hightail it to a hippie commune in New Mexico or somewhere else far away where Barrow would never find them.

I knew they wouldn't do that, though. For one thing, because of the Circle bond, they probably couldn't just abandon us without some kind of backlash. But even without that, I couldn't imagine Jair and Kish and Niko giving up on us.

Which meant we needed to survive until they could free us, if we couldn't free ourselves. I told Barrow: "I'm pretty sure I took an oath of silence."

He mocked my expression. "'Pretty sure...?'"

"Yes." I decided to tell him; I don't even know why, but I did: "I experienced nonlinear time during my initiation ceremony. I don't remember it all. But I know there was supposed to be an oath."

There was, Clive confirmed.

"Ah." Barrow drew a curve in the air. "So it is merely an issue of which you fear more: the suffering that breaking your oath will bring down on you, or the suffering I will wreak to extract the information." I guess I didn't look impressed. We stared at each other for a bit before he added, "You only suffer once when you break an oath, whereas I can cause you to suffer endlessly."

Big whoop, I wanted to say, but I kept my cool. Underneath, I was still trying to grasp any advantage. The others would sense when we broke the oath. Could that help us in any way? Only if they didn't know where we were, I supposed. I let my question out: "What does it mean to break the oath, though, if you already know the group exists?"

Barrow merely shrugged.

"Besides. I told you we don't know much."

He wasn't buying it. "Am I supposed to believe you are naïve and merely have an incredible knack for magic?" He adjusted his britches. "I've felt your talents, remember."

I was too startled to hide it. "You call it magic?"

His gaze traveled all over the two of us. "What else would you call it?"

"They—we—call it the practice of psychometric physiological… wait, that's not it." My thoughts felt jumbled and I couldn't get the words to line up.

Clive filled it in. "The practice of psychophysiological energy transfer."

Barrow wore a bemused expression. "That sounds, dare I say it, rather bloodless? Only Americans would insist on such a thing. I'm surprised you don't have a cute acronym for it. PET or something."

"It's just 'the practice' for short. But we're so new we haven't even had formal training yet. We've just been winging it."

"Was this morsel of a slaveboy how Roland enticed you into their cult? It's clear the two of you are bonded."

His words irritated me. I knew I shouldn't let him get under my skin, but I couldn't help it. "If you must know, Clive and I were already bonded when we joined the Circle."

"That is intriguing." He seemed to examine me with greater scrutiny, then, and maybe a tinge of respect? "And did Roland illuminate for you the dangers and drawbacks of your relationship? Every bond bears a price."

"We haven't had time to get into it."

"Not even the cost of your circle bond? Tut-tut, that sounds suspiciously like uninformed consent."

Don't listen, Clive thought. *He's just trying to gaslight us.*

"I know enough to understand which side respects consent and which doesn't." I told Barrow, "I hear you're not big on consent yourself."

"You see? You do know something." He smiled coldly. "What else have you heard about me and my so-called side?"

Don't answer, Clive urged. *He's trying to get us talking.*

I know, but I'm trying to keep him talking at the same time… It was impossible to have it both ways. "We've heard you won't stop until every member of the Circle is dead."

"I would hope it might not come to that," he said. "But if you keep resisting me at every turn, I will have no other choice."

"If you kill us, you'll learn nothing from us."

"I didn't mean you specifically, just now." He shook his head. "Well, which will it be? You tell me everything or you will suffer."

"I could tell you everything and you could still make us suffer," I pointed out. "If you're going to threaten us, Barrow, at least don't present false choices."

That seemed to set him back on his heels. "You are strange." He said my name like he was tasting it: "Mira."

"Barrow."

"You don't fear my knowing your true name? The name your intimates use? I have power over you by it."

"That's only true if one fears being known." Don't ask me how I knew that. At that moment, I just felt it in my bones. "You only have whatever power over me I grant you."

"Is that so? You're a prisoner here. I can deny you food, water. I can force you."

I shrugged. "You can't force me to believe what I don't want to believe."

Barrow frowned. I think he just wasn't used to his threats having no effect. "Do you have no common sense, woman? You should be afraid."

But I felt no fear. It was just like being in the middle of the fire. There was no space for fear. "Common sense also says a pound of lead should fall faster than a pound of feathers." The only thing that gave me pause was that I had forgotten the edict not to look him in the eye. Maybe that was another part of why I wasn't afraid. He and I had been looking at each other the whole time and I felt no mystical mind control bending my will.

He shook his head. "Cavalier as you may be about your personal safety, you should at least be afraid that you're going to betray your people."

"What else can I tell you? You already know where the safe house is."

"And I know it was maddeningly empty of books or records. A library stripped of its books! Where are they, Mira?"

His question came at me forcefully, and my answer bounced back at him with just as much force: "Burned." Roland had told me the Partisans were out to destroy the Circle's knowledge. But the Circle itself had already come dangerously close to doing that themselves, and I let my outrage over that fact—that stupidity—lend force to my words. "They were all burned."

Barrow gritted his teeth. "You're lying."

"You wish that I was." The best lie is to tell the truth. I knew, of course, that we'd found some diaries in the tomb at Trinity, but I kept that knowledge buried under the story I told him, which was also true: "There was a Wisdomkeeper named Gabriel. The Circle had archived diaries of every member going back for… generations, I guess. But they were paranoid about people finding them and reading them, so Gabriel read them himself and as he finished each one, he burned it."

Barrow looked ill. "Foolish."

"Very." I thought he seemed awfully upset. "I would have thought you'd be happy. Isn't burning the Circle's books yourself high on your To Do list?"

Anger at my presumption flared in his eyes before he tamped it down. "So. Gabriel thought to make himself the only source of the knowledge?"

"I don't know what his motives were other than secrecy."

"Making one's self the sole source of anything is typical of cult leaders," Barrow murmured, almost to himself. "Did he demand favors in return for his blessings, I wonder?"

He's just trying to mess with us, Clive reminded me.

"I have no idea. All I know is he thought he could pass the knowledge on—magically—to someone new, but the transfer didn't work properly." It was surprisingly hard to use the word "magically" without cringing. But it was easy to let my own disgust over the lost knowledge seep into my voice. "Another reason we've been taught so little. The Circle only passes information by word of mouth. There are no instruction manuals." I wondered, if Barrow thought the knowledge was already lost, would he give up his quest to destroy it and the Circle? "My impression is that the Circle was nearly wiped out by AIDS in the 1980s, and what remains is just a vestige of what it once was."

"And what of other Circles? How much contact has there been with other secret-keepers?"

I voiced my surprise. "There are other Circles?"

Barrow licked his lips. "There used to be."

"Before you hunted them down, you mean."

He didn't answer that. "I take your ignorance to mean that your Circle has not been in contact with any others."

"That's kinda the problem with a secret society," I said. I could feel my thoughts shifting to a new perspective, though. Niko and Roland hadn't outright told us we were the first or only Circle, but it seemed obvious to me that Barrow must have wiped out others before us. And it occurred to me that maybe Barrow might even know of other Circles himself, in which case he had knowledge that we might want.

Which was one reason to keep talking to him. He'd already told me more than I knew before. My immediate thought was that if we could contact other Circles, we could band together against him—or at least warn them about him, if they didn't know.

His interrogation of me continued. "You call this Circle ia vestige. Yet they keep an Untouch'd Queen still?"

"A what?" He had to mean Saira, but I'd never heard that term before. "We were told the central figure is the Wisdomkeeper. Gabriel's successor."

"The Wisdomkeeper is the vessel into whom the knowledge was poured?"

"Yes." All I could picture was Niko, cradling a tiny cup of tea.

Barrow rubbed the underside of his chin with his thumb, like he was feeling the stubble there. "Do you know what happens in a spell like that? Where all the lore is thrust into a single mind?"

I felt a prickle at the back of my neck, a premonition that he was about to say something terrible. "No, what happens?"

"The person receiving it becomes an Oracle." He seemed to be gauging me for a reaction. I had none: the word meant nothing special to me. "An Oracle is, in some ways, no longer the person they once were. They are at the mercy of the lore. They are helpless before any petitioner who comes to ask a question."

"What do you mean 'helpless?'"

"Ask an Oracle a question and they are compelled to answer. They will go mad if they do not."

Make no mistake: Barrow was full of lies. But I knew the moment he said it that it was true. The realization crept over my skin like gooseflesh under cold rain, chilling as it sank in. So many little interactions with Niko, from the way he answered certain questions to Jair badgering us away from him, made it clear. But why hadn't anyone told us?

"An Oracle's grip on the present can be quite tenuous," Barrow added.

Jair had said he had lost his mind for a while, but... "Niko seems pretty down to Earth to me."

Barrow smiled. "Is that his name?"

I felt another chill. *Dammit. I suppose I shouldn't have given that away?*

Clive didn't think so. *If that had been a breach of our oath, we would have felt it.* So Barrow must have already known it.

"No one has told me their real name, as far as I know," I said.

His smile was still rather smug. "And the Untouch'd Queen? What of her?"

"I'm still not sure what you mean by 'Untouched Queen.'"

"The virgin whom the circle surrounds. Do you have some pseudoscientific term for her?" Barrow's face wore skeptical sarcasm. "You needn't lie, Mira. I know she must exist."

I let myself be stubborn. "But why? Why must she exist?"

"Because she is the true reason for the Circle's existence." Barrow was looking at the knife again rather than at me. "The core of the knowledge they keep is the knowledge of her and her power. So. How many are you?"

I had to count in my head: Roland, Saira, Niko, Jair and Kish, me and Clive, Dagger. Did C.B. count? I didn't think so or I would have sensed them. Ira and Kanna of course, too. "Ten. At least, I've met ten, and I don't sense anyone else through the bond."

"Very close to the requisite number for the most complex spells," he said. "I wouldn't call that 'a vestige.'"

"I don't know anything about the required number for anything," I replied, resenting his implication that I was lying or downplaying things… except of course I was downplaying things. I let myself be indignant anyway. "They told me they used to have many more, plus whole families living with them. And until this time last year, they would have been only six."

"Very well." He considered for a moment. "So, what's her name?"

I knew he meant Saira, but I still said, "Whose?"

He pronounced each word precisely. "Your precious, pure, potentiate virgin." His gaze shifted, once again looking past the blade right at me. His question was as direct as his gaze. "What is her name?"

"I told you I don't know anyone's real—"

"What is her name?"

Do you think it matters if I tell him?

Probably not. I bet he already knows it. This is just a power play on his part.

They taught us in self-defense class that you could try to meet force with force, or you could deflect, fold, slip away. But you could only do that if you weren't being trapped and held down. I *could* tell him, but it wouldn't save me. I could see that. "No," I said. "I don't think I should tell you that."

He nodded like I'd made a good point. "Well, I appreciate your cooperation up to this point. You realize, of course, that I must verify all that you've said."

"How do you plan to do that?" My shoulder blades itched where I'd been flogged the night of the party, reminding me of one way it could be accomplished.

"You don't play naïve well, Mira You want me to explain it in intimate detail? I have ways of, how would you put it, using the practice of the psychophysiological interface known as erotic sadomasochism to read the truth in your mind." He crouched down. "Did you not experience something like it during your initiation? Or do you not recall it."

"They flogged me," I said. "Before they would trust me."

He snorted dismissively. "Surface truths live on your skin. I will need to, literally, go deeper than that." He was close enough to touch me, to grab me, but he did not. He held out an open palm. "Despite what you may have heard, I would much rather do this consensually. The choice is yours to make."

So. He presented it in such a way that giving in almost seemed like an empowering choice. I had already told him the truth—if a partial truth—and choosing to cooperate further would save me some pain, no? But something didn't sit right with me.

His hand was outstretched like he was offering to help me up.

I went with my instincts. "I've made up my mind."

"You consent?"

"No." I felt my power surge as I refused him. "Come and get me."

FORTY-ONE

I truly believed that if I surprised him, I could take him. I knocked Barrow's hand away and swept one of his ankles with my free foot. As he went down I tried to grab him. But he twisted away and rolled smoothly to his feet, knife in one hand.

He was grinning. So arrogant. But perhaps he had reason to be. I got to my feet and realized my casual telepathy with Clive was gone. Barrow set the shackles on the worktable and I casted around for anything I could use. The table was bare except for a small sharpening steel and some sandpaper. No sign of our knives. Could I grab the stool he'd been sitting on and use it?

He shifted on the balls of his feet like a boxer, lithe and ready, but instead of lunging for me with the knife, his attack came with a soft huff of his breath: The Hand of Lust. I felt the fire in my core leap from smoldering to raging and out of reflex I struck back at him with the same.

He laughed, long and loud, unzipping his fly and exposing himself, quiveringly rampant.

"Thank you, my dear," he said, sucking a long breath through his teeth as if savoring the sensation. "You've just made it even easier to do what's necessary."

I didn't answer, edging further away from Clive and wondering if the door behind Barrow was locked. I would still have to get past Barrow to reach it, though, and could I bring myself to leave Clive? I was mentally prepared to suffer through whatever Barrow could muster, but I couldn't stand the thought of leaving Clive to it.

And I couldn't bring myself to simply give in. In the heat of the situation I could not work out why, but I just couldn't.

He darted at me, and as I instinctively tried to avoid the knife, he caught me with a fist in my hair. I tried everything I could to throw him off, but he was too balanced, too practiced. I found myself on the floor, again, one arm behind my back. Where was the knife? I could sense it in the room but it was no longer in his hand. He had one knee tucked behind one of mine, grinding my patella into the concrete.

"I'll let you choose, slaveboy."

"His name is Clive," I growled.

"Very well. *Clive.* My cock or my knife? Which one shall I pry this oyster open with? Surely there is a pearl inside."

The knife, I thought, though I knew Clive couldn't hear me anymore. *The knife.*

"Don't hurt her," Clive said.

"How much damage she sustains will be entirely dependent on how much she struggles."

"The knife, then," Clive said. I swear I felt a wave of anxiety from him—and a pang of disappointment from Barrow. "Mira," Clive went on. "Please don't hurt yourself."

I really wasn't in a position to argue. I felt the touch of steel against one bare buttock.

Barrow's voice was as cold as the metal. "Hands behind your head. Hitch up your knees."

I complied, telling myself that it wasn't consent if someone was holding a weapon to your skin; it was coercion.

"There is no force in the universe that requires balance, tit for tat, but deep down we each crave it," he said. "Whether you call it justice or revenge is merely a point of view."

Then I gasped as he drove a finger deep into me, sparking unwelcome pleasure.

"I didn't expect you to be so well lubricated."

Did he really not know how strong his Hand of Lust had been? I jabbed him the only way I could: verbally: "Aw, does that take the fun out of it for you?" Some of what he felt might be menstrual blood, too, I realized. The flow had slowed a lot after how much I had gushed back at the Sanctuary, but surely it wasn't done.

He patted me on the thigh, chuckling, one more sensual stroke before his hand withdrew.

When it returned, it felt different. Stiffer. Larger. As he slid his finger into me, I realized it had to be his finger *and the blade.*

I held my breath reflexively, even as my outrage kindled again. I craned my neck, trying to see.

"I trust you comprehend the situation. The same blade you sank into my flesh. It is only fair." He drove in and out of me slowly. The sharp edge of the blade was covered by his finger and I wondered, if I squeezed my muscles hard, would it cut him inside me? Or would I cut myself? I resisted the temptation to find out, trying to stay relaxed and not let my anger turn to a self-destructive reflex. I lay back and tried not to move.

But the more relaxed my muscles became, the more arousing the thrust was. And the more aroused I became, the less my thoughts made sense. I could not call it pleasure, exactly, when he was pouring gasoline onto the flames of my outrage. With each penetration, with each pass of the blade, it was like the rope that held my mind together was being sawed through. When it snapped, the curtain that hid my inner self from view would come crashing down.

He withdrew his finger one final time, but the blade remained, along with a mere thread of resistance in my mind. I was quivering all over. I could not feel the knife at all, really, once his finger was gone; it was too slim, too small, to really feel. But I knew it was there. I could sense the threat.

Barrow toyed with me, brushing a thumb over my most sensitive flesh in a parody of tenderness, letting me keep that shred of control for a while. But not for long. "Clive. Your mistress needs you."

I could hear Clive's breath and the rattling of the chain, while I was thinking, good god I despise the word "mistress." I wanted to cut Barrow's tongue out of his mouth and stuff it back down his throat to keep him from ever saying it again, but I didn't dare move a muscle.

"That's it. Closer. You should be able to reach her now. Carefully. Use your mouth. Don't cut yourself."

Clive's tongue sought out my traitorous clit. I'd been aroused so many times that day without release, and they all seemed to flood back at once. Holding my body rigid, the only place my release could be expressed was through my mouth. I screamed when everything flew loose— my thoughts, my mind, my consciousness, and any illusion of self-preservation I might have once held. There was no holding back, so I didn't. I didn't merely scream, I roared, I raged. I let my anger free and hoped that this time it would hurt someone truly deserving of being hurt.

FORTY-TWO

When you've unexpectedly got someone's blood—lurid, copious, and wet—on your hands, which one of you should be paralyzed with fear, you or them? For their sake, it had better be them.

I could sense Barrow chuckling. I can't say I could hear or see him because I was deep enough in my mind that the only sense I had was that all-sense Niko had talked about.

I wanted to stay there, to stay in that realm where I didn't have to do anything yet about the bad things that were probably happening on the physical plane.

But Barrow's voice kept pulling at me. "I have a new name for you." His voice seemed rich and wry, and now I could hear a breathless quality to it. "Lady Macbeth."

So he had seen it. My downfall. Caught red-handed.

This is what I am.

I opened my eyes to find I was lying spread-eagled on the floor, in the same room as before. Barrow was just getting up from a crouch in the farthest corner of the room from me. On my other side, Clive was huddled against the wall where he was chained, his arms over his head. Like they were both guarding themselves from a literal explosion. I could not tell if only moments had passed or hours. Logically it seemed only moments—I was still panting and sweating—but it also felt like I might have been in my head for hours or days.

I watched Barrow limp toward me and I thought: I did that. I had stabbed him in the leg and now he was damaged. Were we even, now that he'd shattered my internal barriers? He stopped at my feet. "I see we need to have a wee discussion about consent and power."

"There's no consent here," I said quickly, trying to find that mental balance I'd had before, but it was impossible when I felt like a complete failure. "We're your prisoners. Don't try to gaslight us into thinking we have choices."

He did not address my comment. "Don't move."

I held still as he bent down and reached between my legs. Where was the knife? I couldn't feel it or sense it.

It was no longer touching me. He retrieved it—miraculously unbloodied—from the floor. He sniffed it, then wiped the blade with a swab and tucked it into the Velcro brace on his arm, which I then realized *was a sheath* and not some newfangled carpal tunnel treatment. "Thank you for verifying that you told me the truth. But as you are no doubt aware, even despite the holes in your memory, this Gleaning exposed far more than your recent dealings with the Circle."

No kidding. I could practically smell the sickly scent of Ethan's blood. Good god there had been a lot of it.

Clive whimpered against the wall, like a puppy having a dream.

I had nothing I could say. My face felt hot from shame. From guilt.

Barrow looked from Clive to me and back. "You say I shouldn't bother to give you choices, Mira. But you need help—"

"Shut up, Barrow."

He drew himself up. "Are you so filled with self-loathing, merely for discovering that you are not the unblemished picture of moral perfection that you pretended to be, that you refuse assistance?"

I didn't dignify that with an answer.

"Were you unaware of your capacity to harm?"

Ethan. Ethan had certainly never believed I could be such a petty, vindictive bitch as to literally endanger his life. And for what? Because I was angry with him? That was what he called me—not that night, but later—*petty, vindictive bitch.*

He'd betrayed a sacred trust. And then so had I. A submissive makes a promise: to be loyal, to be faithful, to be *mine.* My reciprocal promise was to love him and keep him… which meant, of course, not to cause him irreparable harm.

I suppose it's debatable whether the harm to him was repairable or not—no parts of him were permanently severed, at least, but I couldn't attest to whether those parts remained in working order. And in any case, just because he failed to keep his promises didn't mean I should have broken mine.

"Anger is a useless emotion," I said, without realizing I'd said it aloud until Barrow answered me with a laugh.

"Not for working magic it's not." He took a step closer to me. "I fear you are correct about the Circle. They may be so lost that they don't even know exactly how dangerous you are."

My skin prickled all over as he said the word *dangerous.* "Who, me? I would have thought anyone holding a knife to their lover's genitals could have done what I did," I said sarcastically.

"That is not what I am referring to. I'm speaking of the damage you've done to yourself." He crouched beside me. "The gaps in your memory from your initiation? That kind of blackout is going to keep happening every time you use the practice and it's going to get worse the more you do. And in your situation, you cannot simply walk away from the practice." He glanced at Clive and I felt a sliver of ice lodge in my heart. "You cannot afford for it to happen again like it did…" He trailed off and closed his fist like he was grasping a knife hilt. "You know when."

Yes, I knew. The moment when my knife had cut deep into Ethan's traitorous flesh. I had to blink to keep from being absorbed in the flashback all over again. I sat up and forced myself to speak. To the man who was, like it or not, mine now. "Clive, are you all right?"

Clive did not answer.

"He is not conscious right now," Barrow said. "The pure force of your release caused him to retreat."

I had to ask. "Did he see…?"

"What I saw? I don't believe so." Barrow gestured at him. "Your choice, Mira. Shall I wake him up to face the full brunt of the horror, as you are now doing? Or shall I let him sleep peacefully, coming to no harm?"

I have to wonder, of course, how everything might have been different if I had said, *go ahead, wake him up.* Perhaps nothing would have been different because Barrow was prepared for any turn of events. But still, I wonder, had I not been a coward…?

"Let him sleep."

"Very well." Barrow stood and went to the door. Someone opened it from the other side and Barrow accepted some items they had brought. The door clicked shut and I heard the lock engage again—locked from the outside. I was glad I hadn't tried to get past him to it.

In his hands he held a pillow and some bedclothes. He shifted Clive onto his side so that his head was settled on the pillow and he put a blanket over him. Clive looked exhausted—dark circles under his eyes, face wan. I wanted to curl up with him and tell him everything was going to be okay. I wanted to murmur to him not to worry, that I'd take care of him. I'd promise that I'd never hurt him.

And I'd know that promise was worthless. My stomach curdled.

As Barrow tucked the blanket around him, he said, "I suspect the Circle misunderstands the nature of your relationship. Perhaps willfully."

I held that exact suspicion myself, but I just hugged my knees and said, "What do you mean?"

"You are fully aware that you own him, body and soul." It wasn't a question.

He knew it and I knew it, but the Circle… "They know we're bonded, but they don't really seem to know much about ownership bonds at all, much less life debts. They don't really comprehend what that means."

"Apparently not." Barrow handed me a bedsheet. "You can sense it, though, can't you? That you can siphon his power for yourself?"

I stared at him, clutching the sheet in my hands. "What?"

"Your slave can fuel you. On multiple levels. You might be drawing on him even now."

That didn't sound inherently bad. "Just temporarily, right?"

"It needn't be. The dominant partner can willfully take it all. Every iota of life force, if they wish." His expression was particularly poker-faced at that moment.

"I thought killing would cut you off from the practice," I argued.

"Under normal circumstances, it would. But when a slave's soul is consumed, well, it's no different than reabsorbing a part of yourself." Barrow shook his head slowly. "I doubt your Circlemates know this. If they did, I doubt they could accept it."

I remembered suddenly the reactions to Ira's realization that Anlyse was a slave to Barrow. Even Ira was horrified. What would happen when they learned the truth about me and Clive? Would we be Severed? I tried not to think about it—it would have to be dealt with later. Right at that moment I had to focus on dealing with Barrow. "The other Partisans of Fire, are they your slaves?"

Barrow chuckled. "Some are merely subservient at this time." He said nothing about Anlyse or how many others there were.

I stood cautiously, and wound the sheet around myself, frat-party toga style. He did nothing to stop me. In fact, once I was draped like a Greek statue he gave me a sarcastic bow and indicated I should sit on the lone stool at the workbench. "Lady Macbeth."

"If I'm Lady Macbeth, who does that make you? Iago?"

He chuckled and hopped lightly onto the workbench, settling cross-legged in one swift motion. "You think me a villain, but you have not heard the whole story, Mira."

I kept thinking what Clive had said/thought: *we can't trust him. He's going to try to gaslight us.* "Why do you want to tell me anything?"

"You and I have more in common than I thought," he said simply. "I understand you think I have no sense of fairness because you have been taught I am a villain, but this is not a cartoon. Nor even Shakespeare. We have much in common. In both present and past."

"Oh, really? And you think telling me that you, too, own someone body and soul is going to make me trust you? Or is it that you've also spilled the blood of someone you love in anger." My stomach turned again as I came too close for comfort to saying aloud what I had done to Ethan.

Barrow shook his head again. "Mira. Unschooled as you may be in the so-called 'practice,' you are no naif to the ways of power."

I just sat there waiting for him to explain what he meant by that.

"I will start by telling you a few more things your Oracle should have. Arousal is energy."

Arousal is energy. Sure, I thought. I knew that at some level even if those words hadn't been spoken to me before.

"In specific, arousal is a manipulation of the energy between the planes, drawing it from the aetheric realm into the physical one, through the gateway that is your body."

Right. That clicked with what Niko had told us. Niko, I wondered: was I ever going to see him again? And even if I did, would we have a chance to learn from him? Or was banishment from the Circle all I could look forward to if we escaped Barrow's clutches?

I pushed the thought away again and listened to what Barrow was saying. He was literally giving a lesson. Arousal was the manifestation of energy coming from the spiritual plane into the physical one through the gateway that is the human body. Got it.

"At some level, that is all a living being is: a gateway between the worlds. In Christian terms the body houses the soul. When you die, the physical connection withers away, but the spiritual portion can live on. Or not. The Buddhists are also correct: the soul can be reborn, or it can dissipate back into primordial aether. Are you with me so far?"

"Yes." What he'd said fit what we'd been taught about the body being the projection of the whole self into the physical dimension, the island sticking above the water. I let myself be drawn into the abstraction. It was calming to think in abstract terms and turn away, for the moment, from my feelings about Ethan and Clive and the moral implications.

"Your body as a gateway, of course, has various pieces and parts. You have, for lack of a better term, channels through which energy can flow."

"Like the acupuncture channels?"

He paused, considering. "Perhaps even those same channels. I don't know enough about them to say."

"I don't either, but I can at least get it on a metaphorical level."

He nodded. "As you've already gathered, of course, this aetheric energy, like water or lava or pressurized steam, is going to flow wherever it can. If the body is a gateway between the realms, it flows through normally. But various things can disrupt or change the flow." He rubbed the spot on his thigh where I'd stabbed him. "You can punch a hole in the gateway for one."

"I already apologized for that."

"I'm not bringing it up to make you feel guilty about it. If you're experiencing feelings of guilt I humbly suggest they likely have less to do with me and more to do with the submissive you mistreated."

That made me feel ill all over again.

"My point," he went on, and I was grateful for the distraction, "is that the basis of the so-called practice is mastering these ways of manipulating energy, yes? That includes manipulating the gateway that is your own body, as well as the bodies of others. Injury and trauma can cause the flow to be restricted."

"Like scar tissue blocking off a duct."

"Yes. And the thing is, when you are intimate, when you are entangled, when your spirit is enmeshed with another's—"

"When you're having sex, you mean?"

"If by 'having sex' you include all the complex interactions one finds both inside the ritual circle and in the BDSM dungeon—"

"Which I do."

"Fine, then. When enmeshed, if you damage another, you damage yourself."

I broke out in a sudden sweat. It was like I could feel the straight razor in my hand all over again, but this time I was going to slash myself with it and there was nothing I could do to stop it from happening. I hugged myself, trying not to lose the thread of what I had just learned in the rushing tide of emotions. "This… This is why we've been warned not to kill?"

His sarcasm stung. "And the fact that murder is morally reprehensible is not reason enough?"

Being annoyed at his smugness helped me stem that tide. "Of course it is. It's just… it's been implied there was some magical reason, but no one's told me yet what it is."

"I will tell you, if for no other reason than it may deter you from bringing about my demise." He pulled another knife from somewhere on his person—a pocket perhaps?—I didn't see where. It unfolded with a heavy metallic click. "It depends on how it is done, of course. Intention does matter… but not as much as one might think. Think about this. If I were to stab you, cut you, make you bleed… these things would entangle us on the liminal plane just as much as if we were intimate. Think about what happens when someone you are deeply intimate with dies."

"I haven't had a lover die." I knocked wood. "But I have friends who described it as like having your heart or soul ripped out."

"Indeed. It can be so damaging as to leave one unable to access the liminal plane at all." He seemed to be looking at the reflection of his own eyes in the shiny blade.

I shivered involuntarily, as I could not help but think about first Ethan, then Clive. What if Ethan had died that night? And Clive…when I was protecting him, was I also protecting myself from the damage I'd suffer if I lost him? Had it become meaningless to think of us as two separate beings? Any injury to either of us injured us both, right? That meant Barrow was a puzzle. "But you seem to be able to access the power just fine."

"Yes, that is true."

"Even though you killed members of the Circle." Niko's and Saira's parents.

Barrow nodded, eyes shadowed, and he seemed to be waiting for me to say more.

"You're saying… there are loopholes?"

"Think it through."

I could see only two possibilities. "Either you could killed them in such a way that you weren't entangled with them, or you're some kind of monster who can access the power even though you get mangled by the way you use it."

His smile was thin, a pale echo of the grin Niko wore while gleefully expounding about the practice. Barrow was a cold-blooded substitute teacher. "Surely you can guess a method of elimination that might leave no trace?"

In my mind I could hear the sound of the roof cracking and collapsing, the flames roaring and consuming Ira's house. "Partisans of Fire. That's why you're called that."

"Exactly correct." He seemed pleased. "Fire responds to no will. Fire has no intentions and can carry none."

I wondered, had they named themselves that, or had someone they'd tried to destroy named them? I wasn't about to ask that, though. "And it works on books, too, hm? That's what I've been told. That your purpose is to destroy the knowledge that the Circle is sworn to preserve."

"That is one of the aims. What you have not been told is why."

Another round of prickling gooseflesh rose across my back. He was, unfortunately, right about that. I had accepted the fact that the Partisans were villains dedicated to wiping out the Circle and the knowledge at face value. No one had mentioned why the Partisans might want to.

Barrow wasn't finished pointing out unasked/unanswered questions. "Your Untouch'd Queen. Have you given much thought to why she exists?"

"She's, um, some kind of pure access to the aetheric realm for the Circle?" As I said it I realized that really didn't make sense with what else I knew of the practice.

He looked at the folded knife in his hand. "She's a weapon."

A weapon. The word hung between us and didn't make sense. "Is she more like a knife or more like fire?"

He looked up. "You are very perceptive. She is more like fire. A force of nature. Once her power is unleashed, the destructive force cannot be stopped. And like fire, she can destroy huge swaths."

"And why would she do that?"

"It need not be her will, but the will of those who control her." He leaned his elbows on his bent knees, relaxing slightly. "Don't tell me you haven't thought it strange... if not unseemly and unfair... that a young woman should be asked to dedicate herself to so-called purity?"

He was right that in the back of my mind I had been thinking it was pretty weird and downright regressive to ask a girl to spend her life not only without sex but without even experiencing orgasm? You could get away with that kind of thing in the 19th century, but *now?* But I hadn't really had a chance to think it through with all the new things I'd been learning. I didn't approve of vows of celibacy for nuns and clergy really, either, but if a grown man or woman wanted to serve the church I figured it was their choice. Saira, though, as far as I knew, was only a teenager when she'd made hers...

I still didn't want to agree with Barrow, even if he was technically right. "Taking her mother's role in the Circle was Saira's choice."

"Was it?" he asked. "Was it truly?"

"She only took on the role because you killed her mother," I added.

He cocked his head. "Are you sure about that? The fact that her mother bore her seems to contradict your conclusion."

He was right again. I'd conflated Niko and Saira's stories in my mind. I closed my eyes, trying to think of what I knew. Saira's mother had been the virgin… until she wasn't, because she got pregnant.

"She raised her daughter to take her place," Barrow said. "That is… not a typical reaction to having a child, is it?"

That was, I had to agree, pretty fucked up. I reminded myself I didn't know the full story and he was likely to twist the fact to his ends, but still. It didn't sound good.

"Think about why a coven of ritual magicians would need to have a virgin around. Seems a bit strange, right? I'm sure you've realized by now that everyone has sex with everyone in a Circle. Save this one exception."

When he said "everyone has sex with everyone" I had a sensory flashback to my initiation, Jair between my legs, Kish's bosom against my cheek, the scrape of Roland's beard across my palm. "That's the first time I've heard anyone use the word 'coven' outside of a horror movie."

"The old words are sometimes the most accurate, though their meanings in the modern day may have been twisted," he said. "At any rate, you've no doubt heard the term 'virgin sacrifice.'"

"What are you saying? That they're raising her like a goat to be ritually slaughtered?"

He gave a curt nod. "Slaughter is perhaps a strong term, but, like the Oracle, she is not a person. She is the ultimate vessel into which the power can flow and collect. With no outlet, it simply grows and grows and grows. And with it, the destructive force."

"So you're saying Saira is like some kind of… psychic time bomb? And she would what, blow a hole in lower Manhattan if she were set off?"

Barrow tapped his chin, considering my words. "I do not think there would be a physical firebomb, but there very well could be. There may be multiple manifestations in the physical realms of the powerful release." He sounded grave. "Because it is a power of the blood, it could wipe out an entire bloodline. That means not only you, for example, but all your relatives, as well as all those you are entangled with intimately, and probably those one or two steps from them, as well. And by 'all relatives' I mean everyone genetically tied to you going back for many generations."

"How many?" I asked, somewhat stupidly, but I was trying to get some sense, any sense, of how large the scale of destruction he was describing would be.

"When the ancients discovered this power," he said, voice low, "its intent was to destroy an entire nation in one blow. The stronger she becomes, the farther it will reach."

I blinked, shaking my head, trying to wrap my mind around it. "You're saying genocide. The purpose was genocide."

"Exactly."

I wanted not to believe it. "These days, though, people don't just stay in their tribes or kingdoms. People are connected all over the world."

He simply nodded.

"You're saying if she were strong enough, she could wipe out, what? Half a continent?"

He nodded again. "At worst, the entire human race. At best, perhaps a large portion of some ethnic group. I have never seen the power of the Queen unleashed and if I am successful in my mission, no one will."

I suppose it was a good thing I was sitting down. Few things in life have made me swoon, but that thought was so monstrous, so immense, and so troubling, that I felt a wave of nausea and vertigo sweep through me worse than what I'd felt when thinking about Ethan. "I… don't think Roland knows this."

"Are you sure?"

"No." I could not be sure without asking him. But it seemed unlikely to me. "I told you, I don't think they really know much of anything. Niko can't even access the memories he was given in real time. He has to sit down and write it out."

I was, of course, still not telling him about the diaries that had been found in Trinity Cemetery. I think, in that moment, I had forgotten them. But that was part of what he was telling me about myself, wasn't it? That there were holes in my memory and that was a danger.

"And even when he does sit down to write out a memory," I told him, "sometimes what he gets is gobbledygook."

Barrow inclined his head. "No wonder your training has been so limited, if that's the status of your font of knowledge. His ignorance is detrimental to all in the Circle."

"I'm sure Saira has no idea she's a danger."

"Which only makes her all the more dangerous," Barrow said.

"So you have to kill her? You have no choice?"

He rested his arms on his knees. "To use your bomb analogy, it is possible to defuse her, to undo what has been done, if she is deflowered with the proper precautions in place. But if it goes wrong, it could set her off instead. It is a huge risk."

"But you know the defusing technique?"

"It is a series of steps, but yes, I know them." He shook his head. "I know what you're thinking. You're imagining a scenario where your virgin queen submits willingly to me." His laugh was low and bitter. "Not everyone is as self-sacrificing as you, Mira. Most would rather see a few million of their fellow humans die, than suffer the necessary rape and torture."

"It requires rape?"

"She must be Undone." His face was impassive. "Some of the scriptures refer to her as Unbroken rather than Untouched. This does not merely refer to the state of her hymen or her skin." His eyes closed then, and I realized he was holding himself quite still.

Somehow knowing that he didn't want me to see or sense what he was feeling only reminded me that I thought him a monster. I poked him with the only stick I had: "You would enjoy breaking her more than killing her."

His eyes snapped open. "Don't talk like you know me. You don't know me at all."

I merely shrugged. He didn't trust himself to say anything more, I think, because he went to the door and knocked. Someone on the other side opened it for him, and he abruptly left without a parting word.

FORTY-THREE

There are two questions you have to ask yourself in a relationship. The first one is, do I trust my partner? That probably only gets asked once, maybe twice, in most relationships: at the beginning, and at the beginning of the end.

The second question, though, is tricky, because it seems like it either never gets asked at all, or it gets asked far too often. The second one is: do I trust myself?

While I slept, I had no defenses from the memories I had tried so hard to suppress. The moment when I had cut Ethan was inescapable. The sound of his gasp of shock and horror was a sound of distress so intense, so far beyond his usual playacted cries and moans, that it turned heads. I hadn't really even registered it at the time because I had been so enraged all I could hear was static, all I could see was a white hot flash. But unlike my usual dreams, I heard it over and over, like the clanking of the chains of the Ghost of Dungeons Past. The words would tumble from his mouth and then that gasp. Someone nearby would then scream in the moments afterward, but that sound didn't affect me nearly as much as the sickening reality borne by Ethan's breath.

I know. In every moment in time we are moving forward. So, yes, every moment is the precipice between the past and the future. We are constantly changing. But sometimes something happens in a split second that makes everything that came before it, and everything after, forever changed. Like losing one's virginity. That's supposed to be one of those moments, though I had never put any stock in the cultural baggage that made it such a big deal. (Knowing what I do about the practice, now, I can say there's a chance some of that cultural baggage once had a valid basis. But patriarchal gender expectations are still bullshit and don't you forget it.)

Anyway. Ethan and I would never be, could never be, the same again. But I didn't have to remember the moment it all changed in such vivid detail to know that was true.

I clawed my way out of the nightmare-flashback to find myself alone, with no sign nor sense of where Clive might be. I felt disoriented in time, like my sense of how much time had passed had been obliterated by my being stuck on that moment. I tried to push it aside and concentrate on the present. I was in another windowless room of concrete and brick, similar to the previous one. For a moment it felt almost ridiculous. What kind of place was full of windowless rooms? But then a perfectly reasonable explanation came to me: self-storage units. The whole building had once been a factory, then was at least partially repurposed as a storage place, before being put up for sale. Maybe gentrification would reach there after all, and the place would be luxury condos next.

I vaguely wondered if whoever slept here in the future would sense what had happened in this space, while I tried to divine it for myself. How long had I been here? This room looked and felt more like a bedroom than a cell. I was on a thin mattress on the floor, a sheet and blanket wrapped around one leg as if I'd tossed and turned a bit while I slept. Beside the mattress was an upturned crate acting as a night table. On it was a small, lit lamp and in it were a handful of books. One of them—a notebook—had a ballpoint pen protruding from the pages.

I sat up. I was wearing an oversized T-shirt and nothing else. It smelled—not unpleasantly—like it belonged to someone else. A masculine scent. But whose? I was not bound, but there were marks on my wrists from when I'd previously been.

I rubbed them, trying to remember being either bound or freed. Nothing would come to me, though. My head throbbed. Some moment of change had taken place… but I couldn't recall it. I made the assumption I was still a prisoner and that the shirt was Barrow's. (My assumption would be right.)

He'd told me there were holes in my memory. And he'd said they would worsen the more I used the practice. I checked my hands for blood and my body for cuts or bruises. I found nothing I didn't expect to find. But I couldn't remember how I got in there, in what was obviously someone else's bed. Barrow's bed. And where was Clive?

I was just trying to center myself enough to try to find him through the bond when I heard the locks being undone on the door from the outside.

I stayed put instead of trying to hurriedly find a way to attack. The door opened. I was surprised to see a young man I didn't recognize. My first thought was that he was hapa like me. His hair was overlong and straight like Jair's, but he had deep-set eyes (beautiful, really) and a bit of a hangdog mien that reminded me of Roland. So did his tone of complaint when reality wasn't as he expected: "You're not supposed to be awake yet."

"Who are you?" I asked.

"I'm not supposed to talk to you." He was carrying a cardboard box lid like a tray, and he set it down on the floor. He had brought me food. I couldn't remember the last time I ate, but I didn't feel hungry.

"But what's your name?" I insisted. "Or should I just call you 'hey you'?"

"Barrow will be back soon." He seemed nervous, like he'd been sent into the tiger cage with a tray of raw meat.

"Why aren't you supposed to talk to me?"

"Barrow's orders," he said, then seemed to realize he'd already violated those orders. He cursed softly to himself and fled, latching the door from the outside.

I got up to examine the room and stretch my legs. A zip-top duffel bag lay against the far wall, a jumble of clothes—mostly black T-shirts and socks—in it. (Yes, I checked.) Another small pile of books and magazines looked like they could have come from a used bookstore bargain bin. One was a well-thumbed paperback of Grimm's fairy tales. Another appeared to be an old camping guide for British Boy Scouts. (I hadn't known there were British Boy Scouts.)

I sat on the mattress to look at what I'd been brought. Bottled water, plastic-wrapped snack cakes, a sandwich in a triangular box. Convenience store food.

But I wasn't hungry. That was expected. Even though things were calm at that moment, my nervous system was still in fight or flight mode. I expected feelings like hunger to be suppressed until I felt safe again.

I decided to slip the notebook from the crate and see what was written there.

Good thing I was already sitting down. Where the pen marked the pages, there was a note to me. From me. In my own handwriting. It read:

Mira: try trusting this time.

-Mira

My heart began to pound—fight or flight indeed—on seeing those words. What moment of transformation had I forgotten? When did I write that?

A knock came at the door, then, and I slipped the notebook back into place and pretended I hadn't moved. Why knock? Wouldn't that just give me the chance to ready an ambush? Barrow came in, knife in hand. So he wasn't a complete fool. When he saw I was sitting up and wasn't trying to stab him with the ballpoint pen—even though I thought about it—he closed the door behind him and sheathed the blade.

His smile was strangely warm, as if he found the fact I hadn't jumped him endearing. "How are you feeling?"

I let myself give the automatic answer, even though I'd spent years training myself out of it: "Fine." In truth, my palms were prickling and my heart continued to race. What exactly was going on? "I'm fine."

His smile turned a bit wistful at my curt tone. "What's the last thing you remember?"

I tried to calm myself enough to dredge it up. "We talked about Saira being a tool of genocide. And how dangerous the… gaps in my memory are."

His face fell a bit, but he recovered and crouched down, voice again warm. "The danger to you and to your slave most of all."

"Don't call him that."

His eyes darkened and he sat crosslegged on the floor next to the cardboard tray. "And what else would you have me call a man whom you own wholly, body and soul? Do you recall us discussing that?"

I did. And I recalled thinking that if the Circle knew the true nature of my hold over Clive, we might not be part of them much longer. I looked at my hands. "I didn't ask for that. Nor did he."

"Forces of nature don't ask for consent."

"So you're saying a bond like that can just happen naturally?" I was angry—at myself, mostly—and I raised my voice. "That you can trip and fall into a… a situation where your life can be forfeit to someone else?"

He didn't rise to the bait. "That is not what I said. Think about what a bond is, Mira. It's an entanglement of your being with another's. That can happen many ways, on many levels. What you and Clive have achieved is rare—"

"Achieved. Like it's some lofty goal." He'd told me I could drain Clive like an external battery.

"For some, it would be." But he said it with a bit of a sneer. "For those who think it proof of their moral rectitude."

I felt bile in the back of my throat. Once upon a time I had believed that my lifestyle, my relationship, was superior in some way to that of those who were "less evolved." That was before my exalted submissive partner—whom I believed regularly threw himself onto the sacrificial altar for me, to worship *me*—turned out to have been cheating on me all along. Ethan had a lot to answer for.

I covered my eyes with my hands, then pulled them away as if they were still blood-covered. I had to look to make sure. The apparitions of the past weren't limited to my dreams, apparently. "What did you do to me?" I demanded, staring at my palms.

"Was that a rhetorical question? Or do you need the real answer again?"

I looked at him, trying to determine if he actually resembled Ethan at all or if that was my memory gone mad, superimposing the image. (No, they really did not look alike.) "You'd give me the real answer?"

"You don't remember it, but I already did." He looked concerned. "Take a deep breath. Center yourself. Close your eyes if you have to. And listen."

I did not close my eyes, but I let myself focus on the concrete floor between us instead of looking at him.

"The Gleaning technique I used on you is called Pandora's Box. Perhaps for obvious reasons. I thought your most tightly held secret would be something about the Circle, but no. You had a different set of skeletons in your closet. Pandora's Box blows the lid off your most tightly held feelings and memories, and sends them flying."

I stared at my hands. "And they're still flying around. I can't… stop seeing what happened that night."

"The more deeply buried they are, the more havoc they wreak when they emerge." His voice was near. "Mira, for what it's worth, you've needed to deal with this."

My hands shook. "You don't understand how close I came to—" I couldn't even say it.

"To doing real damage? Is that what you were going to say?"

My blood ran cold. That was *exactly* what I had been about to say.

"Mira, you nearly—"

"Shut up." Ethan and I had gone to a party, one of the secret ones that are hard to get invited to. But he and I, we were always invited to those—he said—because to not invite us would have been like Hollywood snubbing Kim and Kanye or whoever the "it" couple was. He would actually say things like that.

Such bullshit. But I indulged his egoistic impulses, sometimes, because I knew I would relish taking him down a peg or three. It was part of our dynamic. And it wasn't a coincidence that a cross in the middle of the main room would always free up for us. People liked watching us play, liked watching me take him apart with my whips and knives and words. I liked the attention, too. I liked the thought—don't laugh—that we were setting a good example.

"Accidents happen, Mira."

Okay, laugh. I did when Barrow said that. Because I found it laughable to label it an "accident." There had been people watching us, as I said. The party space was not large compared to the number of people packed into the Manhattan loft, so they were close to us. One woman in particular was beside us, staring at him like she was really into him. None of that was unusual. None of that was notable.

It was also not unusual in public scenes for me to make Ethan confess and atone for his sins. Depending on our mood—his mood, really—they could range from the petty and ridiculous, like leaving the toilet seat up in the middle of the night, to more serious things like childhood transgressions or being a disrespectful pill to a friend of mine. It wasn't always how we played, but… sometimes.

That day, though, he had been a pill all day. All week, really. Maybe all month.

Maybe all year. I'd been very wrapped up in volunteer work and my career advancement at the gym and spa. I had worried I hadn't been giving him enough attention, but I thought a public party would be just the thing to patch things up. I hoped we could bask in the glow of a really intense scene for weeks afterward. Maybe when we were both feeling good, then we could work on some of our issues.

"You can't call something so premeditated an accident," I told Barrow. "For weeks I'd been building up how I planned to use the straight razor."

"But did you intend to cut him so? Think, Mira, *think*."

"I don't want to think about it!"

"You no longer have a choice about that."

True. That was true. I could feel the handle in my hand, antique whalebone, circa 1910, the blade feather light…

It went from apparition to reality as Barrow put an actual straight razor into my hand. "Tell me what you were going to do with it."

Was he crazy? He knew what would happen when I held a blade. "Does it matter? Isn't what matters that I placed the cutting edge against his skin and—"

"This isn't a court of law. Maybe you don't care about your intentions, but I do." His hand was still covering mine, holding it still, and he looked into my eyes. He had handed me a weapon. The lump in my throat made it hard to breathe. "Tell me what happened that night. You went to a party. Your submissive was surly. You intended to—"

"Beat it out of him." I found myself trying to breathe in time with him, to slow myself down and keep calm. "It was part of our dynamic. He would act out and expect to be punished, and that would clear the air and we'd be hunky dory for a couple of weeks."

Barrow gave a short nod, but I cringed. When I said it like that, when I imagined what he must be hearing, it must have sounded like a terrible relationship. Well, to be honest, it was. In my defense, I added, "I thought he'd change. I thought we'd grow. Together. That he'd mature into a dependable, loyal, obedient partner, who would thrive on being cared for. I thought that was what he wanted."

"Sounds like you wanted a golden retriever, not a man," Barrow said.

I yanked my hand away and flicked open the razor. It wasn't mine—that one was at the bottom of the Hudson, and I felt a little pang of loss. That razor had been older than I was by a lot. It might have been a hundred years old. Thanks to me, it was nothing. I'd practiced with it in the weeks leading up to the party, flipping it over and over in my hand. Sharp side, dull side. Sharp side, dull side. Barrow's razor felt similar in my hand; it moved the same, feather light. Did he shave with it? How well did this blade know his skin? I felt the rush of desire I knew would come once the blade was bared, thirsty for blood. How long could I hold it back? I grimaced.

"Don't be angry because I'm right," he prodded. "Tell me more about that night."

I looked at my own reflection in the shine of the blade. It was bright as a mirror but the curve distorted my face. "There was a woman there I'd seen before. She had just finished getting spanked herself and she watched us play. Well, lots of people did. And it wasn't weird for someone to be focused on Ethan. He was…"

"A centerpiece of attention," Barrow gently prompted.

"To put it mildly." When Ethan was on the cross, usually everyone in the room ended up watching. The handle in my hand seemed to throb, but it was probably my own pulse I was feeling. "This woman, I didn't even know her, but I suddenly felt… jealous of her? It was strange. Like I suddenly got this vibe. I thought, that's weird. I don't even know who she is. Maybe it's my hormones or something. Ethan didn't seem to notice her."

"Why didn't you blindfold him?"

"I wanted to see the fear in his eyes when I showed him the razor. I'd been telling him about it, threatening him with it, for weeks. I'd told him I was going to shave his testicles with it to prove how sharp it was." I was remembering it as I said it. I'd suppressed all that in the aftermath, but the details were coming back. "But that's why I say it was premeditated. I literally built him up for a month or more."

"But it wasn't the first time you'd cut him?"

"No. We did all kinds of knife play and blood play." I drew the blade through the air and felt the thirst increase. "I'd sometimes pierce him."

"So what made this time different?"

Indeed. "Knife play was a different kind of torment from flogging or spanking. Knife play was never punishment or to atone for wrongdoing. It was always pure sadism on my part— something I loved, and that he loved to fear. He loved being pushed to the edge of terror. To the point he lost himself."

"Interesting."

I had closed my eyes again, centering my breaths, but there was no staying calm with a live razor in my hand. "He said it was why he knew I was the one. Because no one else could dangle him off the cliff like that and then pull him back. No one else could take him apart completely and then put him back together again."

"He was not entirely wrong about that, Mira. We can't access the true depths of our power until we are shattered."

"Ethan said it was the closest thing to a spiritual experience he had in his life."

"No wonder he worshipped you like a goddess, then?"

Goddess. That was another one of those words that left a bitter taste in my mouth. "Deities are supposed to be infallible."

"And their followers are not." Barrow shifted, sitting beside me on the mattress. "The churches are filled with sinners."

"Yes, but I'm not actually a goddess and I didn't have the right to do to him what I did." I could slit Barrow's throat, I realized. I could just grab him and kill him right there…which I was tempted for a moment to do, to get out of having to tell him all that had happened that night.

But I told him. "I was menacing him with the razor, all along his inner thigh, and literally shaving hairs off his balls, when he started to confess." That wouldn't have been unusual if I'd been flogging him until he broke down. But it wasn't one of those scenes—or it wasn't supposed to be. "He did that sometimes when we played. Begged for me to punish him for infractions he'd committed. But usually I was the one laying out the charges and the punishment. This was… unexpected."

"Did you resent him trying to take control of the scene?"

"No. There has to be some back-and-forth or it's all just mechanical. It wasn't against the rules of our relationship, per se, just… unexpected. I was startled for a moment, but then I went with it. I thought, maybe this is the breakthrough I've been hoping for. Maybe this is what all the relationship angst we'd been having was building up to."

"Mira. It was."

True. "I'd hoped for a better outcome, though."

"Because you're an optimist who believes in the good in people."

"Or I did, before that moment." That moment. His confession started out about how he had been a bad submissive that week, listing out the things he'd done that had been less than perfect, when he was rude to me, forgot or ignored a house rule, and so on. "I was next to him, his balls in one of my hands, both of us facing out toward the people watching so that I could show them the blade as I shaved hairs off the underside of his sac. I was working toward the coup de grace. I'd practiced so it would look real. And then it all happened at once."

Barrow licked his lower lip. Could he sense how my grip had tightened on the handle of the razor? "'It all happened.' What happened, Mira?"

"Everything. I looked up and he and the woman made eye contact, and he confessed that he'd been unfaithful, and I knew he wasn't playacting, I knew he meant *with her,* and…" I trailed off, mouth dry, needing to swallow suddenly.

"And?"

And I'd intended to use the dull side of the blade. It was a classic technique for mind-fucking a submissive. That was why you worked them up to a lather about how sharp the knife was and all that. To give them that moment of absolute terror when they thought you'd really sliced them to the bone.

But you weren't supposed to actually do it.

I could barely hear my voice, which quavered. "I was supposed to use the dull side."

"Why didn't you?"

Anger at Barrow welled up. "Why? What do you mean *why?* It wasn't like I intended to—" I broke off suddenly with a sob.

His look was sly. "Did you just admit you didn't intend to?"

"I don't know. Does it matter? I injured him badly. That's what matters most."

"It matters because you treat yourself as if you meant to do it."

"How could I not have meant it? I was so angry I could have killed him, and I nearly did."

"Think, Mira, think! Just because you were angry enough to kill him doesn't mean you intended to."

"Shut up!" I grabbed him by the collar, holding the blade against a pulsing artery in this throat.

"I won't." He swallowed carefully. "You've been locking yourself in a prison of guilt over an accident. If it was anyone's fault, it was the woman who distracted you by being too close to your scene right at the moment when you intended to turn the blade over, and then your own lover—"

"Just because he was unfaithful doesn't mean he deserved to be injured." It took all my strength to hold back from slicing Barrow open.

"That's not what I'm saying. But he is responsible for going off-script, and manipulating the scene in the direction it went. When accidents happen, the conditions that create them are never a sole person's responsibility."

I was seething. I hated that he was right. I hated that he, the self-professed villain, was tearing me out of the cocoon of self-loathing and guilt I had buried myself in. "I'm still the one holding the knife!" Yes, both in the past, and at that moment. I focused on him. "You aren't afraid I'm going to do the same thing to you?"

He took a breath, two, three, before answering, "I made a decision to trust you."

"So did Ethan."

"No. He *didn't* trust you. If he did, he would have told you about the woman and her interest instead of sneaking off to philander with her. Would you have blocked him from seeing her if he'd been honest with you?"

"No." He was allowed to play with others if he had my blessing, and he knew it full well because we'd always had that arrangement. He could have asked for permission at any time. But he never did. "I still... feel like a fraud." My hand shook.

Barrow reached up and clasped my stiff fingers. "In what way?"

"Because I let myself believe the reason he never used that privilege, never asked to play with another, was because I was all that he needed. I let myself believe his loyalty was proof of my dominance and our bond."

"So, you were mistaken about him. Being wrong does not make you ungenuine."

"But that's not all. I feel like I not only injured him and endangered him, I went against all my principles."

"Tell me these principles."

"I should have picked something failsafe. Practicing the switch to the dull side wasn't enough. I should have... prepped a replica that wasn't even sharpened. Or... or something." I was starting to hear how ridiculous that sounded. Could I have done more to make sure he wasn't endangered? Yes: I could have not played with him at all. I could have never fallen in love with him. I was trying to rewrite history and that wasn't going to happen.

"'Or something,'" Barrow echoed. "I hear you trying to make it all your fault. But maybe it's time to stop listening to his voice and listen to your own. Maybe it's time to start trusting yourself again." His fingers were warm and firm around mine as he pressed the blade against his own neck.

I fought him, my hand shaking. "Don't! Why are you doing this?"

"To prove a point. Look, Mira. Look what you've done."

I looked again. But even through the haze of bloodlust I could see... I was touching his skin with the dull side of the blade. I'd done exactly as I'd practiced until it was a reflex. And even with the compulsion to draw blood surging through me, I had still protected him.

I let out a shaky sob. He let his thumb graze the corner of the razor, a bead of blood welling up, and I was suddenly free of the compulsion to cut him. I pulled away, the razor falling to the mattress between us.

Barrow tucked his thumb into his mouth and the knife into a pocket, while I hugged my knees.

"In the end, the person who suffered the most damage from that night was you, Mira. His wounds healed. Yours did not." He was trying to give a dry recitation of the facts, but his voice quavered a little with heat, as if he were outraged on my behalf. "You're the one who cut herself off from her friends and community and means of emotional support. You're the one who decided you were undeserving of that support. But you couldn't starve yourself forever. You had to bury it under a thousand layers of twisted logic in order to retain, or regain, any sense of self. But it was a facade. A facade that burned away faster than plaster at a suburban McMansion."

He was right. He was right and I hated that he was right. But he had made me see that night with Ethan in a different light. "And I needed to… admit that before I could heal."

"Yes." He sat on the edge of the mattress, one arm resting atop his own bent knee. "And you needed to know yourself wholly so you can trust your instincts again."

Speaking of my instincts, suspicion welled up once more. "Why are you doing this?"

He put one hand on the back of his neck and rolled his head from side to side. Like a lot of people, he carried his tension in his shoulders. "I won't insult you by claiming altruism, because you'd never believe that."

"Then why?"

"Think it through, Mira."

"You… wanted to know the truth about me so you'd know how to manipulate me," I guessed. But that didn't explain why he made me work out my hangups. What he'd just done had strengthened me, not weakened me.

I realized he'd been right before, when we'd first met. I should have been afraid for him to know me, my true self, because at that point I'd feared anyone knowing. But I didn't fear Barrow knowing anymore. It was a relief rather than a source of fear. He had become the only person who knew me that well, that completely. Even Wex didn't know all of it.

I looked at my hands again and lifted an imaginary straight razor, waving it from one side to the other. "You said we have… a lot in common."

He nodded. "My goals and yours are not so far apart. I want to make the world safe from an ancient evil. I believe if you know what I know about it, you'll want to, also." He pursed his lips. "I'll be blunt. I'm recruiting you, Mira."

That made me laugh. I mean, wasn't it just the most ridiculous thing you'd ever heard? Once I started to laugh I couldn't stop. He eventually gave up and left me to my laughing fit and I laughed until I cried.

FORTY-FOUR

There are some other fragments I've tried to piece together into whole memories of my time with Barrow, but they're fragmentary enough that they seem almost like I could have imagined them. Except why would I imagine Barrow would tell me something like this? "Mira, you have to know that we are all looking for god. For a being to worship."

I didn't believe that at all. "Some people are just fine without a religion."

"I don't mean religion. I mean someone bigger than themselves they can put their faith in."

"Someone or something? An ideal, okay, sure, but I don't go for the thought it has to be personified. Not everyone is looking for the Big Daddy in the Sky, or Mama Earth, or whatever."

He seemed to feel I'd missed his point. "Just because you yourself have moved beyond needing it, doesn't obviate the basic human need for a being to worship."

"Is it really a basic need, though? Or is it just widespread organized religion makes it seem universal?" He was one step from claiming all human relationships and societal structures had to be hierarchical. I didn't believe they did—or at least I didn't want to believe that, even if it was hard to find evidence to the contrary.

I really wonder if those fragments were really Barrow trying to tell me something, or just me trying to tell myself something. They're mostly arguments, these scattered memories, all too similar to my most vivid memories of Ethan. The fights that could never be won.

More than once Barrow told me the key to power was being indifferent to pain. "Think about it, Mira. What is pain?"

I gave the usual physical-therapist answer: "It's a signal from your body to stop doing something before you make it worse."

"So, you have an athlete with a muscle tear, say, in their leg, and yet they 'power through' to win the race anyway."

"Sure, that sometimes happens."

"Because they were able to convince themselves to ignore that signal and perform at a high level anyway. Now extend that concept to your knowledge of aetheric energy. The conduit is the body. The main reason we can't use or transmit more of it is our physical self 'can't handle it.' This is why the vast majority of people will never come close to stumbling upon the Esoteric Mysteries. But human bodies actually can handle quite a lot more than they think."

Something clicked for me: that was why circle workings were necessary, and why they were so parallel to BDSM: the person who was the focus of the ceremony, who was taking the flogging or whose blood was being used, could withstand so much more if they were supported and challenged and led through the experience by someone they could place their trust in.

I had to wonder, though, what pain had Barrow put himself through to become what he was? What was training to become a Partisan of Fire like? Did he burn, or feel like he was on fire, when he was channeling that power? Barrow's indifference to pain in pursuit of power, though, extended to the pain of others, not just himself. I had to remember that.

I remember waking from a fitful sleep at one point, and I thought the room was pitch black. As I moved to sit up, though, I realized I had a blindfold over my eyes. I reached up and pulled it off, then startled: Barrow was sitting crosslegged on the concrete floor a few feet away, writing in a notebook. He looked up as I examined the blindfold. It had a British Airways logo on it, like the ones they give to passengers on long-haul flights.

"When did I put this on?"

He shook his head. "You didn't. I slipped it on you when the light seemed to be bothering you."

I flung it at him but the thing was so feather-light it didn't go very far, not even making it off the mattress. "Don't do that sort of thing if you're trying to get me to trust you."

"My apologies; I was trying to be considerate."

"How about consider that I don't trust you and so that seems creepy."

He bowed his head tiredly. "I keep assuming that one of these times, you'll remember what's happened between us. Also, I assumed that by now you've learned to see through blindfolds."

My snarl was sarcastic. "I can't say that the subject's come up in my curriculum."

He didn't react to my snark. "I can teach you how to see through blindfolds, Mira. I gladly will."

I looked around the room, feeling cranky. I guess I *had* been sleeping restlessly. "Right now I'd rather know what you've done with Clive. How long has it been since I've seen him?"

Barrow looked at me again for a long moment, folded the journal and slipped it into the side pocket of the duffel, and then repositioned himself closer to me, on the edge of the mattress. "You might remember that Clive is asleep."

"Asleep. You mean regular asleep or do you mean in quietude?"

He expression was one of concern. "Mira," he said gently. "You asked me to keep him in quietude."

I blinked. Had I?

"Presumably until you were ready for him to learn what you've been keeping from him," Barrow went on.

I felt a chill. Yes, he was right. I'd made that choice. I put my hand on my forehead. "That much I remember." And I remembered Barrow letting me put a blade to his neck, to prove I wasn't as bad a human being as I felt like I was. But there had to be something still missing from my recent memories. "Now that I remember everything I was suppressing about Ethan, am I healed?"

He snorted. "If the flow were as it should be, you would be able to pick up a knife without being assailed by the undeniable need to draw blood with it." He sounded personally affronted by my difficulty, and I assumed that meant I'd attacked him at some point, though I didn't remember it.

I rubbed at the rope burn on my wrists. "How many times did I try to stab you that I don't remember?"

"Oh, a few." He seemed coy suddenly. "You've left quite a few bruises and other marks on me."

That made it sound like there were whole days missing from my memory. Weeks, maybe. I suddenly wanted to see the bruises. "Show me. Maybe the sight will jog my memory."

"I would love nothing more." He stood and pulled up his T-shirt. What caught my eye was not the bite mark on one pectoral muscle, but the tattoos on his chest, two black birds on either side of his sternum, one in a Celtic knotwork style, the other looking more like mendhi, like henna. I had no memory of them, and seeing the imprint of my teeth spurred nothing in my mind, either. Not even a sense-memory of the salt on his skin or the crunch against flesh that left that kind of bruise. He let the shirt drop, then, and showed me another, on the back of his elbow. "This one is from hitting the floor when you tackled me."

"Ouch," I said. "So I would attack you and then what? We'd wrestle?"

"Essentially, until I could get you into a headlock." He sighed. "Though you would never yield."

"Oh. So you'd put me into a chokehold and then, what, induce syncope?" Meaning knock me unconscious by cutting off the blood flow to my brain. It sounds worse than it is. Sensei Jack would demonstrate it from time to time.

"Just so," he said. "I am relieved to be past that stage. I have much to teach you and would prefer not to repeat it all too many times."

"You already told me about the sacrificial virgin. That part I remember."

"But do you believe it?" Barrow asked.

"No." I didn't believe it both because I didn't trust him and I didn't want for it to be true. "You're making it up to get me on your side. You looked around inside my head and figured out something you knew would hook me."

His laugh was short and bitter. "If only." He stood. "Well? Would you like to learn both to see despite a blindfold and see for yourself how your… how Clive is doing? That may as well be the next thing I teach you."

Right. He was teaching me things that made me better at the practice because he wanted me as an ally. Because he had some grand plan to save the human race. I'm not sure which was a bigger conceptual change to wrap my head around: that things I'd been blaming myself for had been Ethan's own fault or that Barrow really had stopping genocide at the top of his to do list.

He had let me put a knife to his throat, even knowing the kind of compulsion I would have. He trusted me.

I thought about the note I had written myself. Was I supposed to trust him now? I decided to ask him. "Am I supposed to trust you now?"

He spread his hands. "I don't control your beliefs, Mira. You've made that quite clear."

"I believe your methods are evil."

"And I admit my methods may seem less noble than my aim. But I am not a god. I am human." He touched his neck where I'd held the straight razor to his skin. "I realize it's difficult to believe me when everything you've been taught is that I'm nothing but a cold-blooded force of destruction. But if I can get you to trust yourself again after all you went through, perhaps there's still hope."

I tamped down my impatience with him. "Fine. Teach me to see."

"Put the blindfold on."

Of course. I picked it up off the mattress and slipped the elastic over my hair.

"Breathe with me," he said, and I recognized the deep, centering breaths. "Feel your internal energy. It pours through you from inside to outside at several points. Some of those points are where the threads run that connect you to others."

That made sense, I realized. Like how the Circle bond was intensified at specific points by where the ring went through the skin. Only without rings this time.

"For example, your right hand, the one that held the knife that you stabbed me with. Do you feel or see or otherwise sense the connection from there to my thigh? Because I do."

As I exhaled I felt as if there were a glowing ember in my palm, burning brighter as I breathed on it. In my mind's eye I could see the glowing line from there to Barrow's injury. Or was I just imagining it? I lifted the blindfold, blinking rapidly, and... there was a bright line overlaying what I could see, a silver-blue-red trail through the air that seemed to slip away if I looked at it directly, but was definitely there in the same spot...

I pulled the blindfold back down and breathed, reaching out with my senses and letting my brain believe it was my "eyes" taking in the information.

There was another ember burning, but this one wasn't in me, it was deep in Barrow's pelvis...

"Did we fuck?" I blurted.

"If by 'fuck' you mean did I breach your body with my cock, no. And if you trust your senses you will know we did not," he said evenly. "Though not for lack of desire on my part, nor lack of opportunity, Mira, if that was what I wanted. If you think the thread from your hand to where you stabbed is something, the corresponding connection from my phallus to your entry point would be not a thread but a rope."

"All right."

"So, think about Clive. Remember the scent of his skin, the feeling of his arms around you, the physical reality of him. Use your senses to seek him. Where do you feel him in your own body? Your third eye? Your heart? Your gut? The centers of your palms?"

As he named the body parts, I felt a tingle in each one. "All of the above. As well as some others." The tingle between my legs became a throb of need without warning, and I had to clamp my knees together to try to quell it.

"That's because he's very much yours. Your claim over him is quite complete. Now tell me where he is."

"Downward." I couldn't see the threads as clearly, but I could feel the pull. "That way." I reached a hand in that direction. "And like he's down a floor or two."

"Good. Now feel what he's feeling."

All I could feel was my own body, my shoulder stiff where I had been lying on it, and my sex aching to be touched. I tried to breathe more lightly, letting go of the sensations, no longer like blowing on a hot coal and instead like trying to float on a wisp of smoke, barely exhaling at all...

And I could feel... something. "He's asleep. I think I can feel him breathing."

"Can you see him?"

"I think so." What if I was just imagining it? "He's lying on his side. Curled in a blanket." My hand was still in the air, and I ached to touch his hair, to grip his collar. "I think that's what I'm seeing."

"No wonder you are having trouble trusting me, when you aren't even sure you can trust your own perceptions."

"Of course I can't be trusted," I said suddenly. "Every time I pick up a knife, I'm a menace."

"Except didn't we establish that you're not?"

I could "see" my hands through the blindfold. The curve of my fingers, the lines in my palms. The pulse of power through them looked silver-white rather than red in my vision.

"The bloodlust that grips you is because something is still out of balance. This is an energetic problem, not a moral one." Barrow blew out a breath. "There are ways, magical ones, that I could use to speed things up. But you'd have to trust me in order to let me perform them."

"When you say the word 'magical,' I hear the word 'sexual.'" I could see his desire flaring hot.

"Your damage is tied closely to your ability for intimacy," Barrow said evenly.

"You're saying we have to have sex for you to heal me."

"You will need to be open in certain ways."

"Yes or no, Barrow."

Another sigh from him. "Intercourse might be the easiest way. But I will pledge to you that it is not my aim. If it will help, I promise to exhaust all other options first, and even then, you'll have to be the one to insist very strongly that you want it before I would dare."

I let myself breathe, long slow breaths like a tide rolling in and out, feeling the crackle of desire move throughout my body. I didn't want Barrow, personally, but I could sense that hot core in him and wondered what it would be like to merge his and mine. I hadn't had intercourse since learning about the practice… Except that I had. Jair. During initiation. But I only remembered that in fragments. Would it be like seeing arousal pooling like quicksilver and then spilling from one being to another?

I saw Barrow lick his lips nervously. Yes, I still had the blindfold on.

"Barrow," I said. "You want me to trust you."

"Yes."

"And you want me to believe you."

"Yes."

"And you want me to trust myself as much as you trust me."

"Yes."

It was suddenly clear to me what I had to do. A giddy bubble of lust rose up through my chest and I nearly laughed. Oh, he would never agree to it, I thought. And then I would have caught him in a lie. Or at least in a trap of his own making. "Something has to happen for me to trust you the way you trust me."

He didn't seem like he had an inkling of what I was going to say. "I'll tell you anything. Just ask."

I pulled off the blindfold and looked into his eyes. "Asking's not enough, remember? I'll need to verify the truth. Like you did. Teach me Pandora's Box, Barrow."

He didn't move a muscle, didn't blink, didn't breathe, and that's how I knew I'd struck a nerve. It took him a moment to reply. "You don't know what you're asking."

"Why? Is the technique dependent cn genital configuration?"

He stood quickly, agitated, spine straight. "No, it's not."

I'd backed him into a corner from which he couldn't escape. If he really wanted me on his side, letting me pry him open like an oyster—his words—to get at the pearl of truth inside shouldn't have been a difficult ask. In fact, it felt almost standard, given what I knew of the various trials and tests Clive and other recruits to the Circle went through.

"You don't know what you're asking," he repeated.

"No, but isn't the point to find out?"

He stalked to the door, his gait a bit stiff and not from the injury to his leg. "I'll think it over," he said, then exited quickly, pulling the door firmly shut behind him.

The latch clicked loudly.

I grabbed the notebook and hurriedly wrote, "Pandora's Box doesn't depend on plumbing." But a wave of tiredness swept over me then. All that seeing was draining, I supposed. The drowsiness would not be denied. I lay down on the mattress, pulled the blanket over myself, and sank directly into a deep sleep.

FORTY-FIVE

When next I woke I was in the same room as before—same shirt, too. But I couldn't tell how long I'd been asleep. Minutes? Hours?

The last thing I remembered was telling Barrow that I'd trust him if he'd teach me Pandora's Box and let me use it on him. I rubbed the rope burn on my wrist and wondered… if Pandora's Box could dredge up the stuff I had been trying so hard not to think about, could it also get at the more recent memories I had lost access to?

And could I do it to myself? I had to wonder. I knew it was possible to invoke the energy of the practice while solo—that's how Roland had discovered it. But I wasn't sure where to start. Thinking about what I might do to myself, though, brought me to the thought: I didn't seem to have my period anymore. So I really had been there a week or more.

I sat up. The room looked cleaned up. The duffel had been zipped shut and the books neatly stacked in size order, the notebook at the bottom of the stack. There was no sign of the food that had been left, either. Was I missing another memory, or had the place been neatened up while I slept?

I still wasn't hungry. And I was still suspicious. But…

Barrow came in before I could move from the spot, closing the door behind him. Someone outside engaged the latch. Anlyse? That other guy I met once, the young one? Were the three of them all the Partisans?

If Barrow would let me go through with penetrating his mind, I'd know.

His eyebrow twitched. "You're looking at me the way a chef looks at a roast fowl on the table."

"Sorry." My cheeks felt hot suddenly. "I assure you the carving I'm imagining is metaphorical."

That brought out the hint of a smile. "Have a good nap?"

The nightmare-flashbacks of nearly gelding Ethan seemed to be finally gone. So… "Yes." Unlike previous times I'd woken, I felt balanced and well rested. "Did you give my proposal some thought?"

He sat crosslegged on the concrete floor in his habitual spot. "You're a quick study, Mira, but it's still a rather large leap to putting myself in the hands of an untrained initiate who doesn't even know the technique and who still has, shall we say, some issues."

"You mean with my compulsion to draw blood." I made a fist. "I still don't understand why that happens."

He considered me. "What does your intuition tell you?"

"I don't know. It's not like I want to do it."

He frowned suddenly. "How long has it been going on?"

"I'm not sure." I looked at my palms. "After what happened with Ethan, I threw all my blades away and I didn't touch one until…" I had been about to say "a few days ago" but it had to have been longer than that. "Until right before we ambushed you. That day I chose my Circle blade and we discovered the compulsion."

He stared at me a moment. "You went into battle knowing that you shouldn't draw your weapon?"

"It wasn't like I really had a choice." I replied. "Besides, you call that charm necklace a weapon?" I wondered where it was. Maybe when he was out of the room I should try sensing it.

"The amount of damage done in the spiritual realm does not correspond to the size of the gash in the physical body," he spouted, seeming annoyed. "You should know that."

"It was a rhetorical question, Barrow." I wondered if he was as annoyed as he seemed. If so, then I could get under his skin as easily as he got under mine.

Getting under his skin—or through his defenses—was exactly what we were talking about me doing, though. "If I can't hold a knife, I assume that complicates things?"

"Somewhat. A spell doesn't depend on all the ceremonial trappings, but an instrument of penetration is still necessary." He tapped his fingers on his knee. "And you lack… the inborn one."

"I've got fingers. Even a fist."

"Insufficient." His cheeks reddened, though his facial expression remained impassive.

"Does it need to be… phallic?"

After a long pause, he nodded.

It was obvious to me Barrow was uncomfortable with the idea of being the one penetrated. Lots of straight guys have hangups about that—as if being the penetrated partner makes them less masculine or some similar bullshit. I poked that to see if it was tender: "I know I have a lot to learn about the practice, but… last I looked, manhood doesn't leak out the butthole."

The short bark of a laugh was so sudden he covered his eyes. "Mira!"

I took his sudden reaction to mean I'd hit a nerve. "I'd think to be a big, bad sex magic practitioner you'd have to get over any hangups like that."

"I do not have 'hangups,'" he growled.

I let him stew in his emotions for a moment before I went on calmly. "Okay, real question. Does 'the instrument' have to be special in some way?"

He uncovered his eyes. "What do you mean?"

"You know, does it have to be antique ivory and silver? Or would silicone work?"

He thought it over. "The material… probably does not matter."

I let a few more heartbeats go by before saying his name. "Barrow." He met my gaze. "You'd put a straight razor into my hand, but you won't trust me with a blunt piece of silicone?"

I could see his resistance wearing away. "You… have a point."

"So tell me what I need to know. Theoretically. If we were to go through with it."

His mouth curled as if he knew full well I was using that kind of talk as a disarming tactic. "The most important thing, Mira, if you really want to be able to see clearly, is to set your anger aside."

That wasn't at all what I was expecting him to say, and it set me off-balance for a moment. "Why?"

"Now that you can think about what happened with your submissive. Think about that memory, what you felt, what you sensed."

Right. Anger so white-hot it obliterated sight and sound. "I've never liked being angry," I told him. "It's a toxic emotion."

His voice turned testy suddenly. "Did the Circle tell you that?"

"No. It's what I think."

"Anger can be a healthy emotion when you have something to be angry about."

I shook my head. "Anger isn't 'healthy.' When I say it's toxic I mean it: it builds up in the body and wreaks havoc." I knew all too well from what it did to the bodies of my massage clients. "Even a good massage can't undo that damage."

"Perhaps I misspoke. I do mean that expressing anger is far better for one's health than bottling it up inside."

"I suppose." I folded my arms. Why were we arguing? What were we arguing about? Right. "Is that why you stopped tying me up? Because it was better if I acted on my anger than if I didn't?"

"I stopped tying you because I started trusting you." He held out a hand. "May I see your wrist?"

I hesitated a moment, then held it toward him. He examined my hand and forearm gently, turning them over in his own hands and probing my wrist bones. "Does it hurt?"

"Not really. A little rope burn is all."

"I had to make do with what I had." His lip curled against his teeth. "Don't discount your anger, Mira. It has a power all its own."

Niko had said something like that once, too, I remembered. Another thing I needed to learn, I supposed. I looked Barrow over. He was clean-shaven, his hair combed back, his plain black T-shirt molded to his chest, the tattoos hidden.

"You've been bottling it up, suppressing it, feeling like you had no right to it, and—ironically, perhaps—now you are finally free to experience it and express it. But! But. If you want what you Glean from me to be useful and clear. If you want to see it all, you need to set anger aside."

"All right." Right at that moment I didn't feel angry, anyway. I felt mostly intensely curious. "If this is going to work the same way as before, I should ask you a bunch of things now, listen to your answers, and then verify them when I open you up."

I saw the slightest bit of a shiver in him. "If you like. All I ask is that once you see I'm telling you the truth, you give serious consideration to my side."

"You really believe I'm going to join you."

"I don't mean me personally, or even the Partisans of Fire, if you can't stomach that. But if you are working toward the same goals, that will be enough for me."

I put my hand to my head. "Remind me what those goals were again? Because I am pretty sure one of them was killing all my friends. Or am I misremembering that?"

His eyes flared a little, but he said, in a forcibly calm voice, "The knowledge of how to turn an innocent girl into a tool of genocide needs to be taken from mankind and the threat neutralized." He spread his hands. "Don't shoot the messenger. I'm not the one who created this mess. I'm just the one stuck with cleaning it up."

I remained skeptical. Was it just that I didn't want to believe I was soon going to be forced to choose between the deaths of a few over the deaths of many? "There has to be a better way than murder and rape to get this done."

He held in a smile. "Now you sound like you're on my side already."

"Argh! Asshole!" I smacked him and launched myself at him, and we fought and wrestled, but not in that "we're deadly enemies" way, more like the…

The "we're about to be lovers" way.

I got him into a headlock, my legs wrapped around his. He probably let me do it, but it's hard to be certain. "When are we doing it?" I asked in his ear.

"If by 'it' you mean when am I letting you have your way with me…" He swallowed and tried once more to break free, but failed. "I will need to procure the proper supplies."

"So go procure them," I said, letting him go.

He didn't scramble away from me like I thought he might, but merely relaxed against me, our bodies half on the mattress, half on the concrete. "All right. Silicone, you say?"

Good god, we were going to go through with it. He was going to let me do it. "Give me a piece of paper."

"What for?"

I wrote down the address of my favorite sex toy shop in the city along with the words, *Don't forget the harness and straps.*

FORTY-SIX

"You should meditate while I'm out, to prepare yourself for the spell," Barrow told me before he left.

I groaned.

"You still object to the word 'spell'?"

"No, no. It's just… I hate meditation."

He looked at me curiously. "How can that be? Hate should be nearly impossible to experience in an alpha state."

"What I hate is I never get to an alpha state. I just sit there being frustrated and impatient that it's not happening."

To his credit, he did not laugh at me. "In other words… the frustration you feel over your inability to meditate, prevents you from meditating…?"

"I guess."

"Have you tried some specific visualization?"

"You mean like a mandala or something?"

"I mean like visualizing somewhere familiar, like walking through your childhood home, noting each object you pass."

I swallowed. "I have a dream like that sometimes…" Did Clive, too, I wondered?

"The point is that reaching a meditative state is the goal. How you get there doesn't matter as much. Some people are helped by quiet. Others reach it through movement. There's more than one way to trigger alpha brain waves."

"I know that. I'm great at inducing them in my subs and my massage clients. Not so much in myself." Sometimes a long, sensual flogging could send a sub into a hypnotic state. Some doms said they experienced it, too, but I didn't. I felt like it was a dereliction of duty to let my conscious mind slip like that. In massage, too. Other therapists told me sometimes they'd slip into synch with a client and go on autopilot and it would feel like the whole massage was over in an eyeblink. I had it happen once in massage training and I'd tried to avoid it ever since. It just seemed like bad service to not be all there, you know? "It seems like a really bad idea in a scene. After all, the one time I lost my head, look what happened."

Barrow sat down, boots, jacket, and all, and looked me in the eye. "This is important, Mira. I don't mean for tonight. I mean in general. Sometimes it's important to lose yourself."

I recoiled from the whole idea. "What do you mean, 'important?'"

"You've already grasped that there are different levels of consciousness, yes? And you experience different senses of self at each one." He chopped his hand through the air in upward steps as if showing me the layers on an invisible cake. Then he held up both hands, palms facing each other, and stepped them outward from the center. "Think of them not as higher or lower, but as closer or further from your center. When you let go of the tight hold you have on your conscious self…" He made an hourglass shape as if he were drawing me, shoulders to hips, with his hands, and then expanded his reach outward again. "…you become much greater, much bigger than you knew you could be."

I shivered. "But you said… that it was a bad thing when the Wisdomkeeper lost his mind."

Barrow paused, considering. "That is… different. I think." He wasn't certain. "Perhaps it isn't, though. To transcend our limitations, sometimes the barriers need to be shattered. Sense of self is a shell. It acts as both armor and as container, but it also limits growth."

I looked at him suspiciously. "Forgive me if I resist anything that sounds like giving you permission to crack my armor."

He stood in one motion, turning away from me, turning his back. "Need I remind you?" His words were strung on a voice taut with apprehension. "Yours is not the shell that will be penetrated by what we are about to do."

"Barrow—" I wanted to reach for him.

But he was already at the door. "Prepare yourself however you wish. We'll work the spell when I return."

He slipped out the door and latched it loudly behind him.

"Make up your mind," I said to the empty air, even though I knew he couldn't still hear me. "Is shattering barriers a good thing or a bad thing?" Or maybe the practice was just double-edged swords all the way down. That sounded like the most likely thing. Of course.

I decided to try meditating anyway. If I achieved oneness with the universe, I supposed I'd find out why it was such a big deal.

Instead, I think I fell asleep. When I next looked around, I was in Clive's childhood bedroom. It was dark; the only light coming from moonlight through the windows. I could just make out that he was sitting on the bed, crosslegged, eyes closed as if he were meditating himself.

"You too?" I asked.

"Me what?" I could see the glint of his eyes as he opened them. "My lady, are you really here or are you just wishful thinking?"

"Pretty sure I'm here." I was standing in the moonbeam, beside the shelf of action figures I had seen last time. I picked up Wonder Woman and Catwoman. Wonder Woman was wearing a corset and had a golden coil of rope, and Catwoman had a whip. For the first time it occurred to me that maybe these weren't some kind of subconscious signals. Maybe the artists who drew them were just plain kinky and they'd intended it to be plain as day.

I looked down at myself. I was in leggings and flat boots. The T-shirt I wore was knotted at my waist. Such an odd detail.

Clive's voice came out of the dark. "So what's been happening? I assume Barrow's put me on ice so he can work on you."

I had a sudden sinking feeling. Clive being in quietude was my doing. His retreat from the visions that Pandora's Box had unleashed was my fault, and then I'd told Barrow to keep him in the (literal) dark. My voice quavered. "He's trying to turn me into a Partisan of Fire."

His voice was low. "Of course he is."

"It's not going to work, though. I'm just… using him to learn as much as I can."

"Of course you are."

I took a step toward him. "Can we turn a light on in here? Why is it so dark?"

"It is what it is." The glow through the windows reddened, though, as if maybe dawn were breaking.

I began to see his face clearly, and he looked wan and thin. "Clive?" I put a hand to his face and he felt cold. "What is this I'm sensing? Are you all right?"

He put a hand over mine. "I'm fine."

"I need to break you of that habit." I leaned over to kiss him on the forehead. Cold.

"Which habit?"

"Saying 'I'm fine' when I ask you how you are."

He bowed his head. "You're right. I should know you always want the whole and complete truth." When he looked up again, the glow on his face was growing brighter by the second. "I don't know how much longer I can last."

"What do you mean?" I thought if he was in quietude he was essentially preserved in amber. I framed his face with my hands, pulling him close, and in his eyes I could see the flicker of flames. "Clive, what is happening to you?"

He leaned up to kiss me, and his lip seemed dry and papery. "There will always be forces beyond our control." He looked past me to the window.

I turned my head to look, and I saw it wasn't dawn reddening the sky outside, it was fire. Flames leaping off the hillside and drawing ever nearer.

He pulled me back to him. "I love you, Mira."

"What? I mean, Clive—" I kissed him rather than make a worse mess of my words. Good god, I had so much I had to tell him. Would he even say that once he knew what Barrow knew? Would he still feel that way after I told him what I had done to Ethan?

He freed his mouth with a gasp. "You need to go."

"Clive—"

The flames had started to beat at the windows, and then the curtains burst into flame. "Now, my lady!"

"No!" I pulled open the bedroom door as if I could flee, trying to grab Clive with the other hand and take him with me. "Come on!"

But he was on his feet, arms outstretched, like he was making himself a wall between the flames and me. "This isn't a fire you can save me from, Mira. Not this time."

The window shattered and a gust of fiery wind knocked me backwards out the door, tumbling down the stairs or maybe just into the void. When I caught my breath I opened my eyes… and found I was lying in bed like I'd curled up and gone to sleep. I guess I had been asleep.

Had it all been a dream? Or had it been a real communication between me and Clive in the dreamscape? If it were real, then all I could understand was that Clive was in some kind of danger. I found myself pacing the room, casting about for something I could do. I tried the door. There was nothing in here that could help me escape. Nothing. But I had to know. I had to see he was all right.

But I knew how to see him, didn't I?

I sat back down, trying once more to breathe, center myself, and reach out to Clive.

There he was, one arm flung over his eyes, the other outstretched, flat on his back, asleep. He shifted as I watched, muscles bunching as if he were in the throes of a dream. If it was the nightmare I'd just left, there was no sign. In fact, he let out a slight groan as I imagined my hands gliding down his bare chest, checking him for burns or bruises. The glow in my palms flowed thick as tree branches toward him, toward the root of him. How long had it been since I held him in my hand, since I stroked him to completion on my command? Days? Weeks? I had no way to know.

His flesh responded to my connection, and I felt the corresponding ache in my own emptiness. He was sweating, straining upward, hips curved as if he could drive upward into some soft, welcoming target, but he met only air.

I didn't have the knack that Kish did for triggering a release. I could only get him there if I came myself. I slid my fingers downward, finding my own flesh swollen and willing. With the other hand I stripped the shirt off over my head and stroked a nipple.

And then a knock came at the door, followed by Barrow opening it. He set down a shopping bag and looked me up and down.

"Well," he said. "I suppose that is one way to prepare."

FORTY-SEVEN

Outside, someone threw the latch closed. "So, who is that out there?"

"Would you prefer they were in here?" he asked, toeing off his boots.

"What if I did?"

"I would invite them to watch. But this spell is best done between the two of us."

"Because…?"

He slipped his leather jacket off and let it fall to the floor. The black T-shirt he wore underneath hugged his torso. "Because it is an intimate spell." He pulled a box out of the shopping bag and tore it open, then held up a double-headed dildo. "It requires delicate balance."

The toy was bright blue, silicone, one end long and phallic, the other upright and slightly bulbous, like a hammered thumb in a cartoon. One side to go in me, one to go in him. "Delicate balance," I repeated wryly.

I didn't feel the slightest bit balanced. I was flushed with arousal, still confused about Clive, and on the brink of going out on a limb that I didn't know I'd be able to climb back down from. "If you trust me," I said, stalling until I could get my mental footing, "why do you always lock the door?"

He smiled one of those indulgent, too-familiar smiles. Had there really been more between him and me than I recalled? I hoped I'd unlock that secret shortly, too. "Tell me honestly, Mira. If the door had been unlocked, would you still be sitting here?"

Well. "Maybe not." There were things I needed to know from him, but if I could have fled at any point? Assuming I could get to Clive, escape would be a temptation.

Barrow pulled his shirt off, revealing the yellowing bite mark on his chest, his ravens or crows still black as ever, and then took the harness and a hank of rope out of the bag.

"What's the rope for?" I asked.

"In case it's needed." He laid the rope aside and then held the harness out. "Stand up."

"I think I should be giving the orders now." I folded my arms.

He tossed me the harness with a huff. "That wasn't an order, it was a suggestion so that I could help you step into it. See to it yourself, if you prefer."

"We may not need the harness at all, if the two-headed monster works as expected." I shifted on the bed, setting the harness aside. "It may be the first time you've done this, Barrow, but it's not mine."

He looked at me sharply. "Not your first time topping a man, no, but your first time with this spell." Well, that was true. "If I'm going to guide you through the lesson, Mira, you're going to have to listen to me. If that offends your dominant self image, try to think of your compliance with me not as obedience so much as enlightened self-interest."

"Does it not matter which of us is dominant for this spell to work?"

He closed his eyes and sighed. "It does. But stop jumping ahead."

I couldn't help but smile. Needling him meant nothing in the grand scheme, but I reveled in it anyway. "Fine. How about you tell me what the difference between a 'spell' and a 'ritual' is, then?"

"The spell is the specific working of the power. The ritual is the trappings that surround it, but most spells can be worked without the candles and chanting. Especially those that involve only two."

"Okay, so, no candles, no incense." And no circle of containment or protection. Interesting. "Where's the lube?"

"If the scent of you is any indication," he growled, "there's plenty between your legs."

"Not enough for both of us, though." I clucked my tongue, but then spoke seriously. "Barrow, I'd like to make things as easy on you as possible."

"In the bag," he said curtly, as he moved to turn on the small lamp on the crate beside the bed and nearly knocked it over.

He was obviously afraid. And yet he was going to go through with it. A puzzle. I dug in the bag. He'd also stocked up on condoms and some other necessities.

He doused the overhead light.

"Barrow," I said softly. "It'll be easier on you if you just let me be in charge."

He turned away from me and clenched his fists. "All right."

"Trust me. The anticipation is worse than the deed." I put a hand on his bare back. It was crisscrossed with old flagellation scars. Self-flagellation, some of them, judging by the angle. Others looked like where a cane or whip had split his skin and not been properly tended.

"The rope," he said, voice gone rough with emotion, "is for if you… see fit to bind me."

I dug my thumbs into the tendons as stiff as bridge cables on either side of his neck and kneaded the muscle, triggering him to relax. My voice was barely above a whisper. "I'll only bind you if you fight me."

He said nothing to that. I slipped down to the mattress and pulled him with me. "Hand me the toy, Barrow."

He took it from the packaging and then moved to his knees to present it to me with two hands, reverently.

I inserted the shorter, more bulbous head into myself, gasping a little as it surprised me how large it felt. I really hadn't been having a lot of penetrative sex.

The snugger the fit, the better the control, though. If I pressed my thighs together, I could adjust the angle of the long end. I took some lube in my hand from the bottle and sat back on my heels, stroking my fantastic blue phallus. As I settled into a rhythm I could sense the desire building up in Barrow, too. His fear wasn't keeping his cock from being erect.

"You, too, Barrow. With me."

He gripped his own cock and stroked in time with me.

"Yes, that's it." I could no longer feel which of us was being aroused by what. Any arousal to me fed into him and vice versa. It had seemed like that with some of my prior lovers, but I'd always thought that was just empathy. Now I know it was energy.

He groaned. In the soft light, he looked younger again and I wondered again how old he really was.

"So. Is it skipping ahead now to ask how dominance fits into this?"

He shook his head. "You will be breaching not only my flesh but my aethereal defenses. You are already familiar with how your energy rises toward orgasm. But as a female, you may not be as familiar with the, ah, primal drive to… to…"

"Barrow." *As a female.* Honestly. I tried not to laugh. "I discovered knifeplay a long time ago."

"Ah, true." He let that sink in. "Perhaps that accounts for your extremely naturalistic skill with 'the practice.' At any rate, do you grasp that there is an inherent violence in finding your satisfaction through the breach of others? That is the essence of dominance, in asserting not will alone, but will bound together with erotic desire to take."

"'Inherent violence.'" That was like something out of the anti-sex handbook. "But does it have to be violent?"

"No, just as bloodplay can be the most gentle sensation imaginable. And yet, it is still a cut."

Still a breach. A cut would still bleed even if one felt no pain. I knew then what I had to do. There would be no need to use force. "Barrow."

"Mira."

"Slick your fingers with the lube and then reach behind yourself."

As he did so, I continued to make the dildo slick, stroking upward. Every time I did, his breath would catch as if my hand were on his flesh and not an inanimate toy. The threads of desire wove between us like a web. I ran my thumb around the crown and he shivered, then groaned again at the sensation of a finger slipping inside himself. His brow furrowed as he concentrated on getting a second finger in.

"Don't rush." I propped a pillow against the wall and leaned back, watching him. "I'll tell you when it's enough."

He looked younger still, and I could almost imagine him doing that to himself… For the first time? As a teenager? I had a flash then of another room, of a large open space with a high, high roof overhead.

Was I starting to see into his mind already? His cock bobbed up and down as he worked on himself. I had to remind him again to slow down. His eyes were closed and we were not touching, but his breathing came into synch with mine.

I slid down on the mattress and looked up into his face, his mouth hanging open slightly, sweat at his temples. He tried to tuck his lip into his teeth, but it trembled too much. I could feel the space inside him opening, though.

"Good. Very good. Come straddle me."

He crawled over me without ever opening his eyes, his hair hanging and his teeth gritted. "You may take me whenever you wish. I'm ready."

No. All he was ready for was to endure it like torture. He was expecting me to punch through his defenses like a stab wound. I stroked that set jaw. "Barrow," I whispered. "Kiss me first."

There went one veil of resistance as his mouth brushed against mine, little more than a cursory peck, but I felt the connection deepen and the muscles around his mouth relax.

I had no intention of "taking" him. "Rock back against it, rub yourself on it."

He growled a little, as if the only reason I'd ask was to humiliate him, but each time he touched the toy, I cycled that sensation back through to his own cock. He let out a long "ohhhh."

Meanwhile I stroked his flanks, his ribs, the bulges of his arms. I wished I had some good massage oil. Then I could really reduce him to a pile of gibbering Jell-o. Well, later, maybe. I canted my hips slightly, pressing my thighs together, so that the next time he rocked back, the tapered tip would catch him squarely...

There. He held still suddenly, his entrance wrapped around the tip of the toy like a tiny mouth, and feeling that sensation on the tip of his own cock at the same time. He was caught up in the feedback loop, wanting to thrust his cock into that slick, waiting warmth... except to go deeper, he had to sit back farther, had to take it in...

Good god. The thrill that ran through me at having lulled him into that state was like a hit of pure ecstasy. I could feel it inside me, too, every time he rocked back against it, the part of the toy inside me shifting and moving... and making a pure conduit for his innermost memories. I used that lever to pry open the doors in my own mind, seeking anywhere those interconnections between us led, while at the same time I was digging deeper and deeper into him.

His recent memories were easy to peel away—why look, the Circle of Light had attempted a rescue. Yesterday? Earlier today? The image of Jair and Anlyse locked in combat was stunning—righteous violence glittering in every line of their bodies like diamonds on an heiress. Jair had been beaten back, but not beaten.

But where were the memories of me? Were they more tightly held? There was one of Clive, of Barrow saying to him, "Goodnight, Sleeping Beauty" as he submerged Clive in quietude.

Barrow could wait no longer. He trembled, but his need outweighed his fear, and he pushed himself down fully, the penetration reverberating through his pelvis and up through his chest as he groaned.

The vision was sudden and all-encompassing. Altar boy. Caught touching himself.

Whipped.

I settled my hands against his hips to keep him in place, but he did not attempt to pull away, as the memory poured out. After the whipping, he was made to masturbate in front of the priest who had caught him. Again and again. Each time his young flesh responded to his touch and each time the punishment was exacted.

Meanwhile, in realtime Barrow was speaking, something about the sacred virgin, but I couldn't tell if he was telling me about Saira or if he had fallen into reciting a prayer. I was too transfixed by the foundational memory I had seized. The priest pushed him far past the point of endurance. Until not a drop of ejaculate would come forth. And then sought to ruin him with sodomy.

But the pain of that first penetration had burst out of the young Barrow as a gout of flame, igniting the tapestries behind the altar. The priest had screamed and pushed him away, shouting, "Demon! What devilry have you brought to this sacred house!"

And Barrow, his boy's voice just starting to break, shouted back, "You! You are the devil and if you fail to see that, you are blind!"

The priest had fallen to his knees, cursed sightless in that moment, and as Barrow fled, the man was caught in the flames that consumed all that could be burned within that ancient cathedral's stone.

"Partisan of Fire," I whispered.

His head whipped up suddenly, eyes open, as he realized what I had seen. But his hips had begun to pump steadily, as if he could not stop himself, riding the thing inside with helpless need. It rocked inside me, too, sending pulse after pulse of pleasure up my core. Which of us had hypnotized the other?

I had finally reached my alpha state, where I could see all, feel all. Or so I thought.

There was more to see. Much more. Barrow's hands on the pages of a book, illuminated like an ancient Bible, the text black and red with bits of gold and other colors. The monk who kept it. Who healed the boy after the assault and who taught him the secrets of the profane. His master.

"You hated him," I said, each word a breath.

"He hated himself," Barrow answered, gritting his teeth again but unable to stop himself. "And humanity. So you'd think he would have been content for our entire race to disappear from the planet." His breath was ragged. "But no. He used that hate to mold me into what I am, and to instill in me a deep commitment to the mission. I know my own destructive power. But your Untouch'd Queen is a million times worse."

He was trying to close the lid on Pandora's box before anything more flew out, but his body was locked in the cycle of his need and he did not have the strength to resist it. Release was coming, and that would knock free everything he was still holding tight to.

I could sense a bolus of energy forming in his center, like a new flavor of power began to mix in. I let myself see it. Let myself follow the thread from Barrow out of the room, up and up and up…

To the top floor of the building. There was Anlyse on the same cross where Kanna had been bound. Like her, she was immobilized on a dagger. The other man, the one whose name I didn't know, was alternately teasing her nipples with a feather, then a toothbrush.

I suddenly understood. Barrow was drawing on Anlyse's energy to try to break my hold on him. To upset the balance of power. To try to hide what he could instead of letting it all explode.

"Oh, Barrow," I breathed, rocking my own hips. "I thought you trusted me."

He snarled, unable to say a word as I added my own thrust to rise up to meet him each time he drove himself back. My own orgasm was imminent and I felt my power surging to meet him, to drive him forward. Even with Anlyse's energy added to his, he still couldn't withstand me.

I held his hips in my hands and began to lose my sense of where we were, of up and down, as if the only orientation that mattered wasn't gravity or east and west but just the way our two bodies fit together. My senses began to narrow back to just Barrow himself. But as Anlyse faded into the distance, I heard her cry for help.

"What are you doing to her, Barrow?"

He tried to grab me by the throat, then, and under normal circumstances I would have been trapped under him, the life squeezed out of me. But as I clamped my hands onto his wrists, my grip was stronger and I pried him free.

"I am using her as befits her station," he growled, his hands still grabbing for me even as his lower half was incessantly moving. "She. Is. Mine."

Another of her cries pierced through spacetime, traveling along the thread that connected her to him—to us—and I could feel her heart fluttering like a candle about to gutter out. Her scream of anguish came through as a psychic cry because she barely had breath left to draw.

"Stop it!" I could break his wrists, I realized, crack his metacarpals right there, the way I was holding him. I had no idea I could be that strong. I guessed Sensei Jack had taught me something. But was I strong enough to make Barrow bend to my will? "You're killing her!"

"Let me go and I won't need to drain her of her last breath," he said, chest heaving, as I drove upward into him again and again.

Oh, I'll let you go all right. I released him as I'd intended, with the Sunburst, pouring my own pleasure into him. I suddenly understood where the name came from, the heat and light and brilliance rising up out of me and sending everything flying. Barrow cried out, and the last thing I felt was his ejaculation hot on my skin, as a whirlwind of his memories came rushing at me. My body seemed to grow distant, slumping to the mattress, while my mind greedily latched onto the inexorable tide of his secrets. Good god, there was so much… faces, places, years, decades…I had won. I had beaten him. And it was all mine for the taking. I was suffused with pleasure and satisfaction on every level, every plane.

I was still riding out the aftershocks of the orgasm, my consciousness bouncing in and out of my body, when Barrow's voice seemed to come from all directions. "Goodbye, Mira." Where was he? I was lying there alone, and I realized he had fled the room. The connection between us was fading, but I could still hear his voice. "Remember what you've learned. And for what it's worth, I am so sorry about Clive."

Clive? Sorry…? I reached out suddenly, expanding my consciousness in all directions. There was Barrow, duffel on his shoulder, clutching some items to him, his henchman carrying Anlyse, poised on the threshold of a loading dock. And then, one more step, and they were gone.

So there had been a containment circle after all. It had included the entire building. Once he stepped beyond it, not only did he disappear from my senses, it was like my head had been stuffed in a bag the entire time and I was suddenly freed. I could suddenly breathe clear air, and see and feel what had been blocked from me. In that instant, I could sense the guttering stutter of someone's life-energy flagging, and I could suddenly hear the desperate voice from somewhere below me, Clive whispering one word that sliced me to the core, his safeword: "Divinity."

FORTY-EIGHT

Disembodied spirit such as I was, I was frantic to get to Clive. His safeword was an unmistakeable cry for help, intended for me alone, but I feared that it meant more than that. Clive, who took pride in never using his safeword, and who'd told me he was prepared to do anything for me… was I the cause of his distress? My fear crackled through spacetime as I sensed that what was happening to him was the same thing I'd felt in Anlyse.

My first thought, of course, was that Barrow had somehow been able to draw on them both… but a far more terrible thought followed. While Barrow had been purposefully draining Anlyse nearly to the point of death, had I been unwittingly doing the same to Clive? That explained the mysterious, unreal strength I'd had to fight Barrow off when he'd tried to choke me.

I had to get to Clive. I had to set things right, but although an expanded consciousness is great for knowing things, it's not so great for taking action in the physical world. I couldn't figure out how to move back to the physical plane. He was still in the basement room where I'd sensed him before—where I'd been with him when we'd first awoken with Barrow—what had to have been many days ago. I could tell he was slumped against the wall, a blanket over his legs, his mouth open and his eyes closed. But was he alive? By then I was too spread out in the spirit world to be able to sense his breath, his blood, his heart.

He had to be alive, I told myself. If he had died, I would know. I'd feel the loss. I'd be torn apart. Right?

I had to get back into my own body somehow. I could see myself lying there, but I didn't know how to cross over, how to merge back into my own self.

And I could see blood on the sheets and on my thighs. From what? My first thought was that I despite my gentle persuasion I'd managed to rip Barrow up inside… but no, that didn't seem likely. Had he cut me in revenge as he fled? Was I unable to return to my body because *I'd died?* I didn't think so. You'd think I'd know.

Before I could solve that mystery, another flare of energy drew my attention: someone crossing the circle. Coming into the building.

Jair! And Roland and Ira. I could sense them clearly as they entered the space. I swept to them as quickly as I could. Ira was limping and clutching his side, Roland half-carrying him up the ramp of the loading dock.

"Gotta wonder what put them on the run like that," Jair was saying. His knife was out, and he was walking behind the other two, facing back the way they had come, watching for pursuit.

"They certainly seemed ill-prepared to repel our attack," Ira said, panting heavily as Roland lowered him down.

I tried to call Jair's name, but I didn't know how.

"Stay here with him," Jair told Roland. "I'll see if I can find Mira and Clive."

Jair! I tried again. Then I remembered what Barrow had said: if we'd had intercourse, there'd be not a mere thread between us, but a rope. Was there such a connection between Jair and me?

There was. I yanked on it. "Hey!" His hips jerked. "What was that—"

I pulled him toward Clive. At first he resisted, but then he closed his eyes and drew a breath, reaching out to sense me. "Mira?"

I pulled harder.

It worked. He followed my lead through the building and down the stairs. When Jair reached Clive, the first thing he did was check for a pulse in his neck. Then he spoke into his phone. "Found Clive. He's alive, but out cold. And I do mean cold."

"In quietude?" came Roland's voice.

"Yeah, but even colder than Wex. I don't think I can carry him on my own."

"Any sign of Mira?"

"Not yet. I feel her presence, though." I yanked on him again and he yelped. "I think she's trying to tell me something."

I felt that core of desire he had for me, heating up the connection between us. The next thing I knew, he was running back up the stairs to the storage unit where I lay. He threw open the latch and cursed softly when he saw the blood. He rolled me onto my back and looked me over. "Okay, Mira, I know you're here."

"What was that?" Roland asked.

"I found her, but she's unconscious. Soulwandering, probably."

Ira's voice broke in. "This speaks to the importance of daily meditation and developing facility with movement between the states of consciousness."

Save the criticism for later, asshole. Got any helpful suggestions?

Jair threw his hand across his eyes as a gust of wind suddenly whipped up the papers and grit in the room. "I think you just made her angry."

Damn right he made me angry. The pompous ass.

Jair stuck his phone in his pocket and checked me over more carefully. "No markings. Mira, did Barrow kick you out of your own body somehow?" He looked around the room. "When Clive was out and about, you ordered him to come back. Something tells me that won't work for me and you." He sat down beside me and brushed the hair out of my face.

"I can feel you pulling on our mutual attraction," he said. "You've got to use that like a lifeline, Mira. Until you can pull yourself up out of the water and into the air." He cupped my cheek. "Okay?" His face was so close to mine I should have been able to feel the warmth of his breath on my lips. I wanted to feel that warmth, that life, that passion…

And suddenly I was surging up into a kiss, locking my lips onto his like he was saving me from drowning. I clutched onto him, hugging him hard, the sudden scent of his leather jacket and the taste of his mouth and the rub of his stubble against my chin… The physical world is sometimes under-appreciated, but not at a moment like that. "Jair! What are you doing here?"

"Rescuing you, I hope."

"You saw Clive downstairs." My heart flopped in my chest like a fish.

"Mira, he didn't look good."

"Let's go! I'm… I'm worried for him." How could I tell him I was responsible for Clive being half-dead?

Jair got to his feet and held out a hand to help me up. "Maybe you can wake him up the way I woke you up."

As I stood I realized how much blood was plastered to my thighs. Blood that was coming *from me*. I tried to ignore it and run out of the room, but Jair caught me. "Whoa whoa whoa, are you hurt?"

I felt around quickly. Everything was a little swollen, normal post-sex. "I think it's… menstrual blood?" My head spun suddenly. "What day is it? How long have we been here?"

"Since night before last," Jair said. "Why?"

The world spun on its axis again. "Barrow made me think it had been weeks. But, Clive!" I tried to dash off again, but Jair held me back.

"Here." He tossed me a pair of Barrow's discarded sweatpants. Fine. It took only a few moments to yank the clothes on. My ass was quite a bit wider than Barrow's, but I could get the pants on. I turned a T-shirt into a makeshift maxi pad and pulled another over my head. Barrow had fled in such a hurry, he'd left behind most of his things.

As Jair and I raced back to the basement, I had to ask, "What happened out there? Why did they run?"

"I was going to ask you that."

"Tell you later. We have to assume they're coming back to finish us off as soon as they regroup."

"Agreed."

When we reached the basement, Ira and Roland were already checking Clive over. Clive was propped up against Roland. Ira had apparently recovered enough to walk under his own power, and he was examining Clive's back. "This is not good."

"What's not good?" I rushed forward, heart in my throat. Good god, had I truly drained him to the brink of death the way Barrow had Anlyse? "Let me wake him up."

Ira held me back, while Roland insisted, "Mira, listen. He's got markings like Wex's."

"So? That's no reason not to wake him."

"That's not what I mean. He's got different markings. Ones that… we think might mean we should be careful."

Ira had a hand on Clive's back and I wanted to slap him away. But he was pointing to the glyphs etched into the circular design between Clive's shoulders. "These are the three forms of the sigil for Fire: Desire, Devouring, and Destruction. Given what we've learned from the books we found at Trinity…" He trailed off, like he didn't want to be the one to speak the evil. "This seems very bad."

My blood ran cold, then hot, then cold again, and I went weak in the knees. "Barrow told me it was possible to… turn a person into a kind of psychic firebomb." I crouched beside Clive, letting my fingertips rest on his shoulder. Then I felt for the pulse in his wrist. It was thready and weak.

"What do you know about it?" Ira demanded.

"Barrow lies by telling partial truths." I rubbed Clive's fingers as if that would help warm him up, but he felt cold all over. "He told me that the purpose of the Circle was to raise up a sacrificial virgin who would be like a kind of time bomb. Without release, she would just build up more and more and more energy until she could be unleashed as a tool of genocide.”

“Genocide?” Jair recoiled. “What kind of nonsense—”

Ira pointed to another glyph on Clive’s back. “That one means ‘bloodline.’”

“Oh, shit,” Roland said.

“Clive presumably doesn’t hold the power to destroy the human race,” Ira scoffed, and I wanted to smack him.

“But he would have enough to unleash an all-encompassing fire on everyone he’s linked to by blood,” Roland said. “And that means all of us.”

“Yeah, well, the Partisans could unleash fire on this building if we don’t get out of here stat,” Jair pointed out. “Let’s go.”

“We’ll have to bring Clive with us.” Roland shifted Clive against him and I wanted to push him out of the way and take his place. Which was ridiculous, but that was how I felt. “Assuming it’s safe to move him.”

“I’m… not sure about that.” Ira felt the pulse in Clive’s neck. “His vitals are very weak. And getting weaker.”

My heart sank.

“That’s just because he’s in quietude, right?” Jair asked.

I tried to speak, but my throat was tightening. “In the… in the incident that… drove the Partisans away… Clive… he…” I couldn’t finish. I couldn’t say it.

“It may be necessary to entomb him indefinitely, if—” Ira broke off with sudden alarm. “I’ve lost his pulse.”

No, I thought. *No, it can’t be.*

They broke into arguing, but I couldn’t hear the words. The only thing I could hear was my own internal voice screaming *No No No.* I had held myself together for as long as I could but I couldn’t any longer. I broke down in tears, in great heaving sobs. I pressed my cheek to Clive’s, the wetness making him seem even colder, and howled. It wasn’t fair. After all we’d been through, after all we’d suffered, and I had so much I needed to tell him. I needed to tell him I loved him, that I cherished him, that I never meant to hurt him.

I reached out to touch the beads of his collar, to run my fingertips along them as I’d so often done.

Turns out it hadn’t been my will that held it in place at all. It’d been Clive’s. And the whole thing came loose, the beads falling lifeless from his neck, like water escaping through my fingers, slipping entirely out of my grasp.

FORTY-NINE

I knew it was possible to have an emotional shock so great it could make a person faint. I'd just never experienced it before. So I was surprised to find myself waking up with Jair plucking at the hairs at my temple and calling my name. "Mira, hey, come on now."

"Come on yourself," I growled, grabbing him by the lapels of his jacket. My heart felt like it was burning to a cinder. With Clive gone, I wondered, was this what life would be like? Forget the practice, I wasn't sure I'd be able to feel anything other than pain again. Everything was on fire and the sound of flames crackled in my ears.

"Mira, we need you," Jair was saying.

But I'm useless, I was thinking. I abused my power and pushed things too far, and I'm in my own personal hell for it.

I punished myself with a horrible thought. Maybe if I'd told Clive sooner about Ethan, maybe he would have taken the steps necessary to protect himself. Maybe at least he'd still be alive.

I was sick all over again just thinking about it.

The rhetoric we love to push in the BDSM scene is that the bottom cedes power and control. For many that also means the bottom cedes all responsibility for what happens. But it was an illusion that power and control were 100% in the hands of the dom, and that meant it was an illusion that responsibility was also 100%. Responsibility *had* to be shared, and yet I blamed myself, because how could Clive have been responsible if I hadn't given him all the information? I felt so nauseous.

"Mira, listen to me."

I shook my head. I was caught up in reliving that moment, when I'd thought I'd triumphed over Barrow, laying bare all his secrets, all his knowledge, only to find that the price I'd paid would haunt me the rest of my life. Well, maybe my life wouldn't be that long, if Barrow had his revenge.

Or maybe that *was* his revenge.

"Mira, snap out of it! You're the only one who can get Clive under control."

Clive's name hit me like a splash of ice water. I couldn't bring myself to say, *Clive is dead.*

"I know Ira is not your favorite person, but I really don't think—"

"What did you say?" I shook him by his jacket. "What's happening?"

"The demon is back."

Oh. Acid welled up in my throat. "You mean now that Clive is dead, his body's being possessed by the demon we'd been keeping out." Some part of my mind wondered if we could gather up the scattered beads if Clive could be—or should be—buried with them.

"I... I don't know. He's got Ira."

"Fine."

Jair helped me to my feet and I realized two things. One was that we had moved to the top floor of the building, in the same big empty loft space where we'd first ambushed Barrow. It was sunrise; golden light poured through the big windows. The other was that the flame-burning sound I was hearing was actually in the physical world.

And it was coming from the demon. My heart hurt to look at him. After all, that was Clive's body engulfed in multicolored flame. It looked like Clive with his arm outstretched, levitating Ira into the air. Ira was struggling, but there was nothing he could do.

Clive shaped his other hand like a claw and then raked through the air, and Ira's clothes tore into ribbons and fell from him, a few scraps of silk from his boxers fluttering through the air.

"Please," Ira begged. "Spare me! I don't deserve this!"

"Don't you?" The demon spoke somewhat formally, but it still sounded like Clive's voice, only resonating on all planes of existence. "Have you not wronged me?"

"No! Of course not!" Ira flailed in the air as the demon set him slowly rotating.

"Your crime then is either ignorance or lying. It matters not to me whether you lie to me or to yourself." The demon held up his claw hand again, as if next it would be Ira's skin that would be sliced into tatters.

But he hesitated there and spoke. To me. "My lady."

I hurried forward, but nearly stumbled. Was that *Clive* speaking? "Yes, angel?"

"My lady, I must ask your permission before I may serve justice against this interloper."

I put my hand over my mouth, trying to keep from crying again. It couldn't be true, I thought. I just wanted it to be so very desperately.

Clive looked at me when I didn't answer. "My lady. Are you distressed?" He kept one hand in the air—keeping Ira afloat—but he grasped mine gently and kissed it. "What may I do to help?"

My heart beat double-time as I swallowed, still disbelieving. But, one thing at a time. "I am... concerned about what you are doing to that man over there."

"He has wronged me."

"Tell me how he wronged you."

"He has trespassed upon me."

"Ah. And you seek to inflict punishment on him for this?"

"Yes, my lady. I want nothing more than justice." He bowed his head toward me, though, asking for my blessing to continue. "You said I was not to harm any member of the Circle without your permission."

"Mira!" Ira called from where he hung in the air. "Tell it to let me go! I meant no harm."

"No harm by what, Ira? What did you do?"

"Clive was gone. I thought there would be no harm in it."

Jair filled me in on "it." "He tried to draw Clive's blood through the scars so he could read them better, get a better look. But I guess that attracted a demon."

That didn't quite add up to me. I spoke to the demon. "Tell me about these trespasses."

"They are numerous. I have tried to ignore them, but I can no longer."

A random demon wouldn't have Clive's memories, would it? "Choose one."

Clive growled low in his throat. "The very first time we played, that one asked my limits and was told they were few, but immutable."

"Oh?" I couldn't completely keep the surprise from my voice. Clive had never expressed any limits with me. It was clearly not some random demon.

"That one was told that I would not engage in sexual intercourse with him."

Ira tried to put in a good word for himself. "You said no anal penetration and I never did! Not even my pinky!"

The demon rolled his eyes. "This one's idea of 'not engaging in sexual intercourse' was to bind my legs together and put his penis into the space between them."

"You didn't say you counted intercrural sex as se—" Ira broke off, and tried again. "If you had a problem with it, why didn't you say something?"

"I believed I *had* said something." That really sounded like Clive. The flames around him flared. "If I had complained afterward, what would you have said?"

"I would have at least said I was sorry!"

The demon looked at me with an almost sad expression in his eyes, shaking his head. "He does not always speak the truth, and yet he does not always lie."

I nodded. "The fact that just now he tried to invoke a loophole instead of simply getting clarification from you at the time suggests to me he would have mounted the same excuse if you'd called him on it then. I'll also note that claiming one would have made an apology in the past is not the same thing as apologizing."

We both looked at Ira, who did not realize that was his cue to make an apology. "Mira, don't taunt me!" Ira screeched. "Just tell it to put me down."

The demon growled and flicked his arm. A long tongue of flame, like a whip made of fire, extended from his hand.

I could feel Jair standing just behind me, poised for action, as if there were anything he could do. Roland was on the far side of Clive from us, his phone in his hand. I could see his lips moving. He must have been telling Niko or someone what was going on, but I couldn't actually hear him speaking.

"Tell me more about injustice," I said to the demon.

"It is the reason I burn," he replied, and the flame-whip crackled loudly.

Hm. "And if you take revenge on the one who wronged you, does that right the scales?"

Smart demon. He paused, considering, as if that might be a trick question—because it was.

I continued: "Or is the only true justice to be found in the repentance of the guilty?"

"I do not know if that one has the capacity to repent," the demon answered. "But punishment must still be meted out regardless of the result."

I didn't know if Ira had repentance in him either, but it was clear to me he needed to at least be able to admit when he was in the wrong. Maybe if Ira had actually seemed sorry I might have done things differently. "Ira," I said, "I don't think I can just tell the demon to put you down."

"Why?" he cried.

"Because I don't think it works that way," I replied. "I think you have to actually clear the air to dispel this demon."

"Clear the air...?" Ira sounded equal measures hopeful and outraged. "You mean... submit willingly to punishment?"

I put a hand onto the demon's shoulder. The markings and glyphs on his skin glowed bright as if they were cracks that exposed the fire within. "What punishment would you find fair?"

Clive—the demon—frowned. "Injustice must be righted."

"I agree. Which is why the punishment must be fair and that one must consent to it. Otherwise injustice is merely being perpetuated."

"Yes, of course, my lady." He bowed to me again, from the waist. Ira still rotated slowly in the air nearby, his eyes wild. "I am yours to command."

My heart clenched when he said those words, but I tried not to let myself be distracted from the goal, which was to get Ira through in one piece. "Are you saying the punishment is mine to dictate?"

"It is your right." He bowed again. "I am yours, and an insult to me is an insult to you, as well. A trespass upon me is a trespass on your property."

I ignored the hammering of my very excited heart. "Very well, then. Did this man do you permanent physical damage?"

"No, my lady."

"Then when you punish him, you must not do him permanent physical damage."

"Mira!" Ira's voice had an edge of panic. "You can't be serious!"

Clive studiously ignored him. "Are you certain, my lady? A lying tongue can be burned out."

Ira made a distressed squeak.

"I am certain," I said firmly. "No permanent damage."

"Very well, my lady. If that one agrees."

Ira clenched his teeth, but said, "Fine. I see the logic here. I'll submit to this… this… procedure. But Mira, please, do what you can?"

Fine. "Limit your target to his skin." I watched as Ira rotated in the air so that his bare back faced us. I nodded in approval, then added, "Would you also say it would be fair for a full confession to lessen the severity of his punishment?"

"What!" Ira exclaimed.

Honestly. He'd asked me to do what I could, and here I was, handing him a way to mitigate his own circumstances, and the ungrateful wretch was objecting? I was in no mood for that. Instead of putting a time limit or a stroke limit on the scene, I left the conclusion in Ira's hands, too: "You may proceed until he begs for mercy. At which point I expect you to grant it."

"Yes, my lady." He gestured toward the St. Andrew's cross that still stood at the center of the room and Ira flew to it. Glowing cords of energy appeared to bind Ira's limbs. The demon rolled his wrist lazily as he flipped the whip of pure flame against the brick floor, raising sparks and smoke.

Then he threw a wicked grin in my direction, so much like Clive. "First I'll… warm him up."

"Puns are evil," I replied, trying not to laugh.

"You don't believe that." He did laugh, and it was Clive's laugh.

I let myself try to see the truth right in front of me. I'd suspected something hadn't added up in the explanations they'd given me about demons, but I hadn't known enough to even ask the right questions. But as the demon laid a literal line of fire down Ira's pale back, I said quietly to Jair, "Tell me again what a demon is?"

"It's a coalescence of avidity," Jair said. "When someone wants something so much that it literally splits off from them into a spirit of its own."

But what we were dealing with was obviously not just a random spirit who took up residence in Clive's empty shell. At least, it was obvious to me.

Roland came over to us. "That's why demons are usually all about lust, or greed, or revenge. They're a pure force of desire. Which is why they normally can't be reasoned with."

Ira screamed as he was flogged with the flame. He'd probably taken over a dozen strokes by then? Still no confession. I couldn't take my eyes off of Clive, his muscles bunching and flowing as he swung the whip, but I said to the others, "What happens if the demon never splits off from the original person?"

Roland sputtered something like, "We don't know if that can happen!"

"Rol," Jair said gently, "there's a hell of a lot we don't know."

Ira's voice was getting ragged, his screams taking on a torn-up quality. That had to hurt.

Out there in front of us, Clive paused to crack his knuckles. "There, that was a warmup. Now the real—"

"Enough! Enough, please! I confess!" The words almost couldn't escape Ira's mouth fast enough. "You're right! I pushed things too far. I was jealous, all right? I was jealous of Mira. I watched you two play that night at Purgatory, and I… I was petty. I wanted to prove to you I was everything you could want or need."

"When you've got a hammer, everything looks like a nail?" Jair whispered to me.

"Everything I could want or need?" Clive echoed. "What did you think that was?"

"You wanted to be dominated. You wanted to be able to lose yourself in another's will."

Clive did not dispute that.

Ira went on, his confession slipping into justification: "I may have *pushed* the boundary you set when I rubbed off on you, but I did not *cross* it. I thought it would demonstrate my dominance and care for you simultaneously. Come on, Clive, you know perfectly well the juiciest meat is to be had at the boundaries."

Clive snapped the flame whip in the air, growling angrily. "I didn't tell you my boundaries so that you could make a To Do list out of them."

Ira at least had the good grace to look chagrined, hanging his head. "I misread you. For that, I am truly sorry."

Clive snapped the whip again and Ira's confession picked up speed: "I owe Mira as much of an apology as I owe you. When you walked into my party together I just… couldn't stand it. The only reason I let Wexel invite her was I thought I'd show her up. I thought she'd see all the markings I'd put on you and realize that you were mine, not hers. That she could never give you what you wanted, because she would never dare—"

Clive walked up to Ira and placed one claw-shaped hand on the top of each shoulder. His nails dug in right where Ira had cut him and severed his soul. I held my breath as I realized: if the demon took my orders literally, at no point had I said he couldn't rip Ira's soul right out of his body.

Perhaps Ira realized that, the words pouring out more quickly: "I was arrogant and I was ignorant. I didn't know the effect the cutting would have on you! I thought I would get beyond your mental block, I'd know all your secrets, and you'd be bonded to me—!" His words broke off into a scream as Clive must have put some pressure onto those points. "And the other members of the Circle would realize I was the most powerful and defer leadership to me! And Mira would be left on the outside, looking in!"

Wow. I couldn't even feel angry at Ira at that point. All I could feel was pity. He was that pitiful.

Clive dragged one nail diagonally down across Ira's back, leaving a burn as he went, and drawing a long scream out of Ira in the process. "I'm sorry, I'm sorry, I'm sorry," Ira repeated when he got his breath back. "I was a fool! I was blinded by lust and desire for you!"

Clive shook his head and raked another burning trail from the opposite shoulder, eliciting another cry from Ira, and then a new torrent of words: "Mercy, mercy please! I don't deserve it, I know I don't, but please, I beg you. I can't take any more."

Clive just gave a satisfied nod and stepped back to look at his handiwork. "Your confession is not complete until you have repeated it to your wife. But I am finished." And just like that, the punishment was done. "Let this be a lesson to you," he said, and turned away.

He came directly to me, knelt, and placed a kiss on my foot. Then he looked up and said, "That one is going to need some care." Jair and Roland were already hurrying over to help Ira down from the cross. "But this may not be the place to administer it, my lady."

"Why is that, angel?"

"Because the building is on fire."

So the scent of smoke and ash wasn't just from the demon. "Can you help us escape?"

"For a time, but I am nearly spent."

I seized him by the face, pulling him close. "What does that mean, spent? Is your time on Earth done? I don't want it to be done, Clive."

"No, no, my lady. I mean… the fires can only burn for so long before I need rest. This flesh can only withstand so much."

The body is a gateway for spiritual energy to enter the physical world. And it can withstand so much more than we think we can. That much Barrow had spoken true. But I had to be sure. "So you're saying after you rest, you'll be okay? You'll be all right?"

He hesitated, trying to answer truthfully. "Barrow… did something to me, my lady. Something bad."

"I know."

"But I will be alive, if that is what you are asking."

"Yes, that is what I'm asking!"

"Then we better escape from here, so that I will have spoken the truth," he said with a grin.

Every second counts when you're trying to get out of a burning building, but I had to take that moment to kiss him.

FIFTY

The escape from New Jersey was mercifully uneventful. We went out the same fire escape we'd come up on the night we'd ambushed Barrow. The light I'd thought was dawn had been sunset and as we fled the burning warehouse, full night had fallen. That beat-up old "paint" van looked right at home behind a shuttered warehouse a block over and I'd never been happier to see it. Jair drove, Roland took shotgun, and Clive and I made Ira lie facedown in the back of the van so we could work on his burns. His back was crisscrossed by welts that looked like severe sunburn. Some of them might blister, and I was sure they hurt like a motherfucker.

Ira began to sob uncontrollably as the burn cream relieved the pain. When he was able to form words they were these: "Why you?"

Clive was back to his old self, looking exhausted but no longer otherworldly, a drop cloth around his shoulders like a serape. "If you don't understand why we're the ones healing you, then it's no wonder you don't understand anything else I've tried to tell you about boundaries and responsibilities." He seemed to realize that Ira, who was crying his eyes out, was in no shape to absorb complicated arguments. So he put it this way: "We took you apart. We put you back together."

It was best if I didn't say anything. Ira was clearly grateful for the care, but I wonder if, deep down, he found being healed nearly as humiliating as the fire-flogging. (I would mention this to Clive somewhat later and his reply was merely, "Male doms are weird." While I don't think every male dom has more hangups than a coat check, I didn't argue.)

Ira and Clive both fell asleep on our trip north, Ira curled toward one bench with a seatbelt keeping him in place, and Clive with his head in my lap. As we blew past the exit we should have taken to the Sanctuary, I asked, "Where are we headed?"

Roland answered. "After you were captured, we were worried about going back to the Sanctuary in case Barrow found out from you where it was. So we grabbed some hotel rooms in Westchester."

I had a chilling thought. "Do you think he can track us now?"

"Not as such. He can't pinpoint us the way he can Wex."

And that just chilled me even more. "So Wex is still entombed?"

"Mira," Jair reminded me, "it's only been two days."

Right. "Okay, but…how long are we going to leave him there?"

Roland looked back at me. "Hopefully not much longer. Niko thinks there are ways to nullify the markings. He's been working on that while we concentrated on getting you out." His face was even more sober and serious than usual. "Maybe the same technique of nullification could be applied to Clive. Did Barrow know about the demon?"

"I don't know." Barrow's last words to me had been that he was "sorry" about Clive. I'd been thinking he said it as a dig at me, to rub salt in the wound when I discovered I'd been responsible for Clive's demise. But maybe he'd been talking about what he'd done. "Does Clive being possessed change our interpretation of the glyphs Barrow put on him?"

Roland blinked at me. "Where did Barrow say the power for the firebomb would come from?"

"In Saira he said it would be built up over years without release."

"He's a Partisan of Fire," Jair said without taking his eyes off the road. "Presumably he knows how to invoke fire, somehow?"

"What if it's the demon's fire that those glyphs invoke?" Roland was already trying to call Niko.

Of course, he couldn't just ask Niko a simple question. First we had to explain a lot. And before I knew it, Jair and Roland and he—with everyone else listening on speakerphone— rehashed our whole escape. I explained what I'd figured out: that Barrow's "mind control" was probably good ol' brainwashing. He could make you think that you were talking with him and he could spend a lot of time breaking you down—days, weeks, months?—when actually it was all happening in your head and almost no time was passing in the physical world.

"But you turned the tables on him!" Kish exulted. "What did you learn? What did you get out of his head?"

Before I could answer, Niko broke in. "Mira, take your time. Trust me, I speak from experience. When you've taken in a lot from another mind, it can be overwhelming."

I put my hands over my eyes and let myself be calm for a moment. "I think I grabbed quite a bit. Like… now I know something about the guy who shaped Barrow into a Partisan of Fire."

"Interesting." Jair frowned, tapping on the steering wheel as he drove.

"And…" The knowledge felt like it spread through me like a chill. "And that we're the last Circle left. Barrow already wiped out the others."

"There are… were… others?" Jair asked.

"At least, we're the last one he knew of." My head throbbed a little. "I'd been hoping to find a way to contact allies. You know, in case we could band together to fight him."

"That would have been nice," Kish said. "Hey, Kanna has a question."

I could hear Kanna's voice: "Not a question. Just wondering if Ira is still asleep."

Jair answered, "Yeah, he's still out. He's got some things to tell you, Kanna. He told the demon a bunch of stuff."

"And the demon made him promise to give you the full confession," I added. Clive was also still down for the count. I played with the edges of his hair with my fingers. "A couple of other things I know now: there are only the three Partisans, Barrow, Anlyse, and one young guy… I didn't know his name but I feel like it's on the tip of my tongue…?"

"It's on the tip of your brain," Niko said. "We'll sit down later and I'll guide you through a meditation," Niko said. "Don't try to dredge it all up now."

"I also know that Barrow believes everything he told me about Saira."

As far as I could tell, Saira said nothing while we discussed the idea that the Circle existed to create a walking, talking tool of genocide.

Roland had the most strenuous objection. "First of all, the idea of maintaining a virginal state wouldn't have seemed as weird or regressive in centuries past. Second, the practice accomplishes so much more, why would that be the focus?"

"But that's how power works, isn't it?" Kish replied. "If there's something that could lead to the ultimate destructive force, that's what the structure is going to lean toward. No one's going to just ignore that."

They argued a bit more before I finally said, "There are only two points that really matter. One is that it doesn't matter why Circles were originally created, only that Barrow believes that they're a danger to the human race and that's why he's eliminating them. The other is that if a person can be turned into a vessel for the all-consuming fire, which we have to assume is true, what are we going to do about Clive?" Which brought us back to the original reason we'd gotten on the phone with everyone.

"Hang on, hang on." Dagger broke in. "So we think Clive's been turned into the same kind of time bomb as Saira supposedly could be… but how? He hasn't been denied release or any of that kind of thing."

"Clive has his own source of the fire," Jair said. "Unfortunately."

"Ah, of course. It makes sense now!" Niko sounded energized. "Barrow must have found out about the demon. That's how he knew Clive could be transformed into a booby trap."

"But can the demon be exorcised without setting off the conflagration?" Roland fretted.

"I need to see the glyphs and get a sense of Clive's energy before I can say anything more," Niko said. "I do wonder if, paradoxically, harboring a demon is what kept Clive alive, though?"

"Why is that a paradox?" I asked.

"Because one sure-fire trigger for the conflagration would be Clive's death," Niko said, then added. "Jair, please drive carefully."

"Always do."

I thought about the rosary-bead collar slipping free of Clive's neck. "So now the only thing controlling the demon is the glyphs?"

"With all due respect, Mira, it was not the glyphs that kept the demon from burning Ira's tongue out back there." Jair glanced back to make sure Ira was still asleep. "Pretty sure that was all you."

"How long until you get here?" Niko asked. He sounded fairly upbeat. "I need to compare the glyphs on Clive to what I found at Trinity. With any luck, they'll match, and I can show you my theory about them."

If Niko could be upbeat, so could I. "What's your theory?"

"That they can be… rewritten. Some of them, anyway."

"Oh!" Jair jerked a little in the driver's seat. "That reminds me. Here." He started trying to get his jacket off while driving. I helped him get it free. "Mira. Dig in the breast pocket."

In there I found the necklace knife, *my* necklace knife. "Where did you find this?"

"When we were trying to figure out how to fight the demon and you were still out cold, I found it in some stuff Barrow left behind. If you're going to be unmaking the circle on Clive's skin, you're going to need that."

I clutched the little knife in my fist, unaccountably happy that it hadn't been lost. A Circle heirloom. "You think it's safe? Barrow didn't put a whammy on it?"

"It wasn't in his possession long enough to sever the entanglements nor establish much in the way of new ones," Roland said, not even criticizing my use of the term "whammy." "If it still feels good in your hand, it should be fine."

I wasn't about to draw it to see how it felt, given that I might still be seized with the compulsion to draw blood. Maybe all the crap I'd figured out about Ethan would help with that—but what if it didn't? "I'll test it when we get there. Assuming I'm the one who'll be doing it."

Jair jerked his head toward Ira's inert form. "You keep telling me I don't know anything about how dom/sub stuff works, but I get the feeling if anyone besides you tries it, they'll end up like our friend here."

Roland agreed. "It has to be you, Mira."

When we pulled up to the hotel in Rye, I had to hold in a laugh. I'd been there before. I knew someone who ran play parties there a couple of times a year. They'd get a suite and connecting rooms, into which they could fit quite a number of spanking and flogging stations, and then they didn't even have to wash the sheets themselves the next day. I'd last been to a party there about three years earlier...

On the night I met Ethan. I realized it as the details of the memory surfaced. He'd arrived with someone, played with a few others during the course of the night, and at one point I'd realized I was following him around the party. Of all the places the Circle could have picked, it had to be this one? What a sign. If I'd hoped all the shit Barrow had put me through had cured me of feeling haunted by Ethan, I'd been wrong. I knew only one thing was going to get me past it: telling Clive.

It would have to happen soon. Very soon. I woke him gently to tell him we'd reached our destination.

Roland went through the lobby while Jair pulled the van around to one of the back wings of the building and let us in from there. The hotel was nestled against a hill and the property was completely surrounded by woods, making the place feel more remote than it was. The Circle had gotten two connecting rooms at the end of a hall and it seemed nice and quiet. Well, other than how noisy we were when being reunited with everyone. There was a lot of hugging and congratulating and exclaiming. I was happy to see everyone, of course, but I moved through the reunion in a bit of a haze. I saw everything muted through the inescapable fog that came with the thought that I had to tell Clive what I'd done to Ethan.

And I had to tell the rest of the Circle that I held Clive's life in my hands.

The reunion included food—Ira and Niko drank tea—but I don't remember eating. I must have, but my mind was on the words I was going to have to say. How was I going to break the news?

Clive stayed close by me but didn't intrude on my thoughts, until he took my hand and we slipped away from the meal. Clive led me through the master suite to the bathroom at the far end.

He laid out towels and a pair of matching bathrobes monogrammed with the hotel's logo while I ran the water, waiting for it to get hot. "Something on your mind?" he asked.

"Here we are, in another bathroom," I answered, though that wasn't the thought weighing on me. "I can't wait to get Barrow's smell off my skin." That wasn't it either. "Wash him off me?"

"Of course, my lady." He held out a hand though I needed no help stepping over the low ridge of tiles that separated the glass-walled shower stall from the rest of the bathroom. "But I think we should be cautious."

"Cautious? What do you mean?"

"I mean, until we've determined what might trigger what Barrow did to me, I should probably not be allowed release."

He was right. "We should be quick, anyway." I handed him the miniature bottle of body wash. "I want to try to undo what Barrow did as soon as possible. Did he talk to you or give you any hints about what he was doing?"

Clive made suds between his palms. "I was unconscious nearly the entire time. We only spoke in short bursts."

"What did he say?"

Clive started at my shoulders and soaped his way down my back. "Not much. I think maybe he was just determining which of us to focus on, you or me. When he decided on you, he said 'Good night, Sleeping Beauty.'"

"He literally said that?" I'd seen that in the memories I'd grabbed.

"Yeah, and then pushed me down into quietude."

I turned to put my arms around his neck. "Are you aware..." My voice shook too hard to continue and I had to clear my throat. His soapy hands settled in the small of my back, the spray hitting my legs. "Are you aware that when Barrow and I fought, you nearly died?"

He kissed me before answering, long and hungry and slow, like he was trying to tell me to savor being alive. He certainly was. And then he said, "I am well aware, my lady."

I burst into tears, but before I could say anything, he went on. "Mira, my lady, I owe you my life."

"That doesn't mean I should throw it away in a fit of pique," I said.

"I somehow doubt that your fight with Barrow was 'a fit of pique.'"

But it was my turn to cry, to let out so much I had been holding in. "You don't understand," I tried to say. "It wasn't the first time."

He let me cry on his shoulder, murmuring soothing things to me. Part of me felt that I was supposed to be the one comforting him, soothing him, right? But only someone who believed in toxic dominance could think that doms couldn't also need soothing or sympathy or support from their partners.

But I had to tell him. "Clive—"

He kissed me on the temple. "My lady. You've been punishing yourself for over a year. I'd say your suffering has been more than fair. But if a confession would relieve your burden... I'm listening."

I pulled back enough to look him in the eye. "Do you know what happened between me and Ethan?"

He nodded.

"Barrow told you?"

"No." His eyes searched mine. "I saw it. When Barrow blew your mind, I caught the shrapnel."

Good god. "Then you saw—?"

"All of it. I saw all of it, my lady." He bowed his head. "And, respectfully, what you did to him, and what you did to me are in no way equivalent." Clive closed his hands over mine, hot water slipping over us. "I signed up for this."

"I almost killed you!"

He held my hands tightly. "I knew there was always a chance I might forfeit my life for yours, Mira. I've known that since the night of the party. You saved my life at great risk to your own. Please understand! I have no qualms about doing the same."

"But I didn't intend to hurt you."

"I know. That's why I called out to you. But even if you had known that you were draining me, could you have done anything different?"

I thought back to my struggle with Barrow. "I had turned the tables on him, I thought. I'd convinced him that he should let me open him up and expose his secrets the way he'd opened me. And at first he was willing. But when I saw more than he intended, he tried to stop me."

"By saying his safeword?"

I swayed a little, keeping hold of Clive's hands as water cascaded over my hair for a moment. "No. He tried to choke me." Would I have stopped if Barrow had simply said his safeword—or just insisted I stop—instead of fighting me? I bet I would have. That he hadn't even tried it only proved we were never having the interaction that I thought we were.

"So you acted in self-defense."

Quite literally. "Yes. And I couldn't understand at first why I was stronger than he was. He had been telling me all along about the one-sided nature of a master-slave relationship. Harped on it, even." I stiffened as I realized: "He had been warning me, really—!"

"Mira." Clive put his arms around me like he cherished me. "You can't blame yourself for not knowing."

"Can't I?"

"Barrow wasn't trying to help you by teaching you about that. He was hanging you out to dry, so you'd feel it was your own fault for not figuring it out sooner. That's how he tried to cripple you emotionally."

I stood there in shock, water pouring over us. "You… you might be right."

"It's almost the same thing you called Ira on. He could have just come right out and said something instead of playing things close to the vest and waiting to see if things would turn out in his favor." Clive kissed my wet temple and I leaned against him. "Barrow was always playing things out to see where the chips would fall. If he succeeded in recruiting you to the Partisans, then he wouldn't have had to pull the trigger on… whatever he's done to me."

"And you really don't know anything about it? He gave you no hints?"

"None." He shook his head. "I just… feel the wrongness of it pressing against my rib cage like it might burst out at any second."

"Let me see." I turned him in the water and ran my fingers over the markings on his back. Unlike the cuts Ira had left on him, which had disappeared the previous time the demon had awoken, these remained, spiderweb fine but visible. When I traced the outline of the circle, my fingertip could feel the mark. "Roland thinks I have to be the one to exorcise the demon, because no one else can lay a hand on you."

"Roland is right." To my surprise, he chuckled. "I'm not sure who's been slower to accept that, Ira or you, my lady. All of me is yours and no one else's, Mira. I'm yours."

"And I want you to be." I turned him in my arms, and traced his bottom lip with my thumb, while I thought about kissing him. "But we have to survive this to see it through."

"So let's."

I kissed him again then, until we were both breathless, until there was no time for anything more because we really had to get on with saving the world.

FIFTY-ONE

Niko taught everyone the glyphs because it had become clear everyone needed to learn them. But there was no question I would be the one to perform the Undoing. At one point Ira tried, somewhat tentatively, to argue that he had better facility at reading and writing glyphs than I did, so he should "at least assist…" And Kanna literally smacked him with a rolled up magazine like he was a bad puppy and needed to be taught a lesson. He said nothing more.

Niko pointed out a glyph that was somewhat triangular. "I know this is the glyph for the All-Consuming fire," he said. "What I don't know is exactly what that is."

"Barrow told me it might manifest more than one way," I said. "It could be literally a firebomb that could crater the whole county, or it could send the destructive power through our liminal connections, to wipe out everyone we love."

"Don't make the either/or fallacy," Niko said grimly. "The unfortunate truth is that it would probably be both." (Of course.)

Meanwhile, Jair wanted to know how he—and all of them—could help, without interfering between me and Clive. I told them the best thing he and Kish and Dagger could do was their jobs: get Niko and Saira away from us, in case distance helped mitigate any negative effects. Niko insisted he should be the one to draw the circle and then he promised he would get the hell out.

Roland would stay behind to help us set up and—assuming we survived—to provide aftercare, because we both might need it.

The hotel room we picked was one of the bedrooms attached to the suite. It had an extra large king size bed set against one wall, below a dark leather and wood headboard (which was actually attached to the wall, not the bed itself). Roland closed the blackout curtains, making sure they were completely shut. At some point before our rescue, the chest of implements had been retrieved from The Archive, and it looked rather out of place sitting on the beige carpet of the hotel room, as if it had time-traveled from an 18th century ship.

Niko pulled a piece of bright green sidewalk chalk out of the supplies. "This ought to be visible against all the surfaces." He tossed it into the air and then caught it with the same hand. "Turns out the color *does* matter! The brighter it is—or at least the more visible—the better the containment."

"Because whatever happens, good or bad, is likely to be explosive, right?"

"Yeah, and remember, don't break the circle on Clive's back until *after* you've unmade the glyphs, or I'm certain it'll trigger the conflagration." He climbed onto the bed to draw on the wall and I noticed his socks did not match. "You're doing two workings in one, really, both Undoing and Exorcism, so I'm going to draw two concentric rings," he said. "One all the way around the bed, then another directly on it. When you include the one on Clive's back, that's actually three rings in total."

Of course, these weren't circles, they were spheres, and so the larger one went up the wall and then down onto the rug. For the smaller one he stripped away the duvet and blankets and drew right on the fitted sheet over the mattress.

And he wrote out the glyphs on the wall.

"Will those help invoke the powers?" I asked.

"Only in that they're there to help you remember them," Niko said with a laugh. "It's a cheat sheet for you."

Devour sat on the wall next to the crossbar that would change it to *Merge*. *Desire* would become *Passion* with the addition of two dots. And *Destruction* would go from entropy to *Order* with an angled caret on top of it like a roof.

The symbol for *Bloodline* would stay the same.

Niko set the chalk down and held my hands in his. "I didn't say this to the others because it wasn't going to change the course of action. But there's one more thing you should know."

That certainly got my attention. "What is it?"

His face was grave, the circles under his eyes seeming deeper as he focused on me. "If the Undoing fails, in the course of trying to get it under control… you may have a choice to make."

"What do you mean? If the Undoing fails, don't we all just die?"

"What I mean is… you might be faced with a choice to make. A sacrifice to make. And I want to tell you, if you sacrifice yourself, or yourself and Clive, there's still going to be a backlash among us in the Circle."

"But you'd be alive, right?"

"And so would Barrow." He let out a slow breath. "I felt it should be brought up so you could be fully prepared. In the calculus of one thing versus another, I know every life is priceless, but if it's the choice of one versus all of us, it's not as simple as you dying to save us. The thing to remember is… we'd all be tainted by it."

"Morally, you mean?"

He swished the word around in his mouth like Scope. "Kinda? What I mean is the backlash could make us unable to use the practice in the future, as if we'd killed you ourselves. But Barrow being Barrow, well, I assume he'd be able to carry on."

I froze, the chill creeping over my skin. Niko still didn't know what Barrow had told me. None of them did. Because I still hadn't told them. I weighed whether to burden him with the information that I could crush Clive's life in my fist and not lose my access to the liminal plane. I mean, I'd lose my heart and my mind and probably be suicidal if I did, but technically my soul would be fine. But this went even beyond that. What he was saying was that if I tried to save them, but it took my or Clive's death to do it, I'd just be putting off their death sentence. Because then they'd be helpless against Barrow.

I hoped it wouldn't come down to that. These were the kind of questions that kept the Greek philosophers up at night. I already knew I couldn't sacrifice Clive to save the others, even if his heart was in my hand. It went against everything I believed in and everything I believed about myself and my role. But myself? If I were handed the choice between my life or all of theirs? Maybe it was almost a blessing to know that if I tried to martyr myself the only thing it would accomplish would be to stave off the inevitable.

I told myself it wasn't going to come to that. I had to believe that or I'd never succeed at this in the first place. Ira had been right about this one thing. I needed all my confidence, all my belief in myself—and all Clive's belief in me—wrapped around me like armor as I waded into that battle.

Nobody's life was getting sacrificed on my watch, not if I could help it. But I appreciated that Niko brought it up.

"I'll keep it in mind," I told him.

And then came the goodbyes. They were brief. None of us wanted to believe they were real goodbyes: we had to believe we were all going to see each other again in the morning.

Once they had cleared out, the last step in the preparation was to get my tools ready. "What else did you bring from The Archive?" I asked Roland.

"See for yourself," he said, opening the wooden chest. He lifted out one wooden box with an ornately carved phallus depicted on the lid.

"Is the ivory dildo I've heard so much about in th—oh my." I had to stop and stare when Roland popped open the box. The object was far more beautiful than I'd imagined. I'd been picturing a beige replica of a penis, but what lay upon a velvet bed was an elegant taper as white as fondant, curved like a tusk, with a slightly bulbous tip. At its thickest point, the base was carved with intricate, abstract designs and inlaid with silver. The silver gleamed; I wondered who had polished it and how recently.

I lifted it free with wonder. "I see it's everything it's cracked up to be."

"Look under the velvet."

The case had a second compartment that held the straps of the harness. The leather felt well-cared-for. I set both the dildo and harness on the night table beside the bed. Roland set not one but two bottles of lube beside it.

Also in the chest: my whip bag! I was even more happy to have it back than my little knife. Having lost all my possessions, everything from my former life, to have these three trusty instruments—two floggers and one signal whip—at my hand was like getting help from old friends. I laid them out beside the dildo, along with some rope, candles, and other things that might come in handy.

Once everything was physically prepared, it was all a question of whether I was mentally prepared. I didn't want to disturb Clive's own meditation, so I said to Roland, "I don't think I'm going to learn to meditate in the next twenty minutes. I figure I should take this opportunity to ask if you have any last minute advice."

"Here, have a cup of tea," he suggested. "That may help you feel as calm and focused as meditation is supposed to. There is a psychophysiological practice of tea, after all." In the main room of the suite, he filled the coffee maker with hot water to start it heating and then sat down with me at the table. "As for advice… I think if this is going to work, it's going to be because your instincts are sound. I trust you. I believe in you."

"But? I hear a 'but' coming."

"The 'but' is the thing I fear most, for your sake." He wore that haunted look I had gotten used to. I knew by then that he had experienced so much pain and loss, including the deaths of his mentors and peers, not to mention his relationships. I had never had a chance to ask him about the ex-wife Jair had mentioned to me.

"You mean there could be something worse than all of us dying?"

"For you personally, I mean. Think about it. You're performing a kind of unraveling. Everything coming untied."

"Yes, and?" I was going to make him voice it. I wasn't going to let him make me guess, though I already had.

"This working could be the Undoing of your bond with Clive." He swallowed hard. "I know how precious it is to you."

For a split second I could see what he meant: that I should have been afraid. But I wasn't worried that some quirk of liminal connections or some blip in the spiritual radar was going to come between me and Clive. It wasn't only that I had to have faith in us, it was that I understood something I know he didn't. But I couldn't pause to explain then that "the bond" wasn't the precious thing about my relationship with Clive—as if it existed independently of us—but that how precious Clive was to me was what made the bond special in the first place.

So I just said, "I know."

"I think to exorcise the demon, you'll have to unbind him."

"I know."

"And if the demon turns on you, then…" He couldn't look at me, tears forming at the corners of his eyes.

I knew all that, but hearing him say it, hearing the fear in his voice, sent adrenaline flowing through my veins, anticipation sharpening into something spiky and dangerous. I got up to pour the hot water into mugs.

He followed, fiddling with a can of loose leaf tea that definitely did not belong to the hotel. His hands shook too much to open the can.

I set the can aside and planted a kiss on his forehead. "Don't be afraid."

"Mira, even if the bond stays intact energetically, all of your and Clive's barriers are going to have to come down. Most relationships don't survive that."

"I know." I tore open a packet with a bag of chamomile that had been sitting with the hotel coffee and dropped it into one of the mugs. "But true love requires knowing yourself and your partner. Those who are afraid of love are doomed to failure."

"That's advice I could've used many years ago," he said with a quirk of his lips that wasn't quite a smile. "But, Mira, this isn't just ordinary relationship angst we're talking about. Clive harbors an actual demon. He could become a literal embodiment of lust and rage burning out of control."

I patted Roland on the hand. "Which makes him honestly not that different from any other male partner I've had."

He frowned at me brushing off his concern. "I know there's a power imbalance in the practice, but not all men—" He cut himself off, before he could say something truly absurd— even he realized how it sounded.

"This is the first time I've heard you explicitly mention a power imbalance between the sexes in the practice," I said lightly.

"Well, you know, it's usually the male partner who is dominant, the female partner who is receptive, basic biology underpinning the bias—"

I humored him. I'd have to tell him later that he and Barrow spouted similarly gendered bullshit. I was sure that would horrify him once he thought it through. "I suppose there's no denying the fact that some of you are born with nature's can-opener between your legs and some of us are not. But Roland, I don't need a penis to crack a whip." Or wield a knife.

"I didn't mean that women are weak or anything like that—"

"Here. Drink this." I forestalled his disclaimer by handing him the crappy chamomile tea. He needed it much more than I did. "Listen. If there's a power imbalance of men over women in the practice it's because the practice itself was developed by men." Men like Barrow who believed men were more "naturally" dominant than women.

"You think?"

"Now's probably not the time to go into it." I wanted to pat him on the head. The absurdity of trying to argue biological differences in the sexes, when we are luminous beings projected into this space...? "May we have many late nights ahead of us to debate philosophy and worldview."

"I'll drink to that." He lifted the mug in my direction and sipped.

FIFTY-TWO

I probably was more apprehensive in the moment, but the main thing I remember feeling when taking Clive by the hand and pulling him into the ritually prepared bedroom was *finally! Alone, at last!*

"You want to know something amusing?" he asked, as he gave a goodbye wave to Roland and closed the door behind us. "I've been to a play party in this hotel before."

"Me too! I might have even played in this very room." I couldn't help but smile, as if that's all we were doing, sneaking away from the main party for a little private scene, just the two of us. The room was dark except for the light on the night table beside the bed, where all the implements awaited. "Did Ira bring you?"

"No no, this was before I met him. About a year ago." Clive was still wearing only the hotel bathrobe. I pushed it off his shoulders to find his skin still fresh from the shower, if no longer damp. It still looked strange to see his bare neck with no collar. I nibbled his shoulder because I couldn't resist.

As my nibble turned to a bite right on one of his soul points, he sucked a breath in through his teeth and gripped me reflexively, molding his hands around my waist, just above the belt of my robe. Then he caught himself. "Is it all right to touch you like this?"

He was so good, so good for me.

"When I don't want you to touch me, I'll tie you down." I felt the thrill run through him at my words. I wanted him to express his desire for me, to let me feel it. When that desire needed to be trammeled it would be my job to do that, not his.

If we survived, that is. Right then, though, survival wasn't my foremost thought. I would never be able to get through the working if I spent every moment worrying about the stakes. Yes, we could all die. I had to stuff that thought away in order to let things flow. Roland believed in me, Clive believed in me, and I just had to believe in myself. After all, there's power in believing in yourself, and wielding that power is ultimately what dominance is.

My desire for Clive, which had been pushed to the background so many times, was finally allowed to surge, fueling me and filling me. "You know how long it's been since I wanted someone the way I want you?"

"No, how long?"

"That was a rhetorical question, but the answer is… too long." I brushed mussed hair back from his face with my fingers. "Are you ready for this?"

"I am, but does it matter if I'm not? There's no real choice here."

"Are you okay with that?"

His smile was wry. "Mira. My lady. When I submit, having all my choices taken away is the appeal. Doing so doesn't negate my sense of self. It reinforces it."

Which was why he liked surprises. He liked meeting challenges. But I thought about how angry he was that Ira had intentionally pushed his boundaries. "You know once we start this, there's no stopping."

"I know." His eyes were clear and blue. He took one of my hands in his and pressed a kiss against my knuckles.

"It's just that… I know you told Ira you didn't allow certain things."

His tongue swept across his lower lip. "I didn't allow *Ira* certain things. With you, my lady, my entire body and soul are yours to do with as you wish… or as you must."

Good god but that was one of the most arousing things I'd ever heard someone say to me. "You know there will be no secrets left by the end of this."

"Which is as it should be." He held my gaze as he sank to his knees and put his hands behind his back. "Please, Mira."

He didn't need to ask twice. In answer, I seized him by the hair and kissed him—a kiss that was less about pleasure or the intimacy of mouth touching mouth, and more about taking what was mine. There was a hint of resistance, but his hands stayed where they were.

When I stepped back, I unbelted the robe and let it fall at my feet. Clive's eyes worshipped my naked form and I never felt more clad in my power.

"On the bed. On your back. Quick now," I said, and my voice seemed loud in my ears, almost resonant like Clive's demon-voice.

"Yes, my lady!" He indeed moved quickly, stepping into the circle and then lying flat, his head on the one pillow I'd left for that purpose.

I crossed the circle myself with one deliberate step, and under the lamplight the implements seemed to shine, the silver inlay and the polish on the leather gleaming. I climbed astride Clive's legs and raked my nails slowly down his chest, appreciating the way he arched under me and the sheen of heat it brought up on his skin. "You know, if you'd only come home with me the night we met, I would have done this long ago."

"Done what, my lady?"

"All of this." I leaned down to suckle his nipples, one and then the other, before I flicked them with my fingernails, drawing gasps and another beautiful arching of his back. "So sensitive."

"They are when you do that—!" He broke off with another gasp as I pinched them. My goal was on his back, but I was in no hurry. It wasn't even like I was trying to draw out every moment in case these were our last. I'd waited a long time for it and there was just no rushing me.

"Reach up and caress me," I told him, wanting to feel his hands against my bare skin. He slid them up my waist, then used his fingertips to lightly sweep the swells of my breasts. A slight arch of my eyebrow was all the signal he needed to stop avoiding my nipples and instead brush them with his thumbs until they were stiff peaks. "Ever been flogged until you cried?"

"Yes, my lady," he replied without hesitation.

"On the nipples?"

That made him hesitate. "N-no, my lady."

His previous doms had really lacked creativity. "Your front is much more sensitive than your back. Much more vulnerable." Flogging him on the front also meant I couldn't accidentally trigger anything involving the markings. "This way I can look you in the eye and see your face as you crumble and fall apart, as the repeated blows wear down all your inner barriers."

His swallow was gratifyingly revealing. No matter how much he said he wanted to be laid bare, there were things he couldn't help but hold tightly.

"What are you worried about, angel?"

"Nothing, my lady. Merely the usual fear that I will fail to measure up to the test."

Ha. A masochist's bravado. "Don't be silly. This is the easy part. Would you prefer to be tied down or can I trust you to be bound by your word alone?"

Hesitation flickered again. "Just tell me what to do."

"Spread your arms. Legs, too." His wrists fell right at the point on the inner circle where Niko had drawn glyphs. His feet needed to be slightly farther apart, but before I could say anything he shifted them until they were aligned with the chalk marks, a three-dimensional Vitruvian man. He groaned, low and deep in his chest.

"Can you feel where your hands and feet belong?"

"I can," he affirmed.

"Perfect." I ran my fingers over his face, his curved cheekbone. I liked the rugged look a few days of stubble gave him, though I'd make him shave before I let him use his mouth on me again. One more reason to succeed, one more thing to look forward to enjoying if we made it through intact. "Don't move."

I leaned over to grab trusty Number Two, which could really sting. I swatted my own inner thigh to calibrate my swing and hissed at the sudden pain. I would need a very light touch at first.

I trailed the leather strands slowly across Clive's stomach and chest, dragging them over his skin. "This one's got a nasty bite, remember?"

"Feels nice right now," he said.

"Enjoy it while you can," I teased, drawing the flail directly across his sensitized nipples.

Clive hissed appreciatively, arching into the sensation.

A quick swat with the rawhide tails sent him flat against the bed. I made a scolding noise and began twirling the flail around like a propeller.

"Up. Come up to meet it," I said firmly.

He clenched his eyes but arched again, raising his chest until one nipple was being swiped, over and over, by the pointed tips of the laces. I watched him struggle, instinct driving him to shrink away from the blows while his obedience to me pushed him to obey. I migrated the swinging laces to the other nipple, watching his skin redden and his breath grow short as the pain built up over time.

I shifted back to give myself room to caress his balls and then licked my palm, making a tunnel with my fingers.

"Thrust upward if you want a little pleasure," I urged. Each time he pushed his erection up into my slick grip, I swung the flail, stinging his skin at the same moment. I bounced him between that pleasure and its price for a long time, until his groans and cries began to lose coherence, until he was little more than a shaking mass of vulnerable nerve endings.

Time to take the pleasure away, except insofar as pain was a pleasure for him. I put my hand against his breastbone and began to swat him as hard as I could on the nipples with the flail, sometimes catching my own fingers. I didn't mind a little pain myself, not when there was so much pleasure to be had in stripping him down to the basest emotion, laying bare his heart. I struck him again and again, until all his senses were focused on that pain, until he was consumed by it, as if no other sensation could ever exist again. I could feel it filling him up, taking his shape, hear it in his cries.

And I knew it was time. I was more than ready for him. Hitching forward into a better position, I felt the hard length of him pressing against me. I lifted myself until I could work him inside, his slippery roundness like heaven against me, the sudden intrusion as I sat down making me gasp…and Clive weep at last.

Setting the flogger aside, I ran my fingers lightly over Clive's chest, as if the tiny red bruises starting to appear could be read like Braille. My thumbs, sweeping over his nipples, brought forth another sob and I closed my eyes, soaking up the effusion of his surrender.

It was not at all like when Barrow's secrets had poured forth in a torrent. Instead of everything moving quickly, it felt more like time had been suspended. I felt I could see the whole of Clive's soul glowing inside his skin, see the tangled, woven tapestry of his self, with each strand spinning back into the past, images and essences of ex-lovers strung along the skeins like ghostly Christmas lights. My fingers found the tips of his nipples and squeezed, sending a jolt along the wires, the memories lighting up vividly as Clive's pain spiked.

Changing my approach, I alternated between massaging and pinching his chest, each time sampling another of the fruits from Clive's vine of memory. Kanna and Ira tag-teaming him at Purgatory, in the mud on all fours as a pony trainer from Connecticut strapped a saddle to his back, a well-known dominatrix from the city tickling his feet until he begged her to stop….

With each pinch I felt a throb deep inside me, the twitch of Clive's cock.

The words welled out of my mouth like sap. "How long have you had the demon?"

It took a moment for him to answer. "A long time."

"All your life?"

"No. Since…" He trailed off. "I'm not sure."

He was not sure, but hearing him say that, I was. I was certain he had harbored that demon since whatever it was that had happened to create that block in his mind, the barrier I had crashed against when Ira had drawn me back into Clive's memories while Ghosting the Blade.

There was a pink to his cheeks, a flutter to his eyelids, that told me he was feeling a tinge of shame. "What's wrong, angel?"

"Nothing, my lady. That just… worries me." I could see the muscles strain in his arms as he pulled against the non-existent bondage, his wrists against the circle as if they were tied there. "God, I want you. I just want you so much. Maybe… Maybe too much."

Too much? I rose up slowly, wordlessly inviting him to drive upward into me, to work his hips and seek that pleasure, that feeling of completion that came with each thrust. "That's the way, angel, I want you to want. If you don't want me this intensely, if you aren't so hungry for me you can barely control yourself, then why are we even here?"

The guttural moan he let loose sounded very much like the demon. But his limbs stayed put where Niko's glyphs and my power—our power, really, mine and Clive's—kept him pinned.

"Your desire is what fuels this engine," I murmured, pistoning up and down slowly to meet his thrusts. "Your desire rages like a fire. My discipline is what trammels it into something useful, shapes it into something beautiful."

"Yes, my lady!" But I could feel the objection blossom on his tongue, even as he tried to spit it out. "Old habits die hard."

"Who told you your desires were something bad?"

His laugh was bitter. "Everyone. Even before Sunday school."

"You went to Sunday school?" I didn't recall him saying that before.

"Just for the months leading up to first communion. I was six."

I chuckled. "Didn't you tell me that was about the age you quit believing in Santa Claus and Jesus?"

He bit his lip as he tried to smile. "And the Easter Bunny. Am I being ridiculous?"

"Yes and no. Just remember, the same people who said demons were evil also say sex is evil. At least, sex like this." I squeezed the muscles inside me and made him swoon. "I don't think you got possessed because of some moral failing. Did some lazy dom tell you that you wanted 'too much?'"

His eyelids fluttered again as I rode him. "Not exactly."

He didn't have words for it, but I could see it strung out before me like lingerie on a clothesline. The vanilla girlfriend who wanted to lie there with her eyes closed, who called him "needy" when he wanted her to reciprocate, the more adventurous one who enjoyed both spanking and being spanked who nonetheless deemed it less than "manly" for him to express his submissive side, and, yes, at least one lazy femdom. Being kinky is, unfortunately, not a guaranteed antidote for toxic masculinity nor fucked up gender roles. I could see an icy, self-centered woman with perfect tits who considered him "broken" because he needed the "abuse," even though she was happy to be the one to dish it out…!

"Let it go, Clive," I said. I tugged on his nipples and felt his cock twitch inside me. "You can't hang on to self-contempt like that. There's nothing wrong with masochism or with submission."

"I believe that's true for many people, my lady. But it's hard to shake the idea that the demon is proof there's something evil in my soul."

"You doubt me?" I watched the struggle on his face, as if he couldn't decide how to serve me best: answering would be continuing to argue, but not answering was unthinkable.

So he answered. "It isn't you I doubt, my lady. It's myself."

But what your demon wants most is justice. That hardly sounds like evil at work, I wanted to rationalize. But it wasn't Clive's rational mind that needed convincing; it was the raw, emotional core of him that had been twisted.

I leaned forward, keeping him inside me but letting our foreheads touch. I spoke softly, my lips brushing his, as I said, "If you're broken, maybe it's just my luck that you're broken into the shape that fits me perfectly."

His breath caught on a sob. "I want to believe that, Mira. I do. But I'm afraid to."

"So am I," I said. "But at every step, at every turn on this strange journey, you've fitted me like a key made for a lock. Like we were made for each other, Clive."

He opened his eyes, which shimmered with tears. "Don't say that until you've seen what's hidden in the block in my head."

"Clive." I put a finger over his lips. "That's exactly what I'm about to do."

I felt him stiffen under me, holding himself silent and still when some part of him wanted nothing more than to panic like a horse trying to buck a rider. Tears poured down his cheeks but he didn't fight me, only himself.

I brushed the water from under his eyelids with my thumb, suckling the saltiness from the meaty part of my finger. "Are you afraid to find out what's in there?"

He nodded, and I felt a spike of fear lance through him, cold and unforgiving. "What if you find something hateful, something that would make you abandon me? Or something that would make me hate myself?"

"I can't imagine something that could make me change my feelings for you."

He grimaced. "On the other side of the coin, what if breaking open the scars heals me and the result is I no longer burn with the need to submit? What if the last piece of the puzzle doesn't fit between us, after all?"

I leaned down until I could press my mouth softly against his, tasting his objections like incense clinging to his skin. "If any of those things come to light, we'll deal with them, together. Our bond isn't fragile, Clive, and neither are you."

Another round of tears poured forth. "I want to hold you so much that not doing so hurts," he said.

"Then hold me," I said, knowing it was time to change Clive's position. His hands came free from the glyphs and I let myself have that moment of respite, wrapped tight in his embrace, in the strong arms that I hoped would hold me for the rest of my life, whether that life was short or long.

FIFTY-THREE

I almost regretted not showing Clive the work of art that was the antique ivory phallus. A layer of padding that was part of the harness cushioned my pubic bone as I settled it in place and adjusted the supple straps. I had ordered Clive to turn face down and stretch his arms out to the glyphs again. I surely made for an impressive sight, but I felt it was better that he not see what was coming. If we succeeded, he could examine the dildo all he liked, later.

At Clive's side, I ran my hands over the design on his back, tamping down a flare of anger that Barrow had dared to mark him. I felt more violated by that than by his treatment of me. The knife Barrow had put between my legs I could shrug off as merely something that had happened to me. But the knife touching Clive's skin while I was unconscious? (Not to mention while *Clive* was unconscious?) I could not brush that off so easily, even aside from the threat of the spell Barrow had laid.

I traced the design with a finger. Clive held a deep well of burning rage. Everything comes from something, right? None of us make ourselves from whole cloth. Barrow had discovered that fire at his own core and he had made himself a force of destruction and death.

I could not believe it had to be that way.

Clive shivered at my touch, no doubt expecting the flogging to continue. I scratched lightly at his skin with my nails, imagining that sparks rose when I crossed the markings. Flogging would not be the best way to wear down Clive's walls—they were too thick. Even cutting him hadn't been enough, as Ira had learned. To get into the locked vault of his memories, a key-in-lock approach was more likely to be successful—after all, it had worked on Barrow himself.

You showed me your heart, Clive. Now show me the secret locked in your center.

I drizzled oil, fragrant and slick, down his back and massaged it into his skin, working the taut muscles on either side of his spine and ignoring the markings, though I could feel them under the slide of my fingertips.

I kept working downward, drizzling additional oil between his buttocks. Clive's head lifted as he began to realize it wasn't his back I was interested in. I massaged his buttocks, releasing the tension in them, but the moment I lifted my hands I saw him clench them again.

I trailed one finger lightly down that valley, barely touching the pucker of his hole, and he stiffened all the way to his magically bound extremities. Time for me to tread lightly. "You haven't done a lot of insertion play, have you?"

"No, not really," he said.

"Any reason why?"

"No, my lady. It's just not high on my list of preferences."

That didn't ring true. "Did you wear a buttplug tail when you were a pony?"

"I did, but didn't particularly enjoy it."

I toyed with him, circling his entrance slowly with a well-greased finger. "And you've never been pegged?"

"No, my lady."

"That surprises me." Getting it on with a strap-on was such a standard weapon in the femdom arsenal, and he'd submitted to several. "No one's asked you to bottom that way before?"

"I suppose the subject has come up a few times, but somehow I've never gotten around to it."

Somehow. Perhaps some of his former partners were more sensitive to his boundaries than I would have guessed. I would bet that Clive had subconsciously avoided it, since if he didn't do the thing he didn't like, then he couldn't risk disappointing his top or dom. "And you flat out forbade Ira to penetrate you at all."

He was silent for a few moments, but I could see his chest heaving, as he worked himself up to saying something. "I didn't trust Ira. But I trust you, my lady." He was trembling as he said, "I trust you to do anything you think is necessary."

I patted his flank. "Turn over. I need to see your face for this."

The bonds released him and he repositioned himself, drawing a sudden breath when he caught sight of the phallus. "That's... beautiful."

"Antique, or so they tell me," I said, stroking it with oil as if it were a part of me. It almost felt like it was, warm rather than cold, which I suppose was one of the advantages of bone over steel or glass.

I climbed over him and kissed him again, letting him feel the weight of the phallus against his leg. "I'm going to open you up, Clive. Bit by bit. You know that."

"Yes, my lad——" He broke off as I slipped a lubed finger into him, tweaking a nipple with my other hand. I tickled his prostate and watched as his own cock twitched each time I crooked my finger inside him. Soon he was as hard as the bone. I slid my finger in and out of him, adding oil as I went, until I felt he could take two fingers.

He stiffened again and tightened against the intrusion, even as his face showed me he was trying so hard to relax, not to resist. But some part of him couldn't help it.

"Keep your eyes on me," I suggested, hoping that he felt the same warmth I did when our gazes connected. It seemed he did, since he relaxed at last and I finally got both fingers in. He groaned encouragingly.

That part of the male anatomy hadn't been on my massage licensing tests. What I knew of it came from personal experience and long practice. Not every man would come just from having his prostate gland massaged, just as not every woman would come from interior stimulation alone. If Clive couldn't, I thought, maybe I'd start conditioning him to... once we were out of jeopardy.

When Clive groaned again, angling his hips to take more, I deemed him ready.

"This thing should be easier to take than my fingers," I said, coating the ivory one more time in fresh oil. The scent reminded me of orange blossoms and lemongrass and incense. "It's nearly frictionless."

"If you say so, my lady."

I put one hand on his chest, not to physically restrain him so much as to let him feel the solidity of my weight while I maneuvered the phallus to the proper angle. The other hand steadied the base of it against my pelvis and I teased his supple hole with the rounded tip.

He was yoga-breathing, trying to stay relaxed, but the moment the implement slipped in even a half-inch, he tensed.

But I had spoken the truth when I said it was frictionless. Tapered and smooth and slick, even with him tense, it took only a roll of my hips to push it right into him. It went much deeper than I expected for a first thrust. Clive kept his eyes open, gasping, clutching at my hand on his chest with both of his.

"Arms outstretched," I urged him gently. "In position."

He nodded, but his breathing was ragged as he spread his limbs again to connect with the circle. As I began to pump slowly in and out of him, the circle glowed faintly, the yellow-orange-red of a candle guttering. When I picked up the pace, the light brightened, first to yellow and then to white.

Clive gasped again, his legs trembling.

"Does it hurt?" I asked.

"No, my lady," Clive said, sounding somewhat surprised. "It's just very intense."

"A highly intimate intrusion," I said, agreeing. "I'm going to kiss you now."

I bent down and jabbed my tongue between his lips, matching the rhythm to the movement of my hips. I sensed Clive quickening suddenly and felt my own senses flooded with gratification. He was going to come.

I tweaked his nipples and pressed my body against him, trapping his cock between us, giving him more direct stimulation. The sudden rubbing of his cock between our stomachs set Clive literally aglow.

When he whined, I could see the demonlight in his eyes.

"Yes, good, good," I murmured, slowing the pace to draw out the moment. A question seized me, then. "Are you sure Barrow didn't tell you anything about the spell?"

"Nothing. He just…did what he had to do." Clive's breathing grew slow and even, matching my slow pace of penetration.

"Wait. Were you awake for the cutting, then?" I'd assumed Barrow had knocked him out before starting, but Clive refuted that:

"I was when when he first started."

"Did you have flashbacks like you did that time with Ira?"

He struggled to answer, his mind trying to sort out the tangle of memories, some new, some old. "No. Well, maybe a few…?" I took that to mean there was more than he actually remembered. "But then I passed out. I figured Barrow put me under."

But Niko had told us—it felt like a million years earlier—that Wex's mind might have gone into retreat rather than remain present for what was done to him. "Did you consider maybe you put yourself into quietude?"

"I suppose that's possible. Maybe because Barrow was trying to get at the locked door in my head?"

That was exactly what I was thinking. "Let's open it, Clive. Let's open it…" I said, driving into him again with a long, slow thrust. "When you come. We're going to get there gradually, though. So gradually you may be cursing me and begging for release after a while."

"I would be happy to beg for my pleasure, my lady, if it would please you."

I grinned. "Who knows? Perhaps you'll enjoy being on the edge for so long. I will enjoy finding out."

I began to stroke his shaft with my oily fingers, in time with my slow thrusts. It felt as if Clive's mind and my own were slowly aligning, like planets coming into synchrony. I realized that the revelation of Clive's secret would be less like opening a locked box and more like the blossoming of a flower, warming to the sun, the petals gradually loosening, slowly expanding.

It was so gentle and beautiful that as Clive neared climax again, I began to hope that what was hidden in his memories might turn out to be something small and innocuous, something that had seemed huge and terrible to him as a child but would be harmless to an adult…

That hope was torn away as Clive's bellow of orgasm turned to a scream of terror. Suddenly he was fighting me, trying to throw me off. I held fast to him, driving the phallus deep and calling his name.

The memory was ancient and degraded like old film, as if acidic emotions had etched and eroded it in equal measure, but I understood it clearly enough: the fear that he might die, a gag in his mouth, his hands tied behind his back…and was that barbed wire wrapped around his thighs, his balls? His attacker, larger, stronger, taking full advantage of Clive's helplessness.

"Clive, it's Mira!"

Betrayer. They'd fooled around a bit before, that older boy and Clive. Kept it secret, of course. Then came the games with dares and *let's pretend*—not overtly sexual at first. Challenging each other, taking turns hazing one another, but it was clear which one was the sadist and which one the masochist. When things turned sexual, the dynamic became one-sided and the game became an obsession for them both. A craving. A need.

"Clive, Clive! Listen to me!"

The day it ended, they met in the woods by a creek, a spot they often went for privacy. Clive felt the other boy was on edge, angry and nervous. He was sometimes like that; the anger would make him crueler during the act, but also kinder afterward, when they both felt relief. Win-win.

But not that time. That day was an assault. Clive, unable to scream through the gag, unable to free his hands, unable to stop the relentless penetration or the vile things being said—*you're evil, you're temptation, I'm going to prove it, I'm going to kill you.* The "proof" came when Clive did, and I could almost feel the memory-ghost's hand around my own, still wrapped around his cock and sticky with Clive's spunk. As the boy had sodomized him and brought him off against his will, while Clive had screamed powerlessly into the gag, raging against treatment that he did not, could not, would not accept…

The fires of passion and desire had turned to rage. And in that moment, the fires of rage forged a demon.

In the present day, Clive's scream echoed freely off the walls of the hotel before he fell to panting and shivering.

"I'm here," I said into his ear. "That's me inside you. Use your safeword if you want me to pull free."

I could feel the struggle in his mind, to understand, to find his place, to find his focus.

Me. He focused on me at last. Time reeled forward, through all those casual scenes at camps and parties, through the vanilla girlfriends and the disdainful dominatrices, all overshadowed by this boy from the past. Only Ira seemed larger than a speck, but maybe that was because he was closer in time. But as Clive looked up at me, eyes wide, I realized I loomed larger than them all. And I felt Clive pull his submission tight around him like a cloak, like armor. A moment before his sense of self had been shattered. But he pulled everything together once again into the shape of the man that was mine. And he spoke: "No, my lady, only if you are finished."

"I am not finished," I said, trying to sound gentle but unable to keep a bit of a snarl out of my voice. The demonlight in Clive's eyes flared in answer. "I don't think you plucked this demon out of the air. I think you birthed it yourself, not out of an unfulfilled, twisted sexual desire, but out of a desire for justice, to right the wrong that was done to you."

"Don't you mean revenge?"

"Maybe to a demon, revenge and justice are the same thing. You locked the incident away so tightly you barely even recognized your assailant later."

"You can see him?" Clive could only see the looming shadow cast by him.

I could make the boy out dimly. "Can you fill in the details for me?"

Clive's chest rose and fell as he gathered his courage and his fragmented memories. "One of the neighborhood kids, one of the ones I used to talk into tying me up in 'Cowboys and Indians.'" He blinked. "It turned from a game to a crush to…" He shook his head, turning away from the thought but I felt it: Clive had fallen for this boy, adored him, *loved* him. "I wonder if… he moved away? He disappears from my memory after what he did to me. He disappeared from my life."

"At the very least, I'm certain he avoided you after what he did." How ironic, I thought. The boy was trying to exorcise the demons of his desire, but he actually birthed one.

Clive licked his lips. "I'd never been gagged before. He did it so I couldn't protest, so he could pretend he didn't know I was really trying to get away. At least at first."

My heart clenched, imagining it. "Was there any chance he thought…he thought that was what you wanted?"

"Once he was emboldened… he stopped pretending. He broke a broom handle over my back and said he was going to kill me when he was finished. No, my lady, it was never about what I wanted."

"He tied you with barbed wire."

"Yes."

That explained the star-shaped scars I'd seen, those ancient puncture wounds. "You must have been cut badly by the barbs in a few places."

Clive closed his eyes. "My body betrayed me. That's the last thing I remember, screaming as I came."

I wished I could time travel, so I could go back and protect Clive from the experience. "I think you shut down because you knew if you assimilated that memory, it would keep you from something you needed. It would ruin submission for you, or at least your then-rudimentary experimentation with giving power to others. It might even ruin sex for you."

"And I've had this demon locked inside me ever since?"

"Yes. Growing stronger with age, fighting to get out, since you would never let it have the freedom to exact the retribution you so dearly wanted at that time." In a funny way Ira's instinct had almost been right: Clive *could* have set the house on fire. It would have been Ira's own fault, though, for setting the demon free. "Barrow channeled a similar assault into a fire when he was young."

"I suppose that's why he knows how to unleash it."

"That's what I think, too." I began to thrust again, slowly, rolling my hips so that the padded part of the harness stroked over the most sensitive part of me. "But the power in you is not Barrow's to unleash. It's mine." I wondered if the punishment the demon had meted out to Ira had sated the need somewhat or merely whetted its appetite.

I was about to find out. It was time to unmake the spell inlaid on Clive's back. "Here's what you're going to do now," I said, pressing all the way into him again. "I'm going to pull out and you're going to use your tongue on me, to arouse me, to get me to the edge without me actually coming, until you're hard again yourself."

"Yes, my lady. Something tells me that with my face buried between your legs, I will rebound faster than usual."

I slid free of him with a sigh. "When you're stiff and quivering again, tell me."

Unbuckling the harness, I lowered the dildo to the carpet beside the bed and then lay on my back. Clive applied himself to the task and I felt myself begin to relax as his tongue stroked and caressed, softly at first. Amazingly, his stubble was an enticing sensation rather than an irritating one. After a few minutes, he began to focus his efforts, suckling my clit and flicking it with his tongue while it was trapped between his lips. More than once I had to tell him to back off because I had grown so close I feared he wasn't going to pull back in time.

Fortunately he was ready quite soon. Perhaps the magic flowing through him helped him recover more quickly than usual. He had a hopeful look in his eye, perhaps expecting that I would take him into me.

If only my goal were so pleasurable. I surged up to kiss him with some regret, then moved him aside, gesturing for him to get on his knees and press his hands against the headboard. I ran my hands over the lines etched into his skin. "Clive."

"My lady."

"It's time for me to cut you, angel."

I felt the shiver run down his back. "There is nothing in the world I would prefer more. Do as you will, my lady." The words were brave and calm, but I could feel his heart kicking in his chest.

I shifted on my knees behind him, the knife tucked between my thumb and palm, settling my hands atop his shoulders. Time to do it.

But I found myself paralyzed. "So, you saw it."

"Saw what, my lady?" he asked, his voice light.

"Coy innocence doesn't suit you," I said. "My worst memory. When Barrow interrogated me, you said."

I felt him swallow. "Yes, my lady. Now we are even."

I supposed that was true. We'd each lived through each other's secret. But I was still the one with the knife in my hand. "If I lose control, even for a moment, I could really, really hurt you."

"And I accept that. That has always been true and I have always known it, even before I knew about Ethan," Clive said. "That's the nature of being owned, of the deepest level of submission, the surrender to your will, your whim, your power."

I pressed my forehead against the back of his neck. "What happened to 'submission is a thing I sometimes do, not what I am?'"

His voice was patient, but rough with passion. "Mira." My name echoed reverently whenever he voiced it. "That was *before you owned me.*"

Oh.

Why it took until that moment for me to understand it, for me to see it clearly and to accept it, I don't know. In hindsight it had been obvious—or should have been—since the night of the party. Maybe until I'd truly put Ethan behind me, I couldn't. For the sake of clarity, I tried to put it into words. "You're saying that you playacted at submission with various partners for the sake of fun and sex…"

"And maybe a little spiritual exploration, as well."

"…but it wasn't a part of you, until…I came along?"

"It couldn't be, Mira. It couldn't be anything more than play, until the ownership was real."

I drew a breath and realized the circles glowed as I exhaled, as my power coalesced and swirled. "Oh, angel." *Our* power.

"If I am 'a submissive' now, it's because I am *your* submissive," Clive went on. "No matter which plane of existence we're on. I'm yours, whatever you want me to be."

And I was his. Unlike with Ira, Clive hadn't put boundaries between himself and me because he already knew we could be two halves of one whole. And we were. When he said he'd sacrifice himself for me, he acknowledged it. He'd been aware of my ownership far longer and far more consciously than I had.

I'd known it on an instinctive level, but my conscious mind had kept trying to make it fit my preconceived ideas of relationships and consent—ideas that had been warped by my experiences with Ethan. It was time to get out of my own way, because there wasn't time then to work out all the philosophical or moral implications, but I had to be sure of one thing: "Do you think there's a difference between our bond and the one between Barrow and Anlyse? The others want to believe ours is virtuous and theirs is evil." The knife was tiny but felt large pressed between my palm and his skin.

Clive took one hand from the wall and curled it over mine in comfort, leaning his head toward it. "I find it hard to label something based in mutual love as evil. And as a certain demon we know might suggest, our definitions of good and evil may be due for some examination."

Ha. It wasn't lost on me that not half an hour ago *he'd* been the one worrying he was evil and I had been the one assuring him he was not. "Déjà vu."

"Perhaps if you can worry about whether something is evil, you've already inoculated yourself against becoming so?"

"A good thought, but I wish I could be sure."

He sucked in a breath as he squeezed my fingers and power flowed between us. "I think the way to be sure is to succeed in thwarting Barrow's aims."

I pressed a kiss against his shoulder blade, next to the glyph for Desire. "You're right. Here goes, angel."

I drew the knife and both the chalk circles and the one on Clive's back flared in unison, almost brighter than the eye could see.

First: turn Devour into Merge. Instead of one thing consuming the other like a flame burning up fuel, two things joining, becoming one. I held the knife with my thumb along the flat of the blade, preparing to press the straight line needed in the right spot, checking the glyph on the wall to be sure it matched. Clive's skin was warm and alive under my fingers as I traced over the shape of the glyph and then touched the blade to him.

It took almost no pressure at all for the razor-sharp blade to part the skin, blood welling up instantly. But as it did, my hands began to shake. I could hear Ethan screaming in my ears: How could you do this to me? You never really loved me!

Clive's fingers clawed at the leather headboard. "My lady!"

My title snapped me back into synch with him. "Clive."

"You know whether you loved him or not had no bearing on you cutting him or not."

I tried to blink away the vision of blood in my mind, but the blood on Clive's back, the scent of it in the air, made that difficult. "I guess some part of me still believes it, though, that if I really loved him, I wouldn't have ever made such a grave mistake. That deep down I wanted to hurt him."

"Please tell me, my lady, that deep down you want to hurt me *because* you love me, not because you don't."

Oh, angel. You're right. "Of course." I pressed a kiss to the tender place behind his ear.

"Because that's what makes any pain worthwhile. Whether you mark me, scar me, bleed me, or break me. I submit willingly to it. That is my power and that's what merges us together."

I pressed myself against his back, hugging him with my free hand and ignoring the blood smearing across my chest. "You're right. Time for the next one."

I sat back and licked my thumb, tasting iron and my own sweat. Clive was literally a part of me—not devoured so much as annexed. The rush of power I felt was akin to the euphoria of orgasm, a deep thrum in my bones.

Next. In the L of my thumb and forefinger I framed the Desire glyph and set the point of the knife against Clive's skin. Two small circles? I sank the point in and he grunted in pain. Not a nice pain, being stabbed that way, even though I didn't push it deep. I let enough blood well up that the heavy drop ran down his back and then I did the second one the same way. Like leaving a vampire bite, I thought.

As the second one welled up, though, alongside the lust that came as Desire transformed to Passion, came another wave of fear, another flashback. Ethan's words pouring out of him as fast as his lifeblood: You said you'd always protect me! You're a liar! You can't even protect me from yourself!

"Don't listen, my lady. He was weak."

"The weak deserve love, too."

"Not when he didn't love you back. He was never strong enough to love you. He loved what you could do for him, but he could never see beyond his own needs."

"And what do you need, Clive?"

"I need you to accept that I willingly make myself yours, a part of you, that you are my reason for living, and that when I say that, it's not because I think other people will be impressed if I do or that you'll reward me with a blowjob."

I trembled as Clive's words struck right to the heart of the problems I'd had not just with Ethan but maybe with every relationship. How much of a relationship was playacting and how much was real? Wasn't any relationship a certain amount of playacting for social acceptance? But Ethan had changed the rules whenever it suited him, claiming at one moment to want something, at the next that it was only "endorphins talking." Sometimes I was sure I had laid bare some truth during a scene only to have him disavow it later.

"I want you," I heard myself say. "And I want to mark you." Leaving my mark on my lover's skin, wanting him not just for sex but for everything, wanting him, entirely.

His life, literally, in my hands. Even a tiny knife like the one I held could kill with one stroke, a jab into the soft spot behind the ear, for example.

"Breathe, my lady," Clive said. He seemed to be struggling to draw an even breath and I realized I was hyperventilating. Breathe. "And mark me as you see fit."

Right. Final change to make before breaking the circle. Chaos to Order. "This one is going to hurt, angel," I said and Clive's whimper sounded anxious. But his hands never moved; he didn't flinch away. So obedient. Already part of me. Mine. I felt my anticipation rising as I prepared to cut, teasing myself with how much I wanted it.

I would slash the roof-shape with the belly of the blade, where it curved at the tip. He would really feel it. I sucked in a breath, the ripples of lust making my toes curl. Devour/Merge was still bleeding and I paused to lick it, making Clive gasp and shake. So, was untrammeled desire evil? Yes, if eating him like the big, bad wolf was evil.

But it didn't feel bad. It felt good. So good.

Slash, slash, and power rocketed through me. Niko was so naïve! The glyph he called Order, I called Control. That was what it felt like. Utter and complete control. All around me the circles were aglow, wind swirling within them as if the power I wielded were so hot it created its own updraft.

I wanted to keep cutting him. A few slashes at the top of his shoulders would let streams of blood run beautifully down his back! Why not? And then some matching ones along his spine? Like wings…

"My lady," came Clive's voice, as shaky as his breath.

I looked up to see his hands bound in place by bands of light across his wrists, the way Ira's had looked on the St. Andrew's cross during his punishment. Pure control.

But I had to control myself, too. My knife hand shook and I remembered the way I'd stabbed Barrow in the leg, the way the blades in the choosing had almost had a will of their own. Because after Ethan, my power didn't flow properly.

"Because you've suppressed it so much, my lady," Clive said. "It's almost like my demon. The more you've denied it, the *less* control you've had over those desires, those feelings, not more."

He was right. I knew he was right, and yet all I could do was stare at the blade in my hand, gripping it as tightly as if it were a poisonous snake whose bite would kill. "Clive," I was unable to raise my voice above a whisper.

"You must cut me to break the circle, my lady! Even if you cut too deep!"

The entire spell was getting out of control as I hesitated, the wind whipping fiercely. I'd transformed the glyphs into something that wouldn't harm the others but to finish the job, I had to break the circle and separate the glyphs. Three cuts. Two would have to be made right along his ribs and one right along his spine. Even with the tiny knife I could paralyze him, I could puncture a lung, I could…

"Mira, hurry!"

The use of my name jarred me into action. "I need to break the circle in three places!" I told him.

"You have a knife in your hand!"

"I know, but… it doesn't feel right!" Why? Why couldn't I simply slash through? Because with the bloodlust on me I knew I would cut too deep and then I'd never forgive myself. I couldn't bring myself to damage him and endanger him that way, even if he was willing to sacrifice himself.

I have to master myself in order to master this relationship. I have to master this power to make this work.

Trying to quell the bloodlust long enough for me to think it through, I dragged my teeth over the top of his shoulder and clamped on where his neck and shoulder met, suckling hard as if I could draw his blood right through his skin. It would leave a mark for certain. I remembered wanting to do that at Purgatory and holding myself back… how much it had almost hurt to hold myself back that night…

I had a sudden thought. Could it work? I stabbed the knife into the leather of the headboard, nearly grazing his cheek as I did, and grabbed the signal whip off the desk. It uncoiled smoothly as I waved it, testing the feel of it. *Hello, old friend.* I could strike accurately and hard with it. I cracked it in the air and Clive's flinch followed by a moan was intensely gratifying. I struck the pillow next to him as another test and he sucked in a breath.

"You know what's coming now, don't you?" I asked, balancing on the balls of my feet, right on the edge of the largest circle Niko had drawn. *Yes, this was it.* Was Clive thinking of Purgatory, of the first time we met, as I was?

He was. "You are going to whip me three times, and draw blood with each strike."

"That's exactly right." Once I was back in control, I could see with great clarity. The lines on his back were so sharply limned with eldritch glow that even where blood was smeared I could see them. Power flowed up through my feet and down my arm and into the whip. Normally one wouldn't be guaranteed to break the skin with a whip, but it wouldn't just be the whip I was meeting his skin with, it would be all of my power. "A knife isn't the only way to cut."

"Yes, my lady."

"Breathe, Clive. Breathe with me."

As our breaths synchronized, I felt the ever-present liminal connection strengthening between us.

My first strike needed to separate Passion from Merge. I swung the whip back and forth a few times, then raised it. Breathed.

Struck.

Clive's scream seemed to go straight between my legs. *Yes, oh yes.*

Sadism had never felt so good. The nagging worry that hurting him was wrong had finally disappeared. I felt the relief strongly, a thing that could only be appreciated once it had stopped, like an incessant noise that I had become accustomed to.

The second strike needed to break the circle on the left side, along his ribs, to separate the glyphs for Merge and Control. I swung the whip again, slashing across his back, vicious yet surgical. Again, his scream made my blood surge.

Without giving him time to recover, I struck directly at the last connection, between Passion and Bloodline. I cried out as orgasm hit us both simultaneously, my spasm making me stagger and nearly fall to my knees. I clung to the edge of the bed, unable to move, unable to even touch Clive while in the throes of my release.

Clive's screaming did not stop. His hands stayed where I had told him to put them but his shoulders shook and I saw his skin begin to glow, the marks turning red hot.

No! I had been so sure that would do it. That should have been all that was required—right? The spell was broken and all needs had been satisfied!

But something was still not right. I clenched my fist. My fingers itched to pull the tiny knife from where I'd embedded it in the leather.

Sudden doubts assailed me. Maybe Barrow had been right. Maybe the power would always corrupt. Maybe I would always want to take more than Clive could give… maybe I could never be satisfied with less.

I placed a hand on Clive's shoulder.

The fire was roaring and he was weeping.

"What's wrong, angel?"

"Please don't." It was the demon's voice. Clive's voice, but I could hear that resonance because the demon spoke on the liminal plane at the same time.

"Don't what?" Was the demon trying to safeword out?

No, not at all. The demon had something else entirely to worry about. "Please don't banish me." Demons can weep. Who knew. "I can't bear it."

"Clive, you've carried this burden with you like a stone in your heart—"

"No."

"Are you saying, you want to keep the demon? That you want to stay?"

Demons can whisper. "Yes. Please."

I hadn't thought to ask anyone earlier what would happen to the demon once it was cast out? Presumably it would still be able to possess others. That didn't seem like an ideal situation. And the demon…

… was Clive. "This demon is part of you."

"Yes, my lady."

"Which means… it answers to me."

"As all of me does." He leaned his forehead against the leather of the headboard, panting. Blood still trickled down his back. "You said you loved and accepted all of me. And that I was not evil. If this is true… it feels… unjust… to be banished from my lady's service."

Merely for being a disembodied coalescence of power and will. No, not disembodied. Embodied.

In Clive. "Do I have the power to banish you?"

"My lady, need I remind you? You have the ultimate power over me."

In other words, I could destroy the demon. I could technically liberate Clive from it. But it didn't feel right. "If it is in my interest neither to banish you nor destroy you… then I must collar you."

I can only describe the surge of power that flowed between us then as pure joy. The flames shot through from red all the way to white. "Yes, please, my lady!"

The only problem was that I had no collar handy. Well, that and the knife pulling at me harder than ever, wanting his blood.

I seized him by the hair and licked the dark spot I had left where his neck met his shoulder. The taste the salt of his sweat and the scent of his skin combined with the insistent pull of the bloodlust… how could I do anything at that point but move on instinct? I yanked the little knife free and found myself teasing him with it, shaving away fine hairs on the back of his neck and then sinking my teeth and leaving my mark. I did that all the way around, leaving a collar of bruises and making him pant with anticipation each time I drew the blade near one of his arteries, under his chin, along his Adam's apple, oh he was terrified and thrilled at the same time, both of us as aroused as it was possible to be.

And still the bloodlust did not abate. Because I still had not cut him in the way that I finally understood that I must. I had teased myself and held off and denied myself—and us both—for far too long. I kept a hand in his hair while the other held the knife to that spot on the back of his neck where the clasp of a necklace would have sat.

One, two, three. I slashed the curved "M" of ownership, my mark, into his skin.

Yes. That had been what was missing, what had been burning inside me for so long, shining in that moment as pure as white light. Mine, then and forever.

Clive sagged back against me, tipping his mouth upward, into a kiss of utter surrender.

FIFTY-FOUR

Poor Roland. He must have been dying to know what was going on. Clive and I were so focused on each other that we forgot about him until he knocked on the door. By then it was quiet, and we were wrapped in the duvet, snuggling in the afterglow of making love three (maybe four?) more times after the workings were done. We were very ready for a shower but not really ready to quit cuddling.

"I'll get it," Clive said, when the knock came.

"It's not locked," I pointed out, before raising my voice. "Come on in, Roland. Everything's fine."

He poked his head in like he wasn't really sure if he was going to find the entire room upside down or what. Really, the place wasn't in bad shape. Other than the chalk smeared here and there, and a bit more blood than usual, it didn't look all that different than it would have after a honeymoon. Though the chalk and blood did prompt Roland to say, somewhat wryly, "This is how those sensationalist news stories about satanic cults get started."

Clive yawned and stretched. "We can get into the maid closet, change the sheets, and dispose of these if we're worried we'll get charged with a crime."

"More likely a charge on Ira's AMEX, but that's a good idea." Roland sat on the corner of the bed. "So. I guess… it went well?"

"I'd call it a success." I hadn't looked at Clive's back in a while. I sat up and patted my duvet-covered lap. "Let me see, angel."

He shifted to show us, laying his head on my thighs. Roland's breath caught and his hand hovered in the air. "May I… touch him?"

"You may," I answered, watching as he ran his fingertips over the markings. Each glyph had turned dark red, looking more like tattoos than the raised scars they had been before. A vestige of the circle itself remained: thin arcs between the glyphs seemed to demarcate the blank canvas of Clive's back, awaiting the next stroke of my paintbrush. The only place his skin was raised was where I had cut the "M."

"I have good news and bad news," I said, stroking Clive's hair, letting my fingers comb through his waves, noticing some gray hairs that I was sure hadn't been there before. Clive closed his eyes.

"Presumably the good news is that we're all still alive?" Roland said.

"The bad news is that Barrow is still alive. Oh, and Clive is still possessed."

"Beg to differ, my lady, I consider that good news." Clive blinked and sat up.

I grinned. "Yes, I consider that the good news, too."

Roland looked back and forth between us. "What do you mean?"

It seemed so clear in my head, but putting it into words felt awkward. "It means I'm keeping the demon. Clive's own demon." Words, Mira. Use them. I felt like my brain was working a bit slowly. "Clive birthed this demon himself from an incident when he was young. But instead of shooting off as a disembodied spirit, this one stayed with him. I think he kind of clung to it, in fact? And it was trapped along with the memory of how it was created."

Roland stared at Clive. "You've been possessed all along?"

Clive nodded. "Ira's attempt to see what was behind my mental block set it free."

"But the demon is you, essentially?"

"Essentially."

I gave Clive a kiss on the cheek. "I think having a demon on our side probably gives us a fighting chance against Barrow."

"You might be right." Roland did something I don't think I'd ever seen him do before. He smiled. "This is some of the first optimism I've felt in… years really."

"Good." The wheels in my head were starting to turn again. "What's our next step?"

Roland ticked the items off his mental To Do list. "Hole up at C.B.'s cabin upstate while you recover from what you've just done, study up on glyph writing, fix Wex and presumably initiate him if he's still willing after all this, train you all, and, I guess, figure out more about demons?"

"Sounds like a full slate." And that didn't even take into account anything else we might learn from the Trinity diaries. But I had more immediate concerns. I pulled Clive by the hand in the direction of the bathroom. "Let's get cleaned up."

Roland shook his head wonderingly. "I'm amazed you two are even awake. Workings like that are usually very draining. And that was some of the most powerful transformative magic I've ever seen."

"Ha! You said—" I got caught yawning partway through my words. "—Magic!" Once he'd mentioned rest and recovery, the fatigue seemed to catch up to me suddenly.

I made it through the shower without drowning, and into clean clothes, but the intense need for sleep was catching up to me. It felt almost like it did when Barrow would put me under, except I knew I had good reason to feel that way. I don't remember taking part in cleaning up the room or even getting into the car.

The next time I woke, I found myself in the middle of a king-sized bed with Clive on one side and someone else on the other. I was even more surprised to find that the other person was Niko, sleeping with a hand folded under his chin and his mouth open. On the floor on either side of the bed were Kish and Jair.

Jair was awake, lounging under a blanket and doing something on his phone. He smiled at me when he saw me looking at him. Moving carefully, trying not to wake Niko, I began to work my way out of the bed. Clive gave me a bleary look and I patted him, telling him with that touch to go back to sleep. He conked back out as I slipped from the bed.

Looking for the bathroom, I opened the bedroom door and found myself in a short hallway. At one end was a living room, where Ira and Kanna were asleep on a fold-out couch and Roland was curled up on a sofa too short for him. The bathroom was at the other end of the hall. I almost laughed at my reflection in the mirror: I was wearing a Catwoman T-shirt. Someone must have helped me into it when I was too sleepy to remember.

After using the facilities, I tiptoed through the living room to the kitchen at the back of the house, summoned by the telltale hiss of espresso being made. It felt like weeks since I'd had a good cup of coffee.

Standing at the counter, working a professional-looking espresso machine, was a man who gave me the impression of hardness and softness at the same time. He wore a crew-cut and snarl as he fought the machine, but his cheeks and middle were generous, and so was his smile when he saw me standing there.

I said, "You must be C.B."

"And you must be Mira." His voice was higher and sweeter than I expected; this was before I knew he was trans. He poured from the container he held into two smaller cups and handed one to me.

I breathed in the aroma of the freshly-made coffee and gave a happy sigh. C.B. chuckled.

"Those boys can go on and on about tea magic all they want," he said. "I say coffee magic's stronger." He took a sip, wincing from the heat of it.

"You used the word *magic,*" I said casually, blowing on my drink to cool it.

"I don't let anybody tell me what I can or can't say," C.B. responded with a shrug. I liked him immediately. He took a bigger sip of coffee, either without burning himself or without showing it. "Ah. Need this. What with Dag and Sai in my bed and the rest of you spread out on every other available surface here, I haven't slept."

"Sorry about that."

"Don't be. I'll take a nap in the hammock out back later if the flies aren't biting." He glanced longingly through the back door, which had been propped open to let in a warm April morning. "So. You're the Demon Dominator."

"That sounds more like I'm going into pro wrestling than the practice."

"Put that on the back of a vest," he said with a chuckle. "You're the first thing in a long time that makes me think we might finally have a fighting chance."

I know, I know, I hadn't even finished my coffee and I was already asking, "Any idea what our next move is?"

"Some book-learning and training for everyone and then, if the kids are safe with you and your boy, maybe Kanna and her other half go to England to check things out, and Roland and I might give San Francisco a try."

That was surprising news. "Oh?"

C.B. grimaced. "Just wait'll you read the journals. Found a couple of leads on other Circles."

That was some of the best news yet, assuming they hadn't already been visited by Barrow. "That's exciting."

"Not half as exciting as the prospect of getting Ira out of my vicinity," C.B. said. "I take it he's not your favorite person, either."

"Anyone whose arrogance endangers others is not my favorite," I said.

"I heard that," Ira said from the doorway, so quietly and contritely that I didn't at first realize who had spoken. He stepped cautiously into the room.

"Kettle's on the stove," C.B. said without apology. "I'll be on the front porch if you need me."

I watched him go into the living room, then heard the front door open and close. Ira stood very still, looking at me. His hair had been cut shorter, perhaps to trim parts that had been flame-singed, which made him look ten years younger.

Apparently deciding that I wasn't going to bite him, Ira crossed to the stove, picked up the kettle, filled it at the sink, then put it back on a burner. To my surprise, he had to light the gas stove with a match. I bit back a smile, amused at the contrast between the archaic stove and the new-looking, high-end espresso machine. Priorities.

Ira turned to face me, hands folded. "I owe you an apology."

"Déjà vu." I sipped my coffee.

"Another apology," he amended. "I owe it to you to say this directly. From the moment I saw how enthralled Clive was with you, I saw you as competition. I told myself it was about the practice, about the Circle, but I was simply jealous. Envious of the way he looked at you. Covetous of him as a prize. I believed the only way I could make him mine was to be the one who broke through his block. I failed to realize that I had it backwards: breaking through his block wouldn't make him mine. Only the person who had already made him theirs would be able to do that."

That was similar to what he'd said while under the demon's lash, but hearing it soberly delivered gave the words a quiet gravity. And his words finally explained things like why he had gone so far in that long-ago scene, why he started it before the others could arrive to censure him, and how unprepared he was for the consequences. But he went further:

"I should not have pushed him the way I did in that scene and I've paid for that, but for one reason in particular I felt I should apologize to you directly, and it's this: I've treated you as an enemy wrongly from the beginning and I never saw you as a person."

You never saw Clive as a person either, I thought, looking at him steadily.

"I don't deserve your friendship," he said. "But I would like a chance to know you as a person."

I took another calm, patient sip of coffee.

Ira bowed his head. "I don't deserve your forgiveness, either. But if there is any way I can make it up to you, to pay this debt, please let me know."

I considered a moment, wondering how long I might want to savor that advantage.

Perhaps not long at all. I had other concerns. "Well, for a start, you could teach me about tea magic."

He looked up, searching my face for sarcasm. Finding none, he said, "Of course. We can start right away."

"And one other, important thing," I said, setting my coffee down. "Wexel."

He met my gaze, looking wounded. "Wexel is dear to me as well. I would help restore him whether you asked me to or not."

I nodded. "Good. But I want you to promise you won't touch him afterward. He needs to make his own decision about whether he's joining the Circle."

Ira frowned but nodded. "If you think that's necessary."

"Wex has a habit of falling for the biggest, baddest top in the room," I said. "I don't need him latching onto you as his rescuer."

"Wexel is better at setting boundaries than you give him credit for, Mira. But if that is your wish, I shall honor it." He bowed his head again. "But I would suggest you move carefully, yourself. As you advance in the practice, you will find the power quite seductive."

My gaze locked with his. The working with Clive had tested me sorely, giving me a rather large taste of bloodlust and a hunger for power that could become its own madness. And I had passed that test. But perhaps Ira didn't know that. And it wasn't the first time I had questioned whether I held too much power over another, and wouldn't be the last. "I think as long as I'm constantly questioning the power I hold, I'll do all right. Isn't the whole point of the Circle structure that the power is spread evenly throughout the group? No one of us should dominate."

He bowed from the waist. "May the lessons I've learned…. stick this time."

"Did someone say lessons?" Niko stood in the doorway, stretching his arms upward, his too-short shirt riding up as he yawned. Bedhead made his hair stick straight up.

Ira lifted the steaming but not yet squealing kettle off the burner and swirled the water around in it before placing it back on the flame. "I was just about to show Mira the basics of tea magic."

"Perfect timing, then." Opening a wooden cabinet beside the stove, Niko blinked sleepily at an assortment of tea cans and boxes. "I could certainly use some." He pulled out a square tin and handed it to me. "Oh, that reminds me!"

He hurried out of the room without explaining. Ira and I just watched him disappear down the hall, and then return, a stack of notebooks in his hands.

In the stack was mine, though all I'd had time to write in it was my name. He took back the can of tea and handed me the notebook instead. "Don't just write down facts in this. Write down what happened to you, what you felt, and not just what you learned, but how you learned it. Like you're writing it for someone joining the Circle in the future who might need to know what you know. Start at the beginning, like, all the way back to when you first discovered the practice."

When I first discovered the practice, hm? I didn't have a story like Roland's—or Barrow's—of discovering the power when I was still inexperienced, did I? I'd have to think it over how to start.

"Because this isn't just for you to chronicle what you know for yourself. It's for everyone in the Circle who comes after you and who needs to learn from your journey even after you're gone." Niko handed the can of tea to Ira. "Brew it strong, please? I have a lot of reading to get through today."

Ira clutched the tin to his chest. "I shall do my best."

Niko retreated to the front porch and Ira and I looked at each other. He turned off the gas a moment before the kettle whistled. "It is healthful to the spirit to imbibe warm liquids," he began.

For the next while, I listened to Ira explain the theories of tea. When the first lesson was done, I took a cup of tea and the notebook out onto the back porch. There was a small table there, and one rickety chair. A rope hammock hung between a tree and one of the porch posts, and the view was of an overgrown yard ringed by forest.

Soon after I sat down at the table, Clive emerged from inside the house, a piece of toast in his hand. He settled himself at my feet to eat it, enjoying the warm breeze and the rustling sound of the trees.

I tore a page from the notebook to start, and wrote *Dear Mom & Dad* at the top. I still couldn't explain what was going on, but maybe I didn't have to. My parents had never wanted to know the intimate details of my sex life, after all.

So I wrote to say that a fire at my apartment building had forced me to move and that I was staying with good friends for a while. I was happy and healthy and eager to explore new opportunities. And I loved them and would write when I could.

Then I looked down at Clive, and I reached out to brush a bit of crumb from the edge of his lip with my thumb. His hair was bed-tousled and he was wearing the hotel robe. He looked up at me and smiled.

Yes, I'd start there. With the night we met. I opened the notebook to the first page, intending to do so, and wondering where I'd be in my journey when I reached the last page.

Reader, here we are.

ACKNOWLEDGMENTS
& AUTHOR'S NOTES

Like Mira's journal itself, this book has had quite an adventure to come into being. As some of you know, it was originally supposed to be published by Tor Books back in the 2010s. I had always wanted to be published by Tor, not just because they have a track record of publishing women, queer, and trans authors, but because two folks from there gave me invaluable advice very early in my career. First was editor John Ordover. At Lunacon in 1991, I struck up a conversation, nervously told him I was a writer and I wasn't sure if what I wrote was "any good." However I was sure that the last thing an editor at a con wanted to hear was that I had a manuscript print-out in my bag.

I was wrong: John took me to lunch on the spot and then sat there ignoring his food to read my short story "Telepaths Don't Need Safewords." (For the record, he found four typos.) The story was already circulating through the primordial internet via the Usenet group alt.sex.bondage. John told me two important things that day: 1) Yep, you sure can write. 2) The market isn't ready for what you write (kinky science fiction), but you could be part of what makes it ready. Here we are more than 30 (!) years later and John was right.

The other key advice-giver from Tor was Tom Doherty himself. After that fateful lunch, I decided to self-publish and founded a publishing house called Circlet Press, through which I published not only *Telepaths,* but the works of many other speculative erotica writers. Tom gave me both advice and encouragement, and over the years was always open to my questions. His insights into science fiction/fantasy readers in the 1980s-'90s (much more diverse and female and than previously assumed) validated many choices I made in my career. Tom, thank you.

So when Tor bought The Vanished Chronicles, I thought it was a big full circle moment. The marketplace was finally ready for my brand of kinky sf/f. In those heady days, Obama was still president, *50 Shades of Grey* had just become literally the best-selling book in the history of the English language; it seemed like the stars had aligned.

But internal difficulties at Tor, many of which I wasn't fully privy to, complicated things and the editorial process was slow. So slow that years went by, times changed, and my editor was let go. The end result was Tor decided to give the book back to me, and I decided to self-publish. Full circle, indeed.

I could not have reached this point without the support of many, many people. Some supported in literal fashion by contributing to my Patreon—they were the first readers to read the finished book, as I serialized it 2024-2025. Love and appreciation of course to corwin, my partner in life and in kink for almost 34 years as of this book's publication, who has lived through all the ups and downs of my career. I'd also like to thank the folks who co-hosted an epic kinky "asb party" with me at the 1991 Gaylaxicon in Tewksbury, Massachusetts—D!, Ian, Zonker, and a few others I probably shouldn't name in print: this book is really for you guys. (Long live NELF!) By the way, anyone who attended the old Lunacons at the "Escher Hilton" in Rye will recognize the setting for Mira and Clive's climactic shebang.

A shoutout to my recent con-going posse, especially Francie and Alyse who beta-read the very very early draft of the manuscript, as did Nona F. and Joe C. (and Tris Lawrence, right?), and to all my Frolicon folks (Ed, Mel. Marrus, Julian, Bishop, et. al.) and NY/NJ kink-eventers (hi Greg, Martin, AuntieMisha) who very definitely understand the power of erotic ritual. Mmmm. I also got knife play advice and suggestions from numerous folks, including Carol Queen and Robert Lawrence, Jennifer Williams, and especially Corey Alexander (aka Xan West). A round of beta-readers read the final draft, including Charlie Jane Anders, Lisabet Sarai, Lauren P. Burka, and Jules Behrens.

I need to add one more note about Corey Alexander/Xan West. Between the first draft of these acknowledgments and the last, Corey passed away, leaving a gaping hole in the Twitterverse and in the Venn diagram crossover between romance readers, BDSM practitioners, sf/fantasy fans, and trans/nonbinary queerfolk. The C in C.B.'s name stands for Corey. The loss still hurts. The B. also stands for someone I lost. Both Corey and Brian's influences live and breathe on every page of this book.

I'd also be remiss if I didn't thank some of the many people who have helped me to understand bodywork and healing arts, even though almost none of them know of my erotica writing life. I got certified in massage years ago, and it was inevitable that some healing arts knowledge would eventually land in my books. Thanks to Professor Tom Ryan, Doug Musser, and Steve Balzac. Thanks also to the insights of Maria Spuller, Thabiti Sabahive, Kahuna Mark Saito, and Chris Matsuo, as well as Guru Abundio Baet of the Filipino knife fighting academy Garimot Arnis Training in Florida. There's a little of all of them in "Sensei Jack."

Last: my parents, Peggy and Sergio Tan. A friend who has read a lot of my work recently commented that in my books my characters are often either totally estranged from their parents or actively in conflict with them. "That's weird," my friend said, "because you get along so well with your folks." It's true. My parents are/were awesome. (My dad passed away in 2022.) I'm pretty sure that parents in my books are metaphors for something else in life. My real-life parents always encouraged me to be myself and find my own way of understanding the world. Mom, Dad, that was the greatest gift you could give a young writer. Thank you.

P.S. Don't attempt ritual sex magic at home. Although if you do, please practice safer sex and BDSM—that includes disinfecting your knives and never, *ever* leaving someone alone in bondage. In books, the line between fantasy and reality can be blurred to make the fiction hot. Knives and whips are dangerous and not everything my characters do is something I'd condone being acted out in real life. There are good resources on safe play out there, including books like *SM 101* by Jay Wiseman, and the classes and publications offered by community groups such as TES in New York City, or websites such as The Kink Academy online. Be safe, be well, and I will see you at the next stop on the journey.

ABOUT THE AUTHOR

Cecilia Tan started writing books before she could read them. While some folks spend their lives trying to make their fantasies real, her life has been spent turning her realities into fantasies like this one. A longtime activist and educator in the BDSM community, she retired from community organizing in 2018 to concentrate on her writing. She has been writing erotic fantasy and science fiction ever since self-publishing *Telepaths Don't Need Safewords* in 1992. Her awards shelf has grown crowded in recent years, but she feels the best reward is getting to write more books.

Enter her world (or at least her newsletter ranks) at CeciliaTan.com to find out more about her cats, cooking, and cafe writing excursions.